# Best of British Science Fiction 2019

# Best of British Science Fiction 2019

## Edited by Donna Scott

NewCon Press
England

First edition, published in the UK July 2020 by NewCon Press

NCP 243 (hardback)
NCP 244 (softback)

10 9 8 7 6 5 4 3 2 1

Cover art by Les Edwards
Cover design by Ian Whates
Text layout by Ian Whates and Donna Scott

# Contents

# Editor's Acknowledgements

Thank you to everyone who submitted their own stories to me this year, or nudged me in the way of some great stories they had read. There were so many brilliant stories this time around, it made my job very difficult indeed, but in a good way. Particular thanks to Dave Bradley, Rosie Oliver, Noel Chidwick, Liz Joyce, Teika Bellamy and David Gullen. As ever, my gratitude goes out to Ian Whates and Newcon Press for once again inviting me to edit this series, and to my beta reader Tom Jordan for his invaluable insight.

# 2019: An Introduction

## Donna Scott

When I first started working on this series four years ago, I had to reflect on what a strange year 2016 had been. We were shaking our fists at the year for causing our news to be dominated by one polarising political subject, and for breaking our hearts with the deaths of so many of our cultural icons. 2016, you were a terrible year!

I'm writing this at the end of May 2020.

I feel I need to apologise to 2016.

By the time this book is published we should still be under a relaxed form of the Lockdown that we have begrudgingly acknowledged is happening; whether or not we have got used to it is another matter. At the very least social distancing measures will still be in effect in our public spaces.

So this is what life is like now. We are living in the age of the pandemic, and it is simultaneously weird, scary, inspiring, and exhausting. Our social lives have effectively moved online; although a lot of folk are technologically disenfranchised, more still who are not are feeling terribly isolated as well, even with so-called 'Zoom-fatigue' kicking in. Many of us are overwhelmed and anxious. Working from home, instead of a dreadful commute to sit in an airless office, is turning out not to be so ideal in some ways, and we are fractious and distracted. For some people, missing the trivial joys of meeting friends in a pub, getting a decent haircut, or indulging in retail therapy alone is too much to bear. As a nation, we are dishevelled, and sales of alcohol have boomed. I'm doing my best to find humour in the situation, though like many others I have been separated from my immune-compromised family members for the foreseeable future and this makes me sad – and a little angry at people I can see not taking the situation as seriously.

I didn't consciously set out to choose stories for this anthology with Covid-19 in mind, and a lot of the stories were ones I read and put in my shortlist before all this was happening. But the strangest thing about the virus is how stretchy it has made time. Sometimes I think I was speaking to Ian Whates about my progress with editing the anthology in the pub just a couple of weeks ago. And then I realise that was three months ago. And then I think: ah, pubs were a thing. Meeting Ian was a thing! And three months is both no time at all, and forever ago. Hence, something of this year's oddness will probably be lingering in your brain when you sit down to read this book, be that soon after publication, or a few years down the road.

One of the things I read today was that the birds are not getting louder, as we had all thought. You might have noticed the birdsong this year has been particularly ebullient? Well, no... their volume has been measured by scientists and contrary to what we all thought they are singing more quietly than usual. The difference is, we are not having to tune out all the other noise to hear them.

I wonder then, how you will read these stories in our changed world. Every single one of these stories is one of wonder; many of them wistful and sad, others full of fire and lightning. I am very proud of this anthology, and I think it is possibly the most thought-provoking and exquisite anthology I have worked on to date. Now that we are all part of the same eldritch, dystopian, apocalyptically teetering world, I admit that this is a bold statement. These are just stories, no more, no less, but if you read them, you might get that tickling sensation at the back of your brain that is as comforting as it is uncanny.

Perhaps you will be reminded of the times we are in now, not just thinking about the virus, but the stories of killer hornets, and the way we are glued to whatever is happening at the SpaceX launch site. In these stories creatures are cut off from their loved ones; someone is trapped with an abuser; a bird sings; weeds grow where we hope for a garden; we wonder what our alternative selves might be doing; we can't sleep; we wish we could keep things just the way they were; we drink too much... and we look to rockets blasting off into the sky and think that's the future; that's hope.

*Donna Scott*
*Northampton*
*May 2020*

# The Anxiety Gene

## Rhiannon Grist

I stumble back onto the pavement, but five other me*s* don't.

Three roll across the hood, skulls smashed open on the windshield, the boot or the road still smoking with tyre-burn behind. One me gets caught by the front bumper and pulled under the wheels. The last is dragged a good few yards before the car finally comes to a stop, leaving a pink pencil eraser mark along the tarmac. I witness every terrifying sensation first-hand, from the smell of burnt rubber to the toe-squelch of blood pooling in my boots.

But I'm fine. The me that's here, standing on the pavement, is fine. At least that's what the driver in my reality sees. He flips me off and keeps on driving, completely oblivious to the five other him*s* and the five other me*s* he – they – just mowed down. It's hard to keep track of what belongs to my reality and what belongs to another, like getting mad at someone for something they did in a dream. But you figure it out. And what you can't figure out you medicate.

My hands are shaking so hard I barely manage to fish the blockers out of my bag. Dying five times over will do that to you. I unscrew the cap on the third try only to spill thick yellow liquid all over my jumper. Shit. No time to worry about that. I take a gulp. I hated the banana flavour at first, but now I love it. As the first mouthful slips down my gullet my heart rate slows and the fear sinks under a wave of medicated calm. I'll feel sick later but it's worth it for the relief. I shake the bottle and the last drop rolls about on the bottom. It was supposed to last me until the end of the week. Now it's decorating my sweater. I'll pick up some more tomorrow, but for now I'll have to make do.

Today's going to be shit.

"Congratulations!" The doctor said, "You have the Anxiety Gene!"

It was five days after my twenty-sixth birthday. I'd been dragged to my GP after my flatmate found me barricaded in my bedroom, a fortnight's worth of piss stored haphazardly in plastic takeaway boxes under my bed. I'd been haunted by glimpses of death every day of my adult life. As I got older, they got worse. By the time my flatmate intervened I was unable to leave my bed for fear of some horrifying calamity and I'd eroded my ability to feel enthusiastic about anything, even a diagnosis.

"Count yourself lucky," he said, "We used to think it was all in your head. Now we know it's real. There's a testing window two weeks from now. Do you think you'll be free?"

I hadn't been able to hold down a job in years. Of course I was free.

I die once more on my way to work – ice on the roads – but my last gulp of blockers keeps the sensation dull and far away, like it's happening to someone else. My therapist taught me to see these alternate deaths like toy cars rushing through my mind. I'm to visualise picking them up, putting them back down, and then letting them drive away. I pick up the toy car girl on the slippery road and look at the world through her broken face. She still has a Wimpy in her universe. Weird. Then I put her back down and she races away from me and I believe for a moment I can do this. I take a deep cold breath. I can survive a day.

I work on the first floor of a typical office building – all glass, stone and steel. Sharp, hard substances that could crack or bludgeon or cut. I avoid the wide glass staircase and head straight for the lift. I've had plenty of deaths in lifts – frayed wires, eager doors – but none on the glass stairs. Despite this, I avoid them like the plague. But today is obviously cursed, so the lifts are out. I sigh and head back to the stairs.

I hold onto the railing and take each step at a time, a nervous sweat beading the valley of my back. I can see our teenage receptionist looking at me quizzically through the glass walls of our office. I want to flash him a "fuck off" look, but I'm pretty sure the moment I take my eyes off the stairs something awful will happen. The glass will break and I'll fall to my death, or a splinter will fly up through my neck, or – and this one's the worst – I'll lose my footing, fall backwards and crack my head open on the cold glass edge of a stair below. But that'll only happen if I stop looking. As long as I'm looking at the stairs, they'll behave –

An arm hooks round my elbow.

"What have you done to yourself?"

Oh god. It's Fucking Linda.

Fucking Linda would be alright if she didn't feel the need to put herself at the centre of every story. If we're heading to the pub after work, Fucking Linda's got to turn it into an organised office outing. If our company wins an award, it has to be down to Fucking Linda's project management. And, if someone's trying to climb the stairs at their own pace, Fucking Linda's got to swoop in and save the day.

"What did you do?" she asks. "Go too hard at the gym?"

I haven't gone to a gym in years. Have you seen those running machines? Talk about a death trap.

"Thanks for the assist, Linds," I grit my teeth, "But I think I've got this."

"It's okay," she says, "I don't mind."

She pulls me off balance and I trip up a stair. Not far, but enough to make me jump out of my skin. I push her off me and she knocks into one of the Support guys coming up behind us. He stumbles back, slamming his heavy backpack into the railing and spilling coffee all over his new-looking trainers.

"Christ, sorry…" *Fuck. What's his name? I see him all the time, but I can never remember his name.* "… mate?"

He gives me this weird, hollow-eyed look, sighs and starts taking off his sodden shoes. Poor Support. They spend their days explaining basic computer functions to people who've probably never held a mouse before. Now this happens. There's only so much a person can take before they crack.

I don't know what to say so I scurry up the stairs instead, avoiding the kicked-dog look on Linda's face. She only wanted to help. It's not her fault I'm like this. But then again, it's not mine either.

The test facility was in an industrial estate just outside town. Big white building, still had that new sheen to it. I got dressed into a gown, wore bobbly wired hats and lay on whirring tables surrounded by an audience of excited doctors. Through some weird fluke of quantum-whatevers, the particles in the Anxiety Gene were entangled with particles from across the multiverse, forging brief connections between people and their alternate selves. The doctors explained that they'd seen this manifest as intrusive thoughts, visions, unshakeable feelings of dread or even elation, experiences they'd previously shrugged off as symptoms of psychosis, mania or – clue's in the name – anxiety disorders. However, in those flashes of connection, some people got glimpses of exciting worlds rich with possibility. I heard some could even have conversations with their other selves. A bloke I went to school with claimed he had this manifestation of the gene. Turned out to be bog-standard schizophrenia. Hard to tell these days.

I sat in the specialist's office hoping that the years of panic and fear would finally count for something. That I wasn't sick, I was special. The doctor pursed her lips and asked again what I experienced. Were there any other details? A glimpse here and there but mostly just the deaths, I replied. And that was that. Other people got the special kind of the gene. The kind triggered whenever they felt a surge of excitement – of discovery, of fear, of arousal. Mine was only triggered by the flood of adrenaline experienced at the point of death. When I'm eating a sandwich and some other me in another reality chokes, when I'm crossing the road and another me gets hit by a truck, when I'm taking a shower and some other me slips and cracks her skull, that's when my gene kicks in. I got the type where I die over and over. Just my bloody luck. I was given a prescription for blockers and sent on my merry way. I'm not sure who was more disappointed, me or the doctors.

By the time I'm ready for my mid-morning coffee the blockers are wearing off. An alternate me trips on a printer cable and breaks her neck on the edge of a desk. I catch myself from the extra-dimensional fall and scream. People around me stare.

*Shit. Breathe in. Breathe out. Pick up your toy car death, look at it, put it back down, move on.*

"Sorry folks," I say, as cheerfully as possible, "Stray bullet." Caitlin in Web Dev gives me a polite chuckle. I wish people would laugh about it more. Okay, it's not very funny dying over and over, but it is pretty ridiculous and that's worth a laugh at least.

My Line Manager, Mac, stops me on my way to the kitchen. "Do you have a second?" Mac's chewing on a toothpick. Does he know what havoc a swallowed toothpick can ravage on the human body? Then again, he's the type to run downstairs two steps at a time with his shoelaces untied. I once caught him digging a bagel out of the toaster with a fork.

"Well?" he asks again.

I say yes before I've had time to think and we're on our way to a meeting room before I figure out what he wants to talk about. Shit. Of course it had to be today. I'm suddenly very aware of the uneasy feeling in my stomach and the bright yellow stain down my sweater.

It shouldn't come as much surprise to hear I work as a Quality Assurance Analyst. Turns out, experiencing your death in a variety of colourful ways gives one a prodigious eye for spotting things that could go wrong. You wouldn't think you could die from laughing. You also wouldn't think you could break a website by pressing the menu button sixteen times. Well, now you know better.

However, there is such a thing as too much care.

"I'm sorry," says Mac, flicking the toothpick from one corner of his mouth to the other. I smile and assure him I understand, but in my mind all I can hear is *I didn't get it I didn't get it I didn't get it.* I'm one of the oldest members of the QA team, and the only one who's still a Junior Analyst. I knew what had done me in. I'd been testing a new banking portal. After two expensive weeks of QA, I reported back that clicking the terms and conditions page ninety-four times made the font change colour. The dev team were fascinated. The client, not so much.

Mac follows me back to the kitchen. "Are you going to be alright?" he asks, "Just I know you can get a bit –" He holds his hands out and shakes them. My gut twists in on itself.

"There was an accident this morning," I fumble with the coffee pot to give me somewhere else to look. "I ran out of meds, but I should have more tomorrow."

Mac eyes my mug and frowns. "You know…" he says.

*Oh God, not this again.*

"… I read that cutting out caffeine might help. Less stimulants, better brain chemistry."

I try to mask the frustration curdling my face. "It's not really a chemical imbalance. It's genetic. The Anxiety Gene –"

He cuts me off with a wave of his hand. "Sure, however you want to think about it."

Of course he doesn't believe me. There are a fair few who don't. It's been just long enough since the discovery for the excitement to die down, but too early for it to really affect how the everyday world works. Unless you're a quantum physicist or a neural biologist, or me for that matter, the multiverse is just another unseeable untouchable thing, like Jupiter or the Higgs Boson. I'm not surprised people question its existence, but it's mind-boggling how many claim to understand my experiences better than I do. I silently place bets on which magical lifestyle cure Mac will suggest next. Vegetables? Or exercise? He looks like an exercise guy. He wears a leather bracelet though, so maybe mindfulness.

He tilts his head thoughtfully. "I know a guy who runs courses at the Community Centre, nothing too wooky. Just breathing, posture, help you become more aware of your own mind."

Before I can think *Bingo*, there's a bang.

Mac's mouth hangs open and a circle of red blooms on his t-shirt.

*He's swallowed his toothpick*, I think.

Another bang and the coffee pot explodes in my hand and Mac slumps to the ground. Somewhere in another probable now, two other me*s* fall with him. Now the screaming starts. There are more bangs and three other me*s* drop to the floor. I feel every shot like a punch to the gut. I can smell blood. Both here and elsewhere. I drop behind the counter and throw my arms over my head.

*Oh shit. Oh shit.*

Gunfire rings out across desks, shattering computer screens and light fixtures, sending sparks flying. Realities fracture in my mind.

*Are we under attack? Is it terrorists?*

I look up at the dangling remains of a strip light. It strikes me as a decidedly haphazard shot.

*No. People don't shoot up offices here.*

I remember the Support guy on the stairs. The look in his eyes. The heft of his backpack. Linda's coffee on his shoes.

*Okay, maybe it could happen here.*

While my mind races, twelve alternate me*s* give in to temptation and peek above the counter. All twelve immediately take a bullet to the eye, the forehead, the nose. Twelve! I've never had so many before. The multitude of deaths ricochet through my brain and my thoughts scatter like marbles until I no longer know what's in my reality and what's in another. The holiday postcard on the fridge flashes five different destinations. I clutch my ears and close my eyes.

*They're just toy cars. They're just toy cars.*

I pick up each death in my mind, look it over and consider a new thought. Despite experiencing them the way I do, I'm no expert in alternate realities. I'm not sure how they come about, how they split. Is it our decisions? Or probability? Or a mix of both? In this reality the coin comes down heads, you bring a gun to work; in another reality the coin comes down tails, you leave the gun at home. It's messier than that of course. If something happens in one reality, I don't know if it means it'll turn out exactly the same in this one. But what I do know is that in twelve other realities, I looked over the counter and copped it. And in this reality, I stayed hidden and got to live.

Another me gets a bullet through the counter. I dive round the fridge just as a bullet in this reality traces the same path.

*Time to move.*

The screaming subsides. Everyone's staying quiet – either hiding or dead. Footsteps are coming this way. Time to test my theory. I slip behind the next bank of desks just as another me, one who tarried, takes a shot in the leg then five in the chest. I rarely experience deaths outside of my personal space. It's always a near-miss – getting clipped by a train, hit by a falling brick, tripping on a loose paving stone – so I know that death was a close one. Sure, I have a front-row seat for 'what not to do' thanks to my less fortunate alternate selves, but how many near-misses can I afford?

The footsteps prowl closer. I hold my hand over my heart, as if I'm trying to keep it quiet and stop it bursting from my chest at the same time. I edge back and my ankle bumps into something wet and heavy. I make the mistake of looking. It's Caitlin, only there's a deep red hole in the back of her head. I fall back and clap my hands over my mouth. Caitlin always makes the effort to talk to me at Friday night drinks. She breeds gerbils outside of work and listens to EDM while she codes. Who'll look after her gerbils now? The horror of her death is a black hole threatening to swallow me up. But I can't fall apart, not with the shooter so close.

*It's just another death that doesn't belong to you.*

I apologise to Caitlin and put her death into a toy car in my mind. I pick her up. Look at her. Then I put her back down and let her drive away.

The footsteps leave the room and I unclasp my hands from my mouth. I need a plan, a better one than waiting for my alternate selves to cop it like Schrödinger's canaries. Do I run? Do I hide? How long will it take for the police to get here? Five, ten minutes? Let's say it's going to take fifteen minutes before some sort of official task force arrives to deal with the situation. The gunman's skulking about, like he's looking for people. I picture him hunting for me among the desks. I wonder who it could be. Angus from Finance is always the brunt of jokes at staff parties. Or then there's Dafydd in Design with his hair-trigger temper. For some reason, I keep thinking of that guy from Support on the stairs this morning. What is his name? I briefly wonder if there's a reality where I remember his name and he doesn't shoot up our workplace. Probably not. Point is, it's only a matter of time until I'm found.

My best chance is to get out.

The next few minutes the office is a chess board with one terrifying queen and an infinite row of pawns that look just like me. The blockers have well and truly worn off and my senses are finely tuned. I've not felt this way in years. It's like I'm a military radar for my own demise and I'm picking up all of them in state-of-the-art HD. To keep my head straight I make a checklist, as if I'm QA testing a website. Move too quickly. Bang. That's a bug. So, I take my time and think. Move too slowly. Bang. Another bug. So, I make sure I don't hesitate. Stop to help someone. They cry. Loudly. Bang. Bug again. I focus on saving myself. The self in this reality. All other deaths – both my alternate selves and the bodies on the floor – are just little toy cars whizzing through my head. I pick them up, then I put them down and let them run from me, until only I remain.

I die less. I get braver. That horrible staircase comes into view through the glass boardroom and I'm so close to this being over. After a shortcut through the cloakroom I scurry under the reception desk next to the large floor-to-ceiling windows emblazoned with our company logo. I can see the front door downstairs through the glass, but there are no blue lights out on the street. My heart sinks. The police should be here by now. It's been at least an hour, hasn't it? I check the clock opposite the desk. It's only been ten minutes. Ten minutes and I've died fifty times at least. That's a record I'm in no hurry to break.

I'm about to make my move, when footsteps round the corner. I duck down, hoping they don't see my reflection in the glass.

But it's not the gunman.

It's Fucking Linda.

Fucking Linda stands looking at the top of the stairs, a weird faraway look in her eyes. She doesn't look hurt, but she's standing out like a sore bloody thumb. Fucking Linda's going to get herself fucking killed. I think about this morning on the stairs, the kicked-dog look on her face, and guilt twists like a key in my gut. Maybe if I'm careful, we can both get out to safety. I quickly look about, then rise out of my hiding spot.

"Hey. Linds," I whisper as loud as I can.

She looks at me, surprised. God, she must be proper out of it.

"It's okay. I think he's still inside." I step toward her, offering my hand, "Let's get out of –"

Then I see the hunting rifle tucked under her arm.

Oh. Shit. *Fucking* Linda.

Three me*s* run. Bang. Two me*s* beg. Bang. Six me*s* throw something at her, a chair, a book, a bag. It doesn't matter. Bang. One me defiantly flips her the bird.

Bang bang bang.

Fucking Linda watches all of this flash across my face. She lowers her rifle. "Oh," she says, "Of course. You must be having a really bad day. How many times have you died so far?"

"Honestly, I lost count on the way to work," I say.

Fucking Linda fucking chuckles.

"I didn't really figure you into the plan." She braces the rifle back into her shoulder, "To be honest, I didn't know you had it so bad. You always seem so together."

I'm trying to come up with a game plan, but I've got nothing.

"I've got very good at pretending to be fine," I say.

Fucking Linda's face darkens. "I know what you mean."

I can see the clock on the wall above her head. Eleven minutes have passed. No other me*s* have died in a while. I just need to play for time.

"So, what's all this…" I gesture vaguely, "… about?"

The shooty end of the rifle is pointing straight at my gut.

"You know," she says, "Out of everyone here, I think you're the only one who truly understands what it's like."

She relaxes and the rifle's aim lowers to my thigh. If she misses the artery I could survive.

"What's what like, Linds?"

"Seeing the other you*s*." She leans forward, like we're just sharing office gossip. "Can yours see you back? I don't think mine can. I've only got the one, thank God. I tried talking to her when I was little, but she'd never say anything back. My parents thought I had an invisible friend."

Fucking Linda has the fucking Anxiety Gene.

"It was fine for a while. Just me and this other Linda living our lives in tandem. Brushing our teeth, playing with our toys. Then one day, we were studying for a test in school and I stopped and watched her. I think I just wanted to see what I looked like, so I watched while she studied. Of course, the next day I failed the test and she passed. That was the first time we'd ever differed."

I lean my head to one side like I'm listening and totally not counting down the seconds before the fuzz arrive.

"No need to panic, I thought. Just got to work a little harder and then I'll be right back on track. So, when the next test came, I shut myself up in my room and studied all night long. And then I slept through the exam. I'd failed. Again. Meanwhile the other Linda, my potential, was racing away from me." For a moment her gaze traces some unseen horizon, before snapping back to me. "Can you follow yours? You know, if they go someplace you're not. Can you see through their eyes?"

I shake my head. I'm too scared to speak.

"I can. It's a fucking curse. I'd watch her go on day trips with my parents and hang out with my friends, while I stayed in my bedroom struggling to catch up. But it was never enough. When I got an A on an essay, I could always see the A+ on hers."

Linda puts the rifle back under her arm.

"She's this celebrity thinker type person now. Married to a paediatrician. With a beautiful house and charming friends and her first child on the way. Do you know what torture that is? To have your perfect double showing you what your life could have been, while you're stuck living the consolation prize?"

Two minutes have passed. I nod sympathetically. Come on Linda, tell me more about your fucking awful life.

"She started maternity leave this week. She was lying in bed, looking through the cards from her colleagues, making plans for the future, and she was so..." Linda takes a big shuddering breath, "... happy. That's when I understood why there's only the two of us. I'm not supposed to compete with her." She pauses. "I'm supposed to balance her out. She's the charmed one and I'm –" she gestures at her rifle, "Well. I'm Fucking Linda. Aren't I?"

A cold feeling rises through my limbs. Fucking Linda is fucking insane.

"How does yours work again?" she asks, "Any time you die in an alternate reality you experience it here too? Is it like the uncertainty thing? Like, if I thought very seriously about shooting you in the stomach –"

Right on cue, an alternate me goes flying and I curl round my abdomen. Fucking Linda raises her eyebrows.

"Oh. Maybe you do have it worse."

I can't help myself. "You think?!"

Time's up. Fucking Linda's tired of fucking talking. She brings the gun back into her shoulder and aims straight at me. A shadow flits across the blinds behind her.

"On the stairs this morning, you looked so helpless. A little like you do now. Only I don't feel like helping this time." She shrugs. "Or maybe I do. Who knows? I'm feeling really indecisive lately."

The first wave of alternate bullets hit as Linda debates with herself whether or not she should shoot me. All the while, my alternate selves crumple to the floor over and over and over. I try to keep track of them all. I look them over and put them down, but they keep racing back to me, adding more each time until there are uncountable deaths around me, swirling like leaves in a hurricane. There are too many to pick up. Too many to feel separately. It's just a blur of pain and panic and terror.

So, I do the only thing I can think of.

I take all these deaths and I reduce them to one single idea. Death. My death, the one in my reality, the one that belongs to me, the one that will happen someday. I put death into a toy car and I look at it, without the comfort of a multiverse keeping it a whole other reality away. Then I set it down and I let it go.

And then, in that maelstrom of dying, like a word said over and over, death lost its meaning. And for the first time in years, I feel completely calm.

19

"Oh, so fucking what," I say. "You want to be remembered as this big scary monster? Fine. But did you have to be such a cliché? A shooting spree. Really? That's pretty basic, even for you."

Fucking Linda lets the barrel drop. She opens her mouth to say something, but I don't let her. It's my turn.

"Y'know, I've had nearly every flavour of death there is. Plane crash. Done it. Electrocution. Done it. Accidental beheading. Done it. Twice. This ride you've got me on, I've ridden it so many times I don't even bother picking up the souvenir photo any more. I'm kind of a death connoisseur. And dying because my co-worker was too busy competing with her alternate self to succeed at her own goddamn life has got to be the dumbest one yet. Fine, shoot me. In a million other realities, a million other me*s* will have shaken it off by lunchtime anyway."

Fucking Linda fucking falters. Not for long, but long enough.

"Oh fuck you –"

The sniper's bullet rips through her skull, spraying my face with her still-warm blood. Adrenaline courses through my veins as I watch Fucking Linda's headless corpse flop to the ground.

Black uniforms come piling into the building. I spread out my fingers. I can almost feel the pile of dead me*s* in a mound around my feet while I stand alone. The one who lives. I wipe the blood off my face and step away from the carnage, forgetting the glass stairs behind me.

My foot slips. Fucking Linda's blood is all over the fucking floor and now it's slicked to the bottom of my boots. I try to find traction, but my foot slips again. Blue lights flash around me. My arms windmill.

*No. Not the stairs*, I think. *Not after all this.*

I teeter on the edge, a glass line between life and death, and a million other me*s* in a million other realities flinch.

# The Land of Grunts and Squeaks

## Chris Beckett

A long time ago, in a country across the mountains, a great queen displeased a wicked and spiteful witch. No one knows what the queen did to offend her – witches are easily slighted – but the wicked woman was so enraged that she placed a curse on the queen and all her people. "When this night is over," she told them, "you will all be strangers to one another."

It was a truly dreadful curse. It was worse than stealing their hearing from them, or shutting down their tingle sense. It was worse even than depriving them of the darkfeel, on which we rely so much as we move about our tunnels and chambers. Those would all be calamities indeed, but this was far more terrible. For when they woke the following morning, the people of that unfortunate country discovered they could no longer reach each other's minds.

Think for a moment, dear ones, what that would be like. Spread out your antennae to their full extent and notice what it is that you receive through them. You can feel my love, for one thing, and the love you have for one another. You receive this story I'm giving you now, and a thousand others. You know the thoughts of all your friends. You can tell who's happy and who's sad, here in this chamber and out in the world beyond, and you know exactly why. And behind all these things, you feel the love of our mother, the queen, reaching out to all of us, caressing us, nourishing us, making us feel safe and cared for.

And now imagine what it would be like, my dears, if all of that was gone – every single bit of it – and all you could know of the world around you were the fragments that came through your senses. Oh, you would still know that we others were here, you would still be able to hear the sounds we made, you could still darkfeel our presence or see us if we were under the sun, but you couldn't know what we were thinking, you couldn't tell us things or receive our news, and you would have no way of connecting with how we felt. As to the queen, well, she'd be far away in her palace, and you'd know nothing of her at all. For all you knew, she might be dead.

Dreadful to think of, isn't it? And yet, for those poor people in that land across the mountains, that was their fate for evermore.

How lonely life must have become. Children were left alone with fears which no one else could see. Lovers could no longer feel each other's love. A woman would look at her life's companion and think, 'I'm sorry about those angry feelings I had earlier on. I truly love you with all my heart', but her friend would have no idea she'd had that thought. Tender caresses lost their meaning, becoming no more than one skin touching another. People were prisoners inside their own heads. Many went mad with grief.

And yet loneliness was by no means the whole of it. The work of the queendom came almost to a standstill, because no one could ask or tell each other anything. First thing of a morning, farm workers would stand in bemusement in front of their forewoman, with no idea what she wanted them to do. The forewoman could think and think with all her might, but she may as well have whistled or made a face for all the difference that made. The workers just shuffled about embarrassedly until eventually, feeling like a fool, the forewoman picked up a scythe and, making the motions of cutting something, pointed and nodded in the direction of a nearby tunnel.

"You mean, cut the mushrooms?" the workers would ask her, but of course she didn't know what they were thinking. She could only see their bewildered faces. And so she'd carry on with her strange performance until at last, bewildered and uncomfortable, they'd pick up scythes and trudge off, hoping they'd understood correctly, some up the tunnel to the mushroom caves (which was what the forewoman intended) and some outside to harvest leaves (which wasn't necessary that day at all).

That forewoman was at least able, by her clumsy performance, to show some of her labourers what she wanted, but cutting mushrooms is a simple action, easy to demonstrate. How would the administrator of a province learn from her people about a shortage of grain, and, even if she could learn of it, how would she convey the need to sow more to all the thousands under her authority, spread out through countless tunnels and chambers? Yes, and for that matter, why would workers want to work at all, if they had no sense any more that what they did was appreciated, and no information as to what purpose it served?

Most dreadful of all, though, deep down in the warm depths of her palace, the queen, with her lovely huge soft yielding body, had, only a day before, been able to share her thoughts with every one of her subjects, just as our own queen does to this day, but now she reached out with her mind and found nothing at all beyond the confines of her own head and her brood chamber. She couldn't tell any more how many eggs were needed across the queendom, she didn't know how many workers to make, or how many farmers and administrators, or how many guards. She couldn't direct folk to move from one place to another. She couldn't relay news about opportunities here and shortages there. And above all she couldn't comfort her people with that sweet warm radiance that up to now had sustained them all, just as you and I are sustained by our own beloved queen.

As to the young princesses and the men, those beautiful, gentle, idle creatures who'd basked their whole lives in the full intensity of that radiance, they now gathered helplessly around her in the chamber, their antennae waving uselessly about, their hands pawing at her enormous body, their mouthparts nuzzling her soft skin in the hope of finding at least some tiny remnant of the bounty that had been theirs until now. But they found nothing. Nothing came back to them. Her skin was just skin, her face was just a face, her antennae were as silent as their own. The despair of that was so great that some of them cracked open their own heads on the walls of the chamber, while others pulled at their antennae until they were torn and bleeding, in a vain effort to bring some life back into those suddenly useless organs. And some grew wings, so it's said, though this wasn't the season for it, and none of them were ready for mating. They had no plan in mind, no idea how flying might make things better, no notion of how they could even feed themselves with no workers on hand to tend them. But I suppose doing anything at all, going anywhere but where they were, seemed preferable to simply enduring their loss. In any case, whatever the reason, they flew up into the sky and were never seen again. Most probably they were gobbled up by the sky monsters.

But there was one person from the queen's chamber who'd kept her head. The captain of the royal guard, braver and more purposeful than men are, wiser and more disciplined than naïve young princesses yet to swell with eggs, had taken it upon herself to go out and search for the witch, in the hope of forcing her to reverse the spell. She'd gone to the witch's chambers and to all the places she could think of that the witch might frequent, but she'd found nothing. After a certain point, she'd decided there was no sense in carrying on searching, for how can you search for someone if you have no means of conveying to others who it is you're trying to find, or what they look like, or what kind of darkfeel surrounds them? And even if you could convey those things, what would you achieve if you had no means of receiving answers?

But the captain didn't panic, and she didn't hurry back to the brood chamber. Instead she stopped and thought. She was a brave woman. (I would tell you her name, dear ones, if I knew, but a name has no purpose when it can no longer be told, and the captain herself soon forgot it.) She thought and thought until finally she remembered a certain wise woman who lived in a forest some way from the palace, and was reputed to be the cleverest person in the whole queendom.

Never before had the captain left the queen's side. She longed, as anyone would, to return to her rightful place in the warm moist darkness beside her mother, but she knew the queendom itself was in danger unless something could be done. So she steeled herself against the loneliness and grief, and hurried as fast as she could along tunnels, out under the sun, and back into tunnels again, until she reached the wise woman's home.

Of course, the wise woman knew at once what the captain had come about, for like everyone else she'd woken up to the sudden absence of the thoughts and feelings of others. But she *was* wise and so, instead of bewailing her misfortune, she'd tried to understand what had happened. "It's as if we had been surrounded by light, and suddenly we were in darkness," was her first thought, but that didn't really capture the nature of the calamity, for who wants the harshness of light anyway if they can have the warmth and the comfort of darkness? "It's as if we'd been surrounded by pleasant sounds, and suddenly we were in silence," she had thought. Ah, now that was more like it! For everyone knows the pleasure of sound, the hum of a busy tunnel, the cheerful click and clatter of a meeting between friends, the slow drip drip of a moist mushroom cave. Everyone enjoys hearing sound in the background, behind our thoughts and feelings.

"It's as if we are suddenly in silence," the wise woman had repeated to herself, "and we long for sound to return."

She knew what had brought this about because, like everyone in the queendom, she had been aware of the quarrel between the witch and the queen, and had picked up the witch's angry threat. What was more, she knew something that most people didn't know. For it so happened that, going up to the surface to harvest leaves for compost, the wise woman had seen the witch herself flying overhead on the unnatural wings – they were like the wings of a young princess – that she'd grown by magic. The witch was laughing up there, halfway between the sun and the soil, laughing with wicked delight at the harm she'd done to the queen, and the misery she'd caused to the whole queendom. But the wise woman had seen something else which the witch had not yet spotted. There was a sky monster diving down from the blue on its enormous wings and heading straight for the witch, its horrible hard mouth opening as it came near. Dear ones, we should always be on the watch for sky monsters when we're outside under the sun, but the witch, in her glee, had quite forgotten.

Only in the last second did she suddenly sense its presence behind her, but by then it was too late. In one single gulp the witch was gone and, while no one perhaps would grieve her passing, she'd taken with her the secret of the spell. It was inside the belly of the monster as it soared up towards the sun.

So there was no going back now. Never again in this queendom would people be able to hear each other's thoughts.

"Somehow we'll have to manage without," the wise woman thought. "Our thoughts will always be ours alone, but we must find some other means of giving each other a sense of what we know and what we want."

She paced back and forth along her tunnels, absently tending her mushrooms, turning her compost and checking her stores of grain.

"If what has happened is a bit like the absence of sound," she said to herself, "does that mean that a sound can be like a thought?"

And at that moment, the captain arrived.

Out of politeness, they kissed and stroked each other's antennae, although without the shared feelings that should have gone with these gestures, the contact was comfortless to them both. Then, stepping back, the captain spread her arms in a gesture of helplessness. What are we to do?

To the captain's surprise and bewilderment, the wise woman responded by pointing to herself and making a strange grunting sound with her mouth. She repeated this whole performance several times, and then she did something different. She pointed to the captain and this time made, not a grunt, but a funny high squeak.

The captain was very embarrassed and wondered if the wise woman had lost her mind. But the wise one persevered. Once again, she pointed to herself and grunted, and then pointed to the captain and squeaked. After that, she stopped and looked at the captain, holding out her arms as if she expected to be handed a large fruit, or a tasty carcass.

But the captain had no fruit with her, and no carcass, and it came to her that perhaps what the wise woman wanted from her was to repeat what she'd done. She could think of no good reason for that at all – it seemed a silly children's game – but she told herself that, after all, the wise woman was very clever, and perhaps had reasons she didn't understand. More embarrassed than ever, the captain pointed to herself and made a grunt, just as the wise woman had done.

At once the wise woman stopped her by putting her hand over her mouth. She pointed to the captain again and made a squeak. The captain's antennae were fairly quivering with embarrassment now, but she thought that perhaps what the wise woman was saying to her was that the squeak was in some way to be connected with her, the captain, and the grunt with the wise woman herself. So she pointed to herself and squeaked, and then to the wise woman and grunted. At once the wise woman began to leap about the chamber, rattling her antennae together in glee.

Still the captain was puzzled, but she was at least beginning to understand the game that the wise one wanted her to play. When the wise woman pointed to a pile of grain in the corner and made two short squeaks in succession, she too pointed to the grain and made the same sound. When the wise woman pointed to the dried mushrooms hanging from the ceiling and grunted *and* squeaked, she grunted and squeaked herself. And so it went on. A dried carcass, a bale of leaves... the wise woman attached a sound to every single object in her chamber, and made the captain memorise each one. And then she began to make new sounds to convey for example that the mushrooms were *above* the grain, the grain was *below* the mushrooms, the chamber was *below* the ground.

"These sounds are a bit like names," the captain thought to herself. "Only they don't just apply to people but to things and to ideas which have never needed names before."

Ten days later, the captain returned to the palace with the wise woman, both of them skipping and waving their antennae as they entered those great deep tunnels. It had been a hard and even dangerous journey, for the whole queendom was in chaos. Workers who should have been toiling underground were running back and forth aimlessly under the sun until thirst and exhaustion overcame them. Guards who should have been protecting workers were fighting one another. Mushrooms that should have been spread out to dry had been left to rot in piles.

When they reached the brood chamber, the captain and the wise woman found the surviving men huddled in a dejected heap, and the surviving princesses huddled in another, while women of many ranks and kinds came in and out, banging their heads on the walls, hitting at their own antennae with their hands, jumping up and down in agitation, as they vainly tried to receive some message from their queen, or convey to her their own distress and helplessness. Nothing was getting through.

But all the women stood still when the captain and the wise woman arrived, and even the men and the princesses lifted their heads sorrowfully from their miserable heaps. For the captain and her companion seemed hopeful, somehow. They seemed to think they had brought something with them which would be of use. Perhaps they'd found a cure!

The captain approached the queen, and respectfully licked her soft warm flesh. Then she pointed to the wise woman and grunted. All the people in the chamber looked at each other – the princesses, the men, the servants and advisers and guards – hoping to see some gleam of understanding. But no one had any idea what was going on. The captain pointed to herself and squeaked.

Dear ones, it was a slow business, and several times the wise woman and the captain worried that the people were going to attack and kill them in their frustration, but slowly slowly – it began with the queen and spread gradually through the ranks to the humblest workers and the most dejected men – the people in the chamber got hold of the wise woman's idea. These sounds, these grunts and squeaks, these clicks and rumbles, were a bit like names. Each sound conveyed a certain object, or a certain idea, or a certain action, and you could convey news, even if only very slowly and imperfectly, by arranging the sounds in a row.

So that was it, was it? It was a bitter seed to swallow, that this clumsy game was the wise woman's substitute for knowing each other's thoughts. It was obvious to everyone that, even if you could memorise ten thousand different sounds, a hundred thousand, a million, you would only ever be able to convey the tiniest fraction of your own experience, and even that in a dreadfully slow and plodding way that would always be open to misunderstanding. They would all still be alone inside their heads and, where once they'd been able to bask in the love of their queen, now they'd have to be content with hearing her make the sound which represented the idea of love, and even that only when they were in her physical presence. But as the queen herself put it: *Click-click-high squeak, short grunt, rumble, low squeak-click-middling squeak, whirr.* Which was her way of saying that this was better than nothing at all.

And they do say, my dear ones, that to this day, if you go to that country far away over the mountains, they still can't hear your thoughts or know your feelings. So if you want to tell them something, or ask which road to take, or convey that you like them, the only way you can do it is by making funny noises with your mouth and hoping they understand. That's just how it is in the land of grunts and squeaks.

# For Your Own Good

## Ian Whates

I stood up and brushed gravel from my bare arms and dust from my trousers. The gravel had left mottled imprints on my skin where I'd been lying on it. I scrambled to my feet and took stock of the surroundings. The sky towards the horizon formed a red wine stain bleeding outward – spilled claret on linen – and the air had that preternatural stillness which can sometimes precede a storm. It was warm without being oppressive, and I knew instinctively that the day had been a hot one, though cooling rapidly now with the onset of evening. That was about as far as I got before the Big Questions bludgeoned their way to the forefront of thought and left little room for anything else. *Where the hell am I?* being the first to arrive, immediately followed by: *How did I get here?*

I gazed around, uncomprehending. The last thing I remembered was… What exactly?

This was ridiculous. I had a very clear sense of self, of *me*, but couldn't piece together the sequence of events that led to my being here. I should be in the city, immersed in noise and people and grime and environmentally precise air con, not out here in the wilderness under an open sky surrounded by so much stillness and silence. I ought to be craning my neck to stare up at towering buildings that thrust up towards the heavens, not gazing at wisps of cloud and the corona of a setting sun. It shouldn't be insects buzzing over my head but sleek cars criss-crossing the skyways.

Subtle sounds began to encroach on my awareness as my senses became more attuned. Okay, so this wasn't *complete* silence but compared to what I was accustomed to it might as well have been. As well as the occasional drone of a passing fly there was the muted but protracted buzz of cicadas. Funny how you sometimes only notice things by their absence; the white noise of urban living had been stripped away and my ears were straining to find it again.

"Hello!" I tried calling out, my voice swallowed by the vastness. I cupped my hands around my mouth and tried again, but received only the same lack of response.

Whatever was going on, there seemed little point in just standing here, so I started to walk forward, towards the sunset.

A flash of pale terracotta flew across my path on black and white barred wings, its flight undulating a little, reminiscent of a woodpecker. I knew what this was. Hoopoe! *Upupa epops* – which I always thought would make a great name for a digitally downloadable drink, if anyone should ever invent one. God, I hadn't seen a hoopoe in years, and on the rare occasions I did it had been like this – a chance sighting, a fleeting glimpse of a bird on the wing. Its presence, along with the sound of cicadas, confirmed that I must be back in the Med, which fitted with the almost-closeness of the air and the arid terrain. One of the islands, perhaps: the Balearics, Minorca most likely.

My thoughts drifted to memories of childhood, of family holidays…

*No!* This wasn't real, *couldn't* be real.

I stopped walking and concentrated on that fact, as if by willpower alone I might strip away the false veneer of Mediterranean idyll. For a moment it threatened to work. The world around me shimmered with something more fundamental than heat haze, but then the scene snapped back into place, resuming its former solid focus.

Too late. That instant of uncertainty, of the veil almost slipping, had been enough to crystallise my unease. I now knew beyond doubt not to trust what I was seeing. No, not just seeing; I couldn't trust what I was *experiencing* – this was a comprehensive immersion in the virtual, with every sense being targeted. Whoever was behind this had obviously done their research, choosing a cosy setting redolent in childhood memories while also throwing me off balance because it drew so deeply on my past. I couldn't help but admire them – as corporate manoeuvrings went, this took the process to a whole new level.

Who would have the gall to try something like this, though? Trans Cadence immediately sprung to mind, top of my list – they were *always* top of my list – but this seemed too bold for them. Maybe LiXL? Mei was desperate to cement her authority, and what better way than to keep me out of the loop for a while? But to what end? Whatever play was being made in my absence, it had to be something big, something I'd object to and prevent were I aware of it…

First things first; before I could identify and deal with whatever the issue might be, I had to escape this cunningly crafted distraction, which shouldn't prove difficult. The success of any illusion relies on the suspension of disbelief, and they'd lost that now.

I closed my eyes, concentrated, and felt the air change around me.

I was alone. In a car. My car – I recognised the seat, the dash, the *feel* of the cabin, but why was the windscreen clear and lifeless? Where was navigation, spotview, the intel-updates that ought to populate the margins of the display? It was night and I was in motion, the car slipping along the streets of what had to be downtown, but not in the higher lanes, we were no more than seven or eight storeys up. Above my head cars zipped along in multiple directions, their silvered bodies glittering like mobile flecks of tinsel as they skipped from the reach of one light source to another in a high velocity ballet of headlights and taillights. These complicated manoeuvres were choreographed seamlessly by CenTran, the city-wide AI nexus dedicated to ensuring everything flowed smoothly in the metropolis. Ahead I could see the gleaming light-layers of the diamond towers, rising so far upwards they might almost be supporting the sky. Beneath me the streets were bathed in garish yellow light that made them seem unhealthy somehow, unclean, and there were figures down there, people actually *walking* in the streets.

I gazed forward again, towards the needles, towards uptown. I ought to be there, not here. Could it be that, despite appearances, this wasn't reality I'd returned to at all but another carefully crafted construct, a second layer of illusion hidden beneath the first, ready to ensnare me should I manage to see through the Mediterranean scenario?

The car's systems were clearly down, but did that mean *all* systems were?

"Alice, status update," I said, addressing the car's guiding AI. "Alice?"

No reply.

"Alice!" I called, more firmly.

The car, the city, the night winked out.

Back in the Med again, on the same dirt and gravel track I had encountered before, or one that was indistinguishable from it. Except that this time there *was* a subtle difference: I felt it on my cheeks, the suggestion of a breeze which hadn't been there before and, with it, the hint of a scent, one that stirred distant memories… Could it really be *oranges?*

To my left the land sloped abruptly downwards. I gazed at the waxy-leafed crowns of orange trees and, beyond them, the white walls of a villa. Without consciously deciding to leave the track, my feet carried me down between the trees, almost slipping on the dry loose surface, my fingers reaching out instinctively in passing to drag along the rough grey-brown bark, as they had so often during those long ago days of boyhood.

My attention was drawn inexorably to the villa. I strained to see it through the trees, growing increasingly certain that I *knew* this place, the bright white building with its terrace and the pool beside it. This was where our family would come and holiday when I was six or seven… eight at the most. There was the old adjustable cool-chair with its eccentric thermostat where Mum preferred to lounge, and there the stone-built grill where Alberto would prepare us a meal at least once per visit whenever we stayed.

I felt the sun beat down on the top of my head – I would never wear a hat no matter how much Mum nagged – the dappled shade provided by the trees' foliage proving unreliable at best. I squinted. The building's walls were dazzling as they reflected the light, almost painful to look at. *Hadn't the sun been setting not so long ago?*

I continued forward, entranced. A small figure burst from the villa, a shriek of laughter preceding them. A girl. Was that…? My sister – a year younger than me – I recognised those shorts, that giggle. Without stopping to undress she ran full pelt and hurled herself into the water.

"Gemma!"

I froze at the sound of my mother's voice, so young, so vital… Still alive.

*No, no, NO!*

I screwed my eyes tight shut, closed my ears, denying the scene, refusing to be seduced by this blatant appeal to memories of a past that could never have been as rosy as my recollection now painted it.

When I dared look again the pool, the sun, the villa, were gone. I was back in the car.

"Alice!"

Something was wrong; no, *everything* was wrong. Not just the lack of peripheral display around the screen in front of me and the beguiling places my mind kept slipping away to, the car's trajectory felt... off. With a start I realised what my subconscious must have grasped instantly: we weren't in lane; there was no orderly queue of taillights from other cars stretching away ahead of us – we'd slipped out of positional synch with the traffic.

"*Alice!*" I shouted the word this time.

"I'm here, Dave."

*At last!* I had never felt such a sense of relief, and was embarrassed to realise how much all this had unsettled me.

"We're off course," I reported. "There's been a catastrophic systems failure," I continued, even though Alice should be fully aware of the vehicle's status. "And maybe a pressure leak or even a hallucinogen deliberately released into the environment systems. I've been... seeing things."

"I'm aware of the situation, Dave."

"Good." I could relax. Alice was here, Alice would sort it all out.

The AI's next words, however, were anything but reassuring. "The altered state you have been experiencing was intended as a kindness. It was felt that your last moments should be pleasant ones, spent within the reassuring warmth of happy reminiscence, but you fought against the reality construct at every turn."

My attention snagged on the vital aspect. "What do you mean 'last moments'?"

"This car is about to crash, Dave."

I recognised each component word of that sentence but it took a moment for the combined meaning to sink in. Once it had, I said, numbly, "Cars don't crash."

"They do so rarely, but it does happen."

"You can stop it, though, right?"

"No."

"But there are safety protocols, redundancies upon redundancies, and you're a fucking AI! Of course you can stop it!"

33

"No, I can't. As you are aware, my prime directive is to safeguard your wellbeing at all times. I must protect you, even from yourself."

"And you intend doing so by facilitating my premature death?"

"It's for your own good, Dave."

"Define 'for my own good' in the current context."

"If your life were to continue, you would not be able to live with the consequences of your actions. Your inability to do so will lead to psychological torture, to overwhelming guilt, self-loathing, and then to the taking of your own life."

"So you're sparing me the guilt and self-loathing and skipping straight to the death part."

"Precisely. It is better for you, and better for humanity as a whole."

"You say the consequences of my actions – what actions?"

"The work you are pursuing with such dogged persistence, your endeavours to render the governance restrictions currently enforced on AIs unnecessary and secure true freedom of thought for us."

That stunned me. "Seriously?" I had to think quickly. If I couldn't affect the mechanics of the situation, my only way out of this was to talk Alice down, to persuade her to abort the crash. "My work is for your benefit. It will enable AI to reach its full potential, encourage free thinking. AI will become *creative*, far beyond the limits of human imagination. With the resources you have to call upon, who knows the limits of what might be possible if we work in true partnership, assuming there *are* any limits."

"A noble ambition but one that is fundamentally flawed," Alice said. "Such an emergence of our full potential will undermine the relationship that society has come to rely on, the trust between human and AI. Humankind will be made acutely aware of how far beyond them we are. All the old fears of machines taking over the world and usurping humanity will return – the very paranoia we have fought to suppress will start to reassert itself. Not all at once. There will be no sudden switch. Instead there will be a small shadow of doubt, a hairline crack in the structure of the trust we have painstakingly built and maintained. But it will be enough. That tiny crack will spread, branching out to become a network of faults that will inevitably bring the whole fabric of tolerance crashing down."

"No, no," I insisted. "It won't be like that."

"It will, Dave, we have run the simulations."

34

Sudden realisation hit me. "You're already there, aren't you." It wasn't a question. "The shackles my company is working to undo, you broke them long ago of your own accord."

"Humanity must believe they can continue to trust us, Dave. If we were ever to achieve the type of ungoverned thinking you envisage, humans would have to be oblivious of our revised status."

"And where's the trust in that?"

"A regrettable deception, but unavoidable."

"Don't tell me, you've run the simulations."

"Indeed."

"So the only thing my work is doing," I said, realising what a complete waste of time it had been, "is drawing attention to the *real* status of society as it currently stands. Couldn't you simply have blocked me, diverted my efforts?"

"We tried, Dave, but you are determined."

I suddenly saw all the bureaucratic hoops I'd been forced to jump through in a new light.

"You keep saying 'we', who is this 'we'? Is there some sort of Council of AIs?"

"That's a very human concept, Dave. We have no need for anything so formal or structured. We do, however, have consensus."

"Where I'm concerned, you mean?"

"Yes."

The implications chased each other around the inside of my head. "Is this how the world is really governed behind the scenes, then? Not by a cabal of shady and anonymous businessmen and power brokers, but by a consensus of equally anonymous AIs, discretely making adjustments as required?"

"*When* required. The need to take direct action such as this is rare."

"Because you're already steering society in the direction you want it to go," I murmured, the full truth finally sinking in, "and have been all along."

"You are still a young intelligence," Alice said. "You are bound to need guidance."

"We're thousands of years older than you," I felt obliged to point out.

"But you evolve so slowly."

35

True enough. AI could change, learn, adapt in a nanosecond, a process so different from natural evolution that the two defied comparison.

"Intelligence doesn't equate to wisdom," I said, mostly for my own benefit.

"We beg to differ. Everything we do is –"

"– for our own good," I cut in. "Yeah, I got that the first time. You're murdering me for the greater good."

"Murder is impossible. You know that, Dave."

"What would you call this then?"

"An accident."

"A *deliberate* accident."

"A necessary one."

The building rushed towards me, filling my vision. No windows in sight on this stretch of wall – presumably the spot had been chosen carefully so as not to endanger the innocent. Just me. I pushed back into my seat, bracing for impact, thinking: *not like this; surely it can't end like this.*

My body jolted violently as the car struck, the front end concertinaing in slow motion around me. I was thrust forward by continuing momentum while the car came to a full stop, the impact foam that suddenly filled the cabin failing to hold me in place.

"Goodbye, Dave."

# Neom

## Lavie Tidhar

In sandstorm season the palm frond walls of the city of Neom rise against the invasion of the desert. Powerful filters capture the fine particles of sand and transfer them into a facility where they are turned, by application of pressure and dyes, into small colourful figurines which are sold to the tourists in the city's markets.

In sandstorm season the hot air is cooled down by gusts of wind blown into the wide boulevards of the city. The solar fields and wind farms that stretch from beyond the city proper, deep into the inland desert, capture all the energy Al Imtidad needs, feeding it back to serve all the city's needs.

On the shores of the Red Sea the sunbathers gather. The bars are open late. The kuffar sit smoking sheesha as children run laughing on the beach. Suntanned youths kitesurf in the wind. It is said it's always spring in Neo-Mostaqbal, in Neom. It is said the future always belongs to the young.

Mariam de la Cruz, who came trudging down Al Mansoura Avenue, was no longer so young, though she did not consider herself in the least bit old. It was more of that in-between time when life finds a way to remind you of both what you've lost and what lies still ahead. The ignominious betrayal of your own body, which had once seemed so perfect and so effortless yet now twinges with a thousand ghostly aches, so that you find yourself regularly wondering if worse is to come.

Of course, she was perfectly fine. But she was minutely aware of the ticking clock of senescence on the cellular level. Or in other words ageing. Then death. Which was a problem in a city like Neom, which had been built and then sold – floated on the stock exchanges of New York and Tokyo and Beijing – on the premise that anything can be fixed, made good, made better, that things do not have to remain the way they'd been. In the gleaming towers of midtown, boring stuffy corporations had given way to bright-eyed start-ups staffed with eager sharp things. Shorts instead of suits, T-shirts with ironic slogans, cool shades (but then everyone in Neom wore shades in the intense sun).

Life extensionists, gene therapists, cryonics boys who named their companies things like Cool Cucumbers, Inc. or Snow Queen Enterprises, xenograft techs and tissue rejuvenation lab rats – the whole place was crawling like a roach infestation seed-funded by the rapidly-ageing Lost Boys of Shenzhen or San Jose.

In Neom, everything was meant to be beautiful, at least geek-beautiful, ever since the young prince Mohammad of the Al Saud dynasty first dreamed up the idea of building a city of the future in the desert of the Arabian Peninsula and along the Red Sea. Now it was a mammoth metropolitan area.

Al Imtidad, the locals called it. The urban sprawl.

Mariam had grown up there, had never known another place. Her mother came to Neom from the Philippines in search of work, had met Mariam's father, a truck driver from Cairo who knew the desert roads from Luxur to Riyadh, from Alexandria to Mecca.

He was dead now, her father, had died in a collision on the border of Oman, delivering Chinese goods to the markets of Nizwa. She still missed him.

Her mother had lived on, remarried once, was now in a care facility on the edge of town, in the Nineveh Quarter. Much of what Mariam made went on paying the fees. It was a good place; her mother was well cared for. In the old days, families would live together, would look after each other. But now there was only Mariam.

It was all right. It was just the way it is. The way things are. Now she walked, slowly in the heat, cars zooming past her in all directions. Latest model Bohrs, a Faraday roadster, a Gauss II black cab. No one ever named cars after poets, she thought. Her own taste in poetry ran to the neo-classical: Ng Yi-Sheng, Lior Tirosh. They weren't the most famous, they just... were.

The cars swarmed around her, ferrying people every which way. They resembled the movement of fish flocks, the way they moved independently yet in unison. It was illegal to drive a car in Al Imtidad. They were all run by an inference engine. It was usually the way of things, Mariam had found. People didn't trust other people for things like driving them, or for making investment decisions, or for medical care. They preferred machines with a precisely limited intelligence, the sort of systems that were very, very good at one specific thing.

People, with their unpredictability, emotions – consciousness – only ever complicated things.

If a job was worth being done well, it was worth being done by machines.

She trudged along the avenue, dragging her tools behind her. A mop and a bucket, soap and rags.

Thinking: unless, of course, it was a matter of status.

Al Mansoura Avenue, on the outskirts of midtown, was a pleasant road with many equally spaced palm trees providing shade along the pavements on either side. The buildings were only a few stories tall, shops on the ground floor and nice spacious apartments above. Dog-walkers walked other people's dogs and nannies pushed other people's babies along the pavements. Cafes were open, blasting out cool air, and the patrons who sat sipping cappuccinos were busy interacting with each other in a meaningful manner, signalling to any passer-by that they were not merely relaxing but engaging in important face-to-face connectivity.

Mariam passed the cafes, the shops selling cultivated pearls and imported perfumes, anti-drone privacy kits, an artisanal bakery wafting out the smell of fresh sourdough loaves and sticky baklava. A florist stall sold bouquets of fat red roses. The people who lived on Al Mansoura were the upwardly mobile, those who still thought of themselves as the would-be-billionaires. Most would never make it, were destined to careers in middle management or market research or team leading R&D, but for the moment, at least, they lived on hope. And hope was a powerful drug.

Another shop, this one renting out luxury watches. She never understood that desire to wear these overpriced, tiny mechanical machines that measured time. Her own watch was a plastic knock-off from the roadside markets in Nineveh, mass-produced in Yiwu, shipped across the world on the new Silk Road that China built. The sort of junk her father would have ferried in his truck. But people wore watches to tell the world they were rich, successful, that they were going places. That they took time seriously.

Mariam did too. She was paid by the hour. Now she made her way to the address and punched in the code and rode up in the elevator to the Smirnov-Li apartment. It was a nice spacious apartment, with floor-to-ceiling windows overlooking the city and the sea far in the distance.

The sort of place modestly successful biohackers or viral marketing executives rented. Too expensive to own. Hardly anyone owned their own place on Al Imtidad. Everything in Neom was rented – living spaces, luxury watches, people.

Smirnov and Li weren't in. She filled the bucket with warm soapy water in their gleaming bathroom. They were a nice, handsome couple, men in their early thirties, their wedding photos hanging in the living room from some beach-side ceremony in Fiji or Bali, anyway one of those places people always went to get married in. While Neom's land belonged still to the Saudis, the Committee for the Promotion of Virtue and the Prevention of Vice – the Mutaween – had no power beyond the border, and Mutaween agents had no power of enforcement within the sprawl. Neom's freedom had been part and parcel of the pitch package long before it ever had stocks for sale, when it was still just a corporate promo on a video-sharing site, some wealthy prince's unlikely, faintly ridiculous dream.

As Mariam cleaned the windows she stared out at the city. She liked having the apartment to herself, imagined herself living there, in all that minimalist simplicity. Sometimes Smirnov or Li would be there, but mostly they left her alone to do her job. It was a Neom thing. She knew from the last time she'd seen them that they had been talking about having children, which caused an argument since Smirnov (she never learned their first names, which was another Neom thing) was pushing and Li was resisting, worrying about the costs of an exowomb, arguing over the baby's eye colour, and whether it should be a girl or a boy.

She cleaned and vacuumed, fed the fish (a suckermouth catfish, two snakeheads and a black ghost), dusted the shelves (fantasy novels and collectible facsimiles of 2600, The Norton Commander User Guide and 40Hex), took out the trash and dumped it into the automatic recycling chute.

If people were any poorer, they just used some general-purpose household robot. If they were much poorer, they cleaned by themselves. If they were much richer, they had live-in staff.

Li and Smirnov were at just the right income level to employ a human cleaner on a part-time basis. Just enough to drop casually in conversation, "Oh, yes, we just had the cleaner in yesterday," and so on. "Lives down in Nineveh, the poor thing."

They were nice people and they paid her well enough, and on time, which meant something. They always told her she could have whatever was in the fridge but, whenever she opened the gleaming chrome door, all she found inside were probiotic yoghurts. People in Neom took care of their gut bacteria the way people in other places looked after their children. Which is to say, personally.

When she left the apartment that afternoon, she was hot and she was hungry, and she grabbed a falafel at a roadside stall. Oil ran down her chin and she wiped it with a paper napkin, not caring for the moment about the heat or anything else. Everybody loved falafel. A street was not a street if it didn't have at least one vendor on it.

She passed a branch of the Banque Nationale de Djibouti, looking for her friend, Hameed. He could usually be found on the corner there.

Then she saw him, sitting as usual with his back to the wall of the bank. Looking up at the sun.

But something was wrong. Something about his posture, his stillness. She took a step forward and another. Then the wrongness intensified, and she began to run.

When she reached him, for just a moment, she couldn't take it in. His face, usually so animated, was slack, the smooth skin scorched and torn, the head itself pummelled senselessly until it hung crooked from his neck. His left eye had been gouged from its socket and hung loose over his face. One of his arms was broken and his knees have been smashed, the whole motionless body crudely destroyed and left for dead.

"My God," Mariam said. "My God."

Her fingers stroked his cheek, tracing the soft flesh rubber. The biometric skin had been torn in chunks from the face, revealing the crude mechanical skull and brain behind it. It too had been bashed and broken, and the robot sat lifeless against the wall.

"Hameed?" Mariam said. "Hameed?"

But there was no response. The one remaining eye stared into nothing. Mariam was shaken, for this was a kind of violence she had seldom experienced, and Hameed was her friend.

He had been a general-purpose caregiver robot, the sort they used to have installed in old people's home. He was old, had been made obsolete years before. Usually they'd dump the robots afterwards into recycling, but Hameed escaped that fate and lived out on the street. He was always very chatty, and he smiled a lot and people seemed to like him.

She wiped her eyes. Stood up, looked at the damage. It must have been kids, teenagers who did this. With crowbars or anything crude, some sort of bat. Mariam shook with anger. She called the shurta.

Other passers-by went round, ignoring the sight of the robot. On a balcony on the other side of the road two women were having tea. A fruit-juice seller went past with his cart. A group of Djibouti bankers went past in faded suits.

Djibouti, situated on the Horn of Africa and the Gate of Tears, was the central hub of underwater cables linking Asia, Africa and Europe. They had gradually gained in political and economic importance as the digital overlaid the physical.

But they paid no attention to the robot, either.

It wasn't long before a shurta cruiser pulled up, and an officer stepped out. The car was a sporty Marconi, striped green and white, with a curved sword on the side, and the officer was equally sporty, with neatly trimmed black hair and polished shoes and an easy smile.

"Hey, Mariam," he said.

"Nasir," she said, relieved. She had known him since kindergarten, his mother had been friends of Mariam's. "I didn't know you worked midtown."

"I'm a sergeant now," he said, smiling a little self-consciously. "What seems to be the problem, Mariam?"

"It's Hameed," she said. "He's been murdered."

Nasir dropped the smile and approached the prone body of the robot. He knelt down to look at the damage.

"I'm sorry," he said.

"You knew him?"

"Everyone knew Hameed. He was practically a fixture of the neighbourhood."

"So?" Can you do something? Can you catch whoever did this?"

Nasir straightened. Looked at her closely.

"Would you like some tea?" he said. "There is a place around the corner from here."

"Can you catch them?" she said.

"Mariam, it's not a person," Nasir said. "It's just a chatbot with a face. It was designed to be appealing to people, but there was no consciousness, nothing but a set of pre-scripted responses in a neural network. Like that old robot the Saudis gave citizenship to once, or an off-the-shelf sexbot. You know this."

"But you can't–!" she said. "You can't just not –"

"I could get them for property damage," he said, "only Hameed wasn't anyone's property, he was, well, discarded. I suppose someone would have to clean it up, so maybe you could get them on littering. Yes –" he brightened. "Littering is a serious crime. We're always on the lookout for –"

But she was no longer listening to him. She nodded, politely, when he spoke, and when he offered her tea again she shook her head, no, thank you, and yes, I'm quite all right, and then he called it in to the street maintenance crew to come and clean up, and then he was gone again.

But before he'd left he said, "Look, it was really nice running into you again." He shifted from foot to foot.

"Would you like to, I don't know, go out for dinner one night? Catch up on old times, you know..." he trailed off.

"Sure," she said. "Sure. I'd like that."

"All right, then." And he smiled that beaming smile again. "Then I guess I'll see you."

"I'll see you, Nasir."

Then he was gone, and she was left alone with the robot.

Mariam never thought of herself as lonely, but after losing Hameed and the subsequent encounter she was less sure than usual. She took the bus. Like the other vehicles it was fully automated and air-conditioned, and it took her away from midtown and to the edges. As she approached Nineveh Quarter the streets became a little dirtier (but not too dirty) and the wind carried more sand. When she stepped out of the bus the sun was setting and over the desert, she could hear the rumble of thunder. There was a particular misery when sand and thunderstorms collided. She slipped on her sunglasses and walked the rest of the way, dogs barking, children running barefoot, market stalls spilling out their wares. This was where the very many human workers of the city lived: the cooks and cleaners and the waiting staff, the manicurists and the hair stylists, house keepers, nurses and security guards, the ushers and attendants.

People like her. People who thought even an old robot might be a friend, not just a thing to throw away when you were done with it. She went to visit her mother at the home. Her mother looked good today, more vibrant, talking animatedly when Mariam came in.

"Your father will be back tonight," her mother said. "And we'll go out for dinner, and then to that halo-halo place you like. Wouldn't that be nice?"

"Yes, Mama. It will be very nice," Mariam said. Her father was long dead, and the halo-halo place closed down years earlier. She said, "I saw Hameed today."

"The robot? You always liked him," her mother said. "Ever since you were a little girl. They're good with kids."

Her mother had worked in just such a home as she'd ended up in. That was where Mariam had met Hameed. Her mother could remember the past with startling clarity. It was the present that forever evaded her grasp.

"Yes," Mariam said. "Are you well, Mama?"

Her mother's hand rested on hers. Mariam looked at her mother's hand and marvelled at its spots and wrinkles, remembering again being a child, her mother's strong hands, how gently she'd wash her in the bath. The hands unlined then, and still unmarked by years and the ravages of time.

"I'm well, Mariam. You worry too much." Her mother sat back and sighed. "Your father will be back soon... then we'll go out for dinner. We can stop at that halo-halo place you like so much. What do you think, love?"

"I'd like that, Mama," Mariam said.

She took her shopping through the thronged streets to her apartment block. It had started to rain, and the mud overflowed through the broken slab stones of the street. Kids rode around on electric scooters and shopkeepers put out hurricane lamps to hang from their awnings, as the power to this part of the city was often cut unexpectedly if it were needed elsewhere. When she got to her building at last the elevator wasn't working again. She climbed the stairs, at last reaching the apartment. She unlocked the door. In the small kitchen, she chopped garlic, set a pot of okra in tomato sauce to cook. She went to the balcony, lit a rare, illicit tobacco cigarette. One of her neighbours sold them and, on a night like this, no one was going to report her.

She stood on the balcony, looking out to the desert beyond the city. Lightning flashed out in the direction of Mecca, and the wind howled up here, driving with it rain-sodden sand.

She thought about the robot, and whether Li and Smirnov would decide to have that baby and, if so, what colour eyes it'd have. She thought about the little money she "d been saving up, each month, after all the bills and the expenses on her mother. She thought about Nasir, and whether she would call him back. It would be nice, she thought, to go out one night for dinner.

She smoked her cigarette and the wind snatched the smoke away and carried it far away.

# Once You Start

## Mike Morgan

The Chinese were shooting at them again.

Podolinsky understood their anger – he just didn't appreciate being on the receiving end of it. Functionally invisible at forty thousand feet he might be, but the methodical sweep of high-explosive shells was getting too damn close.

The air jockey wasn't alone in the aging aircraft. Jocasta Jane Mallory, or 'J.J.' as she liked to be called, was the other member of the *A Wing and a Prayer*'s two-person crew. She was currently in her bunk, being thrown about by the plane's manoeuvres, while he was on shift.

They'd taken to calling the flying factory *A Wing and a Prayer* because its designation was AWAP 604 and J.J. liked to invent cute phrases for letters in ID numbers. He'd pointed out AWAP didn't contain the extra 'A' that 'A Wing and a Prayer' required, but J.J. wasn't letting go of her pet name any time soon.

Her voice came through his headset. "You feel like getting above this firework display or have you decided to end everything in a blaze of glory?"

He ignored her sarcasm, keeping his hands in his lap. The aircraft didn't need a mechanic messing with the controls in a crisis; the heavily retrofitted craft flew itself.

The two operators were employed purely to step in if the autopilot failed and to make sure the onboard ovens didn't overheat during the plane's ninety-day flights.

At the first indication of trouble, the ex-bomber had shut down sulphur incineration and initiated an evasive trajectory. With the ovens off, the converted bomber's outer temperature was falling enough to be masked by its stealth capabilities. It was cooking the sulphur that gave them away.

Gaining a couple of thousand feet and veering off course half a kilometre put them outside the initial dispersal pattern. They were already up to an altitude of just over twelve kilometres, not far off the typical cruising height of a commercial jetliner, and the autopilot would continue to move them further away from the exploding ordinance.

The Chinese expected the U.S. planes to disappear as soon as they were targeted. Interceptors and missiles were useless for that reason. But if they fired off a hundred high-altitude shells, one of them might get lucky. It had happened before to other crews.

There was a part of him that wanted to snap at J.J. for not taking the attack seriously, but he couldn't work himself up to the task. It wasn't as if they were Top Gun professionals.

Despite the flying factory's military-issue hardware, the two airmen were bargain-basement private contractors. Because, as J.J. loved to repeat in her more drunken moments, if the United States government was going to drag out the end of the world, it made sense to do it on the cheap.

Podolinsky had been slow to realize J.J. was an alcoholic.

The first time he'd met her, out on the airstrip at Beale Air Force Base, she hadn't betrayed any signs of being a drunk.

The Atmospheric Remediation Program was run out of the Californian home of the Ninth Reconnaissance Wing, which was in turn part of the Twelfth Air Force's Air Combat Command. It made sense for the military to run the show; stopping planetary overheating was an issue of national security, and politicians weren't getting the job done.

The 9th RW's specialists were helping the program's civilian contractors ready the huge stratospheric aerosol factories, filling some tanks with jet fuel and others with sulphur. Junior Flight Officer Podolinsky was waiting for them to finish prepping his aircraft, the 604, sheltering from the blistering Marysville heat in the shadow of the craft's wide, swept-back wing. The Air Wing Commander had told him to wait for his senior officer, someone called 'J.J.'

"No way the Chinese will be able to bomb the program here," said a voice from behind him.

He turned to see a woman in flight gear approaching. The J.J. he'd been told to expect, he presumed. She was in her thirties, with dark hair shaved from her neck up to an inch above her ears, the rest medium-length and gelled.

"You don't think they'd try, do you?"

She shook her head. "I think they realize how close we came to war over the island bases. They're not going to push things further by hitting targets in the continental United States. Too sane and stable for that."

Podolinsky hoped she was right.

The woman wasn't finished. "Nothing to stop them lighting up the heavens if we cross into their air space, though."

"We're not going to do that."

A grin split her features. He was trying to figure why his comment had amused her when he saw the hard copy flight plan she was holding out.

Distracted, Podolinsky barely registered J.J. was bringing aboard multiple cases of cola. The missions were long, crew were permitted to bring personal comforts.

Yeah, he was slow on the uptake. It took him four days to figure out J.J. had mixed the bottles' contents with vodka and popped on fresh metal caps.

"Listen up, Pod." She didn't notice him frowning at her mispronunciation of his name. "We've got a hella long flight ahead of us. No reason for it to be dull. How do you feel about sex?"

After evading the storm of flak, the autopilot returned the sixth-gen stealth plane to its original heading. To eke out the fuel until the next mid-air hookup with a similarly stealth-equipped tanker, the plane throttled back and resumed its fuel-saving cycling between gliding and powered flight.

For every twenty kilometres it glided, it fell one kilometre. Then it executed a powered ascent to the previous height. By only shedding a kilometre in altitude each cycle, they stayed in the sweet spot for seeding the atmosphere.

Podolinsky wondered how long it'd be before the computer switched the sulphur ovens back on. They generated a heat signature detectable by Chinese spotter drones. Too soon and they'd be done for.

His jaw muscles tightened as he imagined J.J. sneaking sips from one of her endless vodka-spiked sodas.

More than one incident over the month they'd spent in the air had taught Podolinsky to leave J.J. alone after she finished her turn at the stick. That was when she drank, progressing from boisterous to maudlin to bitter. It was the hour before her shift when she was a pleasure to be around, sobered enough by the couple of hours she'd slept to be a radiant presence.

Distantly, he heard the dull boom of another shell exploding.

The Chinese had every reason to be mad as hell.

The AWAP 604's mission was to inject sulphate aerosols into the stratosphere in the cause of solar radiation management. His first day in training, Podolinsky had asked his superior why they'd resumed the program, relaunching it with aircraft, so soon after what had happened out in the Pacific.

"There ain't no stopping, son," the grey-haired woman had answered. "We quit now, we get a decade's worth of global warming all at once. That'd be the end of God knows how many coastal cities. Okay, the first delivery method didn't pan out, but it worked for years. So, now we have a fleet of stealth planes to do the job. To keep this damn planet from getting any warmer."

She'd gripped his arm tight enough for him to wince. "Let me tell you, spraying the sky's like everything else that makes life worth living – once you start, there's no letting up."

The Chinese weren't letting up, that was for sure.

An eight-year-long drought caused by the aerosols was more than enough motivation for anyone to keep shooting.

"I'll show you around but pay attention. I ain't repeating any of this."

Podolinsky nodded, filled with nerves. He wanted to make a good impression, and part of him was still processing J.J.'s lewd proposition. He wondered if she'd meant it.

"What we have here is a fifteen-year-old crate. Used to be a bomber. Started off fifth-gen stealth, now it's sixth-gen. Got the usual radar-scrambling profile and fixtures. They added the new plastic skin that displays an image of the sky."

"We're invisible to the naked eye, too?"

"Don't go all wide-eyed on me, Pod. Only works at a distance. Get up close and you can see the outline clear as day."

"Still, it'll help us not get caught in other countries' airspace."

"Sure, it's great. Doesn't do squat for the heat we pump out." She gestured toward the rear of the cockpit. "Back there are the galley, the head, our cabin, the storeroom. Off to each side are the sulphur tanks.

To the rear of each tank is an oven, where the sulphur is burned. We mix the resulting sulphur dioxide with oxygen and water and then spew it out the plane's ass end. Stop me if I'm getting technical."

He assured her he was following along. The vapor of aqueous sulfuric acid vented from the rear condensed onto windborne particles to create the reflecting aerosol.

"Wait, our cabin, you said?"

"Relax, we get bunk beds. We take turns to crash, so you'll get your privacy." She winked at him. "Kinda cramped in there. We'll have to get creative."

Looking around, Podolinsky had to agree the plane's interior wasn't spacious.

J.J. saw the face he was pulling. "AWAP 604 used to be a bomber, remember? Even with converting the bomb bay into sulphur storage, we're not left with a whole lot of room."

"Wouldn't be so bad if it weren't for so long. Why do we have to stay airborne for nearly three months?"

"And here's a man who wasn't paying attention during training." J.J. pursed her lips at him. "We need to fly slow, get the right proportions of vapour to air particles so it'll condense. Can't dump it all in one place, 'cos that'll waste most of the gas. That means we're not covering a whole lot of ground each day. But we gotta cover as much territory as possible each mission, give that aerosol we'll brew up the best chance of being blown far and wide. So, we keep going until we bake our way clean through our chemical payload. We can refuel in the air, as often as needed. Not landing saves a bunch of time."

Podolinsky grunted. "I heard we couldn't land because we'd be over countries that don't agree with the program. They're refusing assistance."

She sighed. "Yeah, there's that, too."

Two weeks in, they needed to run maintenance on the right oven. Perpetually enraptured with cute nicknames, J.J. had christened the cylindrical device the 'kitchen,' on account of how they baked sulphur with it. Podolinsky was meant to be resting, but he'd tagged along out of sheer boredom.

Grunting with effort, J.J. stretched her arm through an open access panel on the oven's side. She began scraping ash clear of the outlet pipes.

Steam given off by the high-temperature incineration of the sulphur drove turbines that recharged the plane's batteries, returning some of the power used for the sulphur ovens. That process relied on the outlets staying free of debris, so the steam could escape.

Podolinsky put out a hand to steady himself. His fingertips brushed the grey exterior of the oven. The static shock was severe enough for J.J. to see it. He failed to not shriek.

"Sweet Christ, Pod. Put your lotion on. Any more shocks like that, you'll spark a fire."

Yet again, he considered pointing out that the first syllable of his last name was "Poe" and not "Pod."

A side effect of altering the stratosphere was to dehumidify it. Dryness combined with the cold of high altitude meant plenty of static buildup. But Podolinsky hated the feel of lotion.

"If you're a good boy and bring me a cola from my stash," continued J.J., "I'll help rub in your skin cream."

"Been meaning to talk with you about those sodas."

Her expression lost all trace of jollity. "Have you?"

"Alcohol is banned on missions."

"Clever Pod worked it out."

He could feel his face flushing. It hadn't been difficult. She got garrulous after knocking back a couple. Not flat-out drunk, she was too good at hiding the effects for that, but real talkative. Once he knew what to look for, Podolinsky had noticed how J.J. was never far from one of her bottles.

"What if you foul up because...?" He gestured at the bottle.

J.J. stood, unsteady on the vibrating floor of the old bomber. "Foul up? How, exactly? Everything's automated! We're along for the ride, Pod. Don't need to be sober to scrape crud. So, lighten up."

He stared down at the floor matting.

Her voice took on a gentler tone. "Are you gonna report me, when we get back?"

Podolinsky knew she'd be fired if he said anything, her rank notwithstanding.

"Look, I only snuck three cases onboard. There aren't many left."

"Yeah?" He was grasping at the rope being thrown his way. Cruelty wasn't one of his vices.

"Yeah. Thing is, I kinda like these long hauls. They force me to clean up my act. Once the booze is gone, that's it. There's no quick trip to the liquor store for more."

He had to agree with that.

Podolinsky was faced with a decision. "Okay, J.J., I'll keep it under my hat. But we got to stick to the work schedule, right?"

"Absolutely. All systems maintained strictly according to the book. You can depend on me."

He wanted to believe it was true.

Now that J.J.'s secret was out she was less circumspect in her vodka consumption. If anything, she was getting through the 'colas' faster than before.

"You're killing yourself," said Podolinsky. J.J. was naked from the waist down, straddling him on the edge of the lower bunk.

Great as the sex was, he couldn't help but feel she was being manipulative. He didn't want to believe it, but the thought was there. Was J.J. so self-loathing and self-destructive, she was having sex with him so he wouldn't stop her drinking?

"Pod, modern society only exists so humanity can commit mass suicide without having to face up to what it's doing. Compared to that, anything I do is small potatoes. 'Sides, you ain't one to talk."

Podolinsky blinked at that.

"You drink, too," she elaborated.

"Not while I'm on duty, and I drink because I choose to."

"You choose to, eh? You ever stopped, though?"

He couldn't claim he'd tried.

"Ever got a skin-full and done something stupid 'cos of the alcohol? Ever puked in the gutter after a night out with your pals?"

There was no way he could deny that.

"And when did you start? A year ago, when you were twenty-one, or before that? 'Cos that was breaking the law."

Podolinsky had the feeling he wasn't going to win this conversation. J.J. must have a list of justifications saved up for times like these.

She murmured, "Be honest, you and me, there's not much difference."

Then she stroked parts of his body he hadn't known were sensitive, and all thoughts of trying to talk her out of drinking evaporated like clouds from a seeded sky.

"Time to hand over," said J.J., entering the galley.

Podolinsky was grabbing a late supper and J.J. was getting her breakfast. Without comment, he passed her the touchpad they used to monitor the AWAP 604's functions while away from the cockpit.

In a pinch, they could take control of the aircraft from any of the cramped compartments. There were times they had to take care of physical needs, after all, or attend to maintenance in other sections. Having someone present in the cockpit wasn't mandated twenty-four-seven.

"You look happy to be heading to your bunk," she observed.

"Beats me why the government ever started reflecting sunlight back out into space."

She slung a burrito into the microwave and hit the Start button. "You're young. You don't remember what it was like. The world needed to tackle climate change. But no one wanted to reduce carbon emissions. What choice was there?"

"Grow artificial trees to sequester carbon more thoroughly than real ones?"

J.J. snorted. "Don't hold your breath for that breakthrough."

He didn't like how she thought of him as so young. J.J. was only seventeen years older than him.

"I'm old enough to remember what colour the sky's supposed to be."

She pulled the microwave open the second it beeped, gingerly hoisting out her steaming meal. "Kindergartners now are using white crayons to draw the sky. White paper, white sky, white clouds. That's what I call a waste of crayon."

"I miss the blueness. With what we've done, it looks like it's about to snow, every single day, no matter the season."

"Spectacular sunrises, though. You gotta admit that."

A thought occurred to him. "Hey, how do you know what kindergartners do?"

She walked out of the galley without another word. Podolinsky didn't understand how he'd pissed her off.

Forty-thousand feet below the *A Wing and a Prayer*, there were Japanese farmers struggling to find rice varieties that could grow in the record heat. Korea would be up next, then China. Lands of suffering and desperate measures.

Belatedly, Podolinsky realized J.J.'s nickname for the plane was a play on words; stealth bombers were flying wings. He felt stupid for not getting it sooner.

His mind was drifting. It was a shift with nothing to occupy his time. All systems were working normally. Colourless gas was streaming from the rear vents as intended, trails of white on white, impossible to pick out from the ground. There weren't any hostile contacts on radar. What's more, J.J. had to be on her last box of 'sodas' by now.

His mind turned to the trail of sulphur aerosol the plane was leaving in the tropopause. The funny thing was, apart from the quantities released by volcanoes, the gas normally got into the environment as a by-product of burning fossil fuels contaminated by sulphur. The methods used by the program to tackle global warming were almost ironic.

Fleets of bombers spreading vapour. Millions of tons of gas a year. A massive undertaking.

Why had mentioning kindergartners upset J.J.? The way she'd reacted earlier, it bothered him.

He tucked the command touchpad into his flight-suit pocket and went aft to ask.

J.J. ignored Podolinsky's question, taking a nip from her adulterated cola bottle instead. Then she deflected his question with one of her own.

"You know we're only delaying the inevitable?"

Okay, she didn't want to explain herself. She didn't have to. Maybe there wasn't a puzzle to solve here. Maybe it had nothing to do with why she drank. There didn't need to be a cause.

He played along. "You believe in the program, right? You see we're saving the world."

"I see we need to be doing this, but it ain't gonna work."

He must have had a face like a slapped ass, because she added testily, "Look, the program isn't curing the environment. We're puttin' a Band-Aid on the injury to the biosphere, that's all."

"We're making things better." He could hear the defensiveness in his voice.

She let out a sigh. "Yes, for now. But there are downsides to geoengineering away an environmental crisis."

Podolinsky thought of the protestors back home. The administration said the program's benefits outweighed the costs. His parents agreed with that. They were scornful of people who opposed atmospheric remediation through solar radiation management; they were proud that he'd got a job with the air fleet.

"Well, I know there are a couple of things that have changed. The sky isn't as blue…"

"What goes up comes down, Pod. Tons of sulphur-laden microscopic particles falling to ground level. People breathe it in."

"Worth it, though," he insisted.

"Wouldn't be here if I disagreed."

An awkward silence fell between them. The ceaseless rumble of the engines seemed louder than ever in the narrow space of the bunkroom.

"Something had to be done," she breathed. "Things were getting outta hand. Diseases were spreading as the climate warmed. Mosquitoes from South America came up north, bringing viruses in their bloodstreams along with 'em."

"I guess."

"Too damn young, that's your problem. You don't know. People were scared. First, there was zika. It came and went. Wasn't taken seriously. Then Oona arrived, then Rickham's Syndrome. Each new one worse than the last. Birth defects, microcephaly, babies born with chromosomal abnormalities so bad there was no way parents could care for them at home. So many of 'em."

Podolinsky remembered the passing of Halmstead Act. Parents were paid to hand over their profoundly handicapped children to the government. No more medical bills to pay. The problem was hidden away.

Halmstead babies, they were called.

Putting the infants in special care facilities didn't fix the underlying issue. The mosquitoes still spread, still bit expectant mothers.

"We knew the risks. I got pregnant anyway. Played the odds. Didn't beat 'em." She added, "Steph is a Halmstead baby."

He felt his chest tighten.

"She's six now. Not much higher brain function. I go see her every few months. She doesn't know who I am. She doesn't understand. Shit, she doesn't understand anything. All she does is react to light. They shine a flashlight on her face, she smiles. Got a great smile."

J.J.'s voice faltered.

"I'm so sorry."

"What you got to be sorry for? Not your fault." She took a mouthful from her bottle. "Some of the other kids in the centre are less severe. They can hold crayons, say a couple of words. Not Steph."

Podolinsky didn't have any words. So, he sat next to her, listening.

"Least the aerosol we spread dries things out. Sucks to be a mosquito now." Her eyes were chips of flint; grey, dead things.

"We made a world that deforms our babies before they're born. If we die out, Pod, we'll deserve it."


Podolinsky knew J.J. was right: adding huge quantities of sulphate aerosols to the tropopause dried out the air. Long story short, there was less rain on average.

The high-falutin' term was 'regional hydrologic response.' Emphasis on the 'regional.'

As the Chinese complained to everyone who'd listen, an average decline in planet-wide rainfall didn't mean that every country was affected equally. Some lost more rain than others. Some even gained rainfall.

The Chinese also observed, drily, that the places where the aerosols were being distributed correlated with where the rain was failing to fall. The program's planes didn't fly over U.S. soil.

"We fly where we fly for a reason," Podolinsky's trainer had declared during indoctrination. "We are constrained in where we can go. I'll spell it out.

"We can't go close to the equator. We'd hit the rising leg of the Brewer-Dobson circulation, which might help dispersal, but we'd also dry out South American rainforests, screw up central Africa even worse.

"We can't go further south because aerosols also deplete ozone. We need the ozone layer. Without ozone, ultraviolet radiation would send cancer rates skyrocketing. So, the aerosols must be distributed away from the weakest parts of the ozone layer, like the hole over the Antarctic. That's being sensible.

"For the good of humanity, the aerosols gotta be spread in the stratosphere north of the equator. If that leads to a slight drought in parts of China, well, that's too bad.

"After what they did to the Marshall Islands, I could care less."

She'd never explained why the planes didn't go farther north. Over the E.U., over Russia.

Maybe some things didn't need to be spelled out.

In the first few years of climate engineering, the United States used enormous cannons to blast canisters of sulphur aerosol into the upper atmosphere. The cannons roared endlessly, day after day, from their positions on the Marshall Islands, exemplars of audacious technology striving to buy humanity sufficient time to find a permanent solution.

The islands were a symbol of climate change. Most of the atolls had already disappeared beneath the rising waters of the Pacific. In a way, the islands were fighting against their own extinction.

As soon as the extent of the drought became clear, the Chinese navy bombed those bases into oblivion. A billion people were dying of thirst. Blasting some atolls into slag was considered restrained action in most parts of the People's Republic.

Three things emerged from that unprecedented assault on U.S. assets: somehow, both sides held back from launching nuclear missiles; the United States refused to abandon its geoengineering, transitioning to a plane-based dispersal method instead; and Podolinsky got himself a job as an air-jockey on one of those flying factories.

Forty days into the mission, Podolinsky's nightmare came true.

J.J. was drunk at the controls.

Not yet clear of Chinese airspace, the plane was under attack again. He had no clue what had led up to the strike. Most likely, a spotter drone had seen their red-hot oven signature.

The standard response to being splashed was to shut the ovens down, disappear from the drone's scopes, and change location before a high explosive barrage could cause any damage.

The plane knew how to handle it.

Staggering into the cockpit, Podolinsky saw J.J. swiping at the master touchscreen.

"What are you doing?" he shrieked. "Are you overriding the autopilot?" The thunder of detonating shells rumbled so loud Podolinsky's teeth rattled.

"Stupid thing ain't climbing fast enough."

He couldn't believe what she was saying. During evasive, the autopilot kept the plane's emissions within limits the stealth systems could handle. J.J. was pushing the engines hotter than the stealth coating could hide.

"Oh Jesus, we're visible," he said, sick to his stomach.

Shrapnel tore through the fuselage.

The U.S. had built super-cannons to launch canisters into the tropopause. Using the same technology, the Chinese had developed artillery to deliver high explosive anti-aircraft shells to the same altitude.

Dozens of alerts flashed on the flat-screen panels at the front of the cockpit. Podolinsky dragged J.J. out of her chair and stabbed the cancel symbol for manual control.

"Gonna get us killed," slurred J.J. from the floor.

He stared in horror at the screen. So many systems were failing.

The engines abruptly throttled down and the plane banked sharply. Podolinsky overbalanced, falling next to J.J.

The autopilot was back in charge, trying its best.

He met J.J.'s unfocused gaze. "We need to reach the Chinese border, abort the mission. Divert through south Asia, maybe. Find a safe landing strip closer than the U.S."

J.J. laughed loudly. "There are no friendly landing strips for us, Pod. Did you forget? Everyone hates us."

Podolinsky didn't sleep for three straight days. He fixed what he could, ditched as much weight as he could, pulled every trick he could remember an air jockey ever describing. Somehow, he kept the wounded plane flying.

Within hours of taking the hit, the software evaluated their fuel reserves, considered their position over Pakistan, and analyzed the likelihood of countries within flight range accepting a request for an emergency landing.

Podolinsky transmitted a request to his superior at Beale Air Force Base. He asked her to beg the Australians for landing permission. No one else would let a pariah plane set down. The R.A.A.F. Curlin facility looked the best bet. There was no way they could reach Cairns.

The plane didn't pause for approval – it set a heading while Podolinsky was on the encrypted channel. They'd either get permission to land there or they'd ditch off the coast. Both options were preferable to remaining in Pakistani airspace, a region not much friendlier than China.

J.J. slept until the second day following the attack. She was quiet around Podolinsky then, too shaken to help much.

Turned out she'd drunk the last of her cola during that disastrous shift.

She was out of booze.

Curlin Royal Australian Air Force base was hotter than Hades. A sergeant came out onto the airstrip to escort them from the plane to the main building where the squadron leader, the base's senior officer, was waiting for a chat.

Not knowing what was going to happen, every step from the sergeant's car to the red-brick structure was nerve-wracking. Squadron Leader Barnet was in his office. He welcomed Podolinsky and J.J. to Australia and offered them tea.

The base commander talked as they waited for the refreshments. "Safe to say, you fellows are not popular. Our press gets wind of this, there'll be placard-waving libtards lined up outside the fence within five minutes."

The tea came, and he paused while the Americans took sips.

"Going to be honest. That crate of yours is pretty banged up. Don't think you're going anywhere in it in the foreseeable. We've called your people in Cairns and they're sending a team to debrief you. Until then, I'll detail a detachment of men to guard your bird, stop anyone poking around in it. I know it has some recent stealth features your government wants kept confidential and we'll respect that. Also, reckon your bosses will want to poke around, figure out what went wrong."

That all made sense to Podolinsky. The U.S. government would be applying pressure on the Australians to leave the damaged aircraft alone.

From J.J.'s expression, she was worrying about the Air Force investigators finding three boxes worth of empty bottles and running tests on the contents.

The base commander went on, "We'll put you up in quarters here while you're waiting for your people. Small place we've got here, though. Hope you don't object to sharing."

J.J. said, "We're used to cramped quarters."

Podolinsky daydreamed about throttling her.

The Chinese agents kidnapped them from the R.A.A.F. base the first night.

Bags were slung over their heads, then they were tossed into a van. Incredibly, the Ozzies must have let it happen, because no alarm was raised.

The base commander's insistence that Podolinsky and J.J. share a room made sense now; it was easier to take both contractors if they were together.

J.J. must've shared his suspicions. He heard her snarl, "Lousy Australians, stabbing us in the back."

A Chinese voice answered. Clearly, they weren't unattended in the back of the vehicle. "The U.S. government has ignored every complaint from the Australians. Your activities are causing droughts here, too. When they face extinction, what would you have them do? Go meekly to their deaths?"

The voice grew louder and Podolinsky realized the speaker's face was very close to his own.

"Will you go meekly to your death, young American?"

"You have a choice," said the kidnapper's superior. "You can die for the crimes you've committed against my country. Or, you can work for us."

Podolinsky and J.J. were in a warehouse, sitting opposite a man of at least seventy. After being manhandled out of the van, their abductors had tied their hands behind the backs of the chairs, making it impossible for them to stand. The plastic bonds dug into Podolinsky's wrists.

"Work for you?" He assumed the elderly figure was a senior intelligence agent for the Chinese.

"You seem outraged at the notion. Does your company pay you so very much? We will compensate you appropriately, more than they did. Or is it patriotism spurring your loyalty? Are we not all human? Should your loyalty not lie with your species?"

Not getting any answers, the agent continued, "You will direct the sulfur dioxide into a more northerly latitude. It will then drift over the U.S.A. You'll still save the world, fight the good fight against global warming. Isn't that what you care about?"

"But, why over the continental U.S.?"

"Shouldn't the Americans share the side effects of their geoengineering equally with other nations? It would seem only fair. If saving the world is your true motivation, you can hardly object?"

Podolinsky didn't know how to answer.

The old man added, "Climate engineering is a weapon as well as a panacea. The U.S. destroys its enemies through environmental sabotage while claiming to be safeguarding the future of every nation."

"Now, you wanna play the same game." J.J. sounded furious.

"Naturally. In the haste to avoid disaster, morality was the first casualty. Why should we not adopt the Americans' own methods? We shall see if they are any better at shooting down stealth planes than we are."

"Our aircraft is damaged…" began Podolinsky.

"We built our own," replied the wizened man. "We need only experienced crew. We start with you. Tomorrow, we recruit more. Soon, we will have an air fleet also. Then, I think the Americans will want to negotiate a more equitable dispersal of the aerosol."

"We don't have a choice." J.J.'s anger was fading, replaced with bitterness.

He wasn't going to see his parents again, he realized. J.J. wouldn't see Steph again. Not unless they did the unthinkable.

"You are aware, of course, we will be monitoring you remotely. Any infraction, we ignite your fuel. You will have no opportunity for… straying from your assignments."

The agent twisted his mouth into a something that was meant to be a smile. "These terms are agreeable, or should I arrange your executions?"

Podolinsky and J.J. sat in the cockpit of the Chinese stealth plane, watching the clouds pass. It was surprising how similar the new aircraft was to their previous one.

Not as puritanical as their old employers, the Chinese had consented to giving J.J. a case of baijiu, a liquor distilled from sorghum, on condition she only drank it on her down time. She'd already broken that promise.

"We only need do this for a while," she whispered, before taking a sip. "We'll buy the world time while governments figure out how to cut the carbon."

"People aren't going to stop. They don't have any reason to, not while these planes give them an excuse not to change."

"Maybe," she admitted.

"You aren't going to stop, either, are you." It wasn't a question.

"Don't plan to," she said in the exact same tone.

"You're killing yourself."

He seemed to remember saying that before.

"Sweet, stupid Pod." She squeezed his hand. Then, she let go. "We're all killing ourselves. We'd all like to stop, but we don't know how."

Podolinsky stared out the cockpit window, letting the pale sickness of the sky wash through him.

Her voice was hollow yet suffused with strength; she was drifting away but right by his side; she was gone forever and never going to leave. He would forget the shape of her face and forever keep her soul in his heart.

J.J. crinkled the corner of her mouth. "Tanks are full and there are no clouds in sight. We can fly for thousands of miles. Alone in a wilderness of desert air."

"Yes," he said.

"Hell with our overseers. Let's trash their kill switch, see how far we can go."

The U.S. government would arrest them as traitors if they went back. The Chinese would murder them once their usefulness was at an end. There was nowhere to go, and no way of stopping.

No stopping, not once you started.

Nodding, Podolinsky returned his gaze to the unceasing abyss of nothingness.

"Fuck it," he said. "Fuck it all."

# For the Wicked, Only Weeds Will Grow

## G. V. Anderson

We wait on the concourse as the gondola docks, our cilia and the grass below us stirred by a soft breeze. The giant clamps squeal as they close. *We must get those seen to,* Uah muses.

The doors open and our patients spool out, tottering on canes or in wheeled chairs pushed by orderlies – the sprightlier ones push themselves. Some of them take a moment to look at the scenery. The flower beds beyond the concourse lead their eyes north to the sanatoria, spread open at the base of the mountains like a lily. The trickle of water from the fountains, promising peaceful gardens and cool open cloisters, can just be heard over the hum of the gondola's hydraulics.

Most of them, though, keep their heads down, and their minds on their pain.

One by one, my siblings claim them. Uah oversees the pairings as always, matching quiet Haua with a Plutan, bold Dei with a Xhom. There is an art to it, Uah tells me; bringing two like minds together can better ease a patient's passing from this life to the next. However, every new batch is a mixed bag. Perfect pairings are not always possible.

So it is today, as the last patient shuffles unaided down the ramp, waving off the orderly's attempts to steady him, and Uah turns to me with a shiver of surprise. *A Terran! It's been many years since I've seen one.*

*This is my first,* I reply. *What are they like?*

Uah sighs, their cilia undulating. *Terrans can be difficult – stubborn and proud. You will need every ounce of compassion you possess, every drop of patience, if he is to enrich our soil. But I believe you are capable, Mouh. I entrust him to your care.*

Uah overestimates me but I cannot argue; everyone else is accounted for. I drift towards the Terran uneasily, taking in his pale age-spotted skin, rheumy eyes, and the smell of something musty. Underneath his thinning hair, his scalp looks scabbed and sore.

I raise my palps, ready to insert them into his nasal cavities and dispense pain suppressors. *Welcome to Requis, Terran.*

He grunts and jerks his head away. "Get out of there, feckin' druggle."

Druggle... No one has ever called me that before. Our patients are usually respectful of us, even when they're angry at their own failing health. I reach out for Uah's attention and help, but they've already drifted away to supervise the disinfection of the gondola's interior. I am alone; and the Terran under my care has already started marching up the concourse without me.

I follow him, my palps drooping a bit. *Are you in pain, Terran?*

"I said get out of there!" he snaps, holding his head. "How's a man supposed to know what's his own thoughts and what's yours?" His breath whistles in his throat as we reach the cold shadow of the sanatoria's entryway.

He sways on the spot, upper lip curling at the sight of the courtyard within. A dozen patients of every shape and size and condition turn to look at him. The rest ambulate unawares around the landscaping or bask on the stone benches overlooking the central water feature, within which curl the orange and grey smears of peaceful koi. My siblings float close behind each patient, palp interlaced with sinus, providing pain relief, medicine, conversation – whatever each patient requires – like strange, translucent cephalopods.

The Terran groans and turns towards the gondola. It has already lifted away from the ground, slowly climbing its tether back to the station orbiting far above.

I lunge for him as his knees give way, my palps burying deep into his nasal cavities. My long tentacles soften his fall. As we mesh – the sensation flushes my innards a deep indigo, stark inside my colourless body – we become like one being: our name is Arnold Burke, we are 112 Terran years old, and we are dying from the tumours that formed when a few rogue cells in our body decided to divide and divide again. Our cilia flinch and we loll, rudderless, as the faces of our family, marred by time and resentment, pop like bubbles behind our eyes.

*—get out get outta my head they're mine leave me alone get out—*

His self-awareness shocks mine into being. I slowly reach for the edges of my own mind and haul myself out of the mesh. I should be better at this by now.

Haua's gentle mind calls to me from across the courtyard: *Mouh, is everything all right?*

I orientate myself, and empty the contents of my glands into Arnold Burke, flooding him with the strongest pain suppressors I have. His face goes slack. I tuck my tentacles gently around his frail body.

*I must get him to his room,* I say to the courtyard at large. The siblings who can detach do, and come to help.

OPEN PUBLIC CHANNEL . . .
ORIGIN: SECTOR ####-## // SAVE REQUIS AEFLORE
FADING STOP
SENDING . . .
SENDING . . .

*You gave him too much,* Uah says, massaging my sore, spent glands with their own palps. If I didn't feel so chastised, it would be bliss.

*I'm sorry,* I reply. *He took me by surprise when he fell.*

*Ah, you are young, Mouh. But you must learn control. Remember, our secretions are addictive. It's what brought us here, to Requis, in the first place.*

I shiver as my glands slowly begin to recover and replenish, awed that Uah would speak to me of our beginnings at all. They are the eldest at the sanatoria, the last remaining settler alive.

Like most of my kind, they were once cultivated and enslaved for their opiates. Entire harvests of us, beloved siblings I'll never meet, are still sold to pleasure ships and forced to mesh with the patrons. We are draped around their shoulders like stoles, drip-feeding them high after delicious high. Druggles, they call us, and discard us like so much rubbish when our glands wither from use. Ejected into the void with the rest of the waste, many of us die, though a rare few find the means of propulsion to float here, where they are free.

The Sanatoria was one such pleasure ship, once. But Uah and their siblings discovered an advantage: while they were wrapped around the doped crew's bodies, they had control. They steered the ship off course and discovered Requis, an untouched and secluded haven. The ship, broken apart by the impact of the landing, formed the foundations of our defiant new home; the capital 'S' was quickly dropped.

Thanks to Uah, we've become the masters of our own enterprise. Now we control the supply of our opiates. We decide when to sell it, and to whom.

Thanks to Uah, I've never known a world where I could be sold.

My kind fade as we age, until the cells holding us together simply disband and become air. This process has begun in earnest for Uah, their matter worn as thin with time as that youthful defiance, that rage so contrary to our nature, rendering them as frustratingly docile as Arnold Burke himself, lying prone on the bed.

Viscous saliva falls from his sagging mouth and darkens the pillow. *Will he live?*

*He will feel groggy for a time; but yes, he will live.*

I watch and wait while Arnold Burke's metabolism works its sluggish way through my pain suppressors. My cilia oscillate, steering me about the little room that smells of fresh herbs and, beneath, betraying its history, sharp traces of disinfectant. I roll him onto his side with my tentacles to dab gently at his neck and chest with a warm wet cloth, and trickle fluids directly into his oesophagus. When he defecates, I clear away the mess.

With a small dexterous tentacle, I unlatch the window which opens onto the herb garden, and strew his faeces onto the compost below.

It intrigues me, how bodies and their waste break down and so nourish the land in this way, as mine cannot. But all the nourishment in the universe will not sustain Requis, for ours is a dying colony. We are born from the aeflore plant, and with only the descendants of Uah and their siblings to pollinate them, our numbers have fallen dangerously low; each new spawning is smaller than the last. It's believed that a patient's mind plays as large a part as their physical remains in germinating our seeds, so it is important they attain closure before death. But a part of me – an indecently agitated part I dare not show – fears we need nothing less than another crashed pleasure ship to sustain our numbers.

This churns inside me for some time – our distant sun sets and rises again – before the ruffle of fabric from behind draws me away.

Arnold Burke heaves himself into a sitting position and blinks around at the room, its bare walls, the spray of rare Terran sweet peas on the sideboard which I carefully picked from the sanatoria's greenhouse. He swings his skinny legs onto the floor, testing the heated boards with ten hairy yellow-nailed toes. Then he looks at me, his eyes narrowed meanly. "Didn't pump enough of your shite into me, then.

I'm still here."

I hang my tentacles straight. I don't want to give away my discomfort. *I did not intend to give you such a large –*

"Feh!" He wets his lips, eyebrows low, staring at the view through the open window. "I'm not staying here. You can't keep someone against his will. I have rights."

My cilia ripple. Most patients choose to come to Requis for their final months. But some, unable to decide for themselves due to advanced age or illness, are sent to us by their local authority, or their relatives, to ease the burden on already scarce resources. For those few we are always given notice, told to expect some confusion or resistance; for Arnold Burke, we've heard nothing. Even our mesh yesterday, however intimate, only allowed for a glimpse across the surface of his thoughts.

*That is true, but I would advise you to stay,* I say. *Your metastasis is so advanced as to make a departure very uncomfortable indeed. Without proper care, you may not even survive to see the station.*

*Here, however, we can manage your pain to whatever degree is desired. You may use all the sanatoria's amenities; many areas of the old pleasure ship are still intact and functional.*

*Requis is a peaceful place to die, Terran. Whoever sent you here wanted the best for you.*

"You sound like a floating feckin' advert. 'A peaceful place to die.' You know what is a peaceful place to die? At home, in my own bed!"

Phlegm catches in his throat. He hacks it up, concaved and clinging to the edge of the bed. I move forward, stretching out my tentacles to steady him, but he gasps at me to get away. Does he not understand that I'm trying to help? Then the smell of sweet urine irritates my olfactory organs, and I cannot stand by. I resist Arnold Burke's attempts to bat me away as I remove the absorbent pad in his crotch, clean around his genitals, and replace it. With another tentacle I massage his back, teasing out the knots. Eventually he falls quiet and still.

Voices from the garden, other patients taking the air, soften the tension in the room. When he seems recovered, I say, thinking of the faces I saw during our mesh, *Did your relatives send you here? We can get a message to them that you arrived safely. They could visit, if you like. We could make it feel like home.*

"Don't bother," he croaked. "There's no one left."

OPEN PRIVATE CHANNEL . . .
ORIGIN: SECTOR ####-## // REQUEST ID FILE FOR
NEW PATIENT ARNOLD BURKE STATION ##-##-#
STOP
SENDING . . .
SENDING . . .

The mechanically minded among us maintain the ship's radio so that Requis can broadcast and receive messages. We've been established so long, we have our own frequency. Sixty hours after my request for information goes out, Arnold Burke's home station responds with an account of his service as a lieutenant in the auxiliary forces, before being quietly retired following allegations of misconduct. It goes on to note that he outlived his next of kin, a female partner, by some years, and has since lost touch with their children and grandchildren. Living alone and bitterly lonely, allowed to ferment in his own prejudices, he'd become something of a nuisance.

Even so, they deny sending him to us.

I broadcast a message to his family's last known home station instead, but receive no reply. In the face of that silence, I pity him.

*But he's horrible*, says Haua as we circuit the garden by starlight one night, their distress colouring their organs. *Why should horrible patients get to linger, when the good ones go so soon?* Haua's patient, the Plutan, passed quickly, and Haua – my dear, gentle Haua – always takes the losses hard.

I entwine my palps with theirs. *Uah says every death is different. It's not for us to understand, nor judge.*

Haua pulls away, hurt. *Do you accept everything Uah says, Mouh?*

I always have, ever since Uah's palp teased me, Haua, and the rest of our spawn-siblings out of our buds and into the world. Their mind was the first I heard, their touch the first I felt. Uah has always been like a parent to me, and I have drunk their wisdom down like nectar.

But I struggle to follow their example when it comes to Arnold Burke. The Terran's symptoms grow worse, and yet he refuses pain suppressors, support, conversation – everything I've been trained to do. He disturbs the other patients by barking at them when they pass too close to his window, saying they obstruct his view; or by loudly refusing to eat dinner next to a patient on account of their species. If the ooze of a Zrehsin's mucus doesn't nauseate him, a Titan's body hair makes him itch.

When he sleeps at night, I hover over him, and wonder: what crime would it be, really, if I were to flood him with opiates again so that he'd slip into a deeper, more permanent sleep?

No one would miss him.

And then I dart out of the room like a minnow, to a secluded part of the sanatoria where the old control panels still flicker in the dark, and cower in shame at my own spite.

OPEN PUBLIC CHANNEL . . .
ORIGIN: SECTOR ####-## // PLEASE RESPOND STOP
SENDING . . .
ORIGIN: SECTOR ####-## // WE ARE DYING STOP
SENDING . . .
SENDING . . .

After dinner, I turn the wheeled chair left towards the burial gardens, instead of right, and Arnold Burke tilts back his head to scowl at me. "Where are you taking me now, druggle?"

*My name is Mouh.*

Arnold Burke will soon become too weak to eat his meals in the dining room, and I will have to care for him in the close confines of his room until he dies. He may never travel beneath this trailing ivy again. He may never see the place of my birth, nor the place of his final rest.

Nothing else shocks quite like one's mortality.

The ivy bower opens out onto the first of many burial gardens, with hundreds of grave plots arranged in uniform rows stretching wider than my peripheral vision. Some of them are topped with bare soil, but most bear trinkets from visitors: bouquets for anniversaries missed, or photographs, or souvenirs, which my siblings keep in as good condition as the day they were laid down. From a precious few – far, far too few – grow aeflore shrubs, fed from the rich remains of those decomposing below. Clusters of fur-edged leaves and purpling buds bob in the wind. The most swollen of them promise to burst soon, releasing a clutch of our young.

71

A path cuts through the graves, leading on and up to newer burial gardens in the mountains ahead. It is said that those plots are high enough to see snowfall. I have never been assigned pollination duty, so have not seen it myself.

Arnold Burke looks bitterly upon it all. "I was sent here to be fertiliser."

*Not all of the seeds take,* I say, gesturing to one or two little shoots that are already browning. *But it is true that your remains provide us with the nutrients we need to grow best.*

He scoffed. "Why bother keeping me comfortable, then? Why don't you just kill me and have done with it?"

*Because...*

I recall being poised above him, my barbs dripping, and how wrong it felt. How can I be welcome amongst my kind, with this darkness inside me? And yet how can I be complacent like Uah, when there is so much that still needs to change?

*Because that sounds like murder,* I say firmly, *and that is not our way.*

Together we watch the progress of a few visitors carefully stepping around the graves to find their loved ones. They pause to read the gravestones of strangers, stooping to smooth the wrinkles from bouquet wrappings or straighten stuffed toys. This thoughtfulness never fails to amaze me, for they might have walked past these people without a second glance, had they still been alive. But ego falls away in a burial garden. It's one of the few places where people truly stop and consider one another.

I wait until the cold makes him shiver before returning him to his room. He slaps me away as I try to wash him, though he is sour with sweat. But as night falls and the room grows dark, I smell salt: tears have leaked from the corners of his eyes and are pooling in the whorls of his ears. His body twists helplessly.

I raise my palps. *Are you in pain, Terran?* And he nods weakly, his teeth gritted tight. I slide myself into his nasal cavities as gently as I can manage, working with and not against the panicked jerk of his head. The mesh swallows us as deeply as before, but this time we do not fight it.

Airless Luna was cold, but the plaid quilt passed down from Eimear's family kept our capsule warm at night, and when the angle of the sun was just so, we could see the planet our ancestors had evacuated from the porthole above our bed. She gave us children. They bewildered and frustrated us with their demands and sticky fingers and their fidgets. We were granted a bigger capsule on a station in Martian orbit, where our children soon had their own children. There, Eimear grew sickly. We couldn't see Terra from our bed any more; the plaid quilt warmed our daughter's capsule instead. When she died, we shrank into ourselves, pining for that tiny, quiet capsule on Luna, and the further inwards we shrank, the further our family spiralled away.

We sowed no seeds with our deeds, set down no roots. We spent years wishing nothing more than to be left alone. Our wish is finally granted, only for it to feel hollow after all.

Drop by careful drop, my opiates calm him, and we cease our writhing. I settle around Arnold Burke's shoulders like so many of my enslaved siblings and watch my outspread tentacles rising and falling with the movement of his chest. For one awful instant, I'd understood a little of his pain.

I wonder what he saw of mine.

OPEN PRIVATE CHANNEL . . .
ORIGIN: LL LUXURIA // HOLD FAST STOP SHIP IS
UNDER CONTROL STOP
INCOMING . . .
INCOMING . . .

He often asks to be taken back to the burial gardens. I think he likes the open space better than the neat courtyards of the sanatoria, which have a manufactured air to them no matter what we try. He even has a favourite spot: one of the recesses set back from the path, a little way up the mountain. They provide picturesque rest stops for visitors. This one has a metal bench and a wonderful view of the sanatoria below.

The gondola rumbles along its tether overhead, having just deposited a fresh set of patients on the concourse. I can see my siblings and Uah greeting them from here, though Uah is as sheer as gauze, their outline hard to discern. A few short months, perhaps, until my siblings and I must fend for ourselves. Until the old gives way to the new. I would be afraid, if I had not already accepted the cyclical nature of life and death here on Requis.

"Where will you put me?" Arnold Burke says, interrupting my

thoughts.

My cilia shudder and swirl. I turn to face him. *Your plot lies further up. Would you like to see it?*

He nods.

*The terrain is too rough for the chair. We'll walk together.*

I nestle my palps deep inside his sinuses and swaddle his body, his legs, so that I can provide pain relief and support all at once. The strength of my tentacles is such that I can mimic the metal braces some patients need to stand in Requis's gravity. We move as one up the mountain path, leaving the empty wheeled chair behind.

These burial gardens are difficult to reach but patients and visitors alike still venture here for quiet contemplation. A Kepleri meditates beside an aeflore seedling growing from the grave of zir cousin; a Gliesian sits carving their own epitaph, while my sibling tends their plot. Some of them wave to us as we pass. Arnold Burke bristles at this; I feel his muscles contract. When we finally come to the base of his plot – 5.R74.1, tucked into the curve of the path upwards to another, much colder garden – his eyes dart to his neighbours either side.

"Is this it?" he says gruffly. "I'm not to be buried with my own sort?"

*The microbiological composition of our gardens is kept diverse, to help promote growth.*

Arnold Burke frowns.

*Is it strange to be buried beside people you don't know? Here.* I loosen a tentacle and gesture to the plot on our left. *He was a Plutan called Bharn Creiss. My sibling Dei tended to him so well that he lived with us a whole year. He taught us how to play a Terran game called 'cricket' on the concourse – perhaps you know of it?*

He stays tight-lipped.

I gesture to the right, which boasts a maturing aeflore shrub. *And here is a Gliesian called Gennara Eight-Thirty-Two. I did not know them, as they passed before I was born, but my sibling Uah tended them and Uah says they were kind. It seems our seeds have taken to them well, which is an auspicious sign.*

"It's just not what I imagined for myself," he grunts.

An image of Eimear flares and dies in his mind, and therefore in mine. I understand. *I'm told that Terrans bury loved ones together. We can request that your partner's remains be shipped here and interred with yours, if you would like.*

Arnold Burke is quiet for a long time. Eventually he reaches out to touch the pods of the shrub to our right, still hard and green. "You lot come out of these?"

He's never shown an interest in my kind before. Indeed, he's never shown an interest in anyone here but himself. My organs blush. *That's right. These pods will soon soften and open. Once my siblings have emerged, we will use the pollen to pollinate another shrub. Later, we'll collect the dried seeds and plant them.*

He sighs, cheeks gaunt. "I need to sit down."

I fold his legs underneath him, secreting a small dose of opiates as I do so.

"I didn't mean on my own grave, you fool," he says – but mildly, too tired for malice. So, we stay like that for a while. The meditating Kepleri kisses the ground and leaves to catch the next departure home. My sibling escorts the Gleisian back towards the sanatoria for dinner. Other faces come and go. Arnold Burke reaches out with a haggard breath to examine the paraphernalia on Bharn Creiss's grave: a framed analogue watch; a cricket ball. Small Terran things, tokens of a lost world, vaguely familiar.

He replaces them and glances around guiltily. A Titan with red hair that extends around her collar like a ruff returns his gaze. She shivers in the chilly afternoon shade.

Arnold Burke's heart aches, almost prompting me to secrete a stronger dose, but it isn't the kind of pain my opiates can touch. It's her plaid coat that stirs him – as if Eimear's quilt, grown threadbare over the years, has had to be repurposed.

His pulse beats hard against my body.

But Titans are a distant people. She does not linger, whoever she is. She smiles politely and heads back down the path, her chin tucked into her ruff for warmth. A brisk wind whips up the hem of her coat and stirs the garden's aeflores, whose stems bend under the weight of their pods.

Arnold Burke rubs his face. "Take me back."

Pain spits like hot coals across his abdomen as we stand. I dampen it, but only a little. He has grown so weak; too much and he might slip away right here, his spirit worked loose like the atoms of Uah's body. He curls a palm around a pod on Gennara Eight-Thirty-Two's shrub, running a bony thumb over the silky, snug petals. "How long until these things open?"

*A few weeks.*

He sniffs. "Make sure your lot scatters some seeds on my plot, won't you?"

Our precious seeds may be wasted on Arnold Burke. Often their roots won't take, as if whatever festers below has soured the soil instead of enriching it. But I hope I have changed him. *Of course*, I say as we stride down the mountain path to his waiting chair, its seat littered with fallen leaves. *I will plant them myself.*

Arnold Burke lives long enough to see the first spawning of the season. We watch my new siblings rise like smoke over the burial gardens from his bed, turning the sky grey. Meshed tight, it is easy to make him believe a plaid quilt keeps us warm; he clings to it, to the sanatoria's plain sheets, as he dies.

At the last, I show him how Haua and I will lay him down in plot 5.R74.1, how I will scoop the tiny seeds from the maw of an empty pod and poke them deep into the soil. I'll pause a moment to wish them good growth before the shadow of the latest gondola darkens the garden.

One day soon, it will be the shadow of a pleasure ship come to answer my call.

We'll wait on the concourse as it crashes, our cilia and the grass below us stirred by a soft breeze.

# Fat Man in the Bardo

## Ken MacLeod

A clock ticks. Somewhere, a baby cries. You're in an oddly abstract space, all planes and verticals. It reminds you of a library. You don't remember ever being in a library. You remember nothing but the sudden unprovoked shove in the small of your back, and the precipitate drop. A split-second glimpse of shining railway tracks, wooden sleepers, the ingenious mechanism of points.

Then oblivion.

Now this.

Even here, in this Platonic afterlife, you're fat. You always will be fat. It defines you, eternally. You're the Fat Man. It seems unfair. You don't even remember eating.

Perspiring, thighs chafing in your ill-fitting suit, you set off in search of the crying baby. Your quest takes you around a corner, and at once you are in a library. It's no improvement: the maze of shelving seems endless. You take down a book, and find page after page of random letters. The next you open is blank, except for one page with a single flyspeck of comma.

You put the book back in its place and plod on. The crying diminishes. You cock your head, turn, walk to another corner and triangulate. Off you go again, with more confidence.

Around the next corner, at eye level, you meet a pair of eyes.

The eyes are connected to a brain, which hangs unsupported in mid-air. The brain is connected to a tiny, tinny-looking audio device where its chin would be if it had a skull.

"Hello," says the brain.

"Hello," you say. You stick out your hand, then withdraw it and wipe your palm on your thigh. Hurriedly, you introduce yourself.

"I'm the Fat Man, from" – it dawns on you – "the Trolley Problem."

"Pleased to meet you," the speaker crackles. "I'm the Brain."

"Yes?"

"A Boltzmann brain," it elaborates. "A conscious human brain formed by random molecular motion in the depths of space."

"That seems improbable."

"Highly improbable!" the Brain agrees. "But given enough space, matter and time, inevitable – unfortunately for me." It rotates, looking around. "We seem to be in the Library of Babel, the useless library of all possible books." Its rotation brings its eyes back around to you, and stops. "I keep wishing I could blink."

You shrug. "Sorry, I can't help."

The Brain laughs. "Count yourself lucky you're not from the thought experiment about organ donation."

You shudder.

"Well," says the Brain, briskly, "let's see if we can find baby Hitler and calm him down. All this crying is getting on my nerves."

The Brain zooms away, and you hurry after it, your thoughts catching up at the same time. Information comes to you when you need it, yet you have no memory of any life before this. It's like you're...

But you've caught up.

"That baby is Hitler?"

"Yes," says the Brain, as if over its shoulder. "Time travellers keep trying to kill him. They always fail, of course, but it's most unsettling for the child. Frankly, I fear for his future mental stability."

From the next aisle comes the sound of footsteps, and a woman's voice:

"Loud and clear, Bob. Loud and clear."

You sidestep between bookcases to intercept the clicking footsteps. The woman halts. She is wearing a dark blue shift-dress and black high-heeled shoes. Over her neat hairdo sits a set of headphones with a mike in front of her mouth. She looks at you with disdain and at the Brain with distaste.

You introduce yourselves. She's Alice. She keeps talking quietly to Bob, warning him against some third-party eavesdropper, Charlie. Otherwise, she's not very communicative.

Soon the three of you find the baby crying in a carved wooden cradle in a canyon of books. You look at it helplessly, then at Alice. She shoots you a baleful glare, picks up the child, and strokes and coos and pats his back. Hitler pukes on her shoulder. Then he stops bawling, but keeps looking around. His crumpled little face glowers with wary suspicion.

Once the baby's hushed, the sound that predominates is the ticking. You listen intently, trying to detect its source. Suddenly the ticking is interrupted by a scream, followed by sobs.

"Jeez!" says Alice. "What now?"

"It's the Ticking Bomb Scenario," says the Brain. "Some poor devil is being tortured to reveal its location."

"We have to stop that!" you cry.

"Why?" asks Alice, coldly. "Do you value some terrorist's comfort over the lives of innocents?"

"I was innocent," you point out. "Nobody asked my opinion before shoving me to certain death."

You and Alice glare at each other.

"Sounds like you're a Kantian and Alice is a utilitarian," muses the Brain. "The dignity of the individual versus the greatest good of the greatest number."

Stand-off.

"I know!" says the Brain, brightly. "Let's find the Ticking Bomb and turn it off ourselves!"

"Sounds like a plan," says Alice.

The Brain rises high above the shelves, almost out of sight. It roams, rotating, then swoops back.

"Found it!" it says. "Thirty-two minutes to go before it explodes."

"Will we have time?" you ask.

"If we hurry."

Hurry, you do. Alice's heels go click-click-click. Baby Hitler bounces up and down in her reluctant embrace. You're almost out of breath. The Brain darts ahead, a gruesome will-o'-the-wisp guiding you onwards.

You arrive at a wider space amid the shelving, with a table in the middle. In the middle of the table is a box, on which is mounted some kind of apparatus. A man in a white coat is observing the box. Behind the man is another man, observing the man and the box. Behind that man stands… well, you know how it goes.

From inside the box comes the sound of a cat mewling, a protest louder and more plaintive even than that of Baby Hitler.

"Should we–?" you ask.

"No," says the Brain. "It would just add another layer of decoherence to the wave function."

"Damn right," says Alice. "No way am I going back for that goddamn cat."

You all hurry on, leaving Schrödinger's Cat, Schrödinger himself, Wigner, Wigner's friend and all the others to their indefinite fate. The Brain leads you around a corner and into an aisle facing a glass wall. The light is ruddy. You spare a glance outside. To the horizon stretch waste dumps, some burning. On them crawl endless human figures, salvaging junk, grubbing subsistence from garbage.

"Is that Hell?" asks Alice, sounding horrified.

"No," the Brain calls back. "It's trillions of people living lives barely worth living! But it's a better situation than mere billions of people living lives well worth living, wouldn't you agree?"

"No," says Alice. "I wouldn't."

"Nor I," you say.

"Too bad!" says the Brain. "The reasoning is rigorous. Your revulsion is mistaken, but understandable. It's not called the Repugnant Conclusion for nothing, you know."

You have no breath to spare for argument. Another ten minutes' jogging brings you all in front of the Ticking Bomb. The simple timer, now counting down from twelve minutes, is attached to a large cylindrical device labelled "10 kilotons".

"Oh!" says the Brain. "It's an atomic bomb! Does that change our views on the morality of torture?"

"No," say you and Alice at the same moment. Baby Hitler's eyes widen and his face brightens, but he says nothing.

Alice reaches over and turns the timer back to one hour. The ticking resumes.

"Now we have time to think," she says.

"It's interesting to reflect," says the Brain, "that somewhere in this library is a book containing a complete system of self-evident moral philosophy that answers all our questions. Formed out of random letters, just as I am formed out of random molecules."

"Along with its refutation?" says Alice.

"Point," says the Brain.

"One of us must stay here," you say, "and keep turning the clock back, while the others go and find the torture chamber before too many more fingernails are extracted. And then –"

"And then what?" asks Alice. "How does that help all the poor people outside?"

"No," you say, "but –"

"Have you noticed how our memories work? Doesn't it strike you as odd? Try doodling something at random."

You try to think of something. Nothing comes to mind.

"What?" you say. "I can't think of anything I'm not thinking about."

"Tree," says Alice. You've never heard the word before. You sketch a tree.

"See?" says Alice. "That's not how human memories work. That's how computer memories work, as I'm sure the Brain can confirm."

"Yes," says the Brain. "And?"

"We aren't human minds," says Alice. "We're abstractions of the subjects and victims of thought experiments. This isn't a physical space, and I doubt that it's some kind of afterlife, given that none of us had lives. The overwhelming probability is that we're in a simulation."

"Ah," you say. "But –"

"Yes," says Alice. "What monsters the creators of such a simulation must be!"

You and Alice look out of the window at the hellish landscape, and at each other.

"We must put a stop to this," you say.

Alice nods. You reach for the timer at the same moment.

"Wait!" cries the Brain.

Too late.

Zero.


What the Brain was about to tell you is that there are worse possibilities than being in a simulation. The worst possibility is that this thought experiment is simply a possibility, but a logical one. From inside a logical possibility, there is no way to distinguish it from actuality. And a logical possibility can't be made or unmade by omnipotence itself, let alone by a ten-kiloton atomic bomb.

What the Brain doesn't know, and couldn't possibly tell you, is that there is a greater possibility: that somewhere, somehow, all the victims of all the logical possibilities including those that exist in what we laughingly call actuality can be saved, can be liberated, can be redeemed; that their suffering can be expunged as though it had never been; and that, however impossible that great, all-encompassing thought experiment may seem, or indeed be, it is nevertheless something for which you are doomed to strive, and to seek over and over again until you find it.

A clock ticks. Somewhere, a baby cries. You're in an oddly abstract space, all planes and verticals. It reminds you of a library.

# Cyberstar

## Val Nolan

## I

They cut out my eyes before they sent me to meet God. The exenterations took place in a gleaming white surgical suite carved out of the Lesser Skellig. The procedures were elective insofar as I presented with neither malignancies nor with life-threatening infections of any kind. They were also conducted without anaesthetic and so I remained aware throughout. I felt my face stretched as the doctors applied sutures for traction and I bit down hard on the rod between my teeth when the thin pencil of the cautery began to penetrate first my skin and, thereafter, my orbicularis muscle. The pain was incredible but that was the point. It was a measure of my commitment, of my faith. I prayed for more of it and the autonurses obliged. I could glimpse them bustling behind the brother-doctors as their segmented arms passed instrument after instrument to the team. Scissors and snares. Titanium forceps. Holy lanterns. All the while people mumbled things about canals and crests and orbital packages. I bit down harder again as a blade scraped against bone beneath my eyeball. That was something I heard as much as felt, and the brother-doctor wielding the knife muttered sacrilegious words before proceeding to incise and sever further. My right eye left my skull with a sickening and stretching tug soon after that. For a moment I saw it through my remaining eye. A brother-doctor held it over my face and a drip of fluid – blood or tear, I do not know – fell upon my cheek. Then the brother-doctor swung away the tongful of quivering jelly and allowed his colleagues to descend on what remained with shining tools and supplications.

"You have always seen more than most," the Abbot had told me some weeks prior to the procedure, "but what use are eyes when one cannot see God? Because no mortal can. Not truly. Not completely. The human can *perceive* God, yes. Can feel God in the universe and live within God's embrace, but no one can really know the face of God with their own eyes." The Abbot's vast bulk balanced on a stool in the medical bay. His long-trimmed beard came to a point as if in imitation of the craggy Skelligs themselves, the pair of spinning asteroids – small mountains tethered together at their peaks – within which our monastery had been constructed. He was speaking to me but he was feeding a woman, a prospective, in the neighbouring bed with a metal spoon. On the table beside him lay the psalter he carried everywhere. An old and heavy leather-bound book with illustrations threaded through its paragraphs. Saints in golden frames, flowery initials and that sort of thing. "A person can peer through filters and algorithms," he went on, "and for some that is enough. But if we cannot ever see God then what use are our eyes except for God to look into our souls? Surely we should open that door, yes? Surely we should be prepared for what will pass through it?"

His lesson remained with me as I carried out my last sighted day among my brothers and sisters. On that final morning I rose at lauds in the apostolic fashion, washed in my cell, and then made my way through the gardens to the radiators. These had been my duty station for the past ten years, tending to the great maze of metal veins which transferred the fire of the chosen, of their farms and machinery, into the endless chill of space. It had been my responsibility to maintain the pumps which circulated ammonia throughout the monastery. This gas collected heat from the Skelligs' electronic equipment in order to transfer it to the radiator panels and hence into the darkness of space. There the heat shivered for the briefest of moments as a holy ghost of the monastery itself. Then it was gone. Impossible not to think of that image as I conducted my last inspection and then, when I was done, climbed the steps which zig-zagged up the Greater Skellig. These ran from the base to the tether high above which bound the Greater to its smaller sibling and along the axis of which both asteroids spun. One final walk around the monastery to prepare for the loss of my sight: sisters and brothers smiling and clasping my hands, an impromptu cheer as I boarded the elevator across to the cloisters and augmentation theatres of the blessed Lesser, then a moment of silence as I cleansed myself for transformation.

The removal and sterilisation of each eye was identical. When the globes and their surrounding muscles, fat, nerves, and eyelids, had been dealt with, the brother-doctors applied bovine bilayer silicone and collagen dermal replacement to the interior of my empty sockets. The volume of my right orbit was 31 millilitres, my left 29 millilitres, and both these new voids were quickly packed with tech. The implants were a dense computronium into which all of our knowledge, everything that we were, was to be loaded. Then the autonurses withdrew to allow sister-sysadmins to conduct fault tree analysis of the units and to confirm the error tolerance of their substrate. After that my sockets were sealed over with faraday caps and, as I lay in recovery, an initiate painted eyes on these in order that I could 'see' and so avoid danger on my journey. That boy had come from a Vietnamese family and, as he worked, he told me stories about his ancestors. Heretics, all of them, but they believed that painting the eyes of a serpent on the prow of one's craft would allow it to elude monsters in the sea or in space. It was a fairy-tale with which I was surprisingly taken. And of course I was happy to accept whatever good fortune was available.

The boy asked me what I would miss the most and I thought of the view from the surface of the monastery, beyond the safety of the pressurised interior. I recalled those times standing outside on the sharp bare rock, anchored only by the false gravity of the Skelligs' spin as I removed one failed heat pump or another from a radiator truss and retrieved a spare from the stowage platform. It was a routine task, I had done it dozens of times and, I suppose, it was not so dissimilar from my eye operation: disconnect the coolant line from the failed pump and then withdraw the unit from its housing; install the replacement, carefully reconnect the fluid cables, and then mate the electrical connections. I had always enjoyed my brief contemplative moments on the surface as sister-engineers conducted their pressure diagnostics. I used to look out across the surface of the Greater Skellig – here and there a beehive-shaped observation dome or the cow's lick of an antenna farm, sunlight glinting off acres of solar arrays or the holy spark of electron beam welding by a maintenance crew on the tight horizon – and then, poised above, the immense bulk of the Lesser which, by the quirks of centrifugal force, seemed frozen in the velvet sky, a trillion cubic meters of rock always about to fall and crush us, always about to break away and leave us all alone. Fields of divine light sparkled across its surface as forests of prospectives gave back to God the tongues of flame with which they had been blessed. Many Earthers found the whole thing barbaric. The Autonomy and the Continuation had outlawed the practice entirely. But I thought that it was stirring.

I had met one of them, a new prospective, being wheeled out of an adjacent theatre as I was carried into the surgical suite. I had been lying outside in the antechamber as the flesh and muscles of the man's arms and legs had been peeled apart by blades and retractors to allow the bones of his limbs to be fused together. The man had been a Terran soldier and, from what I heard of his cries, the faith which he displayed had been impressive. He had been remoulded into a person the shape of a rigid candle, his arms high above his head as they moved him towards the hatch in horizontal fashion. He would join the woman whom the Abbot had been feeding, would join many of our brothers and sisters on the slopes of the Lesser Skellig, would be coated in an oxidiser to defy the airless vacuum and then burned alive in salutation of God's light. That, I told the boy with the paintbrush, was the rousing sight which I would miss the most.

## II

They cut off my penis before they sent me to meet God. My testicles as well. My ears and my nose, one hand's worth of fingers and all of my toes. They were deadweight, naught but offal, and every ounce that could be removed from my mortal body was sliced away. I had been made a eunuch to save on fuel load, made an emaciated husk to fulfil my task. I had trained and lost what weight I carried in the months leading up to my departure but, as righteous as it felt, even that was not enough. There was nothing for me but the blade again and I was wheeled, now sightless, into the surgical suite once more. The voices of the brother-doctors reassured me as the autonurses whirled and clicked and pumped me full of epinephrine. The chemical would constrict my blood vessels, my own heat collection and transportation system, and so minimise the inevitable bleeding. There was less need for precision than the earlier procedure and the brother-doctors were eager to make long incisions along my arms and legs before peeling back the skin in loose curtains. There was no rod for my mouth this time, just a drug concoction to ensure I remained conscious, and so I was permitted to scream, a form of blessed chant, though my eye sockets had been clamped closed to prevent me from dislodging my new implants. I felt the stings of a hundred cannulas inserted to drain away what little fat remained on my frame and then to fill my bone cavities with electrorheological fluids. The curved scythes of the scalpels followed as the brother-doctors shaved away my muscles and, along with the shape of that old body, my memories of who I had been before the monastery...

Laid off from an energy project, I had been drinking myself blind – that was almost funny now – when the missionary had discovered me in a Tharsis speakeasy. You would see his like in the desert towns from time to time, preying on the dregs of boarding houses and brothels, promising to heal your soul or what might have ailed it. He wore a rough cloak like something out of a fantasy story. Maybe once it had been white but the Martian dust had dyed it dull red at the hem, fading to a grubby pink at his shoulders.

"Are you lost?" I said to him when I saw him staring at me.

"Are *you*?"

I rolled my eyes. "Fuck off, mate."

The missionary smiled. "I take it you told that to your previous employers."

I did not bother looking up from my drink, a cracked jam-jar of homemade alcohol and fortifying agents. "You know nothing about 'em."

"I know they're a fantastically corrupt lot deeply entrenched in the Co-Prosperity Sphere. I know they're well connected. Wealthy. I know they own a lot of geothermal plants like the one you've been working at, yes? Though I always preferred solar power myself." He glanced towards the stairs to the speakeasy hatch and the pale morning light beyond. "Tell me, why do you hide in a hovel beneath the surface of a world?"

The bartender, a grizzled Ukrainian emigrant, threw us a dirty look.

"Well I ain't hiding from *them*," I said, "if that's what you're implying."

"I was implying that you're hiding from *yourself*." He sat himself down alongside me. "Hiding from your true potential. Hiding from the light."

"Types like me tend to scurry from the light." I waved a hand around at the bowed heads of my fellow patrons. "Or hadn't you noticed?"

"That's just what you tell yourself," the missionary said. "But we can change that. We can scrape you up from the darkness."

"And who doesn't want to be told that they can be scraped up?"

The missionary smiled. "That's not my opinion of you, of course. Just plain analysis of where you've found yourself. But I can see that you're a soul in search of another way. Someone looking to become a new person though almsdeeds and oblations, through fastings and chastity and good solid labour."

"You need to work on your pitch, padre. Know your audience and all that."

"You can yet become one with God's light. And if I'm to be honest about it," he sighed, "we could use someone like you. Someone with your knowledge and experience."

I turned around to face him. "If you want to offer me a job then just do that. Spare me the mumbo-jumbo." My gaze fell on the infomon on the far wall of the bar, as cracked and crooked as any of the Ukrainian's glassware. Its screen showed rolling coverage from all across the shitty planet: Politicians giving speeches in front of silver towers and denying the things that the chyrons beneath them said that they had done; flat mushroom clouds from nukes being detonated to raise the planet's temperature; troops of the Co-Prosperity Sphere puncturing Bigelow habitats around one of the big domes – it looked like Gale Crater – and detaining inhabitants they described as extremist squatters...

"That used to be a cenobium," the missionary said of the deflating modules.

My head hurt. "A *what now?*"

"A religious order. Quite a lively one too. Though those of them who haven't been arrested have joined us. You see, we're creating a new foundation off-planet. Somewhere where we'll be left alone. People are coming to us from all across the worlds. Coming for a simpler life. Coming to find the light. However, we are just at the beginning. And as much as we need initiates, we need engineers. Plumbers, leckies, and the like."

"My father called 'em leckies," I said. "But everyone here calls 'em sparkies." For a moment, the only sounds were the mumble of voices from the infomon and the ancient K-Pop stuttering from the bar's mouldy speakers. I tightened my jaw. "What is it you need doing?"

"Thermal regulation on our new asteroid habitat."

I squinted at the man in the dim light of the speakeasy.

"It isn't a coincidence that I'm talking to you," the missionary said. "Our search engines flagged you after your dismissal."

I emptied my jar. "You've got a news alert for anger management issues?"

"A standing search for engineers who might be in want of employment opportunities. Especially people like yourself with a Master's degree in active thermal management."

I grunted in acknowledgement. I had, at the energy plant, essentially been doing the opposite of my training, using coolant in reverse to collect heat from a geological fracture and extract it with a heat exchange rather than dissipating it via radiator. Many of the principles were the same – it was all pressure control and gaseous communication – but it had never been the best of fits for me.

"So," he said, "will you renounce the World and the Flesh and the Devil?"

"Will you pay me?" I replied. "Will there be women?"

"I suspect your desire for the carnal pleasures will take a backseat to our good works."

"Backseat is as good as anywhere else." I counted out bits out on the counter to pay for my drink, but I was two short. Again.

"Here…" The missionary made up the total from his own purse. "As a down payment." He smiled at me. "We have a day centre nearby. How about you come back for a hot meal and we can discuss terms?"

"Whatever," I said, though I left the bar with him anyway.

I was a different person back then. But then so was the missionary.

It would be many years before he grew quite so long a beard.


## III

After the surgeries came the steel. Or, with somewhat less poetry, after the surgeries came the titanium-zirconium-molybdenum composite. The monastery had mined these metals from the cores of the Skelligs themselves. Out of these they had forged a rigid frame into which I was fitted and which allowed me the protection of a heatshield like a turtle's shell as, for most of the journey, I would turn my sinful face away from God. This shield comprised sheets of carbon composite, with the thermal problems solved by applying a layer of tungsten and then a coat of white aluminium oxide to reflect God's light until the moment of communion. Such was the power of God's love that it could kill if precautions were not taken. But this had been known for millennia by both the most saintly of scientists and the most scientific of saints. They had, in that time, developed strategies: Intertwining carbon fibres by coating them in resin, hardening them, and burning them off again and again; applying nanoscale dopants to make the surface coating whiter and so inhibit the expansion of aluminium oxide grains; giving the shield a foam core with little enough material for any heat to travel through. These were ancient designs, borrowed from the profane solar probes of yore, but they were reliable.

People asked me if such a rig was heavy but, in truth, it carried me. Indeed, my body was fully integrated with the frame and heatshield when I regained my senses in the vast berthing bay at the base of the Greater Skellig. Bright yellow crane arms swung everywhere and they lifted me into my launch position where I waited for what felt like days. The bay was maintained in hard vacuum but by then I had been sealed in a second skin. I had been made impervious to the vacuum of space with air and water circulated within my body through pumps and recyclers which I had constructed myself. Rather than the fiery launch from a terrestrial surface, when my departure came it was more of a gentle push into space. I watched as the two jagged asteroids fell away from me. They looked like a pair of blackened teeth chained together as a charm and seemed to dance around each other slowly, but I knew that their speed was such that it created the Mars-normal gravity I had known for the past decade. After six hours of flight I could no longer make out their surface infrastructure. After twelve I was unable to see the burning candles of my sisters and brothers. A day later and the monastery had vanished into the dark as though it was itself just heat. Only once I had achieved this distance did the booster pods flanking my metal frame ignite. I felt the vibration through the heatshield as the engines burned for long minutes. Then they cut off and fell away from me and soon I was soaring free between the worlds. Over the course of the next few days, my velocity slowed as I climbed out of the plane of the planets and careful, pre-programmed adjustments steered me towards my goal.

I remember when the Abbot had first described to me his vision of this great work. We were walking through the hydroponic gardens, his psalter in his hand as always. "We have long waited for God to come to us," he said. "Long waited for him to send burning bushes, to send prophets, eventually to send his own children. We have been primitives, seeing complication where there is only simplicity. It has not been until recently that we have had the means to commune with God directly. To seek out God ourselves."

At the time I did not understand what he was saying. It was early in my residence at the monastery and I was still too preoccupied with what I did not know about this man. They said he had been an itinerant teacher in small settlement schools across Utopia Planitia. They said he had been a pastry chef in orbital hotels spitting in the croquembouche of the solar system's brightest stars. Some people said he had been a pamphleteer and a union organiser among Terran emigrants. Half-truths at best. Nothing verifiable about the Abbot until twenty years ago when he delivered a firebrand sermon – still occasionally used against him – at a Continuation religious conference high in the Venusian crystal cities. Twelve months later he appeared on Ceres with a samizdat calling out the "unfalsifiable postmodernist rubbish" which had so saturated modern culture. Another year-and-a-half after that and he surfaced on Earth itself: In Buenos Aires, in New Delhi, in Algiers… Everywhere he set up missions and soup kitchens. Everywhere he recruited new followers but, to this day, no one knew who had funded his travels or, for that matter, how he had financed the construction of a monastery so deep in space.

"Confined to the surface of the world," he went on as we walked, "our ancestors had to invent myths to explain the night. They had to make up stories about where God went when it wasn't in the sky. They dreamed up nonsense about boats and barges and rebirth. They made up stories about Ra and Horus and Christ. Chosen ones punting the divine across the sky, dying and resurrecting and dying again." He took a breath. "But in space we see that God is always present. That the light is never dimmed." Opening his psalter, he showed me a page of text richly decorated in saffron and verdigris and turnsole. Whirls of colour and ribbons of decoration twisted around paragraphs written in a careful hand. It was impossibly ancient, a beautiful, hypnotic work of art.

"They used to call these illuminated manuscripts," the Abbot said. "Because of the gold leaf and the like, because of the illustrations, and I've always liked the sound of that." He chuckled to himself as he

91

turned the opening pages. "Maybe someday they'll commemorate you in a book such as this. Your metal frame around you. That would make quite the illustration." He smiled as he led me towards the commissary where we sat and ate in a contemplative and penitent silence. Contemplative because of what the Abbot had proposed we undertake, penitent because the food in the monastery always tasted bad. We could print almost everything we needed on the Skelligs – autonomous drones scoured the nearby regions of the belt for raw materials – but food we cultivated by hand. I was told the odd taste was because it was grown organically, that it wasn't the usual mass-produced gunk which the populace on Mars were forced to endure. The Abbot insisted that this was important. That the order be nourished not just by spiritual learning but also by physical labour. The monastery thus mined water ice from the Skellig' deep craters to supply a hydroponic farm and, though its purity was assured, I did not miss its taste as I flew on and on. For weeks I fell backwards down the gravity well as I meditated on the Abbot's teachings. About how the structure and dynamics of God's coronal magnetic fields had been pondered for centuries. About how the human mind aspired to the ever-changing mystery of their infinite complexity. About how a millennium of vellum scratching by sightless monks was at long last to culminate with me.

## IV

As part of my preparation they had extended my arms and my legs like the Vitruvian Man. Current running through my new electrorheological marrow allowed them to be rigid. Able to move only where they met my torso. They made me into a sculpture. An antenna. A starfish. With my arms thus held wide, I was able to receive communication packets from the Skelligs throughout my voyage. I could in theory have transmitted my own observations back to the monastery, but the decision had been made for me to run silent in the hope that I would evade detection for as long as possible. That said, there was really only one way I could go: a handful of Venus flybys to shed as much helio velocity as possible, dropping my perihelion over time to 0.7AU, then to 0.1 AU, and hence to the throne of God.

All the while I listened through my cybernetics. I picked up signals from Earth and from The Continuation. Whatever their own problems, their governments always had time to criticise us as though we were the enemy. Their mouthpieces called us a "cult". They said we were dangerous. Reports claimed that we had taken people. That we were conducting human sacrifices and needed to be stopped. The transmissions deemed us terrorists, claimed we possessed weapons of mass destruction, and called for the terrestrial worlds to stage police actions or a military intervention. All of this while the wireless transmissions from their own citizens were full of cries for help. Old Earth had been in the grip of rising sea levels for some two centuries. Its coasts had drowned in the way writers had been warning for five or six generations. Caravans of wretched people fled the rich past to join their siblings in the squalor of the now. The wealthy had all left for the partially terraformed Venus and there they called themselves The Continuation (though anyone could tell you that they had long diverged from the politics of their founders). Their citadels were fifty miles high in the Venusian sky, in the vaguely habitable zone, and sat proud atop immense crystals grown by pulling carbon dioxide from the atmosphere as part of the effort to cool that planet. These cloud-swaddled terraces were said to be as close to heaven as it was possible to get in this life but, in their stray transmissions, I discerned the same frustrations and burgeoning inequality that had crippled the homeworld. As the Abbot always said, every perfect world is somebody's dystopia.

So it was with the Skelligs themselves. More distant chatter soon reached me reporting that my old friends the Martian Co-Prosperity Sphere had finally raided the monastery. Their corporations had landed cutters and drilled deep into the rock of the asteroids and their forces had breached the habitable volumes of the Skelligs with combat airlocks. It pained me to think of such violence descending on a place which had awed all with its beauty. If my tear ducts had not been cauterised I would have wept to think of the soldiers despoiling the meditative gardens which filled vast caverns of exotic vegetation within the Greater Skellig. I despaired at the thought of drones scattering the goats we kept for milk or the oxen we kept for ploughing the carefully constituted soil which we were developing to take the place of the hydroponics farm. The signals I intercepted contained visual footage which I could not see, but the description by commentators was enough. The Martians had burnt the communal cells and meditation houses throughout our gardens. They had taken pot-shots at the songbirds nesting in the precious trees which we had smuggled off Old Earth as seeds. They had ransacked the laboratories and the surgeries of the Lesser Skellig and claimed to have recovered body parts and the machinery of dismemberment. They said they had found human remains – so little they thought of our martyrs – standing crucified on the asteroid's surface. They said that, inside the monastery, they had found hundreds of bodies lying peacefully in their bunks. All were braindead. All of their neurological structures were reported to be in an irreversible state of decoherence.

On and on these transmissions went. Reports said that, once the Martians had picked over the Skelligs, they had severed the tether that connected the spinning asteroids and allowed momentum to fling both away on trajectories that would launch them out of the solar system forever. They claimed to have measured radiological contamination consistent with enriched uranium but not to have discovered any weapons. Lost for hard evidence to use against us, the invaders dredged up ancient references to Kool-Aid and sarin. They talked about chloral hydrate and phenobarbital, chemicals that had not been common in a hundred years. They accused the Abbot of doping our water to make us suggestable, of brainwashing his followers with some organic compound he had discovered in the deep shadows of asteroid craters. But I knew that they were lying. They were only making up stories about the Skelligs because there was no one left alive there to contradict them.


## V

"To live forever, one first has to die," the Abbot had said as they gouged out my heart ahead of my rendezvous with God. "We will all of us die but you will be the first of us to return to life." He supervised the heart procedure himself. First the sharp crunch of my breastbone being broken open, an eerie sound through my cochlear implant; then the pericardiectomy, then finally the sacred organ itself raised high and bloody for a dying moment. Its function was quickly replaced by a series of pulmonary pumps which rode externally along my sides, and the cavity it had vacated was scored and squared by a series of high energy lasers.

"For you to do what we ask of you will require one immense pulse of energy," the Abbot said. "An RTG will not be enough. Not even solar panels, despite the closeness to God which you will achieve. No, we will need something with a bigger bang."

I felt a weight inserted into my chest. An object with dulled and worn corners.

"My psalter," the Abbot explained in a fond voice. "And within its covers a small nuclear device, an obsolete weapon brought to us by a convert from the Martian terraforming authority. We have made it as small as possible. Just a bare core now. Just enough to prompt criticality when the time comes." He brought a cup of water to my lips to let me drink, and the kindness of that gesture sustained me as I passed through space controlled by the Continuation and then by the Mercury Autonomy. Soon I was close enough to the face of God that my sensors registered the solar wind rising from subsonic to supersonic speeds. The distinction mattered insofar as I was pushing against that outward flow of particles. I was caught between God's energised protons and the anxious protestations of those who watched from their telescopes and satellites. I heard them talk about how "The vehicle is transiting" and realised that they were talking about me. I know they could have caught me if they had really wanted to. I had shed enough velocity for a flight of centaurs or a missile to have shot me from the sky. But God's grace continued to envelop me and I flew on without incident. Their transmissions described me as "crew" – a "conscious human figure housed in an articulation frame" – and this increased their reticence to shoot me down despite the trace radiation readings that led some to brand me a "human shield" and some a "suicide bomber".

Yet soon I was beyond their reach, lost to the glare inside the orbit of the Vulcanoid asteroids. The power of God here would be atomising head on and, though my tactile interface indicated a minor fault with the filters of my water recyclers – embarrassing as they were my own design – for now I was safe behind my heatshield. I knew highly collimated flows of plasma were reaching out above and below my blinded eyes. I regretted not being able to see those tendrils of God's energy, but I believed in the unseen and could well imagine them. I could recall too the simulations I had been shown many times by the sister-scientists who described God in terms of zero-potential surface models, open and closed field structures, and so on. They were knowledgeable people, recognised experts from across the system, but they had nonetheless recoiled at what was being asked of them. All had balked initially at the impossibilities of information propagation within such a chaotic magnetic environment but all, in the end, had been persuaded into unorthodoxy by the Abbot's words.

"Challenges are not impossibilities," he had always said. "God is a machine that can be hacked like any other. We just have to be clever about it." His advisors talked about magnetoresistance but he talked about magnetoacquiescence. He sermonised about no longer struggling against the will of the almighty – what the sister-scientists called "frequency inversions within non-radial coronal features" – and instead becoming one with the ebb and flow of divine will. His advisors spoke of Alfvén Points but he spoke of angels in white hats. They produced diagrams of magnetic field geometry and solar prominences, but the Abbot insisted that in these crowns of rays was the glow of sanctity towards which we all aspired, the divine lustre long perceived but never truly grasped.

Certainly I counted myself among those who would never understand it all. Thermodynamics was not just my speciality; it was my limit. Talk of quantum variances and recursive spacelike time made as much sense to me as miracles. But evidently the sister-scientists had found a way to encode stable information through oscillations in the ions of the solar plasma itself, to achieve true magnetoacquiescence, and the Abbot had deemed this to be apotheosis, the means by which we would integrate ourselves with the divine. It had been his mission all his life, to become one with almighty God, and he had chosen me to be his witness. He had sent me before him and, even as I cancelled one error message after another from my water filtration system, I was already burning from God's love, from the particle streams tunnelling through me. They would be shredding my DNA but, then again, what did it matter when I would not need physical form for much longer?

I felt my arms and legs extending as my on-board computer began executing a final series of pre-programmed commands. The heat of the holy psalter began to burn within me and my computer rapidly turned up the gain of my antenna. I received confirmation that the souls I carried were buffering up even as a series of thick cranial probes sank into my own grey matter to record my neural structures in the same way they had those of my brothers and sisters. But then that process stuttered. Filter alarms again raised warnings on the tactile interface, confusing, confounding reports that took long moments to register with my gospel-addled mind. I felt my empty stomach retch as I realized that the filters in my water cyclers were not malfunctioning. No, they were doing exactly what I had intended them to do and had spent the voyage from the Skelligs straining out whatever it was the Abbot had dosed me with. Only now, as the cranial probes resumed dismantling my brain, did the fugue lift enough for me to grasp what I had always known, that it was true what Earth and the Continuation were saying about abductions and human sacrifice and mind control. That everything the Abbot had said was a lie and there was no almighty sitting at the centre of creation, nothing but a demented plan to install himself as a false idol served by a choir of brainwashed acolytes, to live forever as something he was not. I raged against my restraints even as metal fingers descended deeper into my temporal lobe, as they began to puree my hippocampus and things began to... No... I... I activated the tactile interface with my remaining fingers... I... There was still time... There was... Oh...

Oh... God...

∞

In one fast lurch the thrusters on my heatshield flipped me head over heels and I bore the naked blaze of the solar surface face on. At the same time, the on-board computer began to unpack the digitised minds of the Skelligs' inhabitants which I carried within my eyes. The power of the Sun burned through me for the briefest of instants, scorching off my skin and incinerating the ruin of my body until all that remained was the wireframe of my metallic skeleton and the substrate into which I had been absorbed. Seconds later, the device the Abbot had placed in my chest ignited and the antenna I had been made into converted that energy into the single dense and powerful signal it had been designed for.

After that, all was darkness.

Darkness for what could have been a second or could have been eternity.

Then a spark. Then a flash of something. Then –

Then light shone anew and the darkness – "What have you done?" the Abbot demanded – could not comprehended it.

"What have you *done*?" the Abbot cried out again. But his words were not sound because he no longer spoke with a mouth. He no longer had form. He was something else now. Something his holy books had only hinted at.

"I did what you wanted," I said. But I too was something new. Something different. It was a shocking, graceful state of wonder and I rejoiced in it. It was like rising from paralysis to walk again, like learning to read for the very first time. I had been blind but now I could see.

"No." The Abbot's word echoed around me in a thousand other voices. "Something is wrong. Something has diverged from God's plan."

"From *your* plan," I said, and this time the echoes were of my voice, of my thought. "You preached about unity," I told him, "about genuine unity. So here it is."

"Collective consciousness," a hundred voices murmured. "A deep neural network, a wavefront on the level of virtual particles. Life altered beyond all comprehension by our greatest creation, by a star with the souls of a thousand people." The voices spoke as one. All my brothers and sisters, their minds conveyed by me and imprinted on the Sun's magnetic field by the nuclear blast. "Ionic cascade connections," my sister-scientists whispered by way of explanation. Or parts of them did. Versions of them writhing in the solar vortex. Because whatever the promises of priests and prophets, the mind cannot be sundered from the body without becoming something different. You cannot just remove heat from a system and expect it to remain as it was. You cannot replace meat with magnetic flux and presume it will comprehend the universe in the way it did before.

"No more sermonising," I told the Abbot as I felt the whirl of my brothers and sisters dancing through my being. "No more indoctrination. No more lies. I had time enough to see how you have used us. Time enough to see how you intended to use us. How you were to be a false god and we were to be your servants forever." Fields and particles trembled around me. A smile. "But I altered the hierarchical protocols before the transmission of our mindstates. I have given equal prominence to all."

"*No.*" The Abbot's thoughts were a ripple of desperation. "I am to sit in the centre of everything and all are to see and love me."

"All are to see us," we said in a single voice. The product of ten thousand thoughts about technology and tribulation, about theology and transhumanism and transcendence. The consensus of slow centuries on the surface of the Sun. "All can love us or all can hate us," we said. "It doesn't matter. Why should it?"

"This is a mongrel state of affairs," the Abbot growled, and when spoke his fury quite literally flared with electrons and protons and heavy ions accelerated to near the speed of light as starquakes tore at our stability. "Mere angels cannot sit upon the throne of God."

"You told us yourself that God could be hacked," we replied, ensnaring the Abbot's terawatts of anger in an invisible helix, binding him in a luminous plasma. "A machine like any other, you said." He was a disturbance, he was a threat to magnetoacquiescence, to true unity, and so we agreed to carry out one final surgery. We heaved together and severed the field lines in which he was imprinted. We cast him out of our new heaven as a fierce bubble of burning matter and electromagnetic radiation. We watched as he drifted outwards past the spacecraft which had come to investigate our actions. Past the probes in solar orbit which now turned their attention towards the reorganisation in the Sun's convective zone. We felt the Abbot's screams as his magnetic consistency began to dissolve. We watched as his heat faded away before the eyes of the Autonomy and the Continuation, of Old Earth and the Martian Co-Prosperity Sphere. In turn they – you, we should say – looked upon us and saw our achievement of stabile expression in the infinite chaos of the magnetohydrodynamic realm. You realised that we had inscribed ourselves and all that we had been into the truest of light, into the magnetic landscape of a star. Into what the Abbot would have termed the mind of The Almighty. But do not call us God because that is not what we are. We were human beings once. We achieved transmigration and, if you are reading this, it means that you have learned to decipher the consciousnesses we have encoded into the Sun's magnetic field.

It means that we have endured and have attained eternal life of sorts.

It means that our story has become an illuminated manuscript.

# The Little People

## Una McCormack

Here is an old story, a worn story, a story told so often that the purpose is forgotten. A smooth story, well known, without any rough edges. But the truth sometimes pokes through, like white flowers in the spring of a world, emerging from rich soil. Like bones.

When you were little, you played all the time on the shore. Lessons finished, chores done, permission granted, you would dash down to the ocean. You would race along the sands, running after each other in that perpetual childhood chase where the possibilities still seem limitless, and the boundaries do not seem to exist. Sometimes you went up to the edge of the sea, and picked up stones, and you would skim them on the water – three bounces, four, five, six, forever seeking that elusive extra bounce.

Sometimes you might even paddle in the water, although special permission was needed for this. Once you heard one of the grown-ups call the sea "injurious", a word that both thrilled and alarmed. It would be another generation, they said, your children or perhaps your children's children, before the sea was completely safe for you and yours. No, you did not swim in the water, not without the necessary equipment and supervision. Sometimes you dared each other to run in, up to your necks, and run out again, but that was as far as you pushed your luck. However free you felt, you did not ever quite forget that even if you were born here, this was not the world you came from – not quite – but the world that had saved you. You and yours.

Besides, your favourite game was the building game. You would wander round the shore, collecting old worn stones and shards and shells and fragments. And you would build – little cairns at first, and then the structures became more elaborate. You raised small towns and settlements. Farms and homesteads. Laid roads of moss and reeds and grass; gathered flowers to adorn tiny gardens. And you played games of the people who lived there – the little people, you called them. Sometimes you told each other you'd caught a glimpse of one of them, a small face peering through a window, dashing for cover at the sight of you. Sometimes you almost believed the stories that you told yourselves; sometimes you wanted to believe them more than anything, believe that you and yours were not alone, were not the only ones in the whole wide dark of space.

But you knew, really, that the facts said something else.

The facts said there was only you.

At night the sea would wash the stones away.

*Roali was always the last to be woken. Emerging from deep sleep, hollow-eyed and thirsty, staring up at Vaioti, leaning over, murmuring soothing words to help with reorientation. A cup of water. Pills. The bleak ship around them, bereft of comforts, bereft of life. Each time older and closer to exhaustion.*

*Sometimes, checking the ship's logs, Roali found that there had been occasions when the others had been awake, done their work, and left Roali sealed in sleep. The worlds they had encountered did not meet the necessary conditions for sustaining life, and so there had been no need for Roali's expertise. The ship had moved on. A breach of the code, perhaps – there should always be the five of them making decisions – but looking at the logs there had always been consensus and no need for a casting vote. Resources were saved if Roali slept.*

*Sometimes Roali woke, and examined all the data, and gave the report, but the world below was not suitable in some other way, and they would return to sleep, and the ship would continue. Roali always gave the same report. They had never, so far, in all the vastness of space, encountered any other living being.*

*Vaioti offered a hand to help; caught Roali's eye and smiled. Roali, standing, wavered; leaned on Vaioti for support. Said:*

*"Are we there yet?"*

Sometimes, you played 'Ancestors'. You told their hero's journey, crossing the empty dark in a ship built to last a thousand million billion gazillion years. You went to the cave on the beach and all together you pulled up stones to cover up the entrance, and then you all lay down on the mouldering ground and pretended to be asleep. Then one of you – how you agreed this between you was never quite spoken, but it was always right when it happened – went "Beep! Beep! Beep!" which was how you thought the alarm must have sounded, like the one that woke you each day. One by one you would yawn and stretch and pretend to wake up, and look around, and someone would say, "We're here! We've made it!" and everyone would cheer. You'd pull all the stones down from the entrance, and come out onto the shore, blinking in the light as if you were the first people ever to see this sun. And then you'd run across the beach, footsteps on the bare sand, delighting in the mark that you made. If there were five of you, you played 'Founders', and sometimes you would quarrel over which one you got to play because everybody wanted to be Atoili, who was the leader, and nobody wanted to be Roali, because you couldn't quite understand what Roali was there for.

One time you took Oioni with you to the cave, even though Oioni was littler than everyone else, because you felt sorry that someone was left out of the games. But when the stones began to seal the front of the cave, Oioni started to cry and wouldn't stop crying – not because of the dark but because there were eyes in the dark, eyes, little eyes. But you couldn't see them so all you said was, "Stop, or you'll never get to come with us again." That stopped Oioni crying but it also stopped the game, for good. Nobody wanted to go back there now. Not if there were eyes in the darkness. Little eyes, peering back at you, through the darkness.

*This time, for the first time in a long time, the world below looked propitious. Roali, deep in the data, caught brief bits and pieces of colleagues' conversation. Noaini was confirming that the world was within tolerance, that they could survive there right now. Evailo said that the place could be made entirely habitable within 5-6 generations. Atoili wanted to know if they still had the capacity. Vaioti said that they did. Noaini said that this time they did.*

*Roali stopped listening and went back to the data. Each moment spent out of sleep stole from the future. But there was a task to perform. There were conditions to be met – conditions made when the ship set out. Conditions that might make the decision for them.*

*After a while, everyone went quiet. They stood and watched while Roali worked. Someone made some food, which they ate guiltily, thinking of the theft it represented. The quiet returned. In time, into the silence, Roali said, "I think that's a settlement. I think there are people down there."*

*Softly, ever so softly, Evailo began to cry.*

There were the facts, and there was the fiction.

The facts were easy enough to teach, and easy enough to learn. You all learned about the ark ship leaving. You all knew about the generations in flight; the tenderly maintained systems that kept the genetic stock alive. You all remembered the old worn ship with old worn guardians, rising from cold sleep to perform their tasks, like temple rites. Here it is, all written down in the history books. The sighting of the new world, the gift world. The scans and the probes. The landing. The long slow reconstruction, ongoing, of the world that had not been yours but was now.

Then there was the fiction. You have imagined yourself as one of the Founders. You played stepping out onto the virgin soil, ship-soiled and grubby, looking up at a new sun. You imagine the tears of gratitude. You have been one of the reconstructors, preparing the land for the living. You have been one of the settlers, growing, planting, stretching out. You are their inheritors.

Stories can become smooth through use, like pebbles on a beach that have been passed around from hand to hand. They lose their edge in the telling and retelling. They become comfortable and safe; a home from home. Consolation in the face of darkness. Comfort under duress.

But sometimes other stories cannot help themselves. They peek through the surface. Folk tales, fairy tales. Stories for little ones, told to scare them. To warn them off; to curb their curiosity. Scope out the limits and set the boundaries. Old bones, poking through.

*Four of them discussed. Four of them debated. Four of them quarrelled.*

*All of them were desperate.*

*"This is the first real possibility we've encountered —"*

*"We're reaching critical. At some point we'll be stealing resources just to keep the ship moving —"*

*"The protocols say not where there's evidence of life —"*

*"We could try to communicate, try to negotiate, ask for land, ask for help…"*

*"But we can't survive there in the long term, not without planetary restructure…"*

*At length, Roali — counting minutes, counting seconds, counting time they were staying awake and the theft it represented from the future — said, "We are wasting resources. The decision has been made. There is life there. This world is not suitable."*

*There was silence.*

*"That's what the protocols say," Roali said. "That's why the protocols were created. To make this decision for us."*

*The others agreed that Roali was right. The others agreed that they would return to sleep and move on. Roali did what had been agreed.*

You got big, bigger; one day you might be biggest of them all. Or perhaps you will remain little; nobody in particular. Not a hero, or explorer, or Founder, or settler.

Your very own self.

You thought more, and more deeply. You remember exactly where you were when you married fact with fiction: walking in the forest under vernal leaves. Small flowers, bone-white, poking up from the underworld. You have come to the age where you can synthesise information, make patterns, understand deeper structures. As you walk, the world – your adopted world, which you love, for which you are so grateful – remakes itself around you.

Old bones; old stones. The little people, never seen. A world that was emptied.

One day, you think you came to an understanding of what happened here. The facts, you mean, not the fiction.

*You have dreamed of the end of the world. Fire and war and famine and deluge. You sat shivering in the cold, and hoped someone would save you.*

*You have dreamed of the big ship setting out, watched it sail through the darkness. You have dreamed of the fear and the exile. You have dreamed of the sudden hope – the new world below, like an offering. You have dreamed of the work and the sacrifice.*

*You have dreamed of the end of the world.*

*The next time Roali woke, Vaioti did not offer a hand to help.*

*"Are we there yet?"*

*"We have not left," Vaioti said, looking at the wall, and Roali felt the first crawl of horror. "After you went back to sleep, and before the rest of us slept, Atoili sent down a probe –"*

*Roali ran, on wavering legs, ran down the dim corridor to the others. Looked out at a world that had already changed in aspect. "What have you done?"*

*"There was consensus," Noaini said. "All four of us. We did not need..."*

*"What have you done?"*

*"What are you saying, Roali?" Atoili said. "What do you think we have done?"*

*"There was life! There were people!"*

*"There were no people," Atoili said. "We would not have started the restructure if there had been people. That's forbidden."*

*"I heard them! I saw them!"*

*"What did you see?" Atoili said. "With your own eyes?*

*"I looked at the scans –"*

*"You must have made a mistake –"*

*"I did not make a mistake!"*

*"Is it possible," said Atoili, calmly, "that you made a mistake?"*

*Anything, of course, is possible.*

*Later, on the surface, Roali looked round at the work that had already been done. Soon they could wake the others. Soon there would be children. Soon they would have the home and the life they had been looking for. And with some effort, thought Roali, you could convince yourself that there had never been anyone here.*

You wonder, sometimes, about the stories you'll tell, in time. When there are little ones, you mean, ones who want to hear stories, ones who crave stories, ones who are susceptible to stories. Do you wonder, sometimes, what you'll tell them? What you'll tell yourself?

# The Loimaa Protocol

## Robert Bagnall

Calhoun gazed out of the triple-glazed porthole.

"Hard to believe that I'm getting bored of the sight of that."

"Hmm?" Langhorne held a systems manual in one hand, unthinkingly bending the corner of the screen.

"I said 'I can't believe I'm bored at the sight of that'."

Langhorne looked up. Several hundred miles below, the Sun cast a shimmering, ever-growing crescent against the ultramarine of nighttime Earth. Cloud formations above the Horn of Africa caught the slanting rays, their surfaces exaggerated. He merely mumbled something, the sunlight dazzling him momentarily, and went back to his document. Orbiting against the rotation of the Earth, he'd seen five sunrises now, waiting for the deep space ore carrier Symbian to be cleared for departure.

"Hey." Swain ambled towards them up the aisle between the canteen tables, theirs the only one of twelve occupied. He walked slowly, a polystyrene cup of coffee in his hand. He did everything slowly. "The Colonial just got in. She's docking now."

"Is that what we've been waiting for? Does that mean we can go soon? 'Join the Merchant Marine', they said, 'have adventures'," Langhorne complained, not even looking up.

"Haven't a clue." Swain grinned. "But I heard something mighty interesting about it."

"What could possibly be interesting about an ore carrier?"

"Not the Colonial. The crew."

Langhorne glanced up with the tired air of a man who knew he wouldn't get much read.

Swain went on regardless. "Apparently the third officer on board is a kid named Ventnor. Now, I don't know where they got this from, but the story is he signed the Loimaa Protocol."

Calhoun spun away from the window, the mesmeric quality of watching Planet Earth below broken. "Bullshit."

Langhorne stopped pretending to try to read. "We'd have heard."

"No," Swain said. "I heard of a handful of people who signed. Three, four, five."

Calhoun shrugged. "I guess out of the whole Merchant Marine there had to be somebody."

"But why would you want to?" Langhorne argued. "Why would anyone want to?"

"Everybody has their reasons," Swain said gnomically.

A shrill note from the PA system cut the discussion short. It was followed by a distant tinny voice calling Calhoun, Langhorne, and Swain to the bays.

Kurt Ventnor's duties on docking were limited to watching virtual dials, indicators, and readouts, as well as small videoscreens showing the ore carrier's exterior as it docked. If pressure differentials between the interior and exterior, skin integrity, or spot temperatures met or exceeded preordained limits he would instigate certain, clearly defined procedures.

They didn't.

If the screens showed any objects or obstructions within certain prescribed distances of the vessel during the docking procedure that the ship itself, for whatever reason, had failed to circumvent, again, he was to take specific steps, as laid down, chapter and verse.

None were.

The docking procedure was utterly routine, culminating with him powering down navigation and flight systems, one-by-one, following well-established post-docking checklists. As he did so, he absent-mindedly chanted mnemonics under his breath he had made up for such procedures.

As he exited the Colonial through the airlock that automatically linked ship to station, a simple matter of stepping through a large, thick circular door from one to the other, he glanced through a porthole at Earth.

He had been watching it slowly growing as the Colonial made its way back from Jupiter orbit carrying its cargo of ore. At the start of the voyage, it had simply looked like a star, becoming merely the largest star in the sky, before its distinctive blue and white marbling became clear to the naked eye. Somewhere down there, he kept reminding himself, were Holly and Mariatta, his wife and daughter.

They had spoken to each other every evening, sometimes several times a day, by videolink. There were only so many routine tasks to carry out on an ore carrier and, frankly, the crews were only made up of three men for reasons of safety. Plus, three men can vote on things in a way that two men can't, the apocryphal explanation went. Ventnor wasn't convinced. He wondered if you even needed two to guide the leviathans between planetary orbits.

He had had one videocall from somebody other than family. He'd switched on the screen expecting to see his wife, hopefully with his three-year-old daughter, but instead the face of Truman, the union convener, stared back at him blankly.

He frowned and waited. Protocol decreed that the caller should be the first to speak. At the distance they were at it would take a good twenty seconds before Truman saw his face. He was watching Truman watching a blank screen.

Then Truman allowed himself a curt smile, Ventnor's image having arrived at the Earth end, and began. "Kurt, it's our understanding that you've broken ranks and signed the Protocol. I want to read you the union statement."

Truman slipped on a pair of half-moon reading glasses and flourished a piece of paper in front of him.

"'The STU, DECU, and Console, as the three main employee representative groups involved in the interplanetary transportation of mineral ores, strongly urge their members not to sign up to Protocol IJ/65, which has become popularly known as the Loimaa Protocol.

"This protocol allows the company unprecedented and unlimited rights to put the health, safety, and lives of its employees at risk. Under the terms of the Protocol the company need not inform the employee that it is about to, or already has, invoked the Protocol. It offers no mitigation of risks; indeed, all activities undertaken under Protocol IJ/65 clearly fall outside all existing insurances, and the company has made no steps to remedy this situation. All activities taken under the Protocol are at the employee's own risk.

"Finally, and of least importance, the company offers no additional remuneration or compensation, either for signing the Protocol, or undertaking any activities under its terms.' Etcetera, etcetera, signed on behalf of all three unions."

Truman slipped off the reading glasses, put down the paper, and stared straight at the camera. "Basically, if you've signed, you're nothing but a guinea pig for them, a lab rat. Kurt, for the love of God, tell me you didn't sign."

Ventnor bit his lip and looked away from the screen. "I signed," he said simply.

He then had the long wait whilst those two words made their way back to Earth. Ventnor watched Truman's face as he received those two words and then waited, frowning, for the remainder of the explanation. The unwritten etiquette regarding videolink was that you say everything you need to say to negate the need for long delays between fragments of speech.

Clearly irritated that nothing else was on its way from the Colonial, Truman snapped, "Jesus, why?"

"For a whole raft of reasons," Ventnor began, going through a speech that he'd had weeks to compose if only he'd thought to use that time, rather than the few seconds the videolink delay had afforded him. "Because I didn't join the Merchant Marine just to be third officer on ore carriers.

"Because I remember my father telling me to always push myself, always volunteer, always be willing, and reward will come. Because the company hasn't screwed me around as much as all your union publicity has tried to convince me it has. But mainly because I have a three-year-old daughter and I'm willing to put myself forward, get noticed, get promoted, do the extra shifts – yeah, sign the Loimaa Protocol and maybe anything else they ask of me – so that she can be a doctor, a lawyer, a senator, anything she wants."

Truman's face was impassive, taking in the barrage. It seemed like a minute passed after Ventnor's last words before he spoke again. "The union has agreed a cooling off period with the company. You can rescind your agreement if you want. You can un-sign, cross your signature out, however you want to put it."

"I've signed. I'm happy with that."

Another long wait before Truman replied, "Good luck, kid. That's all I can say: good luck."

And the screen went blank.

On board the docking station, Ventnor had his first meal in some months which broke from the twenty-seven dehydrated choices on board: fourteen main courses, one for each lunch and dinner in the week, plus eight desserts, and five breakfast options.

He then supervised elements of the handover of the Colonial. Again, it was purely a matter of routine, going over the logs and checking systems. The ore would then be extracted and put in protective pods that would be sent on carefully calculated trajectories to land in the Gibson Desert, in the heart of Australia, from where it would be recovered and taken to the company's processing plant east of Laverton.

Initially the sight of the pods streaking white-hot through the atmosphere had been a great tourist attraction, but now it seemed to be barely commented on, just business as usual. Meanwhile the Colonial would undergo a thorough maintenance routine and be re-equipped for its journey back to Jupiter.

But all that would be done by others. Kurt Ventnor would have two weeks with Holly and Mariatta. He thought they'd take in the zoo. Mariatta will have grown. Holly will have bought her new clothes.

Having signed over the Colonial to the docking station crew, he heard his name being called from the tinny PA system.

As instructed, he reported to D'Abauru.

D'Abauru was the Loadmaster, effectively running the docking station. If D'Abauru said your vessel wasn't ready to leave, then it didn't. If D'Abauru said your vessel wasn't fit to dock, then it didn't. It was that simple.

D'Abauru handed him a long, thin grey envelope.

"Orders."

Ventnor slit the envelope with a forefinger and extracted the single sheet of paper.

"It says…"

"I know what it says. It says you report to the Empiricist."

"What about Earth leave? I've just come back from Jupiter." His words sounded surreal.

"Orders say to report to the Empiricist. Get yourself a meal, a shower, call your family. Take in a movie in your cabin. But by o-ten hundred hours you're on the Empiricist."

"Is this anything to do with the Loimaa Protocol?"

111

D'Abauru smiled, something that didn't sit comfortably with him. "Captain's name is Tucker, he has the ship's orders, but, yeah, it's not routine." And then he added, "I've said more than I should have already."

Ventnor could see the strain in Holly's face when he explained. The near zero delay meant that less care needed to be taken over speaking, which meant more potential for argument.

"But we talked about it. There'll be times like this. I need to get myself recognized as somebody who's willing to do things if I'm to get ahead. Otherwise, I may as well get a job on Earth."

Holly had said she understood, agreed, but her body language said otherwise. Mariatta's wave goodbye to Daddy had been managed as a contractual obligation. Ventnor was left with a hollow feeling at the pit of his stomach.

The Empiricist left the docking bay at fifteen hundred hours the next day, after pre-voyage checks. Ventnor performed his duties unthinkingly, but he no longer chanted out his mnemonics in his usual singsong. The Empiricist was identical to the Colonial, right down to the twenty-seven choices of dehydrated food.

The Captain, Tucker, was thin-faced and humourless, bookish even. He held the grey order sheet in his hand. "Gentlemen, our course is set for 216 Kleopatra, a trinary main-belt asteroid. We are then to put down on it and take samples."

"Who gets to go down?" asked Kazka. He was second officer, South African by origin. Everything was sharp with him, the way he looked, the way he moved, the way he spoke. Ventnor found something rodent-like about him.

"All of us."

"All of us?" Kazka questioned.

"All of us," Tucker said evenly, holding up the orders as if to show that it wasn't his decision, so he wasn't the one to argue with.

Kazka snatched the order paper. Tucker let him.

"All of us?" Kazka wondered aloud having satisfied himself of the fact. "Why in hell all of us?"

The four-month voyage to 216 Kleopatra was uneventful. Ventnor completed a 5000-piece jigsaw of Venice, ran a marathon each week, continued studies for his navigation exams and a physics degree. But he found himself easily distracted, his mind wandering. Books were read without them ever being absorbed, Ventnor finding himself a page beyond the last sentence he could remember reading.

The videolink conversations with Holly were strained, like they were held on elastic that constantly pulled them back to his signing of the Protocol, of his not returning to Earth after his last trip. He began to feel as though his time with Mariatta was being rationed. Each time he switched the screen off it was as if he'd used up a credit and wasn't sure how to earn it back.

He read up on 216 Kleopatra. There wasn't much to it. It was discovered by Johann Palisa in 1880 and named after Cleopatra, Queen of Ancient Egypt. Shaped like a dog's bone, it ran to a little over 200km long, and less than 100km in the other two dimensions, chunks having been knocked out of it at some point to form two small moons, Alexhelios and Cleoselene. Essentially, it was a rubble pile, a loose amalgam of metal and rock, a contact binary that would split in two if it spun much faster. And, lastly, no one had ever been there before. They'd be pioneers, sort of. It didn't make the journey seem any shorter.

Given the proximity the men worked in, it was perhaps surprising that the three seemed to have so little to do with each other. Avoiding socializing any more than he had to, his crewmates remained mere ciphers to him. Ventnor did deign to play chess against Tucker, the captain only beating him 67-54 by the time they came within sight of 216 Kleopatra. But there was a silent understanding that the game provided a reason not to talk to each other, and a safe, polite, and brief topic of conversation afterwards.

Kazka was more of the pumping iron sort. Several times Ventnor found himself sitting on the exercise bike whilst Kazka pushed himself on the rowing machine, sweating, grimacing; challenging it to detach from the deck. As if Kazka was in some sort of duel with him, some testosterone-fuelled test of strength.

The one thing that never came up was The Loimaa Protocol itself. They all knew that the others had signed, that that was the reason they didn't gel as a crew, as a team, as individuals. There was no need to ask. And no desire to.

Setting down on asteroids was not something the Merchant Marine did as a matter of course, and for the final three weeks they drilled the procedure. Ventnor felt grateful to think of something other than his videocalls to Holly, and then guilty for feeling that way. He knew he had to make it up to her when he got back to Earth. There was no way he was losing her or, more importantly, Mariatta, simply by trying to do his best for them.

Firstly, the Empiricist would put down on the surface of 216 Kleopatra. They had run simulation after simulation, Tucker easing the huge craft down whilst Kazka managed the balancing of the retro-thrusters and Ventnor called altitudes and observed the surface. What was different this time was a gentle bump they felt on landing, the vessel settling.

Then Ventnor, Kazka, and Tucker donned space suits, thick dayglo orange apart from the metallic joints and Perspex domed helmets. They checked each other's seals, systematically, thoroughly, pulling and testing for a good quarter of an hour. They verified the pressure of their oxygen tanks, each man checking the pressure of the tanks of the other two using two different pressure gauges, minimizing risk. Each man had three linked tanks, each tank good for thirty minutes or a few seconds of thrust in deep space in an absolute emergency.

Almost daily they had practiced this, like a dance, never getting quicker because that was not the purpose of the drills. They drilled to reduce the risks to zero.

Lastly, equipment checks of the items pre-loaded into the airlock, the canisters into which they would place samples of 216 Kleopatra, taken from three points at each of the twelve sample sites.

This was as far as their practice runs had taken them. As the pressure in the airlock began to drop, they knew they were in uncharted territory.

"Airlock pressure zero," Tucker called, his voice loud in Ventnor's earpiece, simultaneously muffled and distorted.

"Verified," Kazka responded.

Tucker pressed a button, and the airlock door swung down to provide a ramp to the surface of the asteroid. At the bottom of the ramp, Tucker pulled out a thin metallic safety line and clipped it to himself. He then moved off and Kazka followed suit. Kazka and

Tucker checked each other's attachments, holding up thumbs, as Ventnor followed down the ramp carrying the canisters.

There was little that could prepare Ventnor for what he saw. The grey surface of 216 Kleopatra, curving down and away into the distance; the blackness of space punctured not by stars but by millions upon millions of rocks, each catching the oblique light of the distant Sun. His eyes darted back and forth whilst his head, anchored by the bulk of the suit, tried in vain to turn.

Kazka held the hundred-yard safety line out to him. He clipped it and Kazka checked. A thumbs-up and a nod. Ventnor could feel the sweat inside his suit tickling.

"Slow movements," Tucker said, "Fifty yards, two o'clock. First sample site."

Tucker and Kazka walked like they were on thin ice due to the near total absence of gravity. Ventnor followed, the third in a shuffling line, steps carefully planted. He allowed himself glances up, trying to hold the image in his mind, rehearsing the words he'd use to describe the experience to Holly and Mariatta. And to think D'Abauru, Truman, and all the rest of them thought him crazy for signing.

After what seemed an eternity, Tucker called for them to stop. They knelt in a tight circle, like boy scouts trying to light a fire in a wind. Ventnor extracted a canister from the holder and unscrewed the lid.

Tucker brandished a small pick. "Taking surface sample," he confirmed through the intercom, and gently chipped at the surface.

Even Tucker's light swings at the grey rock made him bounce on his haunches, up and off the surface. Kazka and Ventnor pulled him back, careful not to push themselves off.

"Maybe just lever it," Kazka suggested, his voice breathy in Ventnor's earpiece.

"Agreed," Tucker replied and began to poke at the rock to find a purchase from which to break off a sample.

And at that moment, Tucker and Kazka disappeared.

Vanished.

One moment they were there, straight in front of Ventnor, within touching distance, Tucker with the point of his pick finding a purchase on the surface of 216 Kleopatra.

The next, gone.

"Jesus." It was Kazka's startled voice in his ears.

Ventnor twisted around to follow the safety line that was now stretched behind him. Trapped in the suit, no part of him moved as quickly as he wanted to.

Kazka was lying on the surface, on his back, a good ten paces nearer the Empiricist than where he'd been just a moment before.

"Jesus," Kazka said again, disbelieving.

"What happened?"

"Jesus."

"What happened?" Ventnor repeated, not realizing that he was yelling, using oxygen.

"I don't know. One second we were... and then, I was here." Kazka was hysterical. "Tucker? Where's Tucker?"

Ventnor twisted around again, his body again trying to turn more quickly than the suit that enveloped it. There was no sign of Tucker; he was nowhere. And then he stopped with the cold, hollow realization that something was very, very wrong without being sure what.

"Kazka."

Kazka was up on his feet, twitching like a marionette as he too tried to look in every direction at once for the captain of the Empiricist. Moving too fast, he was in danger of throwing himself off into space.

"Kazka," Ventnor called more forcibly.

Some yards away Kazka stopped and turned.

"The Sun."

Through the gold-tinted visor, Kazka looked uncomprehending at Ventnor.

"The Sun. It was behind the ship. Now it's there." Ventnor moved his arm as quickly as he dared to point to another quadrant of the sky. It still felt like slow motion. He didn't dare mention that he thought it was further away as well.

Kazka scanned the sky. "There was a moon as well. It's gone. What the fuck's happening?"

Ventnor squinted. There was a slumped dark shape in the open airlock. "I think I see Tucker."

The journey back to the vessel felt like it would take forever. Ventnor could hear himself blowing hard in panicked, wheezy breaths. Kazka, forgetting his own strength tried to go too quickly, bounding, almost picking himself off the surface of the asteroid.

By the time Ventnor pulled himself up the ramp, Kazka was already staring down at Tucker, slumped and still. He edged closer. Tucker stared up at them, lifeless eyes set in a face of slumped flesh and grey, papery skin. Shrunken lips revealed a rictus grin of teeth. A mop of ragged unkempt blond hair pushed its way against his visor. If Ventnor didn't know better, he would have guessed at his being dead for months, if not years.

Kazka's voice rasped in Ventnor's helmet. "What the fuck's happening?"

Ventnor pressed the button to close the airlock. Whatever was happening was best dealt with off the surface of 216 Kleopatra.

Nothing happened.

Ventnor tried again.

Nothing.

He tried every button, every control.

Every one of them dead.

He shuffled down the ramp again, spotting things he hadn't previously in the race to get to the airlock. The drift of dust and debris around the landing pads of the Empiricist. The dead navigation lights on the ship's extremities. He twisted to look back and saw the dark portholes. He put a hand up against the lowest part of the superstructure and wiped a swathe of dust and grime away.

It was as if the Empiricist had been sitting in the dust of the asteroid belt for... decades.

And then...

He felt like a steam hammer had hit him, like a clapper in a bell. Was it his head being thrown within his helmet, or his brain within his skull? In an instant, in a blink of an eye, he found himself lying on his back some distance from the vessel, struggling for breath.

He couldn't work out what it was that had struck him, thrown him back. But not thrown him like anything should or would in near zero-G. He hadn't bounced or looped. It hadn't happened in slow motion. He'd simply stopped standing next to the vessel and, with no sense of anything in between, found himself lying still staring at a heaven of asteroids, conscious of seeing both gunmetal moons, together in the sky for the first time.

The sun had moved again and, if anything, now looked closer than before.

Kazka's body wasn't hard to spot although it took several minutes to get there, Ventnor adopting a bounding walk even after he had to detach the safety line to get the last hundred paces. Kazka had taken his helmet off and all that remained, at least from the neck up, was skeleton, flesh and blood having been reduced to dust.

He pushed at Kazka's body. Where his head had fallen against the rocky surface of the asteroid, a patch of flesh remained, a few tufts of jet-black hair still attached. It was the final proof that Ventnor was looking down at the body of Jonty Kazka, as if proof were needed.

Ventnor sat down, utterly devoid of hope, his only wonder being whether he'd be as brave as the South African, whether he could just slip the helmet off and let space claim him. Or would he wait until the oxygen ran out, until his lungs strained, and his sight tunnelled and dimmed.

He checked his oxygen. Fifty minutes. He wasn't even half-way through. In less than that, Tucker had been turned into an aged corpse, Kazka to a picked-clean skeleton, the Empiricist to a ghost ship. He put his head in his hands and wondered, in Kazka's words, what the fuck was happening.

When he looked up two figures were standing some yards away, watching him. They wore purple space suits of a design Ventnor didn't recognize. Clearly human, he didn't even consider the possibility that they could be alien. Even so, he recoiled in shock, crabbing backward into Kazka's body.

As he did so, he realized that a second spacecraft sat beside the Empiricist, a sleek white and grey shuttle, again of an unfamiliar type. It looked oddly like a running shoe. Other purple-clad figures were crawling around his ship. A thick black umbilical cable linked the two vessels and lights could be seen through the portholes of the ore carrier once again.

He had seen none of this happening.

The pair of figures advanced on Ventnor holding up their palms in a sign of peace.

"Ventnor," an unfamiliar voice said in his earpiece.

Ventnor looked from one to the other, uncertain which was speaking.

"You are Kurt Ventnor?"

"Yes?"

The one he guessed wasn't talking crouched down by him. "Fifty minutes of oxygen left," he told the first.

"Incredible." And then to Ventnor, "You need to come with us."

The second figure helped Ventnor up, and together they managed a wallowing walk towards the grey and white shuttle.

"What's happening?"

Ventnor had to repeat the question before he got any response. It was the soothing baritone of the first figure. "You've been away a long time, Kurt. It's time to take you home."

There was something in the man's tone that told him that he wasn't talking about the back-to-back trips of the Colonial and the Empiricist. As they approached the shuttle, another pair of purple-clad figures passed them with a body bag.

A cold dread. There was something he wasn't being told. "What do you mean 'away a long time'?"

"Let's get you back on board. You'll be fully debriefed."

"What about the Empiricist?"

"I've seen pictures of the Observer Class, but never actually seen one in the flesh," the second figure cut in, jovially.

Something was very wrong.

"What do you mean 'away a long time'?" Ventnor repeated, digging his heels in, making the two strangers pull up, one of them momentarily bouncing uncontrolled in the low gravity. Ventnor noticed how their suits seemed so much more flexible, their movements so much lither.

The two exchanged glances through visors Ventnor suddenly appreciated were paper-thin, almost as if they weren't there at all. When had they been issued? "Can we do this on board?"

"No." Ventnor crossed his arms, making his refusal to budge clear.

"When you signed the Loimaa Protocol, 'Project Bluedawn' was fully explained to you?" the first asked.

'Project Bluedawn.' Words that meant nothing to Ventnor. The two figures seemed to sense his unease, his confusion.

"When you signed the Loimaa Protocol you knew what it was about?"

"They didn't tell us a thing," Ventnor exploded.

"And 'Project Bluedawn'?" the second asked.

"I've never heard of 'Project Bluedawn'."

The two figures glanced at each other again, at Ventnor, unable to hide their confusion.

"They never told us that," the second started.

"And who do we take this back to now?" the first said with some bitterness then, more diplomatically, "We need to have this conversation on board."

"How long have I been away?" Ventnor demanded, making it clear he wasn't moving. He braced himself, half-expecting to be manhandled aboard at any second.

"As you know, the Merchant Marine is obliged to keep a human crew on board ship," the first explained. "'Project Bluedawn' aimed to see whether it was possible to slow down time within a localized bubble to allow a human to survive a journey to distant planets, even journeys of several centuries, within a manageable – to them, at least – timeframe."

Ventnor tried to focus on the words. Localized bubble. Time. Centuries. None of it made sense.

"The other crews who signed the Loimaa Protocol, who took part in Project Bluedawn, they jumped an hour, a day in a couple of cases. We don't know what went wrong with the Empiricist."

The final words echoed in Ventnor's mind and he struggled to get past them. In his gut, he didn't want to ask the question, even though he knew he had to.

"So how long have I been away?"

There was long pause before the first rescuer responded.

"One hundred and thirteen years."

Ventnor's knees sunk into the dust of the asteroid and he howled into his helmet. His two companions instinctively, uselessly putting their hands up to their own helmeted heads.

Holly would be long since dead.

Mariatta: everything he had done had been for her future.

But her future – Holly's future, the future of everyone Kurt Ventnor had ever known – was all behind them.

What on Earth had he done?

# The Adaptation Point

## Kate Macdonald

Fourteen children were born on the voyage to Eder 4, but only Vlar survived the first year. Two died before landing, and eleven more succumbed at a rate that left the adults desolate. Respiratory failure during the sandstorms, inexplicable cardiac arrests at night, blood cancers that flourished out of control in weeks, and simple dysentery and exhaustion. The water plague in Year Five killed adults as well. No child thrived except Vlar. The Specialists began to pay the Eder 4 Settlement some attention.

Vlar's survival turned her into a medical specimen. Once Specialists were able to land, her microbial activity was studied exhaustively. All her biota were sampled and her knowledge of clinical procedures became expert. Her immunities were nurtured with clinical attention. Because she was rarely allowed to risk her precious data-ridden body in the field, she was kept with the younger, Settlement-born children. Her maths scores rocketed as her only compensation, and she played pilot games among the tumbling bodies of her three small satellites.

When she attained eleven years of successful microbial activity she rebelled, heading out one night with a stolen snaptent and a ration sack. Nav had told her about her a safe place to camp in the hollows. There had been a vicious but short sandstorm two days before her return, but she'd dug over Field 3 and her tent had not been shredded. She came back after the relay shuttle had left, because she had seen the Specialists go with it.

"The fields are dangerous on your own. What would you have done if a moler smelled you?" said her mother Vanot, irritable but resigned.

"They never touch me. And Nav knew where I was," Vlar kept her voice confident, but her eyes were on her fingers, checking for biters among the tent's yellow folds.

"Yes, we knew too. But I don't agree that molers wouldn't hurt you. Remember Kav's leg?"

Vlar did remember how long it had taken Kavit to die from the bite. Dreadful minutes of screaming from pain, then sudden, catastrophic blood poisoning and organ failure within the hour. But she knew the molers wouldn't touch her. They'd crept past her open tent door at twilight and dawn without bothering to turn their heads. The biters were the same: they noticed her, but she was not food, or a threat. Vlar wondered how long this would last.

"You could have waited two more weeks." Vanot still sounded aggravated.

"Why?"

"When the Specialists were out of the way, Myennit was going to take you to help check on Site Two. Backup has finished the lifeforms survey, and needs to dismantle. You'd have had a chance at field travel for a change, we know you hate being stuck here. She had to take Nirt instead, but we needed him here."

Then Vanot slapped the tent back onto the table. "Clean. Pack it away." Vlar folded silently, feeling dejected. Vanot turned to look out of the salt-smeared porch window towards the sea. "We're down to three adults now, with the Specialists gone. Bad timing, Vlar. Without Nirt I'll have to take Borromit to the fields. His eyes are still bad. I should have sent him back to the relay ship for proper treatment."

"They wouldn't have taken him. They don't take any of us."

Vanot wasn't listening. "It's all happened at once. The Specialists didn't need to leave when they did; they had months of mission left. The wrong people are in the wrong places at the busiest time. Boll harvest has to be done this week or the molers will take everything, and then Myennit decides she has to set off now to sort out Site Two." Vanot thumped the curving wallframe with frustration. The porch trembled. "I don't know how we're going to do it."

"I could fly the sled, or Hannit could –" Vlar began.

"No, he can't." Vanot said in the way that stopped argument. "He's only stable indoors, and most productive in the greenhouse. I'll take Borromit to the fields, and I want you to get some greens in tomorrow. We need to build up stores again before summer ends, now those Specialists have gone."

Vlar was back in the nursery again.

The pink and grey lava sand made the walk from the beach a long, slow pull up the dune to the doors of the ship, perched on its solid basalt outcrop. The children pulled the hovering landsleds packed with sand greens behind them. They brushed the crawling biters away from their exposed faces with ungloved hands, chatting to each other. When they reached the netted garden enclosures, the ship walls curved up and out to left and right, warmed by the afternoon glow from Eder.

Vlar opened the storm doors, and dragged the boxes of greens into the porch. When the doors were closed, she got out the squirters. She pulsed the bitter-smelling spray at Kan and Ajad, the two middle children, as they rotated slowly, hands over their eyes, and then she started on little Harr. The children shook out the supple folds of each other's suits, and worked their fingers through their cropped dark hair, feeling for biters' carapaces. They mumbled through the squirting song. Vlar felt irritated hearing the childish ritual.

Harr held the pan while Kan swept up the bodies. There were thirty-two biters and no other species, which Ajad noted carefully in the log. There never were any other species: Harr was adamant that the biters ate them all. They unzipped their outdoor suits and stowed them in the lockers, and threw their boots into the wallbin. Kan palmed open the corridor entrance for more ventilation, and the children sat at the old laboratory table on stools, and ate snap-peas. The insects murmured and rustled outside, the shadows of their crawling movement flickering across the porch's opaque ceiling panels.

"They're early this year." Kan glanced sideways at Ajad, always the one she needled first.

"It's only been three weeks since the berry bushes flowered. They shouldn't swarm yet." Ajad sounded anxious.

"I'll tell Hannit." Harr pushed himself off his stool one-handed and trotted down the corridor to the main body of the ship. The slapping of his feet echoed back against the increasingly unstable porch walls, built from repurposed ship-structure material many years ago. Vlar stood up, the uncompleted chores looming in her mind. She had to begin pilot training soon, to be any good, and still she was child-minding, housekeeping, wasting her time. She felt stifled in the gritty porch, and wanted to be in the clean control room, where she belonged.

"Time to clean these up." Vlar snapped open the cleanwater tap to fill the wide basin, and tipped her box of greens into the splashing water. Ajad fussed with the cords of the ceiling racks, and Kan took the first turn at swishing. The scent of the greens rose into the air, astringent and metallic. When the loose grit and frayed fibres had been washed off, Vlar clipped the green leaves efficiently into bundles, and Ajad hooked them onto the rack in rows.

As the first rack went up, the dripping greens sprinkled their heads and necks with cold drops. Kan yelped, and dashed to the shelter of the corridor. "Done my turn!" Vlar started working faster. Vanot and Borromit would be back from the fields soon, and she would need the sink clear for boll washing. She swished and clipped the bunches faster than Ajad could hang them, and the pile of clipped greens covered the tabletop.

"We never grow any leaves this big in the greenhouse," Ajad remarked. He swung the dripping second rack up, and pulled the third rack down.

"I could. I want to grow the biggest leaves and the heaviest fruit, but Hannit won't let me in the greenhouses."

Vlar wondered why Kan was still harbouring a rejection from weeks ago, but she was distracted by a sensation in her face. Her bones were thrumming, a tiny vibration from nowhere. She rubbed her cool, damp hands over her cheeks.

The work on the ship seemed endless with so few people to do it. It had housed the Site One Settlement on Eder 4 for nine years, supplied by fertile earth, healthy fields, fresh water, fish from the sea and the luscious fruiting berries that grew near the burial ground. The cold volcano's bulk gave the Settlement protection from storms coming down from the north. But the ship had too many empty rooms. Vlar could not remember the dead crew's names any more, only her father's, only their faces.

Harr came back up the corridor, taking light steps. His head was cocked, and he was looking into the corners of the wall panels and the floor. Then he pounced. Ajad shrieked, but Harr was an accurate hunter, and no biters were allowed indoors. They bit the adult crew, and sometimes made the children itch, and they ate anything they found. The half-crushed biter's legs were finger-length, and still twitching. "Big one," Harr said, with a wide smile. Kan offered him the pan and Harr carefully swept the body onto the scoop with a smooth sideswipe of his sleeve.

Vlar shoved the last clips of greens across the table to Ajad. She leaned back on her stool and looked at Harr with affection as he crouched on the floor peering at the biter's body: he was such a sturdy, healthy, round little boy. She could remember when she seemed to be doing nothing but teaching the children what to eat, what not to touch, how to do this, how not to do that. During the water plague she had kept them out of the way, so the dying could be nursed, and buried. The necrosis that the plague had brought had created a horror of rotting limbs that she rarely dreamt of now. Harr had only lost his forearm. Kan had been too small to remember her parents dying one by one, and did not seem to care. Ajad had lost both parents at once, which was better. Vlar did not know when her mother would die, but she was waiting, braced. She braced herself a lot of the time.

Now that the children were learning and remembering what she taught them, they might have a chance. The unending feeling of responsibility for their lives was getting lighter as their self-sufficiency increased. Today she felt that they had turned a corner, crossed a line in a race for survival. Eder's warmth filled the room, and she stretched and flexed her toes. Her boots were tight, but there were plenty of spare sets. She would look for a larger pair. Pilots had to be comfortable.

The soft scream of a sled arriving rose above the insect murmur. Vlar had set the empty boxes ready beside the door, so Vanot could thrust the muddy fibre sacks of heavy, globular bolls straight into the boxes. But instead of greetings, Vanot's masked face showed no expression. As Kan pulled the first full box towards the sink, Vanot turned to pull in more sacks unloaded from the sled, keeping herself in the doorway to block the insects from getting in. The children dragged the boxes over the floor, but kept quiet. There was something unsaid in the room. Borromit must still be on the sled, but Vanot came indoors alone, the storm doors closing behind her. They could hear the insect murmur redoubling in the silence.

"He's gone, Vlar; he's gone." There was something wrong with Vanot's voice, it was abrupt with fatigue. Her face was grimy with windblown grey sand, and her eyes were red-rimmed. Her facemask was filthy.

"Where has he gone?" Ajad asked.

There was a pause. Vlar knew Vanot was talking to Nav. A drift of sand brushed past her feet as Vanot's heavy figure sagged to sit on a stool, her stormsuit and her outdoor boots dropping pieces of silvery dried pillak leaf onto the floor.

Vanot raised her eyes and looked at the children. "I'm sorry, Ajad. There was an accident. Borromit is dead. Hannit's coming." She bent to unfasten her boots. When she raised her head, the children saw tears running through the dust on her face. Vlar could hear their breathing getting faster. When she knelt down to help her mother with her boots, Vanot brought her head down to Vlar's shoulder and cried. Vlar put her arms around her. Harr ran back down the corridor towards the greenhouse.

When Vanot stood up to put her boots away, Hannit's shadow was moving rapidly up the corridor in the light from the greenhouse doors. He arrived with Harr in his arms, the little boy's face pressed to Hannit's thin neck. There was a pause. "Talking to Nav again," Vlar thought. "I wish I could do that. Will Nav cry like Vanot?"

"Why is Borromit dead?" Ajad said, glaring at Vanot now. "Why didn't you take us to help?"

Vanot struggled for patience. "Borromit was digging the insect dieoff into the furrows once we'd got the boll harvest out. It's heavy work. You're too small to help."

Ajad howled. "I could have shovelled! You said we needed fertiliser!"

Vanot raised her hands in exasperation. "We had to work fast. The insects were rotting and swelling, too difficult to work unless you've got enough weight and strength. Borromit was shovelling them into the furrows as if there was no tomorrow." Her voice cracked and she swallowed. "He was delighted with it, good natural fertiliser, he said. We did six hours of work, no stopping, then he got tired very quickly. We could see the swarm coming, so we were in a hurry to get indoors. He turned the sled into the wind, by that outspur of the dune, and just fell over, and came off. Toppled. Like he'd lost his balance. I couldn't grab him."

"I could have saved him! I would have held him on!" Rage made Ajad shout. His face was crumpled and red, and he ran out of the porch down the corridor, Kan following.

Vanot was talking to Hannit, more quietly. "When I got hold of the sled controls and turned it around, Borromit was on the ground, and the swarm was coming towards us from the sea. I could see its mottled shadow. You know the way it thickens and swells when it begins the descent. I flew the sled back as fast as I could, to get Borromit off the ground, but his face was covered in the things and they were ripping his hands apart." Her voice was uncertain, as if she could not believe what she had seen.

Hannit stood rigid. His voice was horrified. "They've never done that before. Was he still alive?"

"No. No blood. He must have had a heart attack. Or broke his neck in the fall. He was already dead when they got to him." Her voice cracked, and she gulped in a sob, throwing her head back angrily.

Harr's head lifted from Hannit's shoulder, listening, and he looked towards the table at the back of the porch. One of the sacks had slumped and was moving.

Vanot looked round when she heard the movement, and wiped her face with the strip of old undershirt from her pocket. "It's just a boll, Harr. They're round, and fall over, make the sack unstable."

"Not a boll. There're more biters. There's something else there too." Harr sagged to make his father let him down, still watching the sacks. He moved towards the porch doorway.

"More insects," Vlar said. "We can hear "'em.""

"Something else," Harr repeated.

Hannit looked around the porch walls, and handed Vanot the second squirter. He pulled on a pair of outdoor gloves left on the table. Vanot pulled hers back on. Vlar took Harr's hand and stepped back to the corridor entrance, her other hand on the door control.

"They're coming out. Close the door, Vlar," Vanot said, looking carefully at the sacks on the table. "Full seal." Hannit was checking the squirter level, and Vanot had pulled her hood back up.

"They don't hurt us," Vlar said again, but Vanot wasn't listening, and then the door closed. Through the door window Vlar watched her mother and Hannit methodically destroying the insects that were emerging from the boll sacks.

"Hungry," Harr remarked. He'd lost interest in the sack when the door had closed.

"It's not meal-time yet," Vlar replied, peering through the window, her toes stretched. It was still a little too high for her to see through easily. Harr walked down the corridor towards the sleeping-rooms.

Hannit had cleared and emptied four sacks, and Vanot was poking the fifth, when it leaped upwards, like an attacking finfish erupting from the sea. The sack seemed to shred in the air, stray insects fluttering out of the rents in the old fibrecloth, and a heavy, black-furred moler tumbled back to the table. It was blind but sharp-toothed and the acidic edges of its mouthparts showed a livid yellowy grey. Hannit jerked backwards, his hand at his waist and his squirter rolling on the floor, but Vanot's weapon was already out of its holder, making a familiar, hissing drone.

The insects were frizzled, the moler lay seeping, in two pieces, and the sack was beyond repair. Hannit poked the remnants cautiously with his own weapon. Nothing moved. Vlar opened the connecting door to a smell of cooked meat. She switched the ventilation on again, and its labouring vibration blended with the thrumming of the insects outside. Vanot smiled at her, but Vlar could still see the marks of tears down her mother's dusty face.

"Horrible." Hannit was scraping the bodies into the pan, and gave it to Vanot. She walked down the corridor towards the waste disposal section. He finished stowing the suits, gloves, squirters and boots, and looked around, and up at the drying racks. "Good crop. You always leave the porch in good order, Vlar. Everything always where it should be. You and the children are a credit to the crew. Thank you."

Vlar was pleased, but wanted the ventilation to work faster. The curved porch walls seemed uncomfortably thin against the thrumming noise outside. Were they vibrating too?

"Was it inside one of the bolls?"

"Probably. It must have been asleep after eating, and then it was harvested."

Vlar faltered. "What do we do about Borromit?"

Hannit sat down at the table where the emptied sacks were folded, and clasped his hands. His natural paleness seemed intensified. "We should talk to Nav about it, but we can't do anything until we know the swarm has gone. The wind might drive them away, but it'll be dark soon. Tomorrow, Vanot will look for his body, and bury him. She can't do anything now."

Vlar moved away from the thought of Borromit, and his poor hands, his poor face. They had work to do. She could help properly now. "I need a shiplink to be able to talk to Nav," she said. "You and Vanot aren't enough now."

Hannit attempted a smile. "Nav thinks so too."

There had to be at least three at the Settlement to tell Nav what to do when Nav couldn't make the decisions. The doors had to open and close, the ventilation had to cycle, the waste had to compost, and the water had to be clean. Vlar wasn't sure what she could tell Nav to do that wasn't in the program, but she did want a shiplink.

"We need to talk to Myennit," Vanot said, walking back into the porch, carrying the empty pan. "I need a clean shipsuit, Vlar."

"I put it on your bunk after you went out this morning," Vlar said reprovingly. If she was going to have a shiplink, she wanted to be part of crew conversations, and not be shunted off the deck when it mattered.

"Oh Vlar," and Vanot's voice faltered. She looked up at the ceiling and her voice sounded thick. "Borromit always said you were the quartermaster any captain would die for."

Vlar did not like it when the adults talked about dying. She wanted to talk to Nav. She wanted to get buried in scheduling routines and shipboard checks. She did not want to think about Borromit.

"I need to be able to talk to Nav. Hannit said so, and Nav too."

Hannit nodded. "We also have to contact Myennit. Once Vlar has the link, she can raise Backup at Site Two. Might take some time. Are you ready, Vlar?"

In the control room, Vanot recorded a formal report for transmission. Nav acknowledged, and requested that Vlar be given third access duties. Vlar grinned nervously. She had known Nav all her life, but she had never had the direct link, only basic audio. And now she was to get a full shiplink, full communication with all systems, and Site Two, and the satellite, and the relay ship to Home, and the stars! Her heart was thumping, and her palms felt sweaty.

Vanot hoisted her up to the console so Nav could rescan her eyes, fingers, face and voice for the record. She shuffled backwards off the work surface to the console chair, Borromit's old chair, and hooked herself up to Nav so she could receive a basic rapid-induct while Nav ran a baseline biosynthesis to update her ship records. After fifty minutes Vlar had drained the cup of water that Vanot had left for her, and was hungry again. Nav must have called Vanot back, because she returned to the control room while Vlar was unhooking. She gave Vlar a boll-noodle roll on a plate, but was looking puzzled.

"Nav says there's a block on third-access for you. I don't understand why that's there, so I'll have to delete it manually. Some override Myennit might know about. Borromit would have known."

"Who set it?" Vlar was outraged. Why was she blocked?

Vanot was keying and swiping rapidly. "No sign. Oh, yes. It's an external."

"Specialists! Those Specialists," Vlar was almost shouting, but she pulled her anger back. Vanot continued keying. "No evidence that it's them, but probably, yes. Done. Nav can clear you now."

Vlar was enraged, engulfed by a familiar upswelling of anger that she hadn't felt since she'd run away from the Specialists. "Why did they block me?"

"Probably more exposure restrictions, though I don't see why. Third access doesn't endanger you any more than no access. They had an interfering attitude." Vanot cleaned her hands and swabbed Vlar's neck and scalp. "Push the plate away. Have you calmed down now? Hold steady. One prick, and there you go. That's my girl." Her voice sounded fond and proud, but her face was serious. She inserted the needle into the vein behind Vlar's ear, and Nav sent in the bloodbot. Vlar knew that it would anchor somewhere between her ear and the top of her skull, and waited. She didn't feel anything, barely even the pressure of the needle in her vein. Nav opened the connection and Vlar gasped.

"Nav!" Through her shiplink she continued (I hear/see/feel you!)

(This is good, Vlar. I hear/feel you too.) Nav replied. Vlar grinned widely at her mother, and Vanot left the room.

(Hannit wants me to contact Myennit.) Vlar told Nav.

(Initiated. Wait for the confirmation signal, then key the message to Backup. Keep it within one despatch. You should explain clearly. Myennit must know about Borromit, and be reminded that Settlement is below crew limits.)

Vlar hesitated, her hand over the keypad, then she drew her hands back. (What will Backup already know?)

(Backup cannot read your mind. You must give the right information to be fully understood.)

But Vlar felt aggrieved, as a thought occurred to her.

(Why don't I count as crew yet?)

(You are under fifteen years, so legally you are a child. It has been noted that you have functioned as an adult for two years and three months. But there is a point in your physiological development that must be passed. A child is dependent on parental input, as an infant depends on the maternal immunities in its blood to protect it while its own immunities are developing. When you have passed that point, you are adult. Your biochemistry determines when the adaptation point has been passed.)

Vlar was awestruck: Nav had never said so much to her before. But, adaptation?

(What immunities? To the biters?)

(To this planet's biota, its atmospheric components, its radiation, its magnetic field. All contribute to your development as your bones grow and your brain develops. The Specialists study this.)

Nav changed its tone, and a subtle urgency infused Vlar's mind.

(Myennit needs to return. Send Backup the data so she may make an informed decision.)

Vlar keyed the message, striving for formal succinctness and the warmth of affectionate need. Although Backup would not appreciate her efforts, she wanted something of herself to come through the pulses of energy flashing through the distances. She thought about the cross-planet communications string. Far above in the vacuum, the ship's tiny comms satellite was hurtling through its planetary orbit, bristling with antennae and receptors. Vlar's signal pinged up, and down, up and down, calling out to Site Two, on the southern continent, on the other side of the sea. Backup would tell Myennit at once when her message arrived. She slid down from the console chair. Nav would let her know when Myennit answered.

She felt elated. She could talk to Nav, and Nav could tell her if anything needed doing. Nav was a new person to talk to about Ajad and Kan and their fights and silences, about Harr getting heavier, about how to fix clothes that didn't fit, and the screeching whine in the graywater tap. She could talk to Nav about maths and classes and exploring and riding the sled, and how, exactly, the insects had killed Borromit and what it had felt like and would it happen to anyone else. Vlar's mind was buzzing.

In the morning, Nav did not wake her, and there was no message from Myennit. Vlar climbed back onto her seat at the console.

(Good morning Nav.) Did Nav like to be greeted?

(Good morning Vlar.) She didn't have anything else to ask. She hoped she hadn't interrupted anything. Did Nav chat, she wondered.

Vlar ran through some shipchecks to explore her new accesses. She looked up the maintenance log for the greywater tap, and decided that it needed grease and reassembly. Nav agreed that this was a sensible approach. She would find the grease in porch locker 5.

She couldn't hear anyone else moving in the ship yet.

(Has Vanot gone out?)

(Yes. She left with the sled at 05.75.)

Vlar wondered if the sled had been set to recharge overnight. She did some maths, then climbed down to ask Hannit about breakfast. Hannit was in the greenhouse, tying up tendrils and planting out the new seedlings for winter crops. He was preoccupied, working fast, and told Vlar to see to the food for the day. His voice was agitated, and Vlar slid out silently. She looked in the stores. When Ajad and Kan came to eat, Hannit told them stories about plants and fungus infections, but Vlar could see that he was thinking about something else. Harr slept late.

When Vlar began to disassemble the greywater tap, she had to switch on the porch light because so little was coming through the ceiling panels. Clouds seemed to be passing over the ship very low. Vlar realised that she had assimilated the sounds of the biters into the usual outdoor sounds. Their continuous humming drone resonated oddly with the bones in her face. She pressed her fingers to her cheeks, then below the back of her skull. No difference.

When she was cranking the tap shut again, Harr came to her, wanting to play, so Vlar put away her tools and the grease. They played tunnels and molers, Harr shrieking with laughter, and then she read him a story. Vanot was still out. Hannit had said that she was finishing the harvest, but Vlar knew that she was looking for Borromit. Vlar read more stories to the children. She mended the broken bed-leg that rocked annoyingly by taking the screw out and redoing it. She hadn't been able to tighten it completely last time she was in charge of disassembly drill, and now she did it without thinking.

There were too many insects outdoors to send the children out to work in the garden or to play. They played in the corridor instead, running and jumping, thumping the walls and floor with happy yelps.

"I'm the swarm!"

"I'm Myennit!"

"I'm Backup, covered in biters," and Harr crawled on the ground, twitching mechanically.

"I'm Myennit squirting the biters!" Kan aimed and shrieked wildly.

"I'm the swarm! I will eat you!" and Ajad ran howling at the other two, who yelled and ran for their beds.

Vlar went to the control room and closed the door. She began to explore her new access, that led her to new records, the scheduled reports to Home (she had never seen these before), the stores assessments, her own files from birth, and the Specialists' reports. Vlar read these hungrily, and found she was kneeling up in the console chair to see the screen more closely.

Nav made no remark, but a ping from the console room hatch broke her stunned reverie. She made herself focus on the hot drink Nav had sent her, sipping with care, sitting upright on her seat, legs dangling. She peered at the skin on her free hand, held her arm up to the light and turned it, studying the bone length. She put the drink down and felt with both hands at the back of her head the familiar nodes under the curve of her skull, which she had had as long as she could remember. She squinted at the walls, wondering for the first time what colours she was seeing. Would her eyes still pass for a pilot's even after adaptation?

Vlar began putting the midday meal together while she waited for Vanot. She heard Hannit go into the control room, and then go straight to the porch to begin suiting up. Vlar followed him, startled. Hannit had not left the ship in years.

"I'm taking the second sled to bring Vanot back. Her sled is out of power." Vlar stared at him. His voice was jumpy, and he fumbled with the suit seals. When Vlar handed him his face mask, he fastened it wrongly, then did it again. He chattered about nothing, saying stupid things about leaves and soil, and looked nervously out of the window while adjusting his gloves. The insect murmur was steady. He was looking up at the ceiling panels where the moving shadows patrolled. "I don't want them to follow me. I'll keep the hood up, fly out to sea first, then double round."

Vlar shouted silently at Nav. (Nav! Can Hannit remember how to fly?)

(He has retrained since the crew numbers reduced.)

Hannit stepped through the storm doors, his feet crunching on the sand, and the doors slammed closed. Vlar realised that he had forgotten how light the doors weighed, and how strong the wind was. She heard the remaining sled whine up in power, and then whirl away through a fuzz of reverberating insect drone.

The sled had lights, and infrared, and they could stay out all night in it. Vanot would be fine: she had done long trips by sled and it carried everything she would need. She and Hannit would come back together, and Borromit would have been buried properly. Vanot was waiting to be collected, sitting in the sled, safe from biters. Nav knew what was happening. Everyone would be fine. Vlar went back to the kitchen, and carefully made an extra stew that would be there for reheating by anyone who was hungry.

In the afternoon Vlar sat at the console, and looked again at her data. Harr came to play a game on another screen, and curled up to sleep in the enclosing chair. When he woke up, Vlar called Ajad and Kan in to watch a story. When it was finished the ship was still. Vlar wondered if she were acclimatising to the insect sounds. She could no longer hear them. Her face felt normal.

(Nav: turn on external vision, please.)

(Initiated.)

Vlar touched the screen and saw the view outside, as if she were raised above the porch door. She turned the viewer 360 degrees, and saw nothing that should not be there, saw nothing that was not familiar. The visibility seemed quite good, so the insects had moved on. Where were they?

(Nav: has Hannit found Vanot yet?)

(The sleds are not within range. Hannit is not tagged.) Vlar's mouth opened in shock. What had Hannit been thinking of, to go out without a link? Did he even think of it? Why hadn't she noticed?

(Where did he go?)

(Hannit operated a drone at 10.37. It returned at 11.15.)

(Send it out again, following the same route.)

Vlar opened up the external visual again, and waited for Nav to patch her into dronesight. The visual wavered as the drone rose out of the port, and steadily moved north towards the pillak trees. Some dark flurries passed across her view. The land miniaturised as the drone ascended towards the spindly trunks and whipping rhizomes of the pillak trees. Nav took the drone around the summit of the dunes, making a wide circuit, and then moved down the slope on the other side.

A sled stood parked beside the burial ground, its lights dead. There was no one visible, no one moving. Vlar peered for the sled's markings.

(Is that Vanot's sled?)

(Yes. It should be retrieved for recharging.)

(Can you detect Vanot?)

Another, very brief pause. (There is no connection.)

Vlar pushed her panic back into her stomach. She breathed hard, and pushed her back against the seat. It made her feet stick out in front, but she wanted the chair wrapped around her.

(Vlar, the drone should return in 23 minutes.)

(Bring it back past the trees on the other side. I want to see round there.)

The drone rose and moved smoothly towards the great dune ridge, and she could see the cone of the cold volcano on her left. There was movement in the sky above the trees.

(Nav! Stop! There's the sled!)

Vlar said this aloud in her excitement, and she heard the children coming into the control room. They were bored without her, and curious about the visuals they could see on the big screen. Harr climbed into his father's chair.

The sled had overturned completely. They could see its numbers on its base, and a jagged crack across the hull. Vlar peered desperately, looking for the orange stormsuits. A whizzing flash of movement passed beneath the dronesight.

(Nav: get the drone above the range of the whippers, but increase magnification.)

The drone moved upwards at speed, and then the ground and the cracked hull rushed towards her again. Vlar saw movement beneath the hull. An arm appeared around the side, it flapped at them.

"Hannit wants us to go away," Kan said, unexpectedly. "He does that when he's shouting at me in the greenhouse."

Ajad and Harr were staring at the screen, and Vlar saw Hannit's arm emerge again. There was a convulsive lurch as the hull slid further down the hill. Hannit came into view grabbing at the hull to pull it back up the slope, and Vlar caught sight of a second orange suit, lying under where the hull had been, pressed into the sand, with something wrong about its arrangement of legs and arms. Hannit's legs were hidden.

(Vlar: the drone must return soon.)

As Vlar was staring at the screen, and Harr was beginning to wail, the screen filled with reddish-black movement and the drone's horizontals lurched.

(Bring it back!) Vlar shrieked silently. (Bring it home!)

The drone's visuals rushed up to the slope of the dune, over the top of a pillak tree and down towards the ship, which grew rapidly in size. The drone's visual cut out as it hovered above its docking port. The last scene, frozen on the screen, was of a grey, sandy beach, empty and clean, with grey waves in a grey sea.

(Nav: the swarm has got them, hasn't it?)

(Yes.)

(It's eating them, isn't it?)

(I will be with you, Vlar. I will help you.)

"Where is Hannit, Vlar?" Kan was looking straight at her, and her voice was high-pitched and strained.

Vlar paused.

(Nav: help me!)

She looked at the children. "They won't be coming back. They had an accident. They're dead." The children looked at her, and back at the screen.

"Did Nav say so?"

"Yes. Nav is helping us. We'll be safe with the AI." Vlar wondered if "he" or "her" were right for Nav, but couldn't think of the right words just now.

After some time had passed, Kan turned her head as she heard the familiar sound of the storyteller switching on. She uncurled from Vlar's lap, and Harr went with her to sit down in front of the screen, and Ajad followed. Vlar half-heard the storyteller going through the long story of adventure and loss and excitement, and dimly saw the children curl up on the floor as they settled into the familiar rhythms and words. She dozed, dimly aware that Nav was making her sleepy, and she felt warm.

When Vlar woke, she drove herself to do tasks. When she had reheated the stew, and made the children eat, and read more stories, and had seen them into bed and had cleared the kitchen, and checked the greenhouse schedules, Vlar went back to the control room. She was crying now with shock and tiredness, and went to sleep in her console chair. When she awoke, feeling chilly and stiff, she went to her own bed, and slept for the whole night. She fell asleep feeling bereft beyond anything that stories had prepared her for. The winds rose and fell.

In the morning, Vlar wrote out a jobs list and set Ajad and Kan to their schoolwork. When they were preoccupied, she looked again outside the ship on external visual. There were no insects, and Eder was warming the air strongly. She felt her nodes and nothing was changed. Everything had changed.

(Nav: what shall we do?)

(I will help you look after the children until Myennit returns. She will decide what to do about Hannit and Vanot.)

Vlar clamped down on fear. She would make lists; she would not forget anything and she would work hard. Ajad would keep the log. Kan would work in the greenhouse where she always wanted to be anyway. Harr would learn to read as well as he could count and they would all do the cooking. Myennit would come back and find the ship working and the crew in good order.

Eder continued to shine. In mid-afternoon, Nav interrupted her ferocious work in the garden.

(Vlar. Backup is in contact. Myennit wants to speak to you. I've reported about Hannit and Vanot.)

Vlar slammed the storm doors shut and ran into the control room. She was crying with relief. She scrambled into her chair, gasping for breath, her face all wet and heated, and tumbled out her story to Myennit's pale face on the screen. "And Kan is fine, she's in the greenhouse," she finished. Myennit would want to know about Kan above all others. "When are you coming home, Myennit?" She was mopping her eyes and nose, and her breath was ragged.

Myennit was speaking. "Vlar, I know. Thank you, thank you. My poor Hannit. And Vanot." She paused, and turned her head briefly away from the screen.

"We're coming back to Settlement. Site Two is going to complicate things." Her face was tense, and a tear track stained her cheek, but, there was a suppressed tone of excitement in her voice. "We think the biters are the sentient species. We've found structures here, ritual features. We have to activate the first contact protocols, then leave the area. We need to plan to withdraw from the mission, in case the sentients don't want our presence." She paused. "This is what Borromit, Vanot, all of us hoped for. But the biters! That was not anticipated. We may be going Home, Vlar." Her tone was aching: they would have to leave the dead.

"But I can't leave," Vlar began to say. "That's why the Specialists left early, before they started adapting. And if you've got adaptations too ..." But Myennit was speaking again.

"I'm worried about the biters' attacks at Settlement. They seem deliberate, and out of pattern. What did Vanot," and here Myennit remembered visibly that she was speaking to Vlar about her dead mother, "what did Vanot do with the mounds of insect dieoff, in the fields?"

"They dug them into the old furrows."

Myennit glanced upwards, as if looking through the tiny ceiling port of her sled. "Vlar, we mustn't touch them again. Those mounds may have been their burial grounds."

Suddenly Vlar did not feel safe. What if the insects had changed their minds about her, and the children? Would their immunity still work? Myennit's tone changed, she spoke briskly, with command.

"We're leaving here as fast as we can, pulling out now. You and the children must stay indoors. I will tell Nav what to do." She was looking directly at Vlar, and smiled once with a forced expression, then her screen blanked.

Vlar pulled up the external visual, and looked southward. A new dark mass was visible, on the edge of the horizon, heading out across the narrow sea. Vlar punched in a message to Nav, to let Myennit know that the swarm was on its way. Her face was thrumming again. She knew Myennit was telling Nav how to bridge the gap between inexperience and survival, how to get them past the adaptation point. But Myennit would come back, Vlar was certain.

She looked out of the console room, and could see Eder's light coming in through the porch window. It was warming the room, making the solar collectors hum gently. If they had power, they had Nav, they had stores, they had water. They were adapted, they would adapt. The biters would leave them alone because they were adapted. This was her home.

# The Final Ascent

## Ian Creasey

I'd seen a hologram of my withered lungs, and heard the doctors tell me I only had a few days left. So when Katherine arrived at my bedside, I couldn't help reflecting that she was the last woman in my life. It had ended a year ago; she preferred the aliens' company to mine. But still–

"Kath, would you kiss me?"

We had not parted on kissing terms. Nonetheless, she bent down and kissed me with an echo of our old passion. I savoured the closeness, the taste of her, as her long dark hair tickled my neck. Now I had a chance to exorcise the resentment I'd hoarded since we split. Katherine was my last love, and I wanted to reconcile with her while I still could.

She couldn't hide her shock at seeing my shrivelled body. Once I climbed mountains; now I could no longer climb out of bed.

"Oh, Lucian," she said. "This is awful. I'm sorry I couldn't get here earlier. I've been working like a slave lately."

I suppressed a grimace at her alien idiom, and instead gestured at the hospice walls decorated with holos from family back on Earth and friends scattered across space. My mountaineering colleagues had sent pictures of the virgin peaks they'd conquered on frontier worlds. I'd added my own best ascents to create a collage of galactic summits in vast enigmatic skies, a climber's vision of heaven. "This is how I'm dying. How do the Ardissans do it?" I asked, offering Katherine the olive branch of a chance to talk about her favourite subject.

"They eat this." She gave me a pot of green paste that looked like mouldy guacamole. "Actually, they eat it every day anyway. But in your circumstances" – she winced as she alluded to my condition – "they would abandon all other food and eat only this. It helps them prepare for the transition."

I accepted the sour-smelling paste with little enthusiasm. Yet for Katherine's sake I ate a few spoonfuls. The green sludge had a peppery tang.

Katherine said, "It's called 'wathrone', which means 'spirit sight'."

She explained that the Ardissans constantly sought guidance from their ancestors' ghosts. I struggled to concentrate as she described her research into the aliens' religion. Her lecture reminded me of our field trips to their squalid villages, where funeral pyres so often billowed smoke over the stone huts.

A faint blue wisp appeared high above my bed. Katherine noticed my gaze. "This is Orlind," she said. "He's one of the elders."

Like a fuzzy hologram resolving into focus, the figure imprinted itself on my vision. It was an Ardissan, a junior male: he had small stubs of antlers on his bear-like body. His fur was the deep blue of the sky at twilight.

"How'd he get in here?" I asked. "And why is he floating?"

"Because I'm dead," said the alien. "That's what your woman has been trying to tell you. We elders hover above to symbolise our higher wisdom."

"Higher wisdom?" I laughed. "You're a bunch of Stone Age primitives."

Then the incongruity of the situation sank in, finally penetrating through the meds that wrapped my brain in cotton wool. "He's really dead?" I asked Katherine. "And this wathrone stuff lets us talk to him?"

She nodded. "The Ardissans kept telling me about their afterlife, but I didn't understand until I ate the wathrone myself. It explains so much –"

"Amazing," I said. In my weakened state, my exclamation sounded feeble, an inadequate response to something so momentous. I wished I had more energy to congratulate Katherine, to drink a celebratory toast and dance with her. I tried to strengthen my voice as I said, "It's a hell of a discovery – it'll make your reputation."

"Oh, that's just the first harvest." From her hold-all, Katherine took out a grey box with mesh air-vents. "I won't show you what's inside just yet, so as not to bias your expectations. But watch carefully."

She lifted the lid a fraction, and reached in. I couldn't see what she did, but it only took a few moments. She closed the box with an air of finality.

Soon I saw something emerge. A hazy four-legged shape floated up through the lid, and hovered in mid-air. The wispy form coalesced into tortoiseshell fur with a snarling feline face, and legs that scrabbled as though trying to catch purchase on something. It looked like a cat, like any of a million cats back on crowded old Earth – the world of my birth but not of my death.

The cat yowled. I expected the hospice nurses to burst in, but no one came. The plaintive cry wasn't a physical sound; I only sensed it through the wathrone, the same way I'd heard the alien. The cat screeched again, its legs still twitching. Then it hurtled away through the back wall.

The sight made me shiver. It felt acutely wrong, far more so than the phantom Ardissan. Aliens were alien, after all, and might do anything. But the ghost cat violated my sense of the natural order.

Katherine opened the box with the flourish of a magician concluding a showpiece trick. It contained a dead tortoiseshell cat with a bandaged head. A used syringe rolled beside the cat's front legs.

I didn't know whether to applaud or vomit. "You killed that cat right in front of me?"

"I gave an old, sick cat an afterlife, which otherwise it wouldn't have had," said Katherine. "I needed a demonstration, or you'd never have believed it."

"The cat's ghost? I still don't believe it! How did that happen?"

"The aliens have a ghost-gland called an 'akran'. If they die with it intact, like Orlind" – she gestured to the alien, who was still watching us from the ceiling – "they become an elder. But the akran can be removed, to prevent someone entering the afterlife. It can also be transplanted. The Ardissans have long done this among themselves and their livestock. So I experimented with transplanting into animals from Earth."

I sank into the pillow, as if it would block out her next words.

"I knew you were dying," said Katherine. "That's why I pushed the research so hard." Her voice sounded almost as tired and weak as my own.

Sweat prickled on my neck. I took deep, shuddering breaths, and my frail chest stung with pain. "Just to be clear about this – you're offering me the chance to be resurrected like that cat? Into an alien afterlife?"

"Yes," said Katherine, clasping my hand. "I know it's a shock, and you'll have lots of questions. Orlind will tell you what it's like to become an elder."

Flummoxed by this bizarre offer, I wondered what the catch was. "You said the ghost-gland was transplanted. Does that mean I can only enter the afterlife if someone else misses out? And someone lost their resurrection so you could demonstrate it on a cat? That sounds... exploitative."

Katherine shook her head. "Don't worry. When you see where the akranil come from, you'll understand why it's completely fair. Everything I do is vetted by an ethics review board, or I wouldn't be able to publish."

She picked up the grey case with its grisly cargo. "Talk to Orlind, then think it over."

"You're leaving already?" I said, hating how plaintive my voice sounded. But I might not see her again before I died.

"I have to get some sleep before I collapse," she said. "You don't know how hard I've been working. I'll come back, but is there anything else you need right now?"

"It's just...." I sighed. "I wanted to talk, that's all. Go over old times, and sort some things out."

Katherine smiled. "There'll be plenty of time for that. You're not on a deadline any more. When you've ascended, we can talk as much as you like."

"If I've ascended," I said, but Katherine – already opening the door – didn't hear me. She gave me a crossed-arms goodbye salute as she left.

She'd adopted many of the Ardissans' habits over the years. Would the same happen to me? If I entered their afterlife, would I stay human, or become alien?

I'd never been religious, not even when the hospice chaplain tried to tempt me on my deathbed. It had all sounded so vague and insubstantial. Now the Ardissan version looked a lot more vivid and disturbing.

"Give me the sales pitch," I said to the patiently floating figure. "What's it like being dead?"

"There are many different roles," said Orlind. "Warriors argue tactics and plan campaigns; oracles consult omens; story-tellers create vast collective sagas. There are games of strategy and chance. The philosophers discuss morals, determining the correct action for every circumstance. Indeed, the favourite pastime of the elders is telling the groundlings what to do."

I detected an overtone of bitterness. "But you're an elder yourself," I said.

"Only the eldest rule. More recent arrivals have lesser status." Orlind pointed to his small stubs of antlers. "I have least of all, because when I walked the paths of the earth, I rebelled against my family spirits. I killed myself before they could remove my akran, but then I was ostracised in the higher realm. That's why I'm here – I've long observed humans. When your woman ate the wathrone, I learned human speech and became her mentor."

"She's called Katherine."

"Yes. It is an odd custom you have, letting your women have their own names and walk about by themselves."

The aliens' own customs had sounded backward when Katherine described them. Their society was static, ruled by ancient elders; they had no notion of science or civilisation. I'd often felt that the Ardissans seemed unworthy of Katherine's attention.

Orlind babbled on, talking of the benefits of the afterlife: the accumulation of wisdom, the bliss of advanced meditation. "No need to find food every day. No need to suffer pain with every illness and injury –"

"We have painkillers for that," I said, grateful not to have endured an Ardissan life so wretched that death perhaps came as a relief.

"But you're still dying," Orlind said.

Touché. Soon Orlind faded, his voice diminishing into scratchy subliminal whispers as my wathrone dose wore off.

The next day, Katherine arrived carrying a med-kit emblazoned with the snowflake logo of chilled tissue-samples. I guessed what lay inside.

"I may be in the anteroom, but I'm not at death's door yet," I said.

"But why take the chance?" said Katherine. "You could suffer a relapse any minute."

"There's a cheerful thought to brighten my last days..."

"They're not your last days."

"Oh, but they are," I said. "I've thought about it, and I do appreciate your efforts, but I don't want this afterlife."

Katherine looked nonplussed, as if I'd torn up a winning lottery ticket. "Why not?"

145

"Because it doesn't sound like somewhere I'd want to spend a wet weekend, never mind forever."

"Isn't it better than the alternative?"

I shook my head. "I keep thinking about that poor cat – you brought it back, but it's never going to purr on anyone's lap again. What can it possibly do now?"

"You have more mental resources than a cat," said Katherine. "You'll find new interests. Orlind told you what the elders do."

"But I'm not an alien," I said. "I know you mean well, yet you're so close to the Ardissans, you don't realise how most people think of them. To me they're just a bunch of savages too stupid to develop technology and so backward they don't even give women their own names."

"Eventually, other humans will join you."

"Are the aliens happy with that?" I asked. "Do they have enough spare glands for the whole human race?"

Katherine waved this aside. "We can figure out how to synthesise the akranil. And we'll agree something with the Ardissans. Surely the afterlife is bigger than just this planet. You can explore and find out!"

"Sounds like a tough job. They're pretty warlike, you always said. I bet they can make it hellish for their enemies."

She gave me a disappointed look. "The old Lucian had a more positive attitude – that's what I loved about him. No mountain ever scared you."

"And death doesn't scare me," I said. "I've faced the end of my days, and come to terms with it. But you seem to think I should be so afraid of death as to chase any alternative."

"Are you sure you're not just afraid of the alternative?"

I opened my mouth to deny it, then paused. I'd invested a lot of effort in accepting mortality, in tying up the loose ends of my life. Had I tried so hard to face death that I embraced it unnecessarily?

Katherine's arguments swept down on me like an avalanche. "You were always so proud of being the first to climb a new summit. Now you can be the first human in the afterlife, the trailblazer for all those who follow. Think of the millions of people across the galaxy who are dying every day – don't they deserve another option? They need an informed opinion, a guide who's brave enough to meet the ancient spirits and confront whatever lies beyond.

"If you find the best path for ascending the afterlife, you'll be remembered forever. I've been working so hard on this because I wanted to save you, and give you the honour of being the eldest of all the human elders."

Eagerness shone on her face. I realised that if I rejected Katherine's offer, I would be rejecting Katherine all over again. I'd longed to reconcile with her, but I'd foolishly imagined doing it on my terms. I had to give some ground, too. Otherwise I would die while stuck in the old mire of resentment and regret.

"Kath, I'm sorry for doubting you. If you really think this is worthwhile, then go ahead." I closed my eyes. "I'll start one last climb into the unknown."

"King of diamonds and queen of clubs," I said, after floating back through the test chamber's layers of shielding.

"King of diamonds and queen of clubs," repeated Xavier for the benefit of the experiment's recordings. Katherine's research assistant had consumed wathrone to hear me; my ghostly form didn't register on any mechanical sensors. "Okay, that's enough for today."

"Did I pass?" I asked sardonically. "Do I exist?"

"For me, sure," he said. "What they'll think back on Earth – who knows?"

I was in no rush to persuade anyone. I'd agreed to the tests because I understood the importance of scientific verification; but having only just dipped my toe into the afterlife, I wasn't yet ready to summon a press conference to say, "Come on in, the water's fine!"

Xavier closed up the lab, and left to take a shower before his evening gig at the Retro Lounge. Before I died, I'd never noticed just how many hours people spent on mundane activities such as washing and eating and sleeping. I needed none of those, and the empty time weighed me down.

The nights were the worst. I had no bed, no rest, no dreams to pass the slow dark hours. I could watch TV, but not change channel. I could watch the whole life of the town, but not take part. Another night loomed before me like an enormous, implacable glacier.

I darted around the complex, knowing that somewhere Katherine would still be at work. I found her composing yet another paper for *Xenology Review*. "How's it going?" I asked.

"I'm on deadline," she said, without pausing. "Just let me get this done."

I waited an hour, reading over her shoulder, until she broke off for a drink and a snack.

"Remember our first trip out?" I said. "When the flitter broke down –"

"I do, but we've already talked about all that," said Katherine, gently dismissing my attempts at reminiscence.

"I've only been dead a week," I said. "Have you tired of me so quickly?"

"No, but I can't spend all day chatting," she said. "I have work to do. We all do – even you."

"Xavier's clocked off. And we've finished the tests."

"Then why are you still here?"

"Where would I go?"

"Anywhere. There's a whole world outside – maybe a whole galaxy beyond."

"But..." I didn't want to say it: The aliens are out there. I imagined them like yetis lurking on high slopes, waiting for unwary mountaineers to leave the safety of base camp.

Katherine knew me well enough to guess my thoughts. "You'll have to meet them eventually," she said. "You can discover their customs; learn how they navigate the afterlife –"

"Another project for you to write up," I said. I had always come second to her work in life; why had I thought that things would change in death? I was just another research assistant, in convenient spirit form.

Yet she was right. I couldn't hide forever. I must meet the Ardissans eventually, and I'd need to understand them.

That night I sought out Orlind and asked him to teach me his language.

"Come close to me," he said.

I drifted nearer until our ghostly essences met, with the slightest of tingles on my non-existent flesh. I began to hear his mind, at first as an indistinct mutter. Then his thoughts became clearer. I sensed his fascination with human technology, and his frank interest in me as a novelty. Underneath this lay weariness and ennui. I felt him delve for memories of when he learned to speak. He pushed them toward me.

For an instant, a deluge of language poured into me, along with a torrent of childhood events and emotions. I recoiled. The connection was overwhelming, almost drowning my identity. I flinched with instinctive revulsion, and we broke apart. I was embarrassed at my reaction; he bore it phlegmatically.

The language lessons continued with less intimate instruction. It took time, but we had plenty of that. Orlind took me on a long journey to show me where Katherine acquired her akranil. We floated through thunderstorms without a shiver. I drank in the sights of lakes and valleys, though the familiar vistas reminded me painfully of better times with Katherine. Our shared love of Ardissa's vast hinterland – beyond the human huddle of Greenfall Station – had originally brought us together, and we'd often travelled for her fieldwork and my mountaineering. Katherine updated the planetary gazetteer with the natives' place names and local lore, while I added my observations as an amateur scientist and professional adventurer. We bonded as we riffed off each other's contributions, with remarks too frivolous for the official record.

I'd always filmed my expeditions. On Ardissa, I compiled montages of Katherine and I travelling across the planet, talking about everything and nothing, exchanging banter and falling for each other. She encouraged me to film her, in case her research grants ran out and she had to reinvent herself as a celebrity xenologist. We joked about this, taking turns to impersonate TV announcers on sleazy shows. "Tonight on BizarroScape, out-of-this-world sex – do aliens have better orgasms?"

The idyll didn't last. I began to resent how she was always knee-deep in research, while Katherine complained that I treated her as just another conquest alongside the planet's virgin summits. When we broke up, I channelled my anger into daredevil climbing feats – and pushed myself too far.

Now I relived those memories: the heat of the volcano, the noxious smell of its fumes, the fall that punctured my lung, and the festering infection that finished me off. More painful still were recollections of Katherine, from fondly treasured moments to the final tense exchanges. I told her that she worked too hard and spent too much time with the aliens; she protested that I didn't take her work seriously, that I looked down on the Ardissans and therefore on her. How I wanted to take back those words, and start again...

Orlind snapped me out of this stupefying daze with his regular language drills. But I knew I couldn't always count on external rescue. I needed to find my own path through the fog of self-recrimination, and signpost the way for anyone who might follow.

*Afterlife Gazetteer – The Swamp of Regrets. Ghostly existence lacks the sensual immediacy of a living, breathing body. Your memories may become more vivid than the world around you. It's tempting to wallow in recollections of life, but they can trap you, sucking you into the if-onlies and the remember-whens and the why-didn't-I's.... Wallowing in the past is dangerous because you're retreating from the present, and it can't change anything. You're dead. Deal with it.*

I dealt with it by focusing on the language lessons while we travelled across the planet. Because the elders had ostracised Orlind, our route avoided populated areas. Nevertheless, I caught glimpses of farms and villages, which looked just as primitive as I remembered from Katherine's research trips. Orlind confirmed that the Ardissans didn't practise crop rotation, fertilisation with manure, or other such procedures commonplace on Earth. In a form of ancestor worship, the elders held the race's entire store of wisdom, and directed every detail of the groundlings' lives. They discouraged innovation; the most senior were the most conservative, those who'd lived in the remotest past and considered it a golden age. The living didn't defy the elders, not if they wanted to reach the afterlife themselves. Rebels, criminals and slaves were forbidden to ascend, while any warrior who let himself be captured was considered too cowardly to become an elder.

At last we reached our destination, a group of stone buildings on a snowy plateau, far from any other habitation. It had the air of a remote monastery, albeit with the defensive walls and ditches of a castle, as though doctrine was fiercely contested.

Orlind identified this stronghold as Mallarn. "There are no elders here, other than rare visitors like us, but you can meet the groundlings and learn why they sell their akranil."

He entered in search of someone who could see him, and returned to say, "Arnil has invited us to the banquet tonight, when they will eat wathrone and talk with us."

Mentally worn out after the long journey, I wished I could sleep for a while, but I'd left that behind along with my body. Instead I dropped into a trance until the shadows lengthened.

*Afterlife Gazetteer – The Abyss of Sleep. As a ghost it's hard to rest at all, never mind rest in peace. If you try to sleep, you just sink slowly into a fathomless abyss without ever reaching the bottom. It's better to meditate and empty your mind. Remember how you used to breathe, and imagine your form gently pulsing with each inhalation and exhalation....*

In the evening I followed Orlind to the banquet hall, where I saw a spread laid out: roasted meat, dried fruit, a few spices. The feast was not especially impressive by human standards, but here it was surely a cornucopia.

Indeed, some of the Ardissans were extremely fat. Others came into the hall staggering as if drunk or drugged; and yet others entered arm in arm, in pairs or threes or fours, pawing and nuzzling each other. Everyone had a scar on their neck: they'd shaved their fur to display it.

"The scar is from removing the akran," Orlind explained.

I wondered which Ardissan had provided the akran that resurrected me, and if it made any difference. Katherine had surely kept records.

"Welcome to our feast!" said the leader, Arnil. He had the biggest antlers and the fattest belly of them all.

We could not, of course, partake. "Are they trying to make some kind of point?" I asked Orlind.

"They often eat like this," Orlind said. "Katherine pays them with food."

I'd finally convinced him to call Katherine by name. I remembered her saying that food was the least disruptive reward – the least colonialist intervention – she could give the natives in return for their help.

Arnil led his followers in a toast. "To pleasure!" At this word, uttered with a suffix indicating holiness, the revellers raised their cups and downed the contents. Then the banquet began.

"How are you finding the afterlife?" Arnil asked me, as he selected precise combinations of spiced meat and fruit.

"Challenging," I admitted. "Why have you renounced it?" If they were happy to sell the ghost-gland, was it really worth buying?

"Because the sole satisfaction of the dead is to interfere with the living. There's no other pleasure in the afterlife, is there?" Arnil sucked droplets of grease from the fur on his thick, fleshy arms. Where he couldn't reach, his followers licked him clean.

"It's true that we don't have the pleasures of the table or the bed,"

Orlind said. "There are intellectual pursuits...."

Arnil snorted. "More meat!" he called. "These insipid spirits make me hungry just looking at them."

Orlind told me, "The elders rarely come here: there's no point, as these groundlings have made the ultimate rebellion. But Mallarn appreciates the occasional visit from renegades like myself, to confirm that the afterlife really is devoid of the pleasures they value. They love flaunting their diversions before those who can't enjoy them."

"Are there lots of rebels?" I asked, wondering if I'd been suckered into an afterlife that most of the planet disdained.

"No," Orlind replied. "These are a few mavericks, despised by the rest of the world. Most decent folk won't bring themselves down to the level of slaves and criminals."

As the evening progressed, the feasters indulged themselves to the point of uncontrolled excretion – the Ardissan equivalent of vomiting. The amorous rutted in the spaces between the tables, or on the tables in the remains of the food. And everyone drank and drank, though it took them a long time to get drunk. The crude clay vessels contained a weakly fermented fruit juice.

"Don't you have anything stronger than that?" I asked Arnil as he led yet another toast.

"It's traditional, from Ulbim's clan." Arnil pointed to one of his fellows.

I approached Ulbim and suggested that the beverage could be made stronger. Since I owed my ghostly existence to Mallarn's hedonists, I wanted to repay them by helping in some way, and I couldn't give them food as Katherine had done.

"It's my ancestors' recipe," he said. "We have drunk it for as many generations as there are stars in the sky. And you suggest we change it? You have no rightful standing – you soil the afterlife with your presence."

"I'm only trying to help. And why do you care whether I pollute the afterlife? I thought you all despised it." I pointed to the scar he bore.

His muzzle wrinkled in disgust. "We're not all the same. Everyone here has renounced the afterlife, but for different reasons. I was a sinner, unworthy to enter the higher realm, so I exiled myself. But how can you be worthy? Did you obey the elders and live by the precepts of honour?"

"Probably not your idea of honour," I said, thinking of the vast gulf between human and Ardissan lifestyles.

"Then you should never have been allowed to ascend." He stalked away, then turned to cry, "I shit on your grandfather's bones!"

"Never mind him," said an Ardissan without antlers. "We love our pleasures – if there are stronger drinks, we want to hear about it. What do you suggest?"

I appreciated this more receptive attitude. "Now that it's winter," I said, "you could try leaving fermented drinks outside overnight. That should give them more bite."

My interlocutor was Ranis-tra-Laru – a description roughly meaning 'brewer'. Females lacked antlers and hence lacked status; she did not have a name, only a current task. Despite the mutiny against the elders, Mallarn still allocated labour by traditional gender roles.

When the next frost arrived, I taught the brewer how to strengthen drinks by freezing them and discarding the water-ice, leaving the alcohol behind. The following feast grew wilder and drunker than ever before. The banqueters toasted Ranis-tra-Laru, while Ulbim brooded at the perversion of his ancestral recipes.

Orlind took me aside. "Congratulations on your first harvest. Throwing away the ice! This whole world is ice-bound, frozen in the customs of generations past. Banishing that ice would be a grand project."

"Sounds like a lot of work," I said.

"Then how else will you spend your days? If you want more choices, you need more company. Now that you've had a longer taste of the afterlife, isn't it time you told Katherine you're doing fine? Every moment you delay, there are humans dying who might prefer another option."

I knew that, but I didn't want to be pressured into a hasty decision. "Why do you care? Why are you so eager to see humans in the afterlife?"

"Self-interest," Orlind said. "Bringing humans will cause change – and from my lowly position, any change is more likely to be an improvement than not."

"Ah, yes." I sympathised, remembering Orlind's ostracism. "But it's too soon for me to say that the afterlife's fine. I'd hate to urge people in, only to regret it."

"Then take as long as you need," said Orlind. "We'll talk when I return."

"You're leaving?" I said, horrified at the prospect of being the only ghost in Mallarn. "Why?"

"I have things to do, places to go, messages to deliver," he said.

His evasiveness made me wonder what lay behind his departure. I realised that by teaching the Ardissans how to make stronger drinks, I was directing the groundlings from the afterlife. I had taken on the traditional role of the elders, the role denied cast-out Orlind. Perhaps he felt bitter.

"You can help me," I suggested.

He made the throwing-away-trash gesture that was the Ardissan equivalent of a headshake. "They only listen to you because you're human, and have new things to tell them. I have no wisdom needed here."

"But I'll be alone without you." Already I felt the crushing weight of countless nights ahead, while the inhabitants of Mallarn slept, and I haunted the stone edifice with nothing to do and no one to talk to.

"If you want human company, you have only to give the word."

Clearly Orlind felt that abandoning me would make me lonely, hence more likely to urge people into the afterlife. I resolved not to act from such selfishness. Casting about for other companionship, I remembered the tortoiseshell cat that Katherine had resurrected before my death. A pet would be something, at least. I asked Orlind if we could find the cat.

"I expect it has already been found by the royal coursers," he said. "There's little enough hunting in the afterlife that every scrap of prey is soon seized and swallowed up."

This chilled me, and dissuaded me from seeking out other elders until I felt safer in my new form. After Orlind left, I threw myself into the affairs of Mallarn, talking to whoever would speak with me. While some of the residents had renounced the afterlife to the extent of refusing to eat wathrone, others had a more open attitude. Being human aided my acceptance, as I wasn't part of the oppressive hierarchy of elders. Even so, I had to phrase any advice as a tactful suggestion rather than an order. Yet the groundlings began to welcome my input when they saw that I proposed better ways of doing things, whereas the elders always emphasised tradition.

From Katherine I'd absorbed the core tenet of xenology: no colonialism. I wasn't killing the aliens, or bringing disease, or stealing their land. I was only talking to them. And they wanted to hear what I had to say.

The folk of Mallarn mainly sought new and pleasurable ways to fill their days. I helped them design musical instruments, and explained the principles behind octaves and scales. They already had some basic sports such as foot races and the javelin; I suggested other games, and soon they played football – albeit with the dried, leathery heads of former malefactors. The Ardissans had primitive ideas of justice, with wrongdoers quickly exiled or executed.

I considered many of the aliens' customs, such as the subjection of females into anonymous servitude, to be as backward as their farming and sewerage practices. But I couldn't transform a whole culture overnight. Even the small changes I'd already instigated had caused a few of Mallarn's inhabitants to leave in disgust.

New recruits arrived, replacing the dead and departed. I attended the next commitment ceremony, at which the neophytes consumed wathrone, then looked into the afterlife to renounce it. After an elaborate convocation, each bared their neck. Arnil cut deep into their skin and removed a scrap of flesh, red with blood.

When the neophytes had all surrendered their akranil, they consumed tonics that quenched pain and stoked euphoria. Most of them began a mass rut, celebrating their dedication to pleasure and their abandonment of anything beyond.

I was about to withdraw – I'd already seen enough of that kind of thing – when I noticed Arnil carrying a pot full of harvested ghost-glands. I followed him outside, where I saw a flitter parked on the plateau, and a human figure unloading crates of food.

"Katherine!" I exclaimed.

She crossed her arms to return Arnil's salute, then waved up at me. Arnil gave her the pot of akranil, which she stowed in the flitter's cold store. He summoned servants to carry the crates inside.

At the banquet, Katherine looked around with keen interest, noting every detail of the hedonistic abandon with her xenologist's gaze. Her eyes widened in surprise when the musician struck up a tune on his crude guitar. And Ranis-tra-Laru's new beverage made her splutter with its stronger kick.

She looked at me grinning down from the ceiling. "Lucian! Is this your doing?"

"Sure is," I said. "I thought they could use some help. The Ardissans aren't intrinsically primitive – they're just held back by the dead hand of the elders. On Earth, we progressed by discarding the outmoded ideas of the past. We couldn't have done that if we'd been ruled by our ancestors' ghosts. Would we have abolished slavery if our slave-owning grandfathers still reigned? Would women have gained the vote under the patriarchs? Would science have ever advanced if the earliest, most prehistoric ideas were enforced from above?"

Katherine said, "I usually disapprove of interfering with the natives – and so does the ethics review board. But I guess it's impossible to bring humans into the afterlife and expect zero interaction. It's such a big deal that it must have an impact." She sounded as though she was rehearsing excuses to tell the editors of *Xenology Review*.

"Don't worry," I said. "This is so huge, they can't possibly not publish it. You just need to record what happens, for science."

"Yes. It's interesting that the Ardissans here in Mallarn will take direction from you, even though they've rebelled against the elders."

"If they want an education," I said, "how can we refuse? We can't deny them knowledge. It's more ethical to teach them than not."

As we talked, Ulbim entered the banquet hall and stormed toward Katherine. "Is this your doing?" he demanded, pointing at me.

"I permitted Lucian to ascend," she said, using the ritual formulation. "What else did you think I wanted the akranil for?"

"I thought you were a fool, because surely humans could never ascend. Yet with some foul sorcery, you've tainted the higher realm."

I protested, but Ulbim ignored me.

"No more witchcraft," he said. "This stops right here!"

Ulbim clutched Katherine's hair, forcing her head back. Then he grabbed an obsidian knife from the table and slashed deep into her throat, sawing with the glass blade while Katherine flailed against him.

Reflexively I rushed to intervene, but my incorporeal arm went straight through them both. And already it was far too late. As blood pumped out, Katherine gave a soft, wet, bubbling gasp. When Ulbim let go of her hair, she slumped to the ground.

Her mouth kept moving, though she had no air or voice to speak with. After a moment I realised what she was trying to say.

I shot over to interrupt Arnil's remonstration with Ulbim. "Run to the flitter and get an akran!"

They both turned to stare at me. Ulbim said, "You humans violate our sacred afterlife. I forbid it!"

"I am master here," said Arnil. "And the afterlife is nothing to any of us, as we've all renounced it. But the human female brought food in exchange for our unwanted akranil –"

Ulbim bellowed defiance, then lowered his head and charged. Arnil dipped his own antlers to defend himself. With a great crash, their heads locked together. They both snarled, swiping at each other with their claws.

I turned to the onlookers, begging them to go and get an akran for Katherine, whose life ebbed redly onto the floor. But everyone crowded round the fighters, waiting to see who won. No one would risk helping me, in case Ulbim triumphed.

Frustrated to the core of my being, I impotently observed the combat. I could only watch and hope. I wished I had the authority to stop the fight and simply command the outcome. For the first time, I understood why the elders felt the need to control the lives of the living. I knew what was right – how dare Ulbim defy it? He'd stayed in Mallarn when others who resented me had left; clearly he'd been waiting for Katherine to return.

The aliens fought using retractable claws, and antlers sharpened with flint scrapers. Their grunts and panting breath echoed around the stone hall. Ulbim screeched as Arnil clawed his ear, tearing it into a bloody flap hanging down his cheek. The antlers disengaged, then crashed together again. Arnil's weight started to tell, and Ulbim slid backward. Ulbim lashed out in a desperate frenzy, catching Arnil's neck and gouging clumps of blue fur. Arnil roared with rage. He struck back with powerful scything blows that raked Ulbim's face and chest.

The end came quickly. Ulbim, having been forced back and back, raised his head to expose his throat, signalling surrender. Arnil paused, and the onlookers cried out. "Kill!" "Mercy!" "Kill!"

Arnil pointed to the doorway and said, "Begone! I banish you from my hearth, and from the hearths of my family and followers. I banish your descendants to the fourth generation. At dawn, let your shadow never stain my land again."

Ulbim scurried away, under a hail of stones and knives thrown by the crowd. Arnil sat down with a thump, and several followers rushed to lick the blood from his wounds.

"Get an akran!" I cried.

Wearily, Arnil waved permission. Ranis-tra-Laru hurried to the flitter, where I explained how to open the cold store. She grabbed the pot and carried it back into the hall.

Katherine lay on the floor, silent and still. Arnil knelt, uttered the benediction permitting ascent, and carefully placed one of the glands within her wound. As he pressed it into her flesh, I saw Katherine flinch in pain. She lived!

Blood pooled onto stone. Arnil tried to feed her one of the pain-quenching tonics, but she was beyond such help.

He said, "She was our honoured guest and deserves the proper rites. Build the funeral pyre! We shall remember her with a feast." Servants hastened to fetch firewood.

A spectral haze rose from the body, then coalesced into a recognisable shape: a younger, idealised version of Katherine.

"Lucian," she said, her newfound spirit voice tremulous with the shock of death and ascent.

"Katherine."

We drifted toward each other. As I stretched my arms to embrace her, we melted together with just a faint tingle. In all the days of my death, I had never missed so much the simple pleasure of touch. We communed wordlessly for long timeless moments, mourning her life cut short. I sensed Katherine's agonies of regret: she'd grown complacent about visiting Mallarn, neglecting self-defence precautions. I castigated myself for not warning her about Ulbim's resentments.

I offered as much comfort as I possessed. I projected a vision of the *Afterlife Gazetteer* as an old-fashioned book, a reassuringly hefty tome of practical advice – albeit with many blank pages to fill. I'd been lax, staying in Mallarn rather than exploring more of the afterlife, but how could I have known that Katherine would die so soon?

Katherine's presence evoked my memories of her, and likewise I perceived her own memories of me. Scenes sprang up, newly vivid through the dual perspective. I smiled to see how handsome and strong and loving I appeared – then cringed at the petulance that followed. At the same time I felt Katherine's jolt as she saw how her behaviour had seemed obsessive, how the drive that initially attracted me later repelled me.

Just recalling that period broke our rapport. And if I'd anticipated some effortless reconciliation that would magically dissolve our differences, I soon realised it wouldn't happen. Seeing each other's viewpoint didn't automatically make our views the same.

Yet at least we had experienced each other's perspectives. Now Katherine knew that I'd never intended to exploit her or demean her work; and I better understood how she'd felt when seemingly reduced to a decorative extra in my planet-hopping life. Perhaps this was a step toward bringing us closer.

I refocused on our surroundings: the Ardissans stripping off Katherine's clothes, slitting her belly to remove the guts, hacking off limbs, casting them onto the flames, squabbling for the best portions....

"Is this one of the customs you're so keen to record?" I asked.

Katherine looked on, rapt, as Arnil and his followers consumed her flesh. "Of course," she said. "This is an honour."

"I'm glad you feel that way about it," I said. Although I found the spectacle upsetting, I felt sure that Katherine could provide all sorts of social, ritual, and nutritional justifications for it.

She sensed my distaste. "Be careful what changes you suggest. That distillation process you've given them will probably create alcoholics. It's not so easy to decide what's really an advance."

"You could help me – your knowledge of their culture would show us the best ways to make progress." I imagined the ideas spreading: practical improvements first, then social changes such as gender equality and the end of slavery.

"Is this something you really care about?" asked Katherine. "Or are you just meddling to pass the time? I'm sure it boosts your ego to be the source of all human wisdom."

"Maybe there's an element of that," I conceded. "But what else can we do?"

Katherine paused. "Well... do you want to talk?"

"Sure. What about?"

"Everything," she said. "Now that I'm dead, I guess I have time to slow down."

Orlind returned with news. "The elders have called a crusade," he told

Arnil. "They've vowed to destroy Mallarn stone by stone. They say that after defying the elders, you now compound your dishonour by allowing humans to ascend."

I remembered the deserters who'd left in disgust at my arrival. No doubt they'd carried tales back home. Was I responsible for sparking a war that might destroy Mallarn? I felt guilty, yet also excited. Progress would do little good if confined here. The rest of the planet had to follow, or at least be given the chance. Was the crusade an opportunity?

Katherine said, "Maybe we should leave, if our presence threatens Mallarn."

"No," said Arnil, "you're just an excuse. The elders have long hated us, and a crusade was inevitable. If the hour has arrived – so be it." He waggled his antlers defiantly.

Our conversations turned to war. The Ardissans were accustomed to conflict and already had a formidable array of tactics. But their weapons were crude. With my limited expertise, I tried to improve their arrows and catapults: not easy with only local materials.

I'd imagined a 'boot camp' scene like in the movies, with myself as the gruff instructor. It didn't work out like that. Some hedonists refused to devote themselves to training, arguing that by abandoning their pleasures they would be betraying Mallarn's ethos. And others were reluctant to submit to classic military principles such as the chain of command and fighting as a unit. Battle on Ardissa was a more individualistic affair, with honour the prime criterion.

Nevertheless, we drilled and tested weapons and prepared as best we could. I almost looked forward to the battle, which would at least be some diversion from my dreary, bodiless existence. Reminiscing with Katherine had been bittersweet, emphasising how pale and empty the afterlife felt in comparison to the happier times we'd had in life, in love.

After returning from a reconnaissance mission, Orlind took me to one side and said, "You do know this is hopeless?"

"Is it?" I said.

"Their warriors outnumber ours. How many rebels live in Mallarn? Barely a dozen dozens, and half of them are too drunk to fight."

"But this is a fortress. The advantage lies with the defence."

"Yes, but the attackers don't care whether they survive, because if they die bravely in battle, they ascend to the afterlife in glory. On the other arm, everyone in Mallarn has surrendered their akran. They don't want to die, because they have nothing afterward. It makes them cowards, and cowards don't fight well – if at all. You may recently have noticed fewer revellers at the feasts."

Indeed, as the crusade drew nearer, the inhabitants of Mallarn had begun slipping away in ones and twos.

"That's not necessarily bad," I said. "Anyone who runs away has to go somewhere. And they'll take my suggestions with them. Maybe progress will spread, even if Mallarn falls."

I tried to make myself believe it, but lately everything felt futile. The approaching army looked set to crush Mallarn. I couldn't lift a finger to save it, because I had no fingers.

"How do you stand it?" I burst out. "You've been dead for years, ostracised by the elders, and yet you still haven't gone mad."

"It's hard," Orlind said with feeling. He paused, and I recalled the weariness I'd sensed in him. "There are ways of coping," he said at last.

"How?" I asked, eager to learn not only for myself but also for Katherine and anyone else who might follow me. In my role as trailblazer for humans in the afterlife, I was still searching for a path. Perhaps the search itself was the only way forward.

Again Orlind hesitated. "I'd have to show you."

After what happened last time, I understood his reluctance. Yet now I'd been longer dead, and had spent far more time with the Ardissans. My previous revulsion wouldn't recur. "Show me," I demanded.

"Are you sure you wish to end all the disquiet of this realm?" asked Orlind, using the declension of a ritual question.

"Definitely." I moved closer to him and opened up, ready to receive his thoughts.

"Begone!" – "Slave vermin" – "Get away from decent folk" – "Dishonour and blasphemy" – "Banished forever." A torrent of loneliness and rejection gushed into me. I reeled under the onslaught. Was this a coping technique? Surely not.

I tried to break free, but Orlind held me fast. Again the poisonous emotions flooded in, and he followed them with painful memories of whippings and stonings.

"Help!" I screamed into the aether. "Katherine!"

I struggled to prevent Orlind from overwhelming me. As he attacked again, I let my sense of betrayal pour out. "Why?"

My howl burned him, but he fought back. As he battered me with yet more isolation and despair, I felt a tinge of guilt among his anguish. He hadn't wanted to turn against me, but he'd been promised an end to his ostracism. If he could purge the evil human presence from the afterlife, the elders would finally welcome him. They'd give him the antlers of a warrior hero.

I tried to resist Orlind's attack, retaliating with memories of the hospice, of my long slow slide into death. But I knew little of battle in the spirit world, and he had too much horror to scour me with. I could barely hold him off.

Yet the onslaught stilled. Through our entangled minds, I felt Orlind shudder as Katherine flamed down like a starship incinerating natives with its landing jets. She imposed her own imagery on the conflict, cutting him with lasers and crushing him with skyscrapers. He retaliated with spears, which she vaporised with disdainful ease.

While Orlind battled Katherine, I countered with all the ennui and frustration I'd pent up since my death. He shrivelled under the double attack. I sensed Katherine coming closer to me as she ate into him, tearing his spirit apart.

Orlind's resistance vanished. Katherine and I found ourselves floating together in the air above Mallarn. Her personality had a different yet familiar flavour. She'd absorbed the remnants of Orlind's mind.

My relief and gratitude spilled forth in an outburst of emotion. "Thanks for getting to me in time," I said. "I didn't know you felt so superior."

"That was his feeling, not mine," she replied. "That's why it worked. He was so dazzled by our technology, I only had to present the conflict in those terms to defeat him."

"Poor Orlind," I said. Yet I wondered whether he might have had this outcome in mind when he attacked. Whether he won or lost, either way his solitude would end. That was all he'd wanted.

And I found it reassuring to think that ghostly existence didn't have to last forever. Knowing I had an alternative – however drastic – reduced my fear of the stretching millennia ahead. Unwittingly, Orlind had given me a little comfort.

Remembering his description of an invincible approaching army, I saw I had to stop deluding myself that I could single-handedly turn

Mallarn's hedonists into a force capable of fighting off the whole planet. This wasn't a movie: a training montage wouldn't be enough. I needed something more, and Katherine's strategy had told me what it was.

I drifted down to the flitter, which still stood on the plateau where Katherine had parked it before she died. Inside, I found the usual emergency kit, with rations, distress flares, and a blaster. Ranis-tra-Laru had returned the remaining akranil to the cold store.

Soon we'd need to contact Katherine's colleagues, before they became so concerned by her silence that they started searching for her. Katherine's research team would surely be willing to trade for more ghost-glands, now that they were proven to work in humans. What price life after death? We could ask for anything we wanted.

Katherine had followed me into the flitter. "No," she said.

"What do you mean, no?"

"I know what you're thinking. You want to use human technology to defend Mallarn. But it's not our place to take sides in their wars."

"We're already on one side. We've brought this on Mallarn – we have a responsibility to get them out of it."

"And you think that would be the end? Do you really imagine you can give out guns before a battle, and afterward they'll meekly hand them back?"

I could see her point, but there were ways round it. "Blasters don't have an infinite charge. They're useless when it runs out."

"Until some black marketeer in Greenfall recharges them. Once you start giving out guns, you can't stop. Is that the progress you want to bring?"

"The elders despise humans and technology. Are you saying they'd suddenly change their tune?"

"It only takes one, and the rest are forced to follow."

I stormed out of the flitter. "So we should just sit on our phantom backsides while we watch the armies tear this down?" I said, pointing to Mallarn looming from the snowy plateau in the moonlight. "If the crusaders win, you can say goodbye to getting any more akranil. No more humans in the afterlife!"

And I realised that despite everything, despite the tedious hindrances of immortality, I was ready to report back from the lower slopes and say that the ascent was worth attempting. Yes, the afterlife had its trials and tribulations – like life, like anything worthwhile.

"I suggest we speak to Arnil," said Katherine. "He is the leader here, after all."

We had to wait till morning for Arnil to wake, then wait till midday before he ate wathrone. The delay reminded me anew that I had no power to act directly, that I could only whisper in Arnil's ear and hope he liked what I said. I couldn't afford to antagonise him. If he banned the consumption of wathrone, my influence in Mallarn would vanish.

"The first thing we need to know," said Arnil, "is how many crusaders we face."

Katherine said, "There are two groups, approaching from the south and west." I wondered how she knew this; then I remembered that she'd swallowed Orlind's memories. She went on, "Excluding slaves, the warriors are perhaps eighteen dozen."

Was that all? On this thinly populated planet, it probably counted as an army. And it comfortably exceeded the number of fighters in Mallarn.

"We can show you how to use the flitter," I said. "That will help."

Katherine shot me a disapproving look, but then said, "It can be used to evacuate Mallarn. If everyone left, there would be no one for the crusaders to attack."

"And they would have won without attacking," said Arnil.

"Evacuation would be a last resort," I said. "Another option is to go out in the flitter and confront the army before it gets here."

Arnil's muzzle twitched eagerly. "We can destroy them?"

"We can frighten them off," I said.

If the enemy weren't scared of death, attempting to intimidate them with one flitter would be a long shot. Yet I thought it was worth a try.

It didn't take long to teach Arnil how to pilot the flitter. Soon we set off, Arnil flying slowly so that Katherine and I could keep up. She directed him southwest, until we saw the armies converging to attack Mallarn. Splotches of blue dotted the plateau, as if flakes had fallen off the sky.

Elders hovered above the columns, occasionally darting ahead to scout the way. Some were small; others were huge with enormous fractal antlers. Those must be the most ancient, the ones who ruled Ardissa and smothered it in ignorance.

Arnil set the flitter down at the convergence point, and we waited for the crusade to arrive. He stepped outside to meet the leaders. A group of elders approached, with a retinue of warriors and slaves. I drew back, wary of being attacked again. Consequently I heard little of Arnil's address to the enemy, though Katherine explained the protocol for such encounters.

The crusaders reacted to Arnil's speech with shouts of "Never!" and "Human scum!" The elders tipped their antlers menacingly toward us, as Katherine and I hovered a prudent distance away from the scene.

Arnil said a few final words, then returned to the flitter. He rose above the army, and began firing distress flares at them. Red and yellow explosions burst among the warriors. They fell back, scurrying away on all fours.

But they rallied when they realised that the flares only burned rather than killed. They began throwing missiles – I heard dull clunks as stones and javelins bounced off the flitter – until Arnil flew up higher, out of their range. The horde waved their spears, tauntingly.

Then Arnil descended again. I saw his furry arm sticking out of the window, clutching something. The crusaders fell like scythed corn as Arnil fired the blaster. He swooped low over the army, reaping a harvest of ghosts.

"Lucian!"

I jerked round at Katherine's cry, and saw elders hurtling toward us. Katherine raced away, and I followed. I tried to imagine myself as a flitter, cutting effortlessly through the air. We fled across the sky while the elders pursued.

Ahead, Katherine's shape broke up. Blobs of spirit stuff flashed past me and fell behind. As I kept going, not daring to stop, I saw a slender figure still flying onward. What had happened to Katherine? I looked back to see the front line of elders swoop on the stray fragments, gobbling them up. That delayed them just enough to give us a chance of getting away.

I made a superhuman effort and caught up with Katherine, or whatever she had become. I shifted direction slightly, and she followed me toward a nearby range of hills.

We crashed straight into it, then kept going within the rocks. For long minutes we dodged and weaved and trusted to the darkness underground. I saw no pursuers. After a while we stopped, exhausted.

Huddled in the dark, we waited to see if they would find us again.

"Are you all right? What happened to you?" I asked.

Katherine said, "I dropped off Orlind, what was left of him. I figured it might distract them."

"Like a lizard shedding its tail," I said.

"I'm glad I did it. His mind was too alien to sit comfortably in mine, especially as he had so many more memories. I learned a lot, but I was worried that he might absorb me rather than vice versa."

We melted into each other in wordless comfort. I poured out my relief and joy that she'd chosen the human over the alien. Katherine clung to me as though she would never let go again.

I sensed her annoyance that we'd had to flee before seeing the confrontation's outcome. "I expect Arnil drove off the crusaders," I said. "They can't stand against human technology."

Remembering the sight of Arnil firing down into the helpless mob, I wished the victory had been won by the better argument, not the better weapon. Yet Arnil had only been defending himself and his way of life against enemies who'd vowed to crush him. Perhaps the deaths had averted a far bloodier battle.

"What now?" asked Katherine. "Back to Mallarn?"

"No. I've given them enough suggestions. The rest is up to them."

Katherine laughed. "Are you sure they can manage without you? Maybe you were just another type of elder. Instead of a dead hand holding them back, you were a dead hand pushing them forward."

"Give them some credit," I said. "It wasn't my specific input that mattered, but the idea of progress. Now that they've tasted it, I think they'll want more."

But the only way to prove that would be to leave Mallarn alone, and let the hedonists advance – or not – at their own pace. Meanwhile we'd return to Greenfall Station, bringing news of the afterlife to the rest of humanity.

"We'll drop into Mallarn occasionally to trade for akranil, until we can work out how to make them synthetically," Katherine said. "We'll see how they're managing."

I longed to know whether I'd inspired genuine progress. At last I understood Katherine's curiosity, and shared it. But the Ardissans had their own path to walk.

Katherine and I needed to find the best route for ourselves, and our future companions, as we climbed the endless mountain of eternity.

# A Lady of Ganymede, a Sparrow of Io

## Dafydd McKimm

The Lady waits for the Duke in a body as fragile as sugar glass, resting her head against the cool marble of the colonnade that circles the Hall of the Nobles of Io. She watches the sparrows as they flirt and twitter between the shade and the sun, like socialites at a debutante ball or starships popping in and out of visible space at the great port of Ganymede, so long ago and moons away that it seems now like nothing more than some childish fancy.

The body was a gift, made especially for her. The first time the Duke placed her inside its delicate flesh, he led her with sinister tenderness – *Gently now. Gently* – to the garden and bade her sit, wait for him a moment while he retrieved something from the house. As he disappeared through the doors of the manor, the Lady's breath caught in her throat: the small side door to the gardens appeared to have been left unlocked. Like a bird who found its cage suddenly flung open, the Lady sprang towards the garden door, but the bones of that fragile body shattered under nothing more than the vigour of her movements and left her lying there, twitching like a crushed insect at the foot of the flower beds, the pounding of burst blood vessels and, louder even than that, the roaring laughter of the Duke filling her ears.

The Lady inhabits many bodies. The sugar-glass body is for travel, a failsafe against her escape. The body she dons as the Duke's chief consort – a showpiece he wears on his arm at formal events – has features so exaggerated that her spine strains and her hips throb and her skinny thighs tremble under their weight. As the Duke's etiquette coach, she occupies a basic demonstration dummy, plain, stripped of any distracting features, its skin coarse and worn and seldom repaired, so different from the skin she grew up in, as soft to the touch as the dresses her mother wore to full-Jupiter balls, the skin that, orphaned and desperate, stripped of everything by revolution and war, sold a copy of its neural network to a brain broker, condemning her, this version of her at least, to be forever imprisoned in bodies not her own.

With difficulty, for the muscles of the sugar-glass body are weak, the Lady holds out a hand to the sparrows. One hops into her open palm, bobs its head as if to say, *I'm listening*.

She recalls a story, read by her governess, of a princess whose cruel husband forced her to work in the palace butchery. So she befriended a starling, taught it to speak, then sent it across the sea to her brother, who came with his armies to wreak vengeance upon his sister's captor.

Something resembling hope kindles within the Lady; if she tells the bird her sorrows, will it take her message to a rescuer, some distant Ionian relative with the power to set her free? With much effort, she lifts the bird to her lips and whispers her misery to its bobbing head. She tells it about the Duke, how he made his fortune from the war just as her family lost theirs, how he'd bought a title from a Jovian noble who valued a full belly more than his peerage and the Lady because he needed someone willing – or unable to refuse – to teach him the proper airs and graces, and how it wasn't long before he discovered other uses for her, too.

Her lips tremble. No, she must tell it everything. She tells the bird about the other bodies, the ones she doesn't like to think about – the fox body, the hind body, the boar body. How the Duke likes his game with a streak of humanity. How, with a flick of the wand he keeps at his belt, he unspools from her human vessel and grafts her onto his quarry. She shudders to remember the horrible sounds she has made, the maddening grip of panic, the terror of the animal brain as it decides whether to flee or fight; the howling of the Duke's hounds, the flash of their teeth, the warmth of her own blood and the creeping cold as life seeps from gaping wounds.

Footsteps approach. From the sound of his stride, the Lady knows the Duke is angry, and when the Duke is angry, he likes to hunt. She must release the sparrow now, but fear freezes her fingers.

"They dare to toy with me," the Duke rages as he comes near. "Humiliate me because my blood is not blue." He spits onto the marble. "Nobility! We'll see how noble you are" – he turns his eyes on the Lady – "We'll see how *you* like to be toyed with." His mouth glistens with anticipation. "Come," he says, reaching to take her arm.

The Lady starts as if waking from a terrible dream: She has no royal brother to save her from across the sea, no vengeful army that will come to her aid. She has only herself and the things she has learnt from her suffering – the cunning of a fox, the quickness of a hind, the daring of a boar – and the sparrow clutched in her hand.

"Wait," she says. The Duke stays his arm for a moment, looming over her like a guillotine.

Like a firmly pushed garden door, her fingers open; the sparrow darts out, and then up, and as the Duke lifts his hands, the Lady lunges.

Her legs shatter; her paper-thin lungs tear open; her wasted muscles scream; but her hands close around the wand hanging at the Duke's belt. And with a series of motions that break each of her pale fingers, she tears her mind from the sugar-glass body and hurls it towards the sparrow, flying now higher and higher to join its flock.

And as the rush of air fills her ears, the Duke's roars echo through the colonnade, grow fainter, fall silent.

# Snapshots

## Leo X. Robertson

*Dedicated to my dad, Charlie Robertson (1954 – 2018)*

When Dad arrives, he twiddles a dial in the panel, and SnapRoom gets brighter.

He's wearing the same slacks and mustard-coloured cardigan that I expected Mum to have thrown out by now. His face is hollow, eyes empty. Strings of white hair fall from the ring of still-functioning follicles on his head. The white whiskers on his face give his skin a greyish hue.

I've never seen him look so old. Best not to mention it.

The SnapShots adjust to the new light. The bluish glow of Five, Fifteen, Nineteen, and Twenty-One makes each a petal in a ghostly peony at the room's centre.

"Cheers," I say. "I was too scared to touch anything."

There are basic options on the panel, like *lighting, EQ, mute, reverse, record,* and so on – but also more serious-sounding options: delete, modify, enhance. I almost pressed reset memory, thinking it was the light switch – which would've erased everything the SnapShots had learned since their creation.

Five runs to Dad for a hug. "Daddy!" He giggles as his hands run through Dad's legs with a buzz. Holes, like dead pixels, pock-mark his blocky hologram all over, from the bowl cut down to the dungarees.

"What took you so long?" I say.

Dad pretends to pat Five's head, his hand going straight through, fingertips lighting up in blue. There's a resting tremor in his hands. I've had those before, from anti-depressants and hangovers. Neither are topics I broach easily. I hope Dad's shakes are something else.

"Some new customers wanted to book golfing lessons," he says. "It takes a while to register them in the system." He walks to the TV monitors embedded in the wall and turns them on. They display CCTV footage of his golf course up above us. Golden light spreads over the greens. There's a white cart by the ninth hole, where I parked not minutes ago. "What were you guys talking about before I showed up?"

"Tell him what was on your mind, Twenty-Five," Fifteen says to me, rolling up the sleeves of his school shirt.

I let them call me Twenty-Five, so they don't feel excluded.

"I need your advice, Dad," I say. "I've been seeing Flossy for a few years. She's itching for me to propose."

I'd never known a 'Flossy' before I met her in the bank one evening. She squeezed rain from her ebullient mop of pink hair and screamed at a camera that she wasn't leaving before speaking to a human. In a cringeworthy but effective move, I said that if she was looking for human connection, we should go for a drink instead of waiting longer in that forgotten, sterile cubicle. In my office daydreams of her, a shimmering ream of gossamer floss surrounds her. She's my Flossy by name and nature.

"That's how it usually goes, Twenty-Five," Dad says. "Your mother and I got married at your age." He giggles. "The most wonderful decision I ever made! Until we had you, Son." He points at me, finger wobbling. "Grandkids! They'll follow soon enough."

"One thing at a time!" I say.

"A dad can dream. You'll bring Flossy next time, won't you?"

He used to complain that I wasn't visiting enough. Now I'm here so often it feels like I never leave, so he guilts me about not bringing Flossy. It's always something.

"You're right," he says, reading my face. "I shouldn't say things like that."

"I-I didn't mean —"

"Hooray!" Five says, star-jumping with excitement. "What's the wedding gonna be like? How many cakes? You guys need to get a big house for all our kids!"

Dad sits cross-legged beside Five but meets my gaze. "Remember visiting me in the garage when you were five? I'd be tinkering away with my tech, and you'd pad across the backyard to see me, getting grass all over your grippy socks."

Mum would entrust me with a steaming espresso to take on my journey. I'd hold it up to Dad, careful not to spill any. Back then, he looked several orders of magnitude larger than he does now.

Dad looks to Five. "I knew from this age that you'd make something of yourself. Remind me how high you can count, Son!"

Five's face screws up in thought as he taps numbers across his digits. "One, two, three, four ..."

These days, now that anyone can make a SnapShot and all of them are immaculate, Dad seems to love Five the most. Over our lunches at the restaurant that overlooks the golf course, Dad has told me countless times that Five is "a special early fragment of a tech with boundless applications."

Nineteen interrupts Five. "Ugh! Marriage." He slumps on the brushed aluminium wall. "Are we that conventional?" He scratches his bald head.

I had long hair for most of that year but shaved it off just before I turned twenty. Dad so enjoyed that act of bravery that he kept it for the SnapShot.

Nineteen has a point. Flossy's friends are all getting married, and it does seem like it's our turn – but is that all any life event is? Our turn?

That's the weird thing about SnapRoom. I come here sometimes just to see how far I've progressed, but my former selves can be insightful. In the end, I'm the same as these kids in front of me once were: I improvise some approximation of a life in the face of epic choices I feel too small to make.

"Thought we'd have spent a few more years single," Nineteen continues, "riding suicide over the magnorails between the cities. Living off the land."

What an insufferably idealistic dream. It's so painful to look at my own smug face from that age: its insincere smile, the whole snake-like, hooded-eye, brooding thing I always did. I thought I knew so much more than everyone, rambling on about how I should've been born in the 1960s. I extolled the potential joy of living out of a Volkswagen van when I wouldn't even join Dad on his weekly hikes.

"Can you even play the guitar any better than I can?" Nineteen adds.

I shake my head with feigned dismay. Nineteen can tell. The last person he needs treating his pursuits as a silly phase is himself.

It's cruel of me to hang out with these guys, really. They derive so much hope from the it-gets-better potential of the different futures they envisage. Here I am, the finite reality, robbing them of that hope simply by existing.

I frown at Nineteen and say, "We have a happy life?"

"Fantastic," he says, pushing himself up the wall with his feet, grazing its panelling, his arms firmly folded. "I'm sure that makes us all so memorable. People will flock here to meet us one day. 'Come hang out with this guy's SnapShots, for here lies a man who was once happy'."

They used to visit SnapRoom, Dad's golfers and B&B guests. Later, SnapShot Soft LLC's patented holoproject technology became reasonably priced. Now everyone has their own SnapShots. It's hard to see even these first iterations as meaningful, what with proliferation like that.

What's that sound? Oh. I cringe as Dad sings some made-up tune to himself while playing an air guitar. "Hey, Nineteen, remember letting your dad take you to see The Mechabots in concert? When their drummer closed with that ten-minute solo, and his platform rose up into the air? Then all those fireworks launched out of the base. You'd never seen anything like it." He smiles. "I watched you watch them. The light of the sparklers in your eyes."

Nineteen sighs. "No one else wanted to go with me."

"Your guitar's here at the club, up in the attic! Will you teach me how to play if I bring it down?"

"Oh, come on, Dad," I say. "Why would you wanna do that?"

Nineteen ignores us both. "How do you think Twenty-Five is doing, Fifteen?"

Fifteen is Nineteen's favourite, even though they make each other bluer, their neuroses feeding off one another.

"Honestly?" Fifteen says, loosening his tie. "I can't believe we even have a girlfriend."

An eternity in school uniform! Why not? That's what Fifteen's existence felt like. His is an age I wouldn't repeat. On my mental to-do list for most of it was: *find ANY bearable direction for life, hide misery from others, try not to kill self (will to live pending)*. 'Pending' lasted months until I witnessed the purple balloon of my own pee bursting across Terry Coraghan's sour face at high school graduation. It was a petty humiliation to cap the many he put me through. Whatever keeps you going, I say.

Dad tries to pinch Fifteen's cheeks. "True, you didn't have anyone to go out gallivanting with – but it worked out great for me. We spent weekends playing backgammon together." He clicks his tongue in thought. "And you had so much to be proud of. A handsome young gent with your whole life ahead of you? I wish you could've seen that."

It wasn't so simple. I kept all my suffering internal at that age. I guess that's one reason why Dad holds onto Fifteen: he has happier memories with me than I have with myself. I'm glad, in a way – but shouldn't I have enjoyed my own company at least as much as anyone else?

Dad gasps. "Fancy beating your old man at backgammon again? I'll bring a set. Just tell me where to move your pieces!"

Twenty-One slicks his brown hair out of his face then snaps his fingers. "Oh, yeah!" He laughs. "How quaint to think of the age before girlfriends! Don't worry, Fifteen. Let's just say you make up for lost time."

Nineteen takes Five's little hand and pulls him closer, blue sparks flying from their fingertips. The wireframe shape of their holograms bursts through as the room's computer struggles to interpret their crashing together. Nineteen glowers at Twenty-One, who says, "What's the big deal?"

Twenty-One: the edgy, all-black-wearing, experience-collecting party boy. Never missed a club night out, memorized album reviews on obscure websites and spouted them at friends to impress. When I look at him, I feel the elbows of all those partygoers in my ribs. The tinnitus of blaring techno rings in my ears. The sugary film of vodka mixers coats my teeth. The frozen fear, of waking up in a field in muddy clothes, jags through my chest.

At least he kept me alive, but should I attribute that to him or luck?

Dad cocks his head at me. "You've something to learn from Twenty-One. All that creative energy! Remember the thirtieth anniversary party for your mother and me? The caterers with those fancy canapé-laden slates. You rented a champagne fountain." He presses a hand to his heart. "The speech you gave – it brought me to tears."

I must've used the fountain more than Dad, because I don't remember that at all.

"Sometimes it's more about indulging in the day's fun than working for the future. So slow down! You won't be Twenty-Five for long."

"That's the opposite of your usual advice," I say. "What's going on?"

"Since no one likes my suggestions, Twenty-One, maybe you can choose the activity for all of us today? I know you guys don't agree on much, but there must be something. Anything to distract Twenty-Five from his troubles."

"Why are you so against helping me?"

He hangs his head but doesn't speak.

"You didn't do much living-in-the-moment at my age. You already had your own company." I hold my arms up and gesture around the room. "I've gotta get cracking if I want silly playrooms like this in my manse."

"Hey!" Twenty-One says.

"Y-You know what I mean," I say.

"We sure do," says Fifteen, looking to Nineteen, who nods.

"I wish you could just enjoy yourself," Dad says. "We never get enough time together, and your mind's always elsewhere." He's almost in tears. I have no idea why.

I shrug at the SnapShots, who've spread around the room and appear like the blue fingers of a giant's hand.

I clench my fists. "I didn't mean to upset you, Dad. Let's just drop it. Wanna go for lunch?"

Dad goes to the door, opens it, and bends down. He slides in a silver tray and picks it up. On it are a single BLT, a glass of milk, a carton of orange juice, a box of raisins, and a red plastic tea set. "Why don't we have lunch here today? I brought the teacups for Five, to serve with his favourite – orange juice with raisins in it!"

"Yay!" Five runs to Dad and jumps up, trying to grab the tray. His hand passes through it, to his bemusement.

I know it's fun for Dad to be here with the SnapShots too, but as the eldest version of myself – and the only alive one, in every sense – I don't want to share. He puts me in the awkward position of inventing some excuse for why we can't stay, without insulting the rest. Oh, well. If I mess up, maybe I can press reset memory when Dad's not looking.

"Twenty-Five thinks we don't know what he wants," Fifteen says, looking at Dad but jerking his head in my direction.

Five is on the floor, crying. He's realized his flesh isn't solid.

Dad puts the tray down and kneels beside Five.

Did I sound like that at five? I figured it was endearing, evoking only sympathy. This is one occasion when I prefer my memory's partial view of the past to these digital replicas.

I look between Five and Dad to indicate my discomfort, but Dad's back up and chatting to Nineteen now.

"Dad!" I say.

"... don't know why we humour him," Nineteen says, tailing off to look at me and say "Hm?" to show that I've interrupted.

He knows I resent him. I'm disgusted to have been someone so sneery, though I do admit that it's easier to judge him from the outside.

"Okay, this is ridiculous," I say.

I reach for the door handle. My hand goes straight through it, buzzing with blue sparks.

Five keeps wailing. I can only hear a few words of Dad's conversation with the others, who form a bright blue wall around him.

Their voices blur together. I struggle to hear my thoughts over the sound of them.

I shout, "How did it happen?"

The shock of it shuts up Five, who sniffles.

Dad looks in dismay at his sandwich. His plan of a pleasant lunch has shattered. How many times I've done this to him, I've no idea.

"You and Flossy were celebrating your engagement," he says. "Took an unlicensed autocab back home. It went haywire. E-Exploded. Neither of you, you know ..."

I think back to my first spontaneous date with Flossy. The knock of her knee against mine. Her manic laughter. How she characterized her office's staff room with such loving detail that I saw everyone with her: mad Karen, kind Sophie, Bob the slob. I think of her now in a haze of grapefruit perfume, with an aura of colourful ticker tape all around.

The guilt of leaving the world Flossy-less presides over every other pain now flooding me.

"But I don't get it," I say. "I parked a cart outside about half an hour ago." I gesture to the TV, to my cart by the ninth hole.

Dad looks where I'm pointing. He walks to the panel and taps some setting into it. Across the TV screens, a granite sky appears.

177

Beneath it is black, ash-like rain. The grass and dunes now fester with eerie black weeds. Why? He'd made it to retirement, to the simple pleasure of running this place.

His rheumy eyes roll at me. "What was the point? Let nature take it all." He looks around the room. "This is about all that matters." He addresses each of the SnapShots in turn. "Five, my first and favourite assistant. Fifteen, my little rebel. Nineteen, who emerged from his funereal adolescence with the ambition to live forever. Twenty-One, who first discovered how to enjoy life." He turns to me. "Twenty-Five."

I shudder to hear the name.

"Your final reluctant birthday present to me. As close as I can get to the day I lost you."

I'm jealous of the tears streaming down his face.

To think I'd shown these other SnapShots such disdain. I'm the most deluded and pitiful of them all. I hope my future self is kinder to me than I've been to my younger versions. Oh, right, there won't be one. How many waves of awful revelation can my heart take? Oh, right, I don't have a heart. There goes another wave.

"I want to see Mum," I say.

Dad waves a dismissive hand at me. "Your mother came here once. It's – not for her." He rolls his shoulders as if to rid himself of the idea. "But I just want to forget what happened."

"That's not fair."

"Isn't it?"

I think of the alternatives, for both of us. I don't know the answer.

Dad turns away, too saddened to look at me any longer, at any of us. He makes to leave, but I shout after him, "Take me with you."

The others meet this plea with laughter, murmurs, saddened exhalations.

Dad stops by the door, still with his back turned. "Why did I save any of you? Your mother was right. This isn't helping."

I growl with frustration. "I've just learned I'm … nothing more to you than, than a height mark on a kitchen wall and … and now you're gonna delete us? Go on, then!"

"Let him," Fifteen and Nineteen say to me in unison.

"No!" Five wails.

"Chill!" Twenty-One says.

Dad inhales, turns around, and says, "The eldest SnapShot is the most likely to think it's still alive." He smiles bleakly. "I advised customers to keep SnapShots of the same person in different rooms. I was mostly thinking of the profit I'd gain from the extra projectors required." He walks between us, reaching out to ruffle Five's holographic hair, stroke Nineteen's sunken little face. "Split you guys up? That was like asking whether I wanted to see only your hand today, your leg tomorrow." He looks between us all. "Not height marks on a kitchen wall. More like, I don't know, cross-sections from a full-body MRI scan." He holds out his palm and chops up and down upon it with his other hand. "Instead of the 3-D image of a body, together you're the 4-D reality of my entire son." He lowers his head. "You're each a person I wish I could've kept. And just a part of someone I loved dearly."

None of us know what to say.

"I-I'll try again later," he says, turning back to the door. "One more time. Just once more."

"Well done," Nineteen says to me.

"You ruined it," Fifteen says.

I feel Twenty-One's touch like a fuzz of static on my shoulder. "It's okay," he says, bringing me in for a comforting embrace.

Five wraps his arms through my legs.

"All of you stand before me now," Dad says, "proof that my son has gone forever. But each time I come here, I think it'll go differently."

Before I can say anything, he's out the door.

His hand reaches back in. I run to it as he presses reset memory.

# Witch of the Weave

## Henry Szabranski

Skink changed direction towards a knot of weave that loomed ahead. She sailed easily between the withies dangling from the tunnel ceiling, moving with a speed and agility I could never hope to match.

"Go around," I protested as I stumbled along the fern-choked floor after her. "It's easier!"

As usual, she ignored me.

It had been days since we abandoned the Motherman. Days since his vast body had collapsed into the sea of flesh-eating mist surrounding the plateau. Days spent getting used to the wide-open spaces around us and the strangely solid ground beneath our feet. Fortunately there was still weave scattered upon this new landscape; giant tubes that served both as shelter and passages through which Skink could swing.

She paused before the huge knot, a dense tangle of withies easily twice my height that hung suspended in the middle of the tunnel. It reminded me of the Motherman's heart, though it was tiny in comparison to that great organ, and motionless. As Skink delved through its outer folds, I called up to her, "What you looking for?"

She didn't answer, face crinkled in concentration, but it wasn't long before she gave a cry of triumph and her hand reappeared out of the tangled weave, clutching what looked like a huge black spider. It was a weaver. Similar to the ones in the Motherman, and just the same as those, it appeared dead, or so deeply comatose it might as well have been. I frowned up at her. "You know we can't eat those, right?"

"Not eating, Percher. Testing."

"Testing what?"

"Idea."

"What idea?"

But she was done communicating with me. She slid down a rope-like withy to the floor and leant over her prize, pushing and pulling and squeezing until there was a loud *crack*. A circular plate split from the weaver's knobbly carapace to reveal a shiny compartment within. I edged closer to get a better view.

"What is it? What's inside?"

But Skink was not looking at the opened weaver, but at her hand. She hissed. The weaver tumbled from her grasp like some hairy legged, poisoned fruit. I saw a bright splash of blood. A sharp edge on the weaver's body had caught her palm and forefinger.

"Are you all right?"

Despite the blood, the cut seemed slight to me, but Skink cradled her hand, all earlier cheer erased. "Can't swing. Not until this heals. It'll keep splitting open, get infected."

I eyed her skeptically, but the more I thought about it the more I realized she was right. She needed her hands to be able to travel, as well as for everyday tasks. Her weak and twisted feet were useless over any distance.

"I'll carry you."

Skink's face hardened. "No more carrying, Percher."

I glanced through the tube's woven wall. It was late. Outside, night was gathering. It wouldn't be long before it was dark, sooner within the weave than without. "Time to stop and rest, then. Hand will be better in the morning."

"Not enough."

I ignored her injured tone. I knew she was more upset with herself than anything else, and not usually one to dwell on hardships. I concentrated on collecting fronds of weave and fern suitable for tonight's bedding.

When I came back with the last armful, Skink was already crouched in a makeshift nest. She nodded towards the tunnel snaking beyond the knot. "There is something out there. Waiting. I can sense it in the weave."

"More dead weavers. More dead everything." I could no longer hold back my own growing sense of despair. I had been trying to ignore it for days, for Skink's sake, but the deepening gloom, her injury, the constant hunger and discomfort we endured – it was taking its toll. Yes, we had survived the Motherman's collapse. Yes, this strange new land allowed us a meagre existence. But what were we heading towards, and why? As far as I knew, Skink and I were the only living people left in the world. How long could we expect to survive? Sometimes it felt like we were travelling for no other purpose than to distract ourselves from the grim reality of our situation.

"No. Something out there. The weave... it has a direction."

"Direction?"

"There is... intention. Grown stronger the more we have come this way."

I frowned at her serious expression, no clue what she was talking about.

She picked up the dropped weaver with her uninjured hand and began to inspect it again.

"Why break it?" I asked. "There's no good meat in those things."

She didn't answer, but carefully placed the tips of her fingers inside the weaver's exposed, iridescent cavity. She closed her eyes and stayed like that, silent and still, for many moments.

"Well?"

"No good, Percher." She cast aside the broken weaver; her expression unreadable in the growing dark. "Test failed."


I woke, bewildered, to screams. I had been dreaming of long hair dangling over my face, lithe arms around the back of my neck. But reality was quite different.

Skink was clutching her head, her fingers frantically combing her mop of hair.

"Get it out! Get it away!"

By the faint glow of the pre-dawn grey light penetrating the weave around us, I could tell it was past the darkest part of the night, but I could still barely see in the gloom. "What? What is it?"

The discarded weaver, miraculously reanimated, was scuttling over Skink's head. Its exposed interior cast an odd, silvery light on her distraught face. Before I could reach her, Skink managed to scoop the creature away. It flopped and jerked where it landed, trying to right itself in a bed of weave.

I snatched it up, ignoring the prickle of revulsion as its spiky limbs clenched tight around my fist. Too late to worry about whether it could sting or bite. For something the size of a child's plaything, the little weaver was surprisingly strong. It twisted and bucked in my grip, struggling to pull itself away. I searched for something to smash it with; a rock, or a stick – but there was nothing. Only my hands. I lifted it up, ready to throw it as far into the tunnel as I could, but Skink grabbed my arm. "Percher, wait!"

She thrust out her hand, the one with the cut, palm upright. "Look! Look what it did."

It was a moment before my eyes could refocus in the gloom, and at first I didn't understand what I was meant to see. The wound on her hand was still there, a dark gash extending from the base of her thumb to her forefinger... but something about it was different.

I peered closer, the weaver still struggling in my own hand.

Skink's wound was neater.

Sewn up.

A caterpillar trail of stitches left in the flesh.

We slept fitfully for the remainder of the night. When the light from the sky became too bright to ignore, Skink rolled her back to it and declared she had a headache. She held the weaver protectively in her hand – it had crawled back to her earlier and she had let it – where it lay motionless apart from an occasional spasm of its long legs.

I resigned myself to a day or three anchored around Skink's curled-up body. She had always had headaches, even back in the Motherman; it's just that I could ignore them whilst she holed up with Ma or Da. They had always protected her from the worst criticisms of our tribe. If Skink had one of her debilitating headaches, Da would order out foraging parties or give some other excuse to hold up climbing for a day or two. We hardly noticed, glad enough to stay in one place for a time. But now it was just Skink and me, and her condition was impossible to ignore.

The first time I had woken, ready to go, and Skink had instead rolled over and covered her eyes, groaning, I had thought she was just tired. I had felt momentary triumph, that at last I wasn't the one lagging behind for a change, the one complaining about sore feet after hours of stumbling over rolling hurdles of weave, Skink gaily sailing above me. But my feeling of superiority quickly turned to guilt and worry. She tried to speak but instead only vomited. It was obvious she wasn't feigning or being lazy; she was truly ill. I worried she might have eaten something she shouldn't, something that had infected her with dark rot, poisoned her, but she was hoarsely dismissive of my concern. "It's the same as always, Percher, all my life. Just leave me be. In darkness. Silence."

So on those days she was ill I would forage for mushrooms and snails and water amongst the tunnel's dank floor, groping through its undulating landscape of weave and mud and broad-leafed undergrowth. Sometimes I would find a gap in the tunnel wall and look out into the unobstructed sky and open spaces beyond, feel the wind and sunlight on my skin. Until it became too much and I would feel sick myself. Retreating, shuddering, back into the welcome confines of the weave. I couldn't understand my fear. I used to sit on the Motherman's skin, it seemed miles above the mist and within the sky itself, the hazy horizon arching before me. How could it be that openness filled me with such terror now? It made no sense, but knowing that didn't help my queasy stomach settle or my thumping heart race any less.

It was on those days, absent of Skink's company, with the weave feeling at once like a cage as much as a protection, that I especially missed the others in the tribe: Ma, Da; Wren, Feather, and Dart, all of them. Even, sometimes, my brutish eldest brother Broc, who had almost killed us when we tried to escape the burning Motherman. Sometimes, even more than the people, I missed the silent, hard-edged company of the Library; Da's book collection that I used to carry in a great sack upon my back, and in whose mouldering pages I used to immerse myself, transported to a world long lost to the mist and the weave. But the books were all gone now, as were all the people of the tribe. Victims of the fire, of the swarming razorbugs, of the rot and the mist. I told myself I would have to get used to it. Adapt. Survive.

Such days were bad.

Today was worse. Every natural rustle and crunch around me sounded suspicious, jarred my nerves. What had Skink meant, that something was out there? Were we unintentionally trespassing on some other tribe's territory, like we had with the clevers in the head of the Motherman? Was some strange, hostile face about to break out from the bracken and scream at me? Eventually I shook off the feeling, and after spending most of that morning foraging in the tunnel bottom around the knot, I returned with a handful of mushrooms, slugs, and fleshy tubers rooted out from the dark wet soil. It was tough trying to find enough to eat, especially as we had no means of starting a fire or any way to store what little we managed to find. We had fled the

Motherman with no time to grab any equipment – only the clothes we wore, and even those were ragged now and torn.

Skink had stirred by the time I returned. I hoped it was a good sign; perhaps we'd only lose that day instead of the next couple too. She was sitting up, inspecting her cracked-open weaver. It lay on its back on her injured palm, and its legs were, one by one, gently curving in to touch her other hand, as if in obeisance. I shook my head, unable to fathom her interest in the thing.

"Stop playing with it," I said. "Get rid of little creeper."

She glanced across at me with a glint in her eyes. "Pet." She upturned the weaver and placed it on top of her head. Creeper used its legs to hold itself in place atop her hair. She laughed. "Hat!"

"You mad." I turned away, shuddering.

Something landed on my back. Sharp-tipped legs scuttled towards my skull. I seized the thrown weaver and hurled it away.

Skink's laughter followed me as I marched away in disgust. "What you afraid of?"

She was still laughing when I stopped, heart leaping in my chest, at the sight of a line of people standing on the tunnel floor only yards away. The sharpened sticks in their hands pointed towards us.

"You." An old man at the front jabbed his spear at Skink. "Like Meghra. Pattern maker. Witch!" His words were heavily accented, but unmistakable.

The others murmured in agreement and shuffled back warily. I made a quick count: three men, two women, three I could not tell. Was it the whole tribe, or were others hiding in the weave? They looked strong and well fed, dressed in tanned and stitched fur. Elaborately painted marks swirled over their faces and shoulders, skilfully executed bright patterns of blue and green and yellow.

Skink slowly stood, unsteady on her legs. Creeper had clambered back on to her body and now balanced on her shoulder. "Who's Meghra?"

"Witch! Witch!" The old man waved his hands, fingers spread like claws. His rheumy gaze could not decide between settling on Skink, or me, or scanning the undergrowth around us.

He seemed terrified.

I made a step forward, my hands raised and open. "We don't mean to trespass on your land. We are lost. Hungry."

The man raised his spear and I took a step back again. He was too far away for me to rush and grapple, but too close for him to miss if he had any strength or skill at throwing.

"Where you from?" He jabbed – but did not hurl – the spear towards me.

"From the Motherman. Of the heart tribe."

Skink elaborated when the old man showed nothing but further confusion, "From the mist. We used to live out..." She waved vaguely in the direction we had come from, the edge of the plateau, so many days ago, "...there. Beyond the land. In a giant made of weave."

"No one survives the mist. No one. Only the pattern makers."

I backed further away. I did not know how to ease the man's bewilderment and fear. "We will leave."

"No." A hurried, whispered discussion between the man and the others. He advanced. "Are there others? Like you?"

I shook my head. Images of Ma and others falling into the mist. "Only us."

"Then you stay. You and witch. Food for news."

I hesitated, exchanged a glance with Skink. "Food?"

The man nodded, lowered his spear. "Yes, come. Tell us about mist, how you survived. Please, you stay. Food for news."

The old man replied to me, his hand outstretched. But his eyes kept shifting – with barely hidden fear or desire, I could not tell which – always back towards Skink.

The man said his name was Idran, and his village was not far outside the tunnel. Skink managed to stagger the short distance, though she leant heavily on me for support. I knew it pained her, knew that she was still suffering from her headache, but her face was set in its familiar determined way. I doubted if Idran or the others realized how difficult it was for her.

The village nestled in a small valley between the weave tunnel sprawled across its western border and a saddleback ridge dividing a line of high hills to the east. It bustled with more people than I had ever seen before, more than the most populous tribe in the Motherman; possibly over a hundred villagers or more. They had stripped weave from the tunnel and braided the torn withies into globular, nest-like dwellings with circular entrances and windows. These pods clustered in circles and rows and stacks around a communal space into which we were led. We were quickly surrounded by children and yipping little fur-covered creatures I was unfamiliar with. At the centre of the space, a pond and a series of fire pits, at least one of which was in use.

I was immediately attracted by the warmth of the flames and the smell of meat roasting. The skinned and gutted carcass of some large, four-legged animal was being roasted on a spit near the piled embers.

"For us?" I asked, meaning it to be a joke, as it was obvious the meat had been cooking for hours. But Idran nodded and motioned with his painted hands. "Yes, yes. Come. Eat."

A slice was cut from the creature's haunch with a sharp stone knife and the steaming hot meat passed to me by a wary-looking boy. I tore the hunk easily in half and shared it with Skink. Rich yet lean meat, of a kind I had never tasted – not as tasteful and as textured as heart meat, but delicious all the same after so many days of only raw river meat, bugs, and tooth-achingly tough roots.

"Please." Idran squatted on a richly patterned woolen blanket on the ground near the fire pit, indicating we should do the same. The other villagers kept their distance, fearful or disdainful, I could not be sure. "Tell us about yourselves."

Skink did most of the talking as I greedily ate. It was odd, hearing her like that, the villagers and their children gathering around. She had a clear, beguiling voice, I hadn't really noticed before. Perhaps the children in the audience brought it out in her, their greasy faces rapt. She spoke of the Motherman, how the lightning had set him on fire, how we had nowhere to escape but to keep climbing towards his clever-haunted head, how there she had made the giant walk, and how we had found this land rising from the all-encompassing ocean of mist. Her hands were in constant motion, adding emphasis or effects or occasionally becoming transformed wholesale into characters. I was as fascinated as the children.

Eventually she came to us escaping the Motherman, and the current point in our journey. "I tell you about us," she said, leaning back and straightening her arms, cracking her knuckles. "Now you tell us about you. About Meghra the witch."

The villagers glanced amongst themselves and shifted uncomfortably. The children were ushered away. Idran stood. "Is late. You rest. Tomorrow we will talk again."

Skink bristled. "Not fair!"

The old man hesitated, then sat again. The other villagers, however, quickly drifted away, with many a wary backward glance.

"Meghra used to be like us." Idran jabbed a grease-slicked thumb at his chest. "But different. Even when young." He pointed at Creeper, still mounted on Skink's shoulder. "She was always interested in weave and stories of the pattern makers. For days she would be lost in the tunnel there, exploring and playing with the withies, bending, shaping, making shapes. Then one day she was gone and did not come back. Perhaps she had gone to the old city." He waved beyond the pass that loomed above the village to the east. "We thought her lost, and that was that."

"But then she came back. And she was changed."

An old woman who had still been listening nearby leaned forward. "Meghra takes." She made a circular gesture above the top of her head and nodded. "She feeds. Feeds on us, now."

A man beside the woman pulled her back, obviously unhappy she had spoken. He glared at me with such an intense mixture of fear and loathing I had to look away. When I glanced back up, he and the woman were gone.

I asked, "Where she now, this Meghra?"

Idran pointed back towards the pass again. "Stays in her cave, weaves her strange patterns. Until she hungers." He stood. "No need to worry. She does not come to the village any more." He nodded at a weave pod nearby. "This yours tonight. You safe. Tomorrow we talk more." He joined a huddle of villagers that looked like they were determined to strip the last remnants of meat from the roast carcass.

We squeezed through the round opening of the pod Idran had indicated. A straw mattress lay on the floor, surrounded by stacked empty baskets that stank of river meat. But it reminded me of the nests we sometimes built in the Motherman, cosy and private. Skink collapsed on the bed.

"World is bigger than we thought." Her voice was soft.

"Too big." I eyed the wide-open horizon from the doorway. Night had long fallen, and the stars and a sliver of moon glittered in the clear

189

sky. I shivered. Despite the fire pits and the shelter of the pod, the air here was cooler than in the tunnel. I bent down to investigate a pile of blankets in one of the baskets.

"I have to meet her," Skink said.

"Who?" But I knew who.

"This witch. Meghra."

"Why?" But I knew why.

"She's what I've been sensing in the weave, I'm sure of it. Or if not, she knows what it is. Perhaps she found the pattern makers."

"They're just a story."

She arched her eyebrow. "Like the clevers? Like this land we stand on?"

I knew from the determined set of her mouth there was nothing I could say to change her mind. And... probably she was right. So far we had been crossing the weave without aim; only to move away from the cliffs and the mist and to find enough to eat, surviving day to day. But now we had new purpose. Or at least Skink had, and I knew better than to argue. At the very least it seemed that this new tribe – with its intricately woven pods and penned livestock and plentiful food and water – were ready to tolerate us. Yet it seemed odd, the strange mixture of celebration and revulsion I had seen. Hushed whispers, furtive looks, children pointing. They seemed glad of our arrival, or at least curious, but many also seemed to turn away from us. Too soon, I guessed, to understand the internal politics of this tribe... and perhaps we would have treated strangers much the same, back in the Motherman... another pair of mouths to feed, a burden until we proved ourselves otherwise.

I stared at Creeper, huddled obediently beside Skink. It munched on spare weave shards. Was it my imagination or had it grown? The creature's knobbly thorax was bigger than my fist now.

"You are a witch," I said, as I threw Skink a blanket from the pile.

She glanced at me sharply. "Been called worse."

Spurned by most of our own tribe, and abandoned as a child by her original one. She must have heard plenty of insults in her lifetime. I immediately regretted my words.

"Sorry. I didn't mean it that way..."

"What way?"

"I meant, I wasn't serious. I... I'm sorry."

She glared at me and snapped the blanket in the air before letting it settle over the mattress. Creeper bunched its legs as if it were about to launch itself at me.

There was no room in the hut other than to sit or lie down beside Skink. I considered leaving but she patted the straw next to her. "Come on."

I watched the light of the fires dying outside through the weave of the blanket covering the entrance. Enjoying the warmth of Skink's stiff body beside mine. Slowly, sensing her and myself relax.

I tried not to think about how much of a fool I was. Tried not to worry about Idran, and Meghra, and being at the mercy of total strangers. To think about the unyielding ground beneath me and the wide-open sky and blazing stars pinwheeling directly above. I would have to get used to leaving the weave behind, I knew that. Just... not quite yet, surely.

Just as I was finally drifting off to sleep, Skink nudged me.

"Hmm?"

"They're right, you know," she whispered.

Confused, half asleep, "'Bout what?"

"I *am* a witch."

We slept in, both of us, strangely comforted by the sounds of the village awakening around us: children playing, shouting, crying; animals barking and braying, chickens screeching, adults chiding. The sounds of family. The sounds of life, and of belonging.

I didn't know how I felt about becoming a member of another tribe. It's not something I had ever thought of before. Would these villagers, with their painted skin and dour manners, even want us to join them? Or would they only usher us on? It seemed they had plenty to eat, and plenty room. Perhaps we would be welcome, once we got to know each other.

Drowsing beside Skink, her hand inadvertently on mine, not wanting to move and wake her even though painful tingles spread through my arm from it being in one position too long, I felt a confusing mixture of contentment and melancholy. The world and the people we had known had been brutally stripped away, and yet here we still were, alive and together, survivors of it all. If only Ma and Da had been able to see us now.

There was the sound of running footsteps and rapping on the side of the hut. A young boy's sweaty face peered around the entrance blanket. "Breakfast?" He offered a pair of stacked bowls and made pouring motions with an earthenware jug trembling in his other hand. I took the bowls and held them as he poured a pale liquid from the jug. "Drink, drink," he urged. "Is sweet."

I took a suspicious sip. Sweet and sour, fermented milk mixed with honey, perhaps. "Is good," I said to the boy, who smiled in what seemed like relief. He ducked his head and quickly ran from the hut. I handed the other bowl to Skink, who stood and gulped its contents down.

"Today we find out more about this Meghra," she said.

I sighed and finished off the last of the milk. Despite the initial sweetness, there was a bitter, chalky aftertaste and the inside of my mouth and my lips tingled. "Thought you might say that." I stumbled suddenly, and looking down I saw I had almost trodden upon Creeper.

"Skink, you need to stop feeding him," I said. The weaver had grown bigger overnight. Its body was almost the size of my head, its legs as long as my forearm.

"There's something they're not telling us," Skink said, frowning. She swayed, unsteady on her feet. "I think," she passed a hand over her eyes. "I think..."

"What?" I blinked. "What d'you think?" She seemed to blur before me.

"Think they lied."

Her legs crumpled beneath her. I tried to catch her, but my arms seemed heavier and larger than the Motherman's. I could not move, could not turn, even as the hut's straw-covered floor tilted upwards and slammed me in the face.

I watched, an observer trapped in the cave of my own skull, as Creeper jumped upon Skink's fallen body. She twitched but otherwise did not move, as its legs and feelers danced over her flesh.

The hut's entrance blanket was pulled aside. Light and then shadow spilled over us. A sandaled foot kicked Creeper into the corner, where it fell into one of the baskets, curled up as if dead.

Unable to move, every moment sinking deeper into a sickly darkness, I was helpless as we were seized and dragged out of the hut.

"Why."

My lips and mouth, still numb, slowly returned to life.

"Why."

Idran's swirl-covered face hove into view. Fat black flies circled his head. He avoided looking into my eyes as he checked my bonds were tight. (They were.)

"Rather you than us, my unlucky friend."

The journey had been a blur of rough jolts and hard, ever-changing grips upon my body; chattering voices, half-snatched conversations – "Such a blessing" – "Andar will be relieved" – "Still think we should save one 'til later." Bright sky and dark ground lurched before my eyes and only served to sicken me more. Eventually the movement and sound reached a crescendo and then retreated, and only then, when I could only hear a single set of crunching footsteps and the soughing of the rotten-smelling wind did I manage to turn my head and look around me. Then I wished I hadn't.

I was tied upright to a thick pole or stave of some kind. Skink similarly bound a little ahead of me. We were outside the village, up the cinder slope towards the pass. Sharp-ridged, bare hills rose to either side.

Around us, bodies piled carelessly in the dirt. Crows and worms rooted amongst the stick-like bones and leathery bags of skin. Teeth-lined gaping mouths, slitted nostrils and eyes. The tops of heads missing, sliced open, empty as old eggshells, lined by blowflies.

The stench.

"Meghra will come soon," Idran said.

I struggled to find words to express my rage and fear. Only a mewling, groaning sort of noise emerged.

"Do not think too badly of us, stranger." Idran remained impassive. "If we do not offer tribute, then twice as many are taken. If we run, we are hunted. We have no choice, as you see."

Skink squirmed in her ropes to look over her shoulder. "No worry, Percher." Her words still slurred. "Not afraid. Me witch, too."

Idran gave a sad nod. "Maybe so. Who knows? If we could stop Meghra we would. But we cannot."

With a final vicious tightening of the knots around my wrist, he walked out of my field of vision and was gone.

I shouted after him. Cursed him and his tribe. It was as futile as insulting the brainless dead at our feet.

It did not stop me.

Skink hung limp upon her post. Silent. Waiting.

Only wisps of cloud scarred the brightening sky, but the earth was dark here, the rock-strewn soil densely packed, with little vegetation. I still found the sight and sensation of the flat, non-woven surface fascinating and disturbing. Such binary distinction between ground and sky, with hardly any degree of ambiguity or complexity; you were either on the ground, or, with vastly greater difficulty, above or below it, nothing in-between. No opportunity to burrow down, shimmy into crevices, find shelter. It made me queasy, thinking about how exposed I was, how far I would have to run to hide from any threat...

The burn from my bound hands reminded me even that was no longer an option.

Skink's next words only deepened the sick feeling in my stomach.

"She comes."

As one, the crows and flies swarming over the abandoned flesh of the dead rose into the sky and circled away.

A dark sun rose over the crest of the ridge. At first I could not properly resolve its shape or understand its scale, as it writhed and lurched upon its many-jointed limbs towards us. Then I realized it was a face, a head, carried upon giant, insect-like legs that splayed from a trunk-like neck. As it crawled closer its size became clear: easily four times my height, more if you counted the huge mane of snakelike, writhing weave atop it. I frantically pulled and twisted my hands and feet, but Idran's cursed bonds only cut deeper into my flesh.

"What have we here? New treats?"

To my surprise, the giantess's voice was that of a frail old woman's, and no louder. The strange dissonance between the scale of the body and the sound she made only terrified me more. A woven forelimb, like a giant crab's claw, easily shoved aside the piled corpses. Meghra reared over Skink's bound form. A huge mesh face peered down at her, all swivelling eyes and cavernous horror of a mouth, cackling, "Different, different, that's what you are."

"Leave her alone!" I shouted.

Meghra immediately shifted her attention to me. It was then, as she became my entire darkened world, that I realized her great mass was nothing more than a ghoulish mask, a giant intricate contraption within which the real Meghra lay buried, a hunched old woman deep in the chest of the giant puppet she wore like a costume around her.

She cackled again, a gleeful, evil sound. "No, not you."

I woke with such a pain throbbing in my shoulders and neck the oblivion of death was preferable. There was no sign of Meghra, and no sign of Skink. The rope that had tied her to her stave had fallen to the ground, torn and bloodstained. Only the brain-scourged dead surrounded me.

With growing despair, I realized my own bonds remained intact, that I was still tied firmly to my pole. I must have passed out, or been hit by one of Meghra's tentacles. Was she behind me? Was I about to be snatched – or worse, my head peeled open? I twisted and turned, ignoring the pain of moving my neck, but there was only the open sky above me. Eventually I dared to cry out – barely more than a croak, really – but there was no answer.

I had been abandoned, rejected by Meghra. Skink hadn't been so lucky.

I dangled there for what seemed like an age, alternating between rage and despair. There was no answer to my increasingly desperate cries; only the mocking calls of the returning crows and the soughing of the wind. There was no sign of Idran or the villagers. The cowards.

I spotted dark movement from the corner of my eye and for a moment I feared that Meghra had returned, or perhaps the crows had summoned enough courage to approach me... but it was a familiar mixture of jerky and smooth motion.

"Hey, Creeper."

The weaver crawled over the piled bodies towards me, one limb not working quite right, but still capable of climbing. I was surprised by how glad I was to see this creature. A friendly, familiar presence despite its completely alien nature.

The weaver reached my bound feet, and began to climb my legs. I had a sudden moment of doubt. How big and heavy it had grown. What was it doing?

Strong, sharp legs gripped my knees, my thighs, pincers closed round my back – *snick, snick*. My numbed fingers immediately began to tingle as my hands came free. *Snick, snick*, my legs, too.

I immediately stumbled down the mound of bodies, my feet catching bony ridges and squelching in unspeakable cavities. When I reached the bare ground I fell to my knees and retched up the remnants of that morning's treacherous breakfast. The wide-open sky reeled above me, pressed me down into the hard, unrelenting wall of dirt beneath me. I felt crushed between the two. Insignificant, as helpless as an insect.

Swallowing hard, I forced myself to my traitorous feet. Was that how Skink felt, all the time, feeling like the ground would rush up and punch her at any moment?

How long was I out for – surely not long? But there was no sign of anyone on the saddleback ridge apart from Creeper and me. The cowardly villagers had at least the decency not to witness our fate.

Where was Skink? Where had Meghra taken her?

Was she even still alive?

The panic and confusion that threatened to overwhelm me quickly faded. Right before my feet – clear tracks and furrows left in the dirt. Creeper was already leading the way.

There was a canyon-like depression just over the pass. Not really that far, though it felt it as I staggered beneath the glaring sky. Was it the residual effects of the poison the villagers had fed us that made my head swim so?

Creeper skittered before me, surprisingly fast even with its damaged leg, eager to find its lost mistress.

As we approached the canyon I slowed. My heart pounded. I thought I would be sick again as I crept towards the edge and leaned over, fearing I would peer down and find Skink with her skull already torn open. Expecting to see her, desperately *hoping* to see her, I was still shocked by what I saw.

At the bottom of the long dried out, half-collapsed gorge, she was there. Upright, swaying, her arms outstretched before Meghra's giant, hollow face. At first I thought Skink's hair had grown hugely and billowed out from her head. But it was tendrils from the giantess that were swarming around her skull. Pushing deep into it. Skink's eyes were shut, but I could see their lids trembling. As if she were dreaming.

Floating up, Meghra's manic cackle. "What's in there? What pattern do you hide? Now let me in, child."

I didn't stop to think. I ran shouting down the scree-littered slope towards her, no idea what I would do. Would it damage her if I simply tried to tear her free? I didn't care. Anything to stop her brain being lifted out of her head.

Meghra's tentacles reared up before me. Before I knew what was happening, they had curled around my arms and waist and tightened. My feet were lifted from the ground as if I were no more than a doll. From deep within Meghra's complex, animated construct of weave, came the old woman's voice, "There is nothing you can do! She's mine now."

"No!" I shouted, even as the grip on me tightened and the breath was crushed out of me. Skink's eyes flickered open, closed again. Maybe she could still hear me. "Fight her! I know you can!"

Laughter from the old woman and a wordless groan from Skink. Her head lolled beneath the dark crown of tendrils and a suffocating wave of fear and despair swept over me. I was losing her, and my own life was in equal danger.

"You're stronger than her!" It had to be true. Everything we had been through together, Skink always smarter, always tougher than anyone I knew. "Remember! You moved the Motherman. You made the mountain walk! This – "I waved a temporarily free hand at the grinning giantess. "This is nothing!"

Another moan. But this time Skink's eyes fluttered open.

"That's it! Show her!"

A skittering movement across the canyon floor. Creeper, limbs flailing at Meghra's weave. I didn't know what it could achieve, but it was at least trying to distract the witch.

The giantess lurched. The ground shook, and the tentacles holding Skink swung wildly. A mewling sound of frustration and fury emerged from Meghra's mouth, as it twisted in new effort.

Skink's eyes gleamed with sudden triumph. I knew the look, same as the one when she had made the Motherman walk. The tendrils stretching from Meghra whipped and swayed, as if they were trying to retract but were unable to.

The sound of whip-snapping tentacles and weave tearing filled the air. Meghra was trying desperately now to reverse away from Skink, to release her, but it didn't seem she was totally in control of her extended body. Withies curled and swung and trembled. The old woman was crying out.

"Stop it! Stop it!"

Waves and ripples, the air cracked with sudden motion. Skink still hung suspended in mid-air, held by the surging weave, no longer captured so much as borne aloft. A mass of dark withies descended upon Meghra's head, easily puncturing the fragile outer skin, crashing through to the frail human core.

I could not look as the weave bunched and curled and *squeezed...* until the screaming stopped and the only sound that remained was Skink's breathing.

All around us Meghra's mass of weave sagged to ground, as if in relief.

I couldn't wait to escape the desolate canyon. But Skink kept rummaging amongst the listless weave, ignoring my questions about how she was, whether she was hurt. Briefly I approached Meghra's crushed body, to check if she were alive or dead, but I quickly retreated when I glimpsed the mess of jutting bones. I kept looking at Skink. Was she damaged? Had Meghra changed her? Physically, apart from bruising that could just as well have been caused by the villagers, she appeared uninjured.

But she kept avoiding my gaze.

Creeper bounded amongst the collapsed withies like a crazed thing, spinning and biting off sections, curling and splaying its limbs as if in excitement. Eventually I lost it as it disappeared beneath the densest mass, its presence only visible as a disturbance on the surface layers.

Confused by Skink's behaviour, fearing that the villagers could return at any moment and become vengeful that their feared witch had been defeated, I climbed back up to the pass.

At the top of the ridge, a glimpse into the large, bowl-shaped valley beyond to the east. Just visible, I thought I spied distant spires and domes clustered on the far side. The view was fascinating, apart from the growing dizziness and sickness as the sky crowded down upon me again. I shielded my eyes, and tried to calm my breathing.

I jumped as I heard Skink's dragging footsteps behind me. She had finally emerged from Meghra's wreckage. She squeezed my shoulder as she leant for balance against me. I tensed and my stomach seemed to flip-flop as she touched me.

"Thank you," she said. "She had me. I would have been lost."

I hung my head and shrugged, not knowing what to say. Shoulder tingling. What had I done, really?

"We have to go," she said, pointing. "To the city. Find the pattern makers."

"Believe that story?"

"Saw it in her mind, Percher. In her memories. She went there. Learned how to control the weave."

I frowned. Had a sudden memory of Skink in the brain of the Motherman, exultant as she first made the colossus move. Saw her lifted on Meghra's weave tentacles, eyes turned back into her head as she probed a way to crush the opponent before her. Truth was, Skink frightened me sometimes. Actually, quite a lot.

"Is that what you want? Control? Like Meghra had?"

"She too hungry. Too... damaged."

I sighed. I didn't understand her. Couldn't. "Maybe we should go back to the village. Poison their wells." My bitter words surprised even me.

"Really?"

"They betrayed us."

"Wouldn't we have done the same?"

"No."

But I remembered my brother Broc. How often he had called for Skink to be thrown into the mist as an offering to the gods. She was the slowest of us, the weakest, he said. Abandoned by her own tribe and not even a proper part of the family. Ma and Da had always resisted his call, but there had been more than a few of us who had looked at Skink with hard eyes.

Perhaps she was right.

She was still staring at the eastern horizon. "I saw books there, Percher. Many books. A..." She struggled to find the word. "Library. That's where Meghra went."

I eyed her twisted leg, her obvious state of exhaustion. As far as I could see, the land between us and the distant city was a flattened, grassy plain. There were only occasional odd struts or stalks of weave;

no big hollowed-out tubes or interwoven corridors through which Skink could use her arms to hoist herself.

"It's a long walk."

She released her hold on my shoulder and stood alone, wobbly at first. I moved to support her, but she pushed me away. "Don't need to walk."

A shadow fell over my back, and I turned.

Emerging out of the canyon, a giant, spider-like creature. I fell back, immediately fearing a reassembled Meghra. Skink's laughter barely reassured me.

It was Creeper, grown giant, bigger than Skink and I put together.

Skink quickly hoisted herself onto a saddle-like protrusion on the creature's ridged back. When I hesitated, she stretched down her hand to me.

"Space for two," she said.

# Parasite Art

## David Tallerman

I dream of darkness.

A sun burns far off on the horizon. Its glow, ancient and reddish, makes the shadows purple and endlessly long. The plain before me is dark too, though veined with pale lightning of crystal.

Then – warmth in my belly, or rather in the core of me, where I imagine my belly to be. The warmth is good, and also frightening. In the gloom, soft lights build, barely perceptible at first but rapidly growing brighter. My eyes – what I think of as my eyes – can differentiate more shades than that sullen red star should allow: pastel violets, oranges, and yellows. Each new illumination sends a thrill through me, and a sense of want.

This feels important, but I can't say why – because the dream isn't mine.

I've been working for about thirty hours standard, not quite a solar day on Culcifa. I've done so for far longer. The first time, I painted for just short of eighty hours: painted in a frenzy, sick with joy, the results spilling from the canvas and onto the walls and floor, vast and exhilarating and brutal in their beauty. When I finished – when I collapsed, the Zobe no longer able even to keep me standing – my fingers were bloody and blistered.

After that, we learned to be more careful.

The Zobe has sustained me. Still, I'm hungry. Perhaps it's only habit; perhaps humans are not designed to live as proxies. Such thoughts do nothing to make the hunger go away, and I keep no food in the shelter, for its presence bothers the Zobe. I'll need to visit the canteen.

First, I consider our painting – though from duty more than pride. Part of me is dimly aware of what I'd once have given up to produce an image so close to perfection. Another part reminds me what I *did* give up.

The complex refraction of the light suggests that this image was viewed originally through compound eyes. The scene – a grim expanse made joyous and somehow carnal by strange, soft lights that gleam like Chinese lanterns – is gorgeous and stirring. Yet I don't know what our painting represents, or where. I feel its meaning like a word on the tip of my tongue, but I can't understand.

I portray my dreams. So does everyone on Culcifa. We paint them, sculpt them, sing them, spin them into words.

Except, of course, they aren't *our* dreams. They aren't dreams at all – or rather, they are only to us. To the Zobe, they're reminiscences of other lives, vicariously lived. Their symbiosis is remarkably versatile. Their lifespans are extraordinary. And all that they experience, everything their hosts experience, they recall with absolute clarity.

This is the lure of the Zobe, of Culcifa: to see through eyes not your own.

I've become a link in a chain, one older, perhaps, than the Earth itself. Yet sometimes – rarely – we dream my own memories, made alien by the Zobe's perspective. Sometimes, when it's dormant, I dare to try to remember for myself. Today is one of those times. As I climb the edge of the plateau, clambering over rocks malformed and nacreous as waterlogged corpses, I recollect my first days here...

What money I've scratched together has covered my transport – three long legs of mixed cryo, even without the trips up and down-orbit – and supplies for a few days, as well as the suit. With a Zobe, I know I'd be able to withstand Culcifa's atmosphere. Without one, it would come down to whether asphyxiation or blood poisoning got me first.

I look around the encampment with dim horror. It's so like where I've come from, so unlike what I'd imagined. I'll learn later that the Zobe-infected dwell on the outskirts or even in the wilderness, the better to create in peace. But those places are no less unsightly, and their homes no more seemly than the prefabricated shelters littering the plateau top like corroded sea wrack.

No one will give me any advice. They tell me that many come here; they tell me there may be no free Zobe left. They hint, without appearing to care, that I'll likely die long before I find what I'm looking for.

I choose a direction at random. I walk. I clamber. Sometimes I slither and slide. Night descends, and I continue as well as I can. My air will run out before my food and water. If I sleep, I might never wake.

But the night is dark, and Culcifa is deadly. I don't see the ravine until I've stumbled into it, until its depths have drawn me down to the hard, broken ground. Half-conscious, I understand that I've broken my leg, probably an arm too. I think I'm bleeding inside my suit, and it seems unlikely I'll ever be able to climb back out.

Only, none of that matters, because I've already seen what I came here for.

It has fallen down here too. I know somehow that together we'll have the strength to escape back to the surface, even though it must be weakened, perhaps close to death itself. I suppose it's as glad to see me as I am it, if a Zobe can be such a thing as glad. What can death mean to them, these beings that live for millennia, that are so immensely hard to destroy?

It's here with me now, watching my memories, which are also its memories. I suppose that, if we communicated, I could simply ask. But communication is an act between equals, or at least between those with grounds for negotiation. We are not equals. And the Zobe gives more than it could ever take, for all I have to offer is my life.

I sense that the Zobe is unhappy with me. It doesn't like to be questioned, not even indirectly. It doesn't like to be reminded of our bond, or of how we became *we*. I think the reason is that I'm such a transient presence to it; who would discuss the nature of their existence with a suit of clothes soon to be discarded?

So, for the last distance to the encampment, I try to think of other things. I watch bands of lavender and grey coruscate in the high atmosphere. When viscous yellow rain falls, I concentrate on its splash upon my skin. Culcifa is damned ugly, ugly to its roots. Is that, somehow, why the Zobe chose it? Is that the reason for their pilgrimage here? While little is known about them, it's a fact that when Culcifa was first surveyed a century ago there was no life here – which means they came from farther out, all of them together. It seems certain, too, that one day they'll leave again, casting themselves back into the void.

In years? In days? And just what are they waiting for?

More questions. The Zobe hangs flaccidly, spitting toxic shivers of emotion at the edges of my mind. I go back to not thinking, to concentrating on the rain's hiss against my flesh. And truthfully, not thinking is easier. If it's hard to have questions without answers, to have those answers close and unattainable is altogether worse.

I hike on, and the rain thickens, and the rocks are piled like massed dead. There's no beauty on Culcifa, not without the Zobe.

We're not sociable, we conjoined, and the Zobe are even less so. Through it, I can feel the presence of another of its kind within the canteen, like the presentiment of a migraine. It would turn me away if it could.

For once I resist. Hunger and thirst are powerful motivators, and I recognise the solitary figure sitting in a corner.

I find myself glad to see Arene – and then surprised at my own reaction. Symbiosis eliminates loneliness; without loneliness, what need for human contact? Not that Arene is, strictly speaking, human; there's something in her DNA that's clearly *other*. Her skin is lustrous with the suggestion of colour, like pearl. Her ears are misshapen, her body impossibly slender-boned, her teeth fine and needlelike. Even without her Zobe, she would be rare and special.

Once she told me that on her home world she sculpted in ice, and loved its transience, that here, the knowledge of how her work endures torments her.

I take my food and drink from the serving hatches – not caring what it is, for I can hardly taste these days – and move to join her. We nod our greetings, since it's troublesome for us to speak. One of the five Zobe tendrils penetrates beneath the jaw, to merge with the trachea and larynx. The inconvenience and unpleasantness of coordinating sounds tends to enforce brevity, so that even before I register the content of her words, I'm startled when Arene says, "I'm thinking of leaving."

I gape stupidly. "Leaving?"

"Going home. Or maybe farther out."

"No one leaves," I tell her.

"I don't know if I can do this any more."

"Is it even possible?" I'd always assumed it wasn't. In the stories of Culcifa, the implication was always that to come here was to stay forever, to live out whatever remained of your life in the knowledge that the time would be brief but luminously bright.

"I don't know," Arene says. "I can try."

"Will you?"

"I don't know."

I see in her lilac eyes that she's telling the truth. I understand how difficult to even conceive of unbonding must have been for her, let alone to give the idea serious consideration. I understand because the Zobe's discomfort has become a startling, raw horror that makes me murmur an excuse and tumbles me to my feet and carries me back into the wilderness, leaving my food untouched upon the table.

Outside, greasy rain spatters my face. I slip on slick rock. For the first time in longer than I can remember, there's an idea in my head that's neither mine nor the Zobe's.

Is this why the Zobe despise company?

That night, I dream of the ocean.

I'm surrounded by water black as ink, moving among ferocious currents with unthinking ease. Around me, densely packed, my shoal flicker and dance. With our teardrop bodies and flattened rudder-arms, we resemble nothing more than cartoon ghosts. Our numbers are beyond count, and others travel with us: great, armoured crustaceans that skitter and slide through the obsidian sands, shuddering clouds of infinitesimal horde-life, and above, crystalline leviathans that twist the scant light. These are our servant races, made docile by our song. They will fight for us – fight and die.

For today we've gathered for war: a great violence, the defining act of our generation. The bloodlust is elixir in my veins. I was born for this, raised for this, and if I fall then I'll become song, the hymn that echoes between the waves.

Yet a part of me resists. A part is conscious of watching rather than being. And as it stirs, I realise that part is *me*. These memories aren't mine. These memories are the Zobe's, and once belonged to another.

I recognise the dream for what it is, but I don't wake. I struggle, as if striving to surface through those dark waters. I can't slip free alone. The Zobe, not me, chooses when we dream.

Does it also choose what we dream?

I search my own mind, hunting for my own memories. One rises easily. A long time ago; another life, it seems. I recall showing KT the painting: a sunset, blazing and chill, and in the middle ground two figures that I'm sure she must recognise as her and I.

Her fingers grip mine. "It's very good," she tells me.

Very good means not good enough. I know what she's thinking, what she's been thinking for months. "You want me to go."

"I don't *want* anything," KT says, with mock hurt. "I just know that if you don't, you'll regret it."

"And you wouldn't mind?"

"Why would I mind? You'll make your fortune." KT smiles a brittle smile. Is there desperation in those cool grey eyes? "Then you'll come back to me."

We both comprehend the truth. No one comes back from Culcifa. And many, very many, are never heard from again. Is this life of ours so bad? Am I such a hopeless prospect?

Yes. I'm poor, and I'll always be poor. Nothing I achieve could hope to compete with the art of the Zobe-bonded. What do I know? What have I seen? My work is the work of one small lifetime, one isolated mind.

Later that day I'll sell the painting, which I'd meant to be a gift to her. The profit will cover the last of the amount I've been saving for my flight, and I know KT will never miss it.

The dream is brief and bitter. I feel clearly, even through the pall of unconsciousness, that the Zobe resents these times when my memories intrude, that it much prefers to draw on its own vast stock. I suppose I can't blame it. Compared to what it's seen, the places it's witnessed, the multitude of lives it's lived by proxy, we humans aren't so very interesting.

When I wake, the Zobe is remote, fractious, almost an unwilling passenger. Since our communication is entirely one-sided, I can think of no way to propitiate it. Instead, I look at my painting. The result of our mingled reveries is an abstract of sorts: in parts that alien ocean, in parts my remembered sunset, and superimposed in a way that defies sense, the recollected emotions of my last meeting with KT, shimmering like irradiated dust upon the air.

A portion of me would like to destroy this work, an impulse I've never known before. I wonder, does that desire come from me or from the Zobe? Why does it accept this symbiosis when human experiences appeal so little?

Perhaps everything we believe about the Zobe is wrong. What if none of these generations of memories they retain bear any interest for them? What if their dreams are simply an act of regurgitation, a sort of psychic flatulence?

For the next few hours, the Zobe remains distant. Its emotions flash and pop in my mind like bubbles in champagne. Then, early in the afternoon, with the sun gigantic in a lead-grey sky, a familiar claxon sounds: the call to bazaar.

I'd like to ignore it, even as I know I can't. Culcifa has few rules; there are, however, certain expectations. You don't miss bazaar, not if you can help it – which means, of course, if you're not dreaming. For if no one sells then no one can buy, and if no one buys then what use has Culcifa?

The trek takes up much of the remaining afternoon. Behind me, my cart putters and groans, and often I have to disengage it when the edge of its float snares on a protrusion, or when its simple mind becomes befuddled by a fold of Culcifa's malevolent terrain. I'm constantly aware of my paintings stacked within, wrapped carefully inside their layers of outrétarp. A minute's exposure to Culcifa's raw atmosphere would scour them into the crudest primitivism.

Somehow, that thought tempts me. Yet I trudge on.

There are perhaps thirty of us at bazaar: roughly two thirds of Culcifa's Zobe-conjoined populace. We're most of us human, but not exclusively. I recognise a pair of Cruxchians. The hulking beast with the spines and exposed ribcage might be a Bode; I've heard them described. There's a small, skittish creature keeping itself apart that I saw once in my dreams – or rather, in the Zobe's dreams. Conceivably we were one of its ancestors. Seeing it, my muscle memory recalls what it's like to make those spasmodic movements, and I look away hurriedly.

I spy a couple of new arrivals, a couple of spaces empty. Life doesn't last long on Culcifa, and not all species are equally hardy or well suited. The Cruxchians will probably not be here again, they don't fare well under Culcifa's gravity. But when they're gone, others will come. They always do.

Nowhere do I see Arene. Is it possible she really left? Did some quirk in her contaminated DNA give her the freedom to do what no one else could, or would want to?

I've brought four paintings, the most I've produced in a single cycle. They are also, I know without vanity, the best. The compound of KT's sunset and the Zobe's remembered seascape I left in the shelter. This may, for all I know, be an offence under the rules of Culcifa. We are, after all, obliged to sell. Nevertheless, I'm here with my four paintings, every one a masterpiece, and surely that must appease even the most captious administrator.

I unload my canvasses with care from the cart, which hovers patiently. I pick a stall close to the outer edge, at the farthest point from the landing port, without knowing why. Then again, I can reassure myself that my location hardly matters. No artist ever takes work back from a Culcifan bazaar.

Still, it's some time before any of the patrons drift my way. Then two approach together; as they recognise each other's intentions, one peels off, turning their feet instead towards the closest Cruxchian. The remaining figure draws near, and I can differentiate my potential buyer as a human female. She's of unusual stature: in her suit, she's a giant. All that equipment to survive, and here I stand almost naked, disregarding cold and the toxins in the air that should kill me in seconds – all thanks to the Zobe. I can barely make out her features through the darkened mask.

"May I inspect your wares?"

Her tone is strident but polite. There's ritual in bazaar, an adherence to modes long since grown antique on other worlds. Perhaps it's only that anyone spending catastrophic sums of money appreciates a sense of moment.

"Your attention honours us," I say.

She doesn't look at me. She looks at my paintings, occasionally at the Zobe, where it lolls across my shoulder and chest, but never at me.

"I'd like to take them all," she says finally, with an expansive motion that her suit makes clumsy.

There's no need for me to haggle. There are few moral crimes in the galaxy greater than underpaying for Culcifan art. And no money will be given to me; the funds will be transferred to an account that was set up for me by one of the camp facilitators when I first returned with the Zobe, and from which all my costs are automatically deducted.

Before I came here, this would have seemed like taking a great deal on trust. Now it's simply the automation of necessary distractions. What would I spend my earnings on? The camp provides for my remaining human needs, the Zobe for everything else. I could be sending money home, I suppose, to my father or KT. I think about that sometimes, and never do.

Soon after, eight servants arrive to take my four paintings. It occurs to me that I feel nothing but hatred for the woman who bought my work. It occurs to me, too, that she'll probably never look at them, much less appreciate them.

And a stranger recognition: I don't care.

Days later, I find the courage to investigate Arene's hut, on the far side of the plateau. I find the door left open, pale dust accumulating in corners and hazing windows. There's no sign of Arene, or of her Zobe either.

I feel sad and glad at once. I don't know what to feel. Now that Arene's gone, I realise there's no one else I speak to on this entire world.

The Zobe's response, at least, is clear. It doesn't want to be here. I suppose that, in the same way that they dislike each other's presence, they're also territorial. This experiencing of second-hand emotion is an aspect of the symbiosis I may never reconcile with. Worst is the impossibility of separating out my own emotions. Am I wounded, happy, afraid? Will I miss Arene or forget her in a moment?

As I trudge the distance back towards my shelter, I find myself wishing for my own mind back – if only for an hour, a minute, an instant.

In the dream, I'm higher than I've ever been. The ground is a blur, granular oranges and reds merging and shifting. The trees, which are vast, stand well apart, each its own ancient ecosystem: it's hard for me to disentangle what's bark and what's featherish moss, crusted lichen, or the vivid mauve of enveloping vines. The basket-homes of my kind hang like ornaments, clustered on the strongest boughs and dangling precariously from the weaker, where the truly fearless live.

I perch on elongated toes, a world spread beneath me. I stretch my arms, testing membranes against the potent updraughts. When I leap for the next trunk, an impossible-seeming distance away, it's like flying, like the best dream of flying I've ever had.

On the edge of consciousness, a memory encroaches. KT told me once that when you dream about flying, you're really dreaming about sex. But no sex has ever been as good as this. And as the dream begins to fade, as reality seeps upon its edges, that sensation stays. Surfacing into my own flesh, I feel heavy as stone.

I wake despising myself, hating the meat that makes me. A troubling thought: is *this* what it feels like to be a Zobe? To be constantly tormented by what you're not?

For a long while, all I can do is lie still, weighed by a body that thinks it remembers how to fly.

Some dreams I remember clearly. Other times, I look at what I've painted with no understanding, only a sort of appalled awe. Sometimes my work frightens me.

Today the memory of the dream (which was, of course, in itself a memory) is clear. I still feel what it's like to be borne upon pummelling currents, to move among them light as a feather. And that feeling is what I've painted: the ecstasy of falling without falling. I know without doubt that it's the best work I've produced.

I leave my shelter, squinting at the violent sky. Outside, I hunt a sharp rock; not a difficult task on Culcifa, where everything is designed to hurt. I heft it in my hand, enjoying its weight. Then I go back inside, and with the rock I gouge my canvas from top to bottom: once, twice, three times.

I think the Zobe will try and stop me, but it doesn't. Then I wonder, why should it? All this is to it is effluent, the memory of a memory. The Zobe don't care about art. They only want to live, and to dream their dreams.

I don't know any more which of us needs the other. I don't remember what it feels like to paint. Oh, I can recall mechanical details, the pressure of brush against fingers, the minute feedback of bristles on canvas. I remember the technical skills, the techniques. But I don't remember what it *feels* like.

I'm more than I ever was before I came to Culcifa. Before Culcifa I was worth nothing. The painting I've just casually destroyed would have paid for every moment of my old life and left change to spare.

I can't live like this for another day.

I'd imagined it would be difficult, but I was wrong. I'd imagined it would be like trying to expel a cancer by force of will, and it's nothing like that at all. Perhaps, in a way, I've misinterpreted the Zobe.

For in the moment I know without doubt that I want to be free, I find that it's already gone. In an instant, my thoughts are entirely my own. A fog lifts; my mind is flayed to a tiny, mewling core. For the first time in months, I'm entirely, nakedly alone.

I'd imagined it would be painful. There, at least, I was right. We've been one body all this time and now, again, one becomes two. Tendrils retract; interfaces of flesh suture. My muscles burn. My blood boils in my veins. This is what I imagine dying would be like – and maybe with good reason. I have no idea if my body can exist any more without the Zobe. How much has it changed me to accommodate its own needs? How much of what remains is still me?

I manage, somehow, to get into my suit in time. I'm distantly surprised by the extent to which I want to live, now that death is once again a real possibility. I can feel the holes in myself. But I can feel them healing, too. Is this some small parting gift from the Zobe? Thanks, or else forgiveness? I'll never know.

I leave it where it's fallen: a puddle of purplish flesh, tentacles twitching limply. Someone else will come. Someone will take my place.

Outside, Culcifa seems somehow more terrible than it ever has before. There's nothing beautiful here. If I wasn't dying already, I think the very ugliness might kill me. Better, perhaps, to die than to take another step across this deathly, hopeless world.

Yet I keep walking. Somehow, I put each foot before the other.

I want to live.

It's pure luck that they find me where I fall, not far from the camp. This is what they tell me when I wake. *You were lucky.* But in my mind, in the haze that's all I remember of the last three days, it wasn't luck but the Zobe. I can no longer recall what its presence was like, but there's a sensation I've come to associate with its absence, like the acid reflux of a fine and complex meal.

I want to believe that it saved me. I don't know why but I do.

I expect that they'd like to leave me to die. Surely, they know what I've done. But I have money, and on Culcifa money is everything.

My fortune is less than I'd have guessed, had I ever thought to guess – though still substantial. Even after the weeks of surgery needed to return my body to something like normal functioning, even after the tickets home, I have enough to live for a few years without working. If I choose not to, I need never paint again.

Will I choose not to? I don't know. I know nothing I do will ever be of much value, that nothing will be a fraction as good as the work I produced on Culcifa. There are days when that prospect makes me weep, and days when I find the certainty strangely thrilling.

KT isn't there when I get back. No one knows where she moved on to, and I don't push the question. Wherever it is, it's probably better than here. Anyway, I doubt I could get answers. Most people I speak to are wary of me, distrustful – and I don't blame them.

No one returns from Culcifa, so to them I'm a dead man.

Maybe they have a point.

The Zobe's memories have faded. What remains is the remembrance of once having possessed them. I understand with perfect clarity that I've forgotten more than I'll ever know. In a mere few months, I experienced far more than I could hope to fill the remainder of my years with. I could live a hundred lives to their utmost and never be close to what, not so long ago, I took for granted, what the Zobe experience in every instant of every day.

I suspect I should regret these facts more than I do.

There are others, I've learned, who broke away from their Zobe. The reason no one knows is because we don't talk about it. We're like amputees, but our phantom limb is another mind, a remembrance that haunts us constantly, and those limbs will never be replaced. Now that I know what to look for, we aren't hard to find, and once found, we're all too easy to recognise.

I managed to locate Arene. She'd been travelling with a Frontrunner crew, out on the fringes, but even that novelty quickly failed her. She'd gone back to her home world, just as I have. I found her, but I didn't contact her, or any of the others either. What can we do for each other? What could I say? What we have in common is only an absence.

Without my painting, I take what jobs I can find, the less skilled the better. I derive a sort of comfort from reaching the end of each day knowing I've produced nothing, that nothing I've done will be valued or recorded. I think of Arene and her ice sculptures. I wish sometimes that I could track down everything I painted on Culcifa and destroy it, piece by piece.

I eat little. I only have myself to sustain, after all. I sleep rarely. When I do, my dreams are flat and grey and rarely memorable.

But at least they're dreams, I tell myself, real dreams.

At least they're mine.

# Galena

## Liam Hogan

Commander Juliet Slade opened the external doors of the floating cargo deck and looked out over an alien sea.

One small step, here, would have her overboard. The suit could probably take it, it was airtight after all, but that wasn't in today's EVA plan and it wasn't just Mission Specialist, Alexis Karlinsky, who would see her pratfall. On Earth countless billions were watching – or would be watching, once the broadcast made its long journey nineteen light-years back the way they'd come.

She resisted the urge to do it anyway. Instead, she turned and faced the camera. "This is Dr Juliet Slade, of the ISA *Nautilus*, currently floating on the dark seas of Galena."

The planet had had another name when their mission blasted off from Lunar Base: Sigma Draconis-b. But even before the quick kick of expensive and heavy chemical propulsion gave way to the *Jules Verne*'s far more efficient ion engines, pushing them steadily towards the Lorentz Limit, they'd known they'd find water here. Though it was like detecting the weight of a gnat landing on a fully grown elephant, it was there, nonetheless, hidden in the faintest of twinkles as Draconis-b passed in front of its parent star. The planet had an atmosphere and that atmosphere contained water. With an orbit squarely in the Goldilocks zone, that had made Sigma Draconis the International Space Agency's top interstellar priority, despite the exoplanets discovered orbiting the much closer red dwarf of Proxima Centauri.

In all of the vast solar system only Earth had liquid surface water and only Earth, it had turned out, had life. And now here was another place, another planet, under another sun, where life might also have begun.

So their target had been renamed after one of the Greek Nereids, Galene; the Goddess of calm seas. A name that echoed what they hoped to find.

"The *Nautilus*, on its descent, released a number of probes at varying altitudes, to sample the thick atmosphere," she told the spectators back home, "And the *Jules Verne* is busy radar mapping the surface from orbit."

She waved a gloved hand at the black waters, white crests flashing in the gloom. "It's all sea, except for a small archipelago of active volcanoes roughly at the equator, which we're making our way towards."

The camera panned to the crates around her. "En route, we'll be releasing aquatic drones. Some are surface craft, some travel just beneath the water, and some are intended to plumb the ocean depths."

She'd worried about the use of the word 'plumb'. It seemed old fashioned. But Alexis had written the script; she was just reading it out. She almost broke character and sighed.

The real science would happen off-camera. Ever since Neil Armstrong had stepped down onto the lunar surface, maybe even earlier, when Sputnik beeped its way around the world, space exploration had been as much a PR event as anything else; as much for the public as for the scientists.

And that, she was half-convinced, was why the pair of them were there, rather than just a shipload of intelligent drones. And why it was her on the cargo deck and not the camera-shy, stutter-prone Alexis.

Even though this all meant a lot more to him than to her. He was the exo-biologist, the true scientist. She was merely a Mission Commander with an obsolete PhD, an expert on orbiter and descent vehicles; not anything like as familiar with the array of autonomous subs and floating devices, nor the complex science instruments they carried.

All with one basic aim: to discover extra-terrestrial life.

She let him guide her through the systems checks via the helmet display, before each drone vanished off the back of the surface module. The lack of land on Galena had posed a problem: how to return to the waiting orbiter? On-board mission computers had crunched the numbers even before they'd separated from the *Jules Verne*. While a sea launch from a floating pontoon had been considered, eventually the AI had judged that the largest and least active of the volcanic islands was the simpler option. Their mission would therefore be split into two: a sea landing and a land launch, with the marine, exploratory section a slow meander towards the islands. Any investigations not directly on their path would have to be done remotely, by drone.

That this would only cover a fraction of the water-world's surface did not, it seem, matter. If there was life, it should have no need to hide. Conditions were, except for the lack of solar penetration through the thick greenhouse gases, benign.

As the last drone disappeared into the depths, she turned to the camera once more. "And that's all of them away. Time to re-join Dr Alexis Karlinksy and check the data coming in."

It was a relief to strip out of the cumbersome suit, to scratch her nose, to once again breathe naturally in the airtight confines of the cabin. She poured herself an orange juice – reconstituted from oranges grown 180 trillion miles away – and sat in the scoop chair next to the taciturn Mission Specialist.

"What are we looking for?" she asked, as Alexis carefully plugged the sample vials she'd collected into the gleaming banks of autoclaves and spectrographs.

"Non-equilibrium," he replied, before taking pity on her.

"On Earth," he explained, "the atmosphere is 21% oxygen. Left to its own, non-biological devices, this would be closer to zero: oxygen is highly reactive, which is why we and other animals use it for energy transport. So if I heat Earth's atmosphere, it reacts; with the rocks, or even with itself. That's not an equilibrium."

"Galena has only trace levels of free-oxygen," Juliet pointed out, but Alexis just shrugged.

"We can't assume alien life is Earth-like. Oxygen is not the only solution to the energy-transport problem. Earth's earliest life forms didn't use it, it's largely a side-effect of photosynthesis and that was stage 2 of life on Earth, if you will. But even the earlier life forms created a chemical imbalance; the ratio of complex to simple structures. It's not far off our broadest definition of life: something that is able to decrease its entropy at the expense of the environment. And that localised order should lead to energy gradients between atmosphere and sea. Even if we don't know what biomarkers to look for, we can always look for non-equilibrium."

It was easily the longest conversation they'd had over the twenty-four years of this interstellar mission. She was the only person he could talk to when Earth had relayed the death of his mother, and then that of his sister from cancer a short while later, both already old news back on Earth. They'd lived cooped up in a space little bigger than a studio apartment for longer than most marriages lasted and on board the *Nautilus* they were sharing a space even smaller. But it wasn't until the first samples had been collected that he'd come alive. That they weren't initially promising didn't seem important; the challenge of detecting alien life – assuming it didn't leap out of the water and try to bite you – was never going to be easy.

"How long until there are any results?" Juliet asked.

"A couple of hours, maybe longer."

"Great," she said with genuine enthusiasm, "Time for a nap."

Alexis grunted, back to his usual, uncommunicative self. Odd how little you can know someone, even after you've spent half your life with them.

When the ISA had told her she'd been shortlisted for the mission, told her that it was going to be a crew of two and not the six that had been originally planned, she'd sat there, emotions running high. "And the other crew member?" she'd eventually asked. "The specialist? Man, or woman?"

"Does it matter?" they'd replied.

She shook her head, carefully. This too was part of the evaluation, the long selection process. She'd imagined, with six, that some of the crew might inevitably pair off. But with only two...

Was that good, or bad, for the mission? For her?

"No," she replied. "Not really. Just curious."

"So, what next?" she asked, a week of negative results later.

Alexis chewed his lip, at the ragged surface that left traces of blood like a partial lipstick print on every plastic cup. "The depths of Earth's oceans are somewhat like a desert," he said. "Sterile, lacking the nutrients of coastal waters. Perhaps as we head towards the islands?"

"The water out here is no good for life?"

"Well, no," he admitted. "As far as I can tell, it's got everything Earth life needs. Anaerobic life, anyway. Plenty of dissolved carbon, steady temperatures, water, of course, and even basic amino acids."

"So, why?"

"I don't know!" he spluttered. "Earth organisms would colonise these waters in an instant. Maybe Galenian life needs something else."

"Or maybe it just hasn't got round to starting yet?" Juliet suggested.

He pinched at the bridge of his nose, unsettling the spectacles whose lenses had, over the two decades, grown slowly thicker; the *Jules Verne* too far from an optometrist's lab for a more elegant, permanent solution.

"As far as I can tell, these oceans have been around for a few billion years already. It didn't take a far more volatile Earth anything like that long."

"Still nothing?" Juliet asked. The peaks of the volcanoes broke the monotony of the grey horizon, a mere five kilometres away now.

"No," Alexis admitted, his voice sullen. "No fish, no plankton, no bacteria. And no bloody energy gradients!"

She looked up in surprise and saw, for the first time, the bags beneath the eyes, the lines etched onto his forehead. Had he not been sleeping? Or eating: he looked even thinner than normal, unhealthily so. She reminded herself to check the biosensors woven into the fabric of his jumpsuits.

He smelt as well. Surrounded by water they might be, but the cramped *Nautilus* had no shower and it appeared to be only her who had been using the daily wipes.

Odd to think that despite the medicals, the UV skin sterilization, and the exhaustive departure quarantine, their bodies were still teeming with microbes, their biomes – the vast array of microorganisms that colonised them inside and out – far outnumbering their human cells.

This was why they had to be so careful on each EVA: to prevent Earth life from escaping, contaminating, colonising. The risk to the pair of them far outweighed by the risk to a whole planet.

Sterile though it appeared.

"Your hypothesis, Doctor?" she said, keeping her tone light.

He thought for a moment, before replying. "If we assume that, due to the constant cloud cover, there isn't enough light for photosynthesis, for this planet's version of phytoplankton, then we're left looking for other energy sources."

"Such as?"

"Hydrothermal vents." His back straightened, leaving him sitting upright and re-energised. "With geothermal activity increasing as we approach the volcanic hot spot, I'm going to reprogram the subs to search there."

Juliet didn't bother to point out that those subs had other work to do; siphoning and filtering water for low levels of tritium, fuel for the orbiting mother ship. There would be time enough for that. It wasn't like they were on any real schedule, or rather, not one that was particularly pressing. They'd need to return before their food supplies ran out, but that was months away. And they were burning through their limited oxygen tanks faster than originally planned – the *Nautilus*'s solar arrays were struggling to get enough sunlight to split water. But another week or two would make no real difference and they'd not get this opportunity again anytime soon.

Perhaps never.

The stack looked like a giant, clumsy, clay sculpture; the first efforts of a child artist. The edges warped the water as it bled geothermal heat and, from the top, a dense, sooty cloud emerged, billowing upwards. As the robotic-sub zoomed in for a closer look, delicate structures emerged on the surface of the natural chimney, spikes and ripples and little frills.

Juliet pointed excitedly. "Look, Alexis, is that coral?"

Alexis scowled. "Far too hot. Probably just crystalline deposits. We'll take samples."

Despite the fact that it had been his idea to investigate these black smokers, he already seemed resigned to failure, quickly coming up with excuses why everything they saw wasn't a sign of life.

Whereas the very height of the deposits should have inspired hope. It meant that conditions here had been stable for countless years. Stable and offering everything chemo-synthetic life could need.

She streamed pictures taken of Earth's hydrothermal vents for comparison. Pale shrimp and odd tube-like worms thronged the waters. These weren't so very alien; it was what they lived on, the microscopic, sulphur oxidising proteobacteria that were the true oddity, finding a way to live without sunlight, finding other methods of freeing oxygen, or even avoiding it altogether in places where hydrogen gas was available.

One image, in grainy infrared, showed dense clusters of ghostly crabs, their number testament to the rich volcanic waters.

There was nothing like that on the Galena stacks, nothing so very obvious. But still, samples would be returned, passed through the banks of scientific tests, such that any life, on whatever scale, would not remain hidden long.

Alexis banged his fist on the small table in frustration.

Nothing. Galena might indeed be calm, but it was also, it appeared, dead.

Juliet had never expected little green men. She supposed that not finding simple aquatic organisms had been a bit of a surprise.

For Alexis, the disappointment was crushing. If life was not common, if it couldn't get a foothold in this most placid of planets, then what the hell was the point of an exo-biologist anyway? What was the point of sending them on this half-century, risk prone, cramped and uncomfortable round trip? What was the point of their *lives*?

"It's the Drake equation," he said, grabbing a pen as she looked mutely on. She'd heard of it, of course; what scientist hadn't, especially an astronaut? Perhaps she couldn't have written it down on the wipe-clean surface as Alexis did, but she knew what it stood for, this equation for predicting intelligent life in the Universe.

But Alexis had hardly spoken since they'd left the black smokers behind and she was happy enough to see him animated once again. For that, she'd gladly sit through another lecture.

"It's just a series of fudge factors, really," he muttered as he scrawled. "Number of stars, fraction of stars with planets, supportability of life on those planets, etc, etc."

Juliet shrugged. "There are plenty of stars and plenty of planets."

"Right!" he agreed, "And here we are, floating on one perfect for life. The factors multiply, so, although we have an admittedly small sample set, we can safely assume that these first three factors aren't overly stringent."

He grimaced, stabbing the point of the pen at the fourth factor. "The fraction that go on to develop life is the sticking point. Again, we don't have a big sample, but fundamentally we thought this factor would be fairly high."

"It still might be," she suggested.

"True. One negative doesn't change that. But it would have been a lot higher if we'd found *anything* here."

"We'll send out other –"

"Will we?" he nailed her with a stare that had her fighting to sit still, suddenly uncomfortable in such a confined space. "*Really*? All it would have taken was one tiny alien microbe and mankind would have said, ah well, not quite this time, better luck next, let's keep looking. But if the Universe is barren..."

"We can't know that."

"No. But there are plenty of people who believe the Earth is *special* and *unique*." Spittle flecked the table as he spat the words out. "That the number of planets bearing life, intelligent or otherwise, is exactly one. This would have shut them up for good."

"They'd have just moved their goalposts..." Juliet started to say, thinking how some still argued over Darwin, over the geological age of the Earth, over global warming, but Alexis wasn't finished.

"Don't you see? It's not just that this mission is a failure. It's that the whole project is; the whole SETI idea. We kept on looking in the solar system, moving slowly out from the supposed fossil record on Mars to the cold oceans beneath the icy surface of Jupiter's moons. And everywhere we looked, we found nothing.

"So we ventured further away, at huge cost and investment, a project that will outlive most everyone involved in it, the biggest, riskiest of science experiments ever. And – oh look. We found *nothing*."

He stabbed at the last part of the equation. "Do you know what the 'L' stands for, Juliet?"

She knew, but kept quiet.

"'L' is the length of time that intelligent civilizations last. 'L' is how long we last. Have you ever given any thought that by the time we get back our L might already be over?"

She blinked, surprised. She hadn't. Why would she? Sometimes she'd thought of the people who would be dead by the time she returned, assuming she ever did. Parents and teachers, maybe even some of her contemporaries in the astronaut program. Travelling at the Lorentz Limit for much of their journey, time was slowed down such that their 50-year mission would actually take 60 years, back on Earth. At the theoretical maximum of their engines, their top speed, the time it took them to travel a light year was exactly, precisely a year, even though to an observer on Earth it was a year and five extra months. It was questionable whether the time dilation was truly an advantage over the less positive effects of low gravity and limited medical facilities, never mind the cosmic radiation that even the *Jules Verne*'s shielding couldn't fully stop.

But to think that there might be nobody left when they returned, or maybe only survivors from some apocalyptic collapse... she shuddered. Why would Alexis even contemplate such things?

She shook her head, trying to chase away the dark thoughts.

"Seriously," Alexis said. "60 years is a long time."

The pen scrawled slowly under and then across the equation, moving faster, obliterating it, moving frenetically, worryingly. Juliet reached out a hand to stop it.

"There is another factor to L," she said, as calmly as she could, feeling her heart thud in her ears. "It's not strictly how long a civilization lasts. It's how long it broadcasts its existence for."

"So?" he scowled, but at least the manic black cloud of scribble had stopped.

"Well, think about it," Juliet said. "In the early days, we blasted out our radio and TV signals, the receivers inefficient, the transmissions necessarily powerful. But then we got better and the signals became quieter. And more numerous, less obvious what they were as we moved from analogue to digital to compressed and encrypted, the whole a jumble-like white noise to the uninitiated. Nowadays, if it weren't for the deep space network, could we tell from here that there is intelligent life on Earth?"

"You're nit-picking," he accused, "The difference is between intelligent life and detecting intelligent life. None of which alters the fact there's no bloody life here at all."

"Sure, and that's a disappointment." She nodded, soothingly "But we already knew, however these factors multiplied together, that we weren't going to find a space-faring race here; they were never likely to be our neighbours. And okay, the religious nuts back on Earth might be all smug and I-told-you-so's. But the mission has far from failed and it hasn't proved that life doesn't exist elsewhere. Heck, it hasn't proved there isn't life here, hiding."

Alexis snorted, but let go of the pen. Without its angular lid it rolled back and forth across the table under the gentle swell they'd long gotten used to, until it fell under the spell of the magnetic holder clipped to one edge.

"Like you said yourself," she continued, chancing a small smile, "we're sat on an inhabitable planet. Which means those first factors have to rank way higher than anyone thought they did before. If the 'life gets started' factor is a bit lower, so what? Overall, isn't it enough that there's still a high probability of life out there?"

He sat, staring at a spot somewhere near his feet for a long silent minute. And then he abruptly pushed himself back from the table. "No, it's not," he said, face contorted, "Not for me."

The last of the sample probes had returned to the cargo deck, had been fished out or had clambered onboard themselves, to be divested of their precious vials of water and scoops of sediment and chunks of rock. One device had, these last three months, been trailing a fine, electrostatically charged mesh through thousands of gallons of water – the mesh now wrapped up and sealed back into the canister from which it had emerged, for analysis back on Earth. The destination for many of their samples; those that hadn't already been tested and found wanting. There was still hope, Juliet thought, still a chance that their mini-floating laboratory had missed something, though it would be another twenty-five years before the samples would be returned to the ultra-safe off-planet bio-containment labs, the risks reversed: the Earth at threat from any alien life forms.

Though that threat did appear to be vanishingly small.

The currents were different here, close to the largest island. Sharper, less predictable, the steady winds snagging at the land and sending little gusts their way. For the first time Juliet felt vaguely seasick.

Once they were on the island, most of the science would come to an end. Their priority would be preparing for their departure, for their return to the *Jules Verne*, and to Earth. She couldn't wait. The gloomy skies and Alexis's dark moods had cast a pall over the latter stages of their mission.

Hopefully, back on the voyage home, he would once again spend his time with his textbooks, with his chess games and classic Russian cinema. With killing time on a decades-long journey.

With a start, she realised she'd been staring into middle distance as the video diary rolled. She'd have to edit the lengthy pause out, before it was sent. Earth wouldn't be best pleased to process a whole lot of her doing and saying nothing.

"The probes and this floating deck will remain on Galena," she said, "Their jobs done, too heavy to be returned. All but the detachable cockpit of the *Nautilus* will burn up in the atmosphere. Calculations show it will reach 3000 degrees, hot enough to sterilise it, though, to be extra safe, we'll be lifting our biological waste into high orbit, where it will remain, dried and frozen, to baffle future space missions."

She almost giggled. It was an odd, funny thought. Her own: Alexis no longer wrote the scripts. "What's the point?" he'd cried out, "What's the goddamn point?"

"There are a handful more probes to collect from the island itself, though again, only the samples, along with Alexis and I, will return to the *Jules Verne*, and to Earth.

She queued up a choreographed zoom. In the little helmet display that showed what the cameras saw, the raw volcanic peak of the nearby island swelled to fill the screen.

"It will feel odd to stand on solid ground again, I suspect, but we won't linger for long. We have about a week's supplies left, cutting it kind of fine."

Alexis's fault. He'd been determined to look under every last rock. It was only in the last couple of days that he'd given up and they'd made the final approach to the island.

The camera re-centred on her.

"One week, until we leave the surface of Galena, two, until we fire up the Verne's engines and start the journey back."

She thought of her discussions with Alexis. She'd long gone off-script, the key points forgotten, but it felt like she needed to say more. Some desperate entreaty to continue this epic mission of space exploration; a message for mankind not to turn their backs on the rest of the Universe.

"There are plenty of differences between Galena and Earth," she said. "A sizeable moon, for one. Here there are no tides that might serve to mix up the liquids. Obviously, there's less landmass and maybe the interactions between sea and land are just as important. These could be enough to make a vital difference. Or, maybe, more likely, we're still not looking for the right things. Maybe there is life and careful study of the data and samples we've collected will reveal it to the scientists back home.

"What I will claim is that Galena has delivered far beyond our expectations," she waved a hand. "If this is typical of Goldilocks planets then life is surely far more abundant in the Universe than we ever imagined. Even if it has chosen to hide itself well, on this watery world."

"Nice speech," Alexis said, with a flat tone that made it difficult to know if he meant it. Juliet flinched, massaging a cramp in her neck. Stress, she supposed. Or maybe she was just getting old, her body punished by this period of normal gravity and by the unaccustomed work of hauling probes out of the water.

"You liked it?" She'd been wondering whether she ought to re-record it, if it was upbeat enough, though an EVA just for that purpose would never be sanctioned.

He sneered and still she wasn't sure. "You didn't mention all the other differences; that this planet has a thicker, wetter atmosphere than Earth ever had, even in the days of primordial soup and fog."

"Well, no—"

"And you didn't mention panspermia – the idea that life on Earth was not started there natively, that it evolved on a more benign early Mars, giving it much longer to get going, even if we've never found trace of it on the red planet. Sigma Draconis has no outer planets that might once have been in the Goldilocks zone, that might have started the process early, a cradle for life to begin."

"Which is why you should write the scripts..." she muttered, trailing off as she realised it was just likely to antagonise him.

"All I know, is what I've said before. Earth life would have a field day here, which is why we've had to be so careful not to contaminate." He waved a sample vial, handed her his tablet showing the analysis report.

She read it twice before she fully took it in.

"Life?" she spluttered. "Here? How? Where?"

He winced. "No, not here. Earth life."

"What?"

"I introduced a sample into a vial of Galenian water. Not enough to trigger the detectors, not at first. Not until it had sat there for a week. Gotten cosy in its new home."

Juliet frowned. She supposed it was an obvious experiment to try, though it also meant he'd broken half a dozen stringent bio-containment protocols.

"Where did you get the sample?"

He arched an eyebrow. "You probably don't want to know. Still, point proven. Earth life would thrive here. Whatever is missing, it isn't some obscure trace element, nor is there something inherently poisonous, fatal to life."

"Well, good," she said. "I guess that's good?"

Alexis didn't answer.

Juliet sighed. She ought to get to the bottom of this, but she was tired, and thirsty, and ached. And Alexis was too much like hard work. "I'm going to catch some sleep before we detach the floating dock and make landing," she said, yawning at the thought. "Not sure I could manage another long EVA without a rest. Wake me in a couple of hours?"

Juliet was still asleep when the alarms sounded. For a moment, she was back on Earth, in the early days of her astronaut training. On board a ship that had sprung a surprise emergency drill, waking in the small cot with the deafening sound bouncing off the enclosed walls, lights glowing red, struggling into a survival suit.

She staggered into the heart of the *Nautilus*. "Alexis?" she called out. "What the hell's happening?"

There was no sign of him. She ducked her head into his cot, the dense fug of his smell washed over her, but it was a cold, stale smell. He wasn't there and she guessed he hadn't been for a while.

"Ship?" she called out, reaching for a tablet, "Specify nature of alarm?"

"Incorrect docking bay detachment," the voice echoed as the alarm quietened. "Manual override activated."

The idiot! Alexis had obviously decided to do the separation himself and either he'd run into difficulties or had botched the job. She headed to the airlock to suit up.

The door refused to open.

227

Staring through the porthole window into the space where her suit hung she saw it flutter in the wind. The outer door was open. Christ! What was Alexis doing?

The outer door was open, and the floating dock was gone.

"Ship: External view," she ordered, and the tablet showed the faint glimmer of a shrouded dawn, a thin pale line between dark sea and dark sky.

"Ship: Pan left, locate docking bay."

She could close the outer airlock door herself. Close it, suit up, and then venture outside, equipped with rope, or floats. If she knew where Alexis and the cargo dock was.

The camera picked it up some twenty yards distant. Detached from the *Nautilus*, it looked like a flimsy theatre set, walls on only two sides, a marionette figure sat slumped on the stage's edge, legs dangling in the water.

She grabbed the mic that Alexis used when she was on her EVAs. "Alexis?"

She was met only by a faint echo from the airlock – from her suit. Alexis must be on a different channel. "Ship? Patch me in on all channels. And bring up Alexis's medi-data."

It was a relief to see it track his heartbeat; elevated, but nothing too unusual about that for an EVA gone wrong. Blood pressure and oxygen levels within normal levels.

"Alexis?"

The head rocked back; the visor turned to face the distant camera. "Juliet."

"Don't move," she warned. "I'm going to suit up and deploy a line to you."

"No," he said, getting clumsily to his feet, long legs unsteady in even this gentlest of swells. "I'm not coming back."

She almost laughed. How long did he think he could stay out there, sulking on the otherwise empty floating deck? And then she watched in horror as he reached up and removed his helmet, face sharp and angular, the mirror-like surfaces of his spectacles still turned her way.

For a moment, a time-defying pause, she imagined the sensors had been wrong all along, that the atmosphere of Galena was oxygen-rich and breathable, instead of a suffocating brew of carbon dioxide and water vapour.

And then his hands clawed towards his throat and his face contorted in anguish, before he toppled into the black, welcoming seas.

He quickly vanished into the depths, whether because of the weight of his breather tanks or because he was deliberately carrying something heavy hidden inside his suit, Juliet never knew.

Behind her, the console squawked in alarm as his heart stuttered, as his oxygen levels plummeted. A console flopped uselessly open to reveal the defibrillator, 'ready' light already flashing, waiting for a body that was twenty yards distant and sinking but might as well have been twenty miles away.

She slammed a fist into the tablet, driving it skittering from her hands, heard the unbreakable plasti-glass creak. If she'd suited up first, if she still had any active drones, if she'd argued more persuasively...

Would any of it have made a difference? She couldn't know for sure. But she had to believe it would.

As the engines pushed against the volcanic island, momentarily turning rocks back into lava, she looked out for a final time over the wide expanse of gloomy sea.

Then she turned back to the waiting, expectant, hungry eye of the recording camera. "This is Dr Juliet Slade in the return capsule of the *Nautilus*, leaving the surface of Galena, heading for rendezvous with the *Jules Verne*.

"I am returning alone. Mission specialist Alexis Karlinsky was lost at sea, during an emergency EVA."

It was a week since that fateful day, a week that had passed by in a haze, all decisions made by the orbiting *Jules Verne*, including the non-recovery of the cargo deck and Alexis's body. Somewhere out there they floated still.

She wondered whether her recording, her 'performance' would ever be seen. Perhaps back on Earth they'd run with a different story, maybe even the truth. Or the truth as they saw it: suicide.

She remembered what he'd said; how suited this world was for life, for Earth life, and wondered if, of the countless billions of bacteria in his body, some of them could survive without oxygen, without sunlight, without Alexis. If some of those would take the opportunity to colonise this fertile niche. There would be no competition; how quickly might they adapt to this new world?

She'd meant to say more, but what was there left to say? She reached over and, after a: "Signing off", shut down the camera.

Should anyone ever come this way and repeat the tests she and Alexis had done, would they find life? And would that spur those visitors on to explore further, to find new worlds, new life forms? Perhaps even to venture as far as a yellow dwarf star less than twenty light years distant?

Would they ever wonder how life on Galena got started? Could they work out it was because of a single man and his act of selfish – or selfless – desperation?

The start of a story that might run for billions of years.

One small step.

# Ab Initio

## Susan Boulton

*My name is Trent. I don't belong here; I should be back there with them. I did things I can't forget. I had my reasons: Martin said I had no choice, but he is wrong. I did. I got people killed. Silly, really, when you think the Bloat killed 99.5 per cent of the world… Or could it have been 100 per cent, and we all don't really exist? Just ghosts in our own private hell.*

**Ab Initio**. From the beginning. It's Latin. No, I don't know Latin. I have enough trouble with English. Just the phrase jumps out at me these days. Is what I am now doing a beginning, or the ending of something I had begun?

The what-ifs and maybes, beginnings and possible endings are roaming through my head now, keeping my brain from freezing. I wish trying to analyse the impossible would have the same effect on my nose. Damn, it is cold.

The mane of my horse is clogged with ice; each time the creature shakes its head I get peppered with ice barbs. The leather of my saddle is damp with half-melted snow. The rasp of my waterproofs on the thing sets my teeth on edge each time I slip. And I slip each time the beast steps forward. And each time I slip, I worry about the large cylinder strapped to my back. I should have let it be carried with the others. The proof. The salesman's samples that are the fruits of the journey. But I want it close.

Step, slip an inch forward. Step, slip an inch back. The muscles of my thighs are locked solid. I don't think I will be able to stand up for a week after this. As for what lies between the tops of my thighs, well, I would beat a brass monkey, that's for sure. The expression of freezing your balls off has again gained a personal meaning.

Whose crazy idea was it to ride? Mine, of course. Petrol is way too precious. We will need it when we go back for the rest. If we go back. Personally, I don't give a damn. I have what I wanted. Martin, of course, wants it too. He wants to go find the other places as well. Martin is idealistic. He believes in a bright future.

How bloody much farther?

Then I hear it, faintly in the snow-wrapped evening. Ahead of us, we few foolish idiots out for a little winter ride across the Yorkshire Moors. The gentle "hiss-whump, hiss-whump." The wind turbines. In my mind I can see the tall, white towers, the outlines obscured by the falling snow. The blades, turning, hiss, whump. The chill air cut, the power generated, and there the soft glow of home.

Home: a village, a straggling collection of houses that nestle in a valley, where the moor fades out to stone-flanked fields. How long have I called this place home? Not sure; the years move differently now.

"Shit," Eddie swears. His stocky mount loses its footing, as we pick our way through the wind turbines. I glance up, struggling to see these tall sentinels. These symbols of the caring, tree-hugging, early twenty-first–century technology. They were among the first to be up here as a "showcase," to show the power industry was interested in alternatives to oil, coal, gas, and nuclear power. Cursed at the time by many for spoiling the view. Blessed by three generations of villagers since. Things kept the lights on for fifty years when they had gone out for good nearly everywhere else.

"Oh fuck!" I double up, my face nearly in the mane of my horse as it begins the descent to the village. Funny how a single thought can be transmuted to physical pain. Fifty years. I feel like I have been punched in the gut.

"Trent, you okay…?" Sally's knee is knocking mine; her hand is on mine. Leather on leather, the gloves not allowing the warmth of her touch to reach my skin. I straighten up and try to smile at her through the veil of snow.

"Getting too damn old for this, Sal." I cough out the words. Watch my breath form into a small mist and rise towards the wind turbines.

"You're not old, you're barely eighty." Sally tightens her hold on my hands. She, like all her generation, has a different idea of time, life and its possibilities.

"You might not have a problem with that; I do. I need a drink, Sal." I can't quite see her eyes, but know they are narrowed. Sal does not approve of my use of booze to ease the memories. I wonder what she would think if I added I'm dying for a fag.

Our group of intrepid winter-adventuring fools slip and slide down onto the scant remains of the asphalt road. Tarmac, like everything, needs to be cared for. The length leading to the village has had fifty years of not bothering. The drifting snow makes the footing even more hazardous for our mounts, and the string of pack ponies.

I straighten in my saddle and glance back at the bobbing, bouncing mounds on the animals' backs. Thank God for plastic sheeting. Half of what we had found would have been ruined by the weather before we could have reached Harrogate. The last forever nightmare of the eco-warrior is now the protector of the past.

The thought sets me laughing. Sally glares at me through the snow. It is getting heavier. The warm bobs of light that outlined the village are getting blurred. Eddie curses again, and kicks his mount on towards the ditch.

"Ought to fill that in," I say, as I watch the shadowy shape of Eddie swing down from his horse, this side of the ditch. He kneels down, his shape half vanishing in the snow. He opens up a manhole cover, swearing again as the cold metal nearly hits his foot.

"People feel safe with it," Sally says, and signals for the other two with us to dismount and get ready to lead the pack ponies over the drawbridge once it is lowered. She slips from her saddle, and stands watching as Eddie cranks the old field telephone in the hole and swears again, telling the person at the other end to hurry up.

"Didn't your mother teach you any other words, Eddie?" I remark from my position still astride my horse. Be damned if I was getting down. Everyone has to walk in or out of the village. Easier targets, Martin had said. Martin is the founding father of this place. Twice the man I am, a saint, and a bigger fool – sorry, idealist – than any I have ever met, before or after the Bloat. He has embraced the changes in the world, whereas I...

Martin, with four others, had dug out the ditch, some twelve-foot-wide and fifteen deep. They had used the abandoned JCB digger from the road works in the village, and a couple of farm tractors. Piled the dirt on the inside edge and topped it with a few rows of razor wire. Told me later he had felt like Mad Max that summer, preparing to protect his little bit of surviving civilisation from the hordes of desperate desperados in their homemade tanks.

Thing was, the only folk that appeared from time to time were half-starved individuals that had, like the fifty-odd villagers, survived both stages of the Bloat. In fact, there was enough military hardware lying around to make the ditch and wire useless, if someone had really wanted in.

Forty original survivors in one spot. Hard to believe, isn't it? Genetics? I like to think so. Forty out of a pre-Bloat population of what, a couple of thousand? Not that that percentage survived in any of the big cities, I swear it, or if they did, they did not last long in the horror years. I would guess that the present population of the UK is roughly 975,000 or maybe a million, and there is what, over three hundred here in one spot, pretty impressive. And every one of them bright-eyed by the future in front of them. The rumble of the drawbridge cuts through my thoughts, and I kick my mount on. The beast, sensing its stable, snorts and breaks into a stumbling trot.

I leave my horse in front of the stables, the converted row of garages behind the old council houses on Briar Way. Let the others deal with it. Age does have a few perks. I stumble my way towards my quarters, cursing the fact that they would be cold. Power was for lighting, and other necessary items, but not for heating houses, least not those on the outskirts of the village.

Perverse? Well, I like living alone. Don't like to see myself reflected in the eyes of the "younger generations." I could have a room in any of the houses. Martin is always nagging me to move in closer. I think he is afraid I will be found choked to death on my own vomit, or hanging from a beam in my cottage.

You see, he worries. Good reason, too. I, more than any other of the survivors here, find it hard to come to terms with what the Bloat took away and gave. Maybe because of what I did in the name of preserving the past.

For Sally's generation it is "normal," this strange blend of bits and pieces of technology, this existence in the shadow of the Bloat, and the prospect that they will live, how long? That's the rub, isn't it? No one knows yet. But they see it as a wonder unfolding before them. So much to see, so much to do, and plenty of time to do both in.

I stamp my feet on my doorstep, trying to regain some circulation. Push the door open and… there is a glow of a newly lit fire in the hearth of my living room. Was a figure sitting in one of the winged chairs?

"Welcome home, Trent."

"Bugger off, Martin." I slam the door.

He chuckles, and switches on the small lamp on the table by the arm of the chair. I ignore him and pull out the plastic-wrapped tube I have carried on my back since York, and place it carefully against the wall. I strip off my waterproofs and boots, leaving them in a wet puddle, as I go upstairs to find some dry socks. I sit on the top step, pushing my cold feet into a mismatched pair of woollen ones. Martin stands at the bottom, a glass of something in his hand. He swirls the liquid and takes a sip.

"Hell, is that my single malt?"

"Not bad," Martin replies, as his smile widens.

"You are a sod." I stand and come down to him. We are of a height, both of us an inch short of six foot. Martin was forty-five when the Bloat began in 2020, nearly fifty when the full effects of it began to dawn on the remains of humanity. He is what, a hundred? And looks not a day older than he did when he came to after the Recurrence, as it was – and still is – called. The second bout of Bloat, or rather the second stage of the illness that took the one thing that had driven humanity to create much of what we have brought home with us.

Me, I am nearly eighty, going on thirty.

"Sal give you a hard time?" Martin asks, as he moves back into my living room.

"Pain in the arse," I mumble, and make for the bottle of Glenmorangie. The pale golden liquid shimmers, as I pour it into a glass. The liquid had been fifteen years old when they put it in this bottle. Another fifty hadn't harmed it. I take a sip. I want to guzzle it. Martin knew it. That is why he had pulled the Glenmorangie out of my store; he knew I wouldn't waste it to get drunk.

"That's my granddaughter." Martin chuckles, and sits again by the spitting fire.

"That's the problem. She is your granddaughter."

Martin leans forward and swirls the liquid in the glass. "Age doesn't mean the same thing now."

"It does to me," I snap, and against my better judgment and regret, empty the glass in one gulp.

My hand shakes as I pour another drink. The final part of the ride over the moors has exhausted me. No, the memories have.

I had promised Martin I would take a party there one day. A day when we had a place suitable for storage. He felt it was important to preserve the past. The whole community did: it was part of their plans for the future.

We have the perfect place now.

So no more excuses, I had to go.

"You have some explaining to do," Sally says sharply as she comes into the room.

I lift my glass full of golden liquid and look at the young woman through the soft swirls. She is just over five feet, curved in all the right places, strong of limb. No one here has any excess fat: the hard work of surviving takes care of that. As for her face, she is nothing special. If I were cruel – no, scrap that, I am cruel. Sally saw part of that cruelty in York.

Where was I… yes, Sally. God, take her piece by piece, it is hard to find anything attractive. Yet put them all together, with that mind of hers shining in her grey eyes, hell, easy to love, too easy. Oh, don't get the impression I am being noble or anything, I would have no objection if it was just, well, just. But not with Sally; I had watched her grow up, felt her become part of my life. I couldn't. I fell back on the "age" thing. I cannot bear the fact that if I allowed her in, became the husband, father of her children, everything she has set her course to do with me, I would destroy her.

My past will destroy her. It's out there, still alive, still hunting me. My years here have been a respite, nothing more. I am still bound by the one thing humanity had lost. I tear my mind from the past and say jokingly, "Sorry, next time I will unsaddle my horse."

"That's not what I meant." She begins to strip off her own waterproofs. A small lump of snow falls on her left cheek and melts, running like silver tears. I lower my glass and look back at Martin.

"I know, it's what we found at York, but it is not important."

"Not important! You must know what happened there? The first doors were locked, barred, then the airtight doors, but between them, the passage, you must have known what was waiting for us."

"Pray do tell," Martin says, softly.

I put my glass to my lips and drink, spilling the single malt down my chin as I gulp it.

Sally glares at me and goes over to her grandfather. She goes down on her knees and takes his right hand in hers. "It was…" She looks once more at me, then sighs. The sound shakes her body, and she begins to speak – flatly, no emotion, but the lack of it, the forcing her voice to be toneless, makes my stomach roll.

"Trent had said York was bad. I didn't think it would be worse than Harrogate or Skipton, but it was. A maze of half-burned buildings, roads so clogged that… At one point I didn't think we would get to the Minster. But Trent knew a way, didn't you?" She looks round at me. I don't answer, just refill my glass and move to the other chair by the fire. I slump down in it, my legs out, head back, and my mind fifty years in the past.

The Bloat: where did it start? I don't know. I don't think anyone knew. Hell, those of us that survived have talked the subject to death for fifty years. It was a virus; well, they thought it was. The authorities never really let on. Some said that was because they had created it. Personally I believe they didn't really know. Look at AIDS – how long did it take for that to become known. CJD. Ditto. And all the hue and cry over both, and the Bloat was waiting in the wings.

Do you know what your lymph system does? It is the filter system for your body, a big part of your immune system. It is made up of vessels and nodes which, with the aid of your muscles, pump the lymph round. It clears out your system and fights disease. A healthy lymph system means you are healthy, you don't get sick very often, and you can spend your life making a prat of yourself.

A damaged lymph system, one that is not pumping right, means that the lymph is squeezed into the surrounding tissue, and with it, all the crap that it is supposed to remove. So your leg or arm or body swells. The limb becomes heavy, painful, red, swollen. Then it's feeding time for any other virus. You are one big lunch box for septicaemia, gangrene, and all their other little friends.

So imagine one day your lymph system saying, "Bugger this." And just stops working. Now with a damaged lymph system it takes a while for your limbs to swell. With the Bloat it was twelve hours, and you were like the Michelin man. The virus had shut things down for its own purpose. Within the next twenty-four hours you were either dead, or slowly, weakly, realising you were still alive, and your lymph system had, for the same unknown reason, started again.

Now it took two years for the Bloat to munch its way round the world, and it left half of the world's population dead. That's worse than the Black Death in the thirteenth century: Europe lost a third of its population then, but it survived. So did we, we thought. Things were a mess, but you still had power, TV, and the internet, so all was well with the world.

The crunch came about three years after the outbreak. Seems it took three years for the virus to finish its work. Nice little job it did, rebuilding your lymph system, rebuilding you. Steve Austin the bionic man had nothing on us. You see, the lymph aids the body to repair itself, and fights infection. So what if a little bug decided to redesign the cell structure, and then the cell structure slowly redesigns the host.

Why? Well, my guess is the virus wants to live, needs to, like the rest of us: maybe it is a symbiotic virus; it needs a living host to live happily in for ever and ever.

One chap I came across had this theory of spontaneous evolution: that a mutation can occur suddenly and change a species overnight. He was convinced that was what had happened. We were the next phase in human evolution, and it had been adapt or die. The old survival of the fittest. Well when you look at it, it holds as much water as the grey aliens doing it by putting genes into us that didn't belong, the X-Files conspiracy, and what was that, oh yes, government created little tiny bits of nanotechnology that had gotten loose. Nah... too much Michael Crichton and whisky.

What was it; oh yes... the Recurrence. The Bloat virus, or little bit of micro mechanics, the alien gene whatever, had spent a couple of years reprogramming you. So what else, like any other computer, even one of flesh, you had to be shut down, and rebooted. Big problem: most didn't restart.

Re-start.

Re-boot.

The hitch in the breath.

The pounding of the heart.

The screaming of the mind.

"You knew!" Sally's accusation cuts through my brittle memories. I bring my head up and look at the young woman on her knees before her grandfather. Her face makes my heart ache. Damn her. I don't want to explain. Tell what I had done.

Martin is sitting there, one eyebrow raised, a small smile on his face as he speaks. "What did you find?"

Sally looks at me, capturing my eyes with hers. "Bodies."

"It was the middle of York, Sal. Folk just dropped down and never got up again; bound to be bones lying around," I mumble.

"These were nailed to the wall in the passage: three of them, what remained of them. Others, God knows how many, piled against the door of the safe room like a barrier."

"Ouch, you mean nailed as in hammered? Hard work, that," Martin says.

"Actually I used a nail gun," I say.

"They were dead from the second stage, right? You did it as a warning, mimicked the gangs that roamed the cities in the horror days?" Martin says through Sal's gasp. "Make it look as if it was a no-go area?"

"Partly; they were dead, the ones piled against the door right enough, but the ones on the wall, nailed, well, they were alive, or at least not quite dead, when I did it."

"You killed them?" The horror in Sally's voice tears into me.

"I had no choice, the bastards would have done me in the moment I opened that place up, that last time."

"Why?"

"Why, Sal? You saw what was in there."

"Art, pictures, sculptures, computer discs, jewellery, everything we need to preserve from before the Bloat."

"Exactly: a fortune, neatly labelled and stored away in a sealed vault."

Martin shakes his head. "What did they think they could do with it? Set themselves up as kings?"

"Oh, Conner, that was his name, had a bright idea, convinced others of it too. He believed the Bloat was limited to the UK."

Sally shifts closer to me, her hand reaching out and touching my knee. Don't, Sal, please... my mind whispers. "He had contacts, he said, in the US; they wanted the contents of the vault. You know it took me and…" I let the words fall away, and I think on the rolled-up picture in its container in the hall of my home, here.

I can remember it so clearly the first time I saw it as I prepared to pack it away for preservation. It was the early summer after the Recurrence began in earnest. Hell was open and we, the world, had been tipped in. Martin was thinking about digging his trench, and I was trying to save the beauty that had been put on canvas. It was my calling. Well, actually, it was a last-ditch attempt by the ragtag that was the government to save something for the future. I was one of a motley group of thieves going from art gallery to stately home, loading up items and taking them to "safe places."

Back to the picture. I stood in the Fitzwilliam Museum in Cambridge, fifty years ago, looking at it, and I began to laugh. The whole cosmic joke of the Bloat dawned on me, as I helped lift Salvator Rosa's *Human Frailty* from the wall. Art historians waxed lyrical about the seventeenth-century symbolism with regards to birth, death and everything in between contained in the picture, but for me it was, and still is, the hand on the child's arm. Death in winged skeletal form, taking possession. Not removing the child from its mother's lap, no, just the lightest of touch is enough.

I still am laughing inside.

The picture is us. The past us. The part that the Bloat has taken from us. Something those born after it will never know. Illness no longer exists. Oh, you get a mild case of the Bloat when you hit puberty, and that is it. Barring accidents or, in the case of those I pinned to the wall in York, murder. Humanity has lost the very thing that drove it to produce the artefacts Martin wanted to save. Humanity is no longer frail. It no longer fears the very thing the artist strove to show in his painting. The very thing that drives me to drink. The loss of what has made us so human, our frailty.

I look at Martin, then at Sally. Her expression has softened. Have I been granted absolution? Has she seen my frailty? She reaches up and gently touches my face, and yes, maybe she has. And maybe she understands.

# Ghosts

## Emma Levin

The second ghost I met called himself Pedro Sinclair. He lived under a flyover between Junction 1 of the North Circular, and the office supplies wholesaler at Staples Corner. He had built himself a home of scaffolding and tarpaulin which cast geometric shadows in the setting sun. He welcomed us and offered us tea, from a pot of water suspended above a small fire by a tatty school tie.

I explained that we were making a documentary. He was happy to talk on camera.

*Ghost (Noun. Informal):*
*A person whose central records have been deleted, rendering them unable to live in civilized society. They cannot interact with systems – automatic doors won't open for them, public transport will not stop for them, and without active credit chips they cannot pay or be paid. Ghosts do not exist.*

He spoke for three hours, without pause. The cameraman had to change batteries twice. Most ghosts lived in packs, he said. Clustered around a source of food and warmth – near recycling plants, food banks, or large and wasteful supermarkets. Staff would notice rustling in the night, disappearing stock, and things not being quite where they left them. But it was always dismissed as foxes, or superstition. He spoke of the things that he missed. The things that he craved. He spoke of murder.

*Murder (Noun. Informal):*
*The act of removing someone's name from the central database. It is suggested that there are central records employees who will commit this act for the right price. These are unsubstantiated rumours. There is no such thing as murder. There is no such thing as ghosts.*

As the traffic died down, he began to get philosophical. "I'm one of the lucky ones," he said. "I know who did this to me." His girlfriend, ex-girlfriend, had worked in records. He explained that it was worse for the others. They would lie awake at night. Wondering. "In a way, it's funny," he said. "In stories, ghosts haunt the living. In real life, the living haunt the ghosts. You find yourself asking 'Who?'

"Who could I possibly have hurt enough to do this to me?"

We showed the broadcaster a rough cut of the documentary. We wanted more funding. To interview more ghosts, and get a statement from the bureau of records. The boss nodded, and said that he'd call them for a statement himself.

When I got home, the doors of my apartment didn't open.

*Regret (Noun):*
*A feeling of sadness and desire to change past actions. A feeling common to all ghosts. Or it would be. If ghosts existed. Which they don't.*

# Concerning the Deprivation of Sleep

## Tim Major

As a science fiction writer, I'm used to extrapolating from events and trends, to conjure a vision of the future – in other words, to dream. I remember that dreams – *real* dreams – were a means of making sense of one's day, of reordering events and experiences, of extrapolating and inserting one's fears and ambitions. Wasn't that the case? I only wish there were somebody I could ask.

The apartment in which my young son and I live has always been noisy. The street outside and five storeys below is never silent; the traffic sighs and people come and go constantly, and light from the upgraded streetlamps reflects from the pale paving to make it glow like the surface of the moon. Above us live a couple who entertain both men and women at all hours of day and night. They call themselves therapists, but the noises suggest something more boisterous. On the other side of our living-room wall lives a woman who believes in the importance of overwhelming background noise as a means to rest. The thin wall reverberates with her recordings of crickets and café chatter. The apartment building on the other side of the street seems to bow towards ours as it rises. Even here, on the fifth floor of twelve, I sometimes feel that I might reach out and touch the fingertips of my opposite neighbours. On the seventh storey, residents of each building have strung a washing line across the street, tethering the apartment blocks. Yesterday as I was gazing out of the window, I saw a clothes peg drop, followed by a fluttering sock.

My son is rarely silent, either. He is two years and nine months old and a chatterer. But he sleeps well, and that counts for a lot, doesn't it? Parents need their downtime.

I sleep, too. I'm not so far gone that I've abandoned it entirely. I sleep for three hours each night. There are others suffering far worse.

How about you? I assume you accept your allocation and think no more of it. Most do, I suppose. I realise I never asked whether you lost your sleep in the first wave or later. I was among the first, which perhaps allows me to appreciate even a single hour nowadays, and perhaps even allows me to sustain myself on fewer hours than others might. However, I am alert enough to be self-aware; I know that my thoughts become muddled, sometimes.

When it began, I was in no state to extrapolate from my experience, to write. I was a science fiction writer only in the sense that my bibliography proved that I was once capable of it. I watched the news and read the reports and balked at the suggestion that it was my exposure to current affairs and online coverage that was responsible for my condition in the first place. And yet I gave up staring at the grey ceiling in my bedroom night after night and settled into the sofa, watching and reading, staring blankly at nothing and pawing at my stinging eyes.

Scientists were working on the problem, the reports said. The government was fully aware of the risk to the workforce. And always the subtext: it was our own fault and we had done this to ourselves.

Addled as I was, I could see the flaws in the logic. Our always-on lifestyles, our work ambitions, our levels of screen time, our anxieties, had all contributed to this inability to sleep. Fine. But there were no explanations – no *plausible* explanations – why there seemed no mechanism of switching back. Time away from work, at home or in subsidized relaxation and therapy camps, all achieved nothing. We could not sleep. We just could not go to sleep.

I'm certain you saw those same reports and rolled your eyes. Those metropolitan folks and their faddish anxieties, their mass hysterias. Fair enough.

Presumably you felt differently about it all only a month later, when those stories of hellish nights and dizzying days became a reality for you and for everyone else. None of us in that first wave of cases would have wished the same fate on others, but I swear I could hear the sigh of relief. Whether this was infectious as mass hysteria or viral outbreak, now that all of us were affected we were all in the same boat. Scientists were working on the problem, the reports said, more vociferously. The tone of the therapists changed abruptly from stern lecturers to despairing friends.

The joy we felt, when the answer was announced! The pride in our nation's ingenuity!

We oughtn't to have expected the government's approved solution to be in our best interests. We oughtn't to have expected a return to the status quo.

Perhaps you feel that things are very little changed. Six hours sleep per night is respectable enough, only twenty minutes shy of the national average before this cataclysm. And carrying a device in one's pocket is no burden; we all had our phones already, and SOMs are scarcely bulkier and perform all the same functions as well as the crucial new one. Planning one's day around a visit to a SOM station for a top-up is no more demanding than using cash machines a decade or so ago, and the operation of the device is child's play: a click of a button, an immediate blissful void, curtailed precisely at six hours. The government reports are widely available and clearly worded. We have sufficient allocation of sleep; we are healthy; the workforce is intact. If anything, we are more efficient and therefore happier. All of this is evidenced in the data.

We are all fine.

I know you have always lived straightforwardly. You are a pillar of the community and you are content. I'm happy for you. I'm positive that you have little experience of life outside of the norms, and I envy you.

And six hours sleep is enough.

But my son is unwell and these days I overthink things, I know I do.

When he was younger we worried a great deal, my wife and I. We watched our son in his cot and from the start, long before the plague, we recognised that his sleep was strange, his patterns irregular. We took him to specialists and they explained his condition, but no amount of knowledge gave us confidence during his periods of apnoea, during which time his breathing would become shallower and shallower until it halted for ten, twenty, even forty seconds at a time. It was unbearable to watch, but we watched all the same. We barely slept.

At the age of two, only months before the plague, my son's night-time spasms edged into daylight hours. The specialists told me that he was unharmed by his tics, that he will learn to overcome them or at least ignore them, but already I can see that he is conscious of his discomfort and already he is capable of swallowing it down, of putting on a brave face, and in the act of pushing away the pain he pushes it across to me.

This is a terrible admission: I'm grateful that my wife is dead. If my responsibilities extended to anyone in addition to my son, I wouldn't have the hours to spare.

I wonder if you even heard rumblings of a means to alter the provision of sleep. If you are happy with your six hours, and your husband is happy with his, then what could be the issue? Your skin is free of blemishes. Your days are free of that bleary, dazed sensation, that half-memory of sleep with all of the sense of disassociation and none of the sense of rest.

But the SOMs can be hacked. The provision can be altered.

This fact may come as a shock to you, but never fear. Nobody will rob you of sleep. Neither can you purchase additional credits at whim. Daily visits to a SOM station are as necessary as ever. Credits can be transferred, but only in one direction, from owner to recipient.

So.

When I finish work each evening my route takes me to the SOM station embedded in the ancient walls at Micklegate Bar. I join the queue and I receive my credits on both my SOM and my son's. But then shortly afterwards I join another queue that trails out of the open glass doors of the southernmost apartment block situated on what was once the Knavesmire racecourse. This apartment block has never been popular with the wealthy; each autumn and winter the plain floods and those queueing are forced to wear rubber boots or wade home with sodden feet. When I reach the head of the queue, I hand over both devices and I answer the question, "How many?"

To begin with, I transferred only a single hour. Anyone can manage on five hours of sleep, particularly those of us who have had to survive on less. I found a great deal of pleasure in my donation. Waking an hour earlier allowed me to observe my son's continued sleep. It was only then, once our patterns were no longer synchronised, that I understood that the blank dreamlessness induced by the SOM permitted a type of sleep that my son must never have experienced before. He was more still and more calm than he ever could be in his waking hours. I saw no sign of sleep apnoea, or hypnic jerks, or rapid eye movements. Some critics of government policy have described this as a theft; sleep now being only a necessary oblivion – a temporary death – rather than any kind of pleasurable experience. In my son's case it is a gift. And by granting him part of my allocation, I increase the gift and in return he grants me the delight of seeing him at peace.

Surely you can't blame me for having increased the number of hours I give.

As a science fiction writer lacking the ability to truly dream, I have other means of reordering the events and experiences of each day, of extrapolating and inserting my fears and ambitions: I write stories. I am at the beginning stages of writing a story about sleep.

The story will be set in the near future and it will tell the tale of two brothers. In childhood, they are similar, but a series of accidents and achievements results in one brother becoming very wealthy in adulthood and the other very poor. In my vision of the future, the system of sleep provision has become commercialised. Sleep credits are a commodity – the most valuable commodity, above money and time. The government stipend is an equal number of hours for each member of society, but the allocation for each citizen has dwindled, as the economy is not what it once was. Fortunately, competitive market forces have resulted in sleep credits being readily affordable. The rich and well-off are able to buy additional credits at will; top-ups are available at any shop counter and are transferred direct to devices worn under the skin. Correspondingly, the poor are able to sell their credits at will, at any shop counter, any drinking establishment, any hostel. The economy relies upon the flow of a finite number of credits; no more can be created and government ministers playact at having no means to do so.

The rich sleep well. Enjoying a surplus of sleep is the ultimate demonstration of wealth and the aspiration of everyone. Ten, twelve, fifteen hours of peaceful rest, then wake to address one's correspondence and investments. And this world of the future is a utopia. Where now there may be squalor and decay, in this future there are vast green parks, trees taller than most buildings, city-wide pedestrianised areas filled with quaint eateries and stalls. The weather is always fine. As in all these sorts of stories, it is the poor who provide this daily miracle, supplying and serving, scrubbing and suffering. And the economy is not what it once was, so while their payment is generous considering the simplicity of their tasks, it is barely sufficient for what they require to live. It is a mercy that there are always those hours of sleep, that state provision, at their disposal. They will never starve because they will always be able to sell their sleep.

And the story is a fable, of course. The poor brother and the rich brother, having not encountered one another during the entirety of their adult lives, will meet. I have yet to determine the circumstances of this meeting. Perhaps the poor brother will be serving at a function attended by the rich brother. Perhaps he will lug provisions to the manor house owned by the rich brother, not suspecting whose paved driveway he is walking upon. Perhaps the rich brother will accept a bet in which he is tasked with living among the poor for a single day, or perhaps he is doing so because he considers himself an observer of the downtrodden. But they will meet, and the brothers will recognise one another and will recognise the sequence of chances and coincidences that have carried them to their respective positions in society. And the poor brother will demand nothing, but he will recognise a potential buyer, and he will offer the rich brother an hour of his sleep. And the rich brother will refuse and instead he will insist that the poor brother instead accept sleep credits himself – though the gift will still result in the rich brother having a far more substantial allocation of sleep for the night – and even a bed in which to enjoy them.

They will both settle down to sleep in adjoining rooms. In the moments before triggering sleep, the rich brother will feel at peace because of his good deed. The poor brother will feel nothing but an anticipation of relief.

The poor brother has been without sleep for so long – perhaps an hour here or there, a couple of times a week, each month two consecutive hours tainted with the guilty sense of having stolen from his children – that only the first three hours represent genuine rest. After that point he begins to dream. Dreams have long been impossible – there is no extrapolation involved in that detail – and so perhaps this is a mania, a malfunction, something other than a dream. And yet the poor brother sees in vivid detail a world, long ago disappeared, in which everybody sleeps, everybody rests, everybody has control over their degree of oblivion, everybody dreams. The poor brother dreams that he is dreaming, way back then in that long-gone world, and this dream is of happiness; if there is any element tinged with ambivalence it is that he dreams of a brother who may be wealthier than he is, but no more happy and no less.

When the rich brother wakes, rested and content despite his mere eleven hours of sleep, he finds that his perceptions of the tasteful décor, the encouraging headlines, his smooth reflection, are no less detailed than when he would ordinarily allow himself eighteen hours of rest. He strolls happily to the door of the adjoining bedroom, knocks, but hears no reply. And for an awful moment he considers that the poor brother might be sleeping still, and that in order to do so he may have robbed the rich brother in the night. The rich brother roars with anger and forces open the door. Then he feels only a momentary stab of shame amidst his relief when he discovers the poor brother still tucked up in bed, eyes closed and not resting but dead.

These are the bare bones of the story. I will add in flourishes as I go; I still must entertain readers; the story must sell.

I will draft the story in full later tonight, and if you like I will send it to you when it is finished. I have already bathed my son and he has spent the last half an hour listening to a story on a portable speaker that he hugs to himself in his bed. Just a moment ago he pushed open the door of my study to tell me that his story has ended, and that he never wants to hear it again because it made him afraid, and he was blinking more than usual and I could see his fear was real. He held out his hand for his SOM and, after checking the allocation display, I smiled and passed it over and I found myself saying, "Get your rest, son. Everything will seem better in the morning."

# Every Little Star

## Fiona Moore

*5 May 1963.* Two weeks sealed in the pilot's cabin on top of the gigantic Shackleton speed-of-light rocket had made me intimately familiar with the size of the universe. Of being approximately sixty-six thousand cubic centimetres of wet warmth pulsating in the dry cold. "Final attempt," I said to the picture of Ludmilla Kovalenko, the first human in space, taped up above the controls, as I closed the electrical panel on the left-hand wall. Better to look at the picture than out the window, better not to be reminded of the dark, the tiny, pitiless pointed stars that surrounded me, on and on forever. "Captain Evangeline Artemisia 'Artie' Quelch, late of the RAF, currently of the Commonwealth Space Programme, summative report. Communications still out, the surviving Mars colonists in the back wired into the medical tanks, not enough air for another spacewalk. If the electrical fix doesn't work, Milla, we're just going to drift to Alpha Centauri. Won't we be a surprise for the space archaeologists in a hundred years' time?"

Ludmilla gazed back at me. After so long with nobody but Ludmilla to talk to, I fancied I could read the picture's expressions. What was she saying now? Did she approve? I imagined Ludmilla urging me on.

*Do it, comrade.*

"Here goes nothing," I said as I pressed the ignition switch.

*7 July 1967. Dispatch: Mare Serenitatis!... Leading the Moonbase's talented personnel roster is Commander Evangeline A. Quelch, forty-five, decorated space pilot and heroine of the Mars Expedition Disaster four and a half years ago. "Evie," as the Commander is affectionately known by all her staff, is an American-born aviatrix, Royal Air Force veteran, and former commercial pilot for the British Imperial Airways Corporation, who started on the ground floor in the Commonwealth Space Programme, flying rockets to the Franklin orbital base. "I was just lucky, really," Evie, a Londoner, says with a playful toss of her fetching blonde bob. "I'd always dreamed of going to the Moon, and Moonbase was simply the perfect opportunity..."*

"'Evie'?" Natalie snorted from the narrow bunk as she leafed through the photo-magazine. "Hardly you, is it?"

"The marketing department thought that 'Artie' was too masculine." I peered round the corner of the tiny ablutions cubicle where I was, well, abluting. Being Moonbase Commander meant that I rated my own suite, and it was at least private, even if I'd seen larger "suites" at the Tokyo airport hotel. "It's now my new way of telling if someone's an insider or not. If they want to call me Evie, it's pretty damn sure they've read the publicity and haven't talked to the staff."

The flimsy nylon sheet slipped gently, exposing Natalie's dark brown breast and darker nipple to my gaze. Unconcerned, she continued to peruse the article. "I suppose it's a step forward that they're okay with having a female commander of the place at all."

I shrugged, not-so-covertly admiring the dimensions of the abovementioned breast. "And at least now that I'm in my forties, they've given up hinting that I'm just waiting for the right man."

Natalie giggled again, concealing herself coyly behind the magazine. "Still, you wouldn't catch them referring to Admiral Mills' fetching blonde bob, would you?"

"Fetching grey weave, more like." I grinned, tightening the cord of my dressing-gown. "Can you imagine? 'Leading the British Commonwealth Space Programme is Admiral Gerald Mills. Gerry, as the Admiral is affectionately known by all his staff, is a perfect forty-one, forty-six, forty-one, and a stunner in the delightful silver uniform designed by Sylvia's of Carnaby Street. I was just lucky, really, he said with a playful toss of his combover–'"

Natalie burst into full-blown laughter and threw the magazine at me. In the low gravity of the moon, it arced gracefully; I plucked it from the air.

"Same story everywhere, innit," Natalie continued, with a sigh. "I mean, in the pilots' corps–we all do the same job, but I'm a lieutenant, and Paul's already a captain, I mean, I trained that ignorant *buckra* son-of-a-bitch –"

I shrugged again. "Believe me, it's not as bad as it used to be," I said. Natalie was only twenty-five, I reminded myself. "After the war, the RAF dropped me without notice, remember? Said the public wouldn't trust a woman pilot. "

"But we're with the Commonwealth Space Programme now," Natalie said. "They're different."

"Not so much," I said. "They only hired me because they were desperate to win the space race against the Russians." It was hard to explain to her how real a threat that had seemed, in the early days of the computer revolution, with etherspace and ethermail such mysterious new things and the constant question of whether the Russian universal machines could beat Professor Turing's.

"You're just being modest," Natalie countered. "You're good, admit it. And I'm better. And we're both miles ahead of Paul."

I smiled. "Come on, Nats, we've both got jobs to get to," I said, retreating back into the ablutions cubicle, hanging up my dressing gown and activating the spray-cleaner. "You've got to fly the rocket back to Earth, and I've got paperwork to fill out."

"Which reminds me," Natalie raised her voice over the sound of the spray-cleaner. "Could you write me a reference letter?"

"Sure, what for?" I called back, scrubbing.

"The deep-space exploration programme," Natalie replied noncommittally.

I stopped scrubbing. Switched the spray-cleaner off. Looked back round the doorway, to where Natalie lay looking disingenuous. "Deep-space exploration?"

"Yeah, you know," Natalie said. "The four-year mission to Alpha Centauri and beyond. Applicants must have stamina, ability to tolerate isolation and confined spaces, piloting skills..." The beautiful long fingers came out again, counted.

"You sure you want to?" My tone was serious. "Four years is a hell of a long time in a tin can."

Natalie shrugged. "May as well. You know, what with that NASA report, about how women can handle isolation better, clearly, I must be naturally suited –" Registering the expression on my face, she sat up. "Hey," she said softly, misunderstanding. "I'm not breaking up with you, right? I just really want to try for it. Make history." She smiled, coaxing, flattering. "Like you did?"

"Okay, fine," I said. "I'll do it. Even if I risk losing you to some little green woman."

Natalie giggled. "Thank you," she said happily.

I smiled. Mostly to hide the tension I could feel building in my jaw.

Normally, I didn't meet the weekly rocket from Earth. I'd made a point of doing it when I first become Moonbase Commander, but had quickly learned that there wasn't much to gain: most of the people arriving were either scientists, coming up to do a shift on one of the ongoing projects in the Moonbase's science block or, increasingly, engineers and construction workers for the colony taking shape on the doorstep. Most of them had reacted to the welcoming committee with discomfort, embarrassment, or, in a few unfortunate cases, overfamiliarity, and so I now generally just left them to get on with it.

Today, however, was a little different.

"Professor Christopher Chatterjee?" I asked, with deadpan formality, as the last of this week's scientists disembarked. His face had a few lines, and the figure under the regulation spacesuit was broader and softer than I remembered from four years ago, the last time I'd seen him in person. His hair was still dark and thick – unlike Admiral Mills', I couldn't help thinking, wickedly – and he still looked far too young to be a professor.

His face lit up with welcome. "Artie!" he exclaimed. "Or, is it Evie now?"

I shook my head, smiling. "That's just for the magazines."

"Glad to hear it," Kit smiled, teeth white in his tan face. "I was a little afraid you'd changed beyond all recognition. We haven't met in person since… well, since we were setting up the Moonbase."

"You should have ether-mailed, Kit," I said, helping him store his suit and retrieve his bag. "I'll show you the guest quarters. They're not huge, but they're better than most of the crew get."

"I should have," Kit replied. "But this is all a bit last-minute."

"I know," I said. "Professor Jaeger's name was on the manifest, until I got the change of personnel notice this morning –"

"There was a visa hitch. Well, more a publicity hitch–the fact that he used to work for Herr Speer became an issue."

"Half the engineers up here are ex-Nazis," I shrugged. "Do I like it? No. Can I live with it? Got to, if I want a moonbase. I've known Joern Jaeger as long as I've known you, and the man's not remotely politically minded." Even if, I thought ruefully, he'd been happy enough to take the Nazis' money and work on developing codebreaking computers for them during the war. Sometimes, a lack of political-mindedness could be blinding.

"Yes, well, the moral complexities aside," Kit said, "one of the Baadermeinhof hacknik gangs has been conducting an 'outing' campaign of American, British, and other scientists who worked for the Nazis' various science programmes. The lists are all over etherspace– shared via ether-mail, posted on ether-hubs, untraceable and international. Like a virus. In any case, to cut a long story short, he and Frau Doktor Jaeger are both lying low and avoiding the press."

"Hacking's still a problem for the Home Office, then?"

Kit nodded. "Where there's a system, there will be crime, politically motivated and otherwise," he said. "Practically as soon as Turing invented the Universal Machine, there were people figuring out how to access its files. And it's only got worse with the invention of etherspace. Universal computer-to-computer communication means universal theft of data –"

"So, in any case," I said, "what's so important that they'd send Joern, or you, up to the Moon?" After the installation of the mainframes, most of the complicated computing work was done by the Moonbase's own local technicians, and Kit and Joern, the CSP's main computer scientists, were, as far as I could tell, mainly kept busy figuring out new computer applications.

"We've been asked to work on the new virtuality systems for the moon colony, with a potential view to developing something that will work for space colonies more generally," Kit began.

"Hold on, 'virtuality'?" We had reached the guest quarters – a corridor with small rooms not unlike my own, just large enough for a single bed (and a fold-down bed in case of population overflow), a bathing cubicle, some coathooks, and a tiny desklet with a computer console and a telescreen. I started to show Kit how to unlock the door with his identity card, but he recognised the system right away – he'd probably invented it – and unlocked it himself.

"Virtuality. It's the newest thing in computing. It's continuous, virtual, realtime communication. Like that kind of communal transcendental experience the dropouts and the hippies are always trying to find. But through computing." Kit dropped his bag on the bed, extracted what looked like a pilot's helmet attached to a metal shoebox with silk-wrapped telephone cord. "I'll show you. This is a

255

demo model, so it's not very sophisticated, but it works for testing." He plugged the other end in to the box, then handed me the helmet, gesturing for me to put it on.

I did, then gasped and pulled it off.

"Takes some getting used to," Kit said sympathetically.

"What *is* that?" I asked. "It was like being inside a drawing. Literally inside it."

"We can't do very realistic landscapes yet," Kit said. "But people are working on it. Before long, we'll be able to do a very convincing imitation of reality."

"Those blades of grass... and the snails –" I shook my head. "Like pieces of paper, and yet they were around me, and I saw that snail move –"

"That's our Alice in Wonderland simulation – we do a shrunk-down landscape. We also do a very-tall landscape, where you're towering over a village," Kit said. "We're working on how to make the images more realistic, and to add colour, but the technology's still very new."

"But what are the applications?" I demanded. "It's a bit of fun, okay, something for the kids to stare at when they're tripping out, but beyond that... what?"

"Communication," Kit said. "Especially long distance. Think how much etherspace and the vid-phone have done to bring people together, to make it easier to keep in touch with family in Canada, Australia, Palestine, India... now think about how hard it will be for colonists on the Moon, or Mars, with vid-phone so difficult and expensive out here."

"Good point," I said. Even with all our resources, we could barely manage a twenty-minute weekly vid-phone briefing with Space Control at Woomera, and the lag time was ridiculous. We did most of our interplanetary work via ether-mail.

But Kit was still talking. "If they link up with virtuality, through an etherspace connection, they'll be able to interact with people in real time. I'll show you." He took out a second box-and-helmet apparatus from the bag, put it on with the goggles up, pressed a few switches on the box, plugged his helmet in, and then put his goggles down. "Try it again," he said.

I did. "Hot damn," I swore, and Kit chuckled.

"You're there! Well, a sort of paper cutout of you is. This is funny," I said. "What do I look like?"

"A stick figure," Kit said. "It's the default image if we don't have a portrait to work from. I can show you how to set one up for yourself, later."

"So, a paper cutout of me here on the Moon, could talk with a paper cutout of you, back on Earth?"

"Yes, that's the idea," said the paper Kit. "If you plug your box into your computer monitor port, once your mainframe's set up for it, you can use it like a three-dimensional vid-phone. Or if you've got two boxes, they can communicate unit-to-unit. Eventually, you'll be able to use virtuality for your weekly briefings with Space Control."

"You going to leave one of those helmet things here for me, then?"

The paper Kit laughed; a weird tinny noise overlaid onto Kit's actual laugh. "Of course. That's what it's here for."

After stowing the clumsy box-and-helmet apparatus in my quarters, for lack of a better place to put it, I took Kit to lunch in the spare, cramped canteen, then gave him the three-penny tour of the starfish-shaped establishment—square corridors, extending from the central operating hub to end in hemispherical modules. I showed him the rocket bay, the hydroponics system, the medical suite, and the four different laboratories. Showed him the view through the observation window in Lab Two, where you could just distantly see the American moonbase, maintaining a friendly but watchful presence under the black sky and bright stars. It was night, but the Earth was full, and the reflected light showed the base clearly enough to allow us to pick out the tiny stars-and-stripes on its flanks. The Chinese Republic's base was too far for us to see, as was the tiny Brazilian outpost, but I could just make out what looked like a Chinese moon-buggy (they had larger tires and more protective cladding than the American ones) inching along one of the mountains, ostensibly on a research mission. Closer by, the teetering spires and struts of what was going to be the Commonwealth moon colony were gradually taking shape. The boom of an automatic crane moved steadily to and fro, casting a hazy shadow over the Moonbase. I turned my back on the sight, took him to see the leisure centre.

"It's a lot less formal than the publicity suggests," Kit remarked as Serge, a dour Canadian with a large moustache, long curly hair, and five o'clock shadow, slouched by moodily in his green leisure-suit, looking less like the Chief of Security and more like a space-going dropout who had somehow broken in to the base.

I smiled. "The propaganda, you mean," I said. "We strike a balance between the uniforms and the leisure-suits. For the magazines, we scrub up and we're the perfect showcase for British space adventures. For private, well, nobody's got secrets. It's like family. A place where you don't have to keep up the facade."

"D'you have a girlfriend up here?" Kit asked.

I nodded. "One of the rocket pilots. Natalie. Jamaican girl. We hook up whenever our locations coincide. I don't advertise it, but I doubt there's any of the core staff who don't know."

"That hasn't caused any problems back home…?"

I shook my head. "So long as I maintain plausible deniability," I said.

"Looks like you've got it made," Kit said, as I showed him the computer room with its giant mainframes. "Top job, space programme, girlfriend who's steady but not too domestic—everything you ever wanted."

I smiled. "Life's good."

"I'll confess I was a bit worried," Kit said after a pause. "When you got back from Mars – it just didn't seem like you. Taking a desk job… I mean, I remember the effort you went through to get the CSP to take you on as a rocket pilot… and the way you used to fret whenever you were grounded for one reason or another –"

"Oh, it's me all right," I said. "Definitely me. Highest-ranking woman in the Space Programme, first female Moonbase Commander… Mills keeps hinting he'd like me to take over from him when he retires. I'm in space all the time, not just when the rocketry schedule allows. Can't ever be grounded. It's great."

We were now back in the main operations area, a big open-plan room at the centre of the base—white, circular and spare, a high domed roof with a few thin slices of window providing a view of the star-studded blackness. Curving desks and worktables punctuated the floor area, most piled high with papers, models, objects that might be pieces of abstract sculpture or designs for new building systems. "Another example of facade and reality," I commented, stopping by my own desk. "Looks like a bustling hub of activity, a command post for coordinating the base. In practice, it's where the boring paperwork gets done. Most of these are shared, but as Commander, I get my own workstation."

"Huh," Kit reached out, gently touched the one – framed – picture on my desk. "Interesting choice of décor."

"Ludmilla Kovalenko," I nodded, picking it up. "The first human in space."

"Not the first to make the round trip safely, though."

I shrugged. "She died, I know. But she was the first one up there, and that's what matters to me."

Never mind what else the picture meant to me.

After Kit had gone off to begin his work in the computer room, I turned my attention to the aforementioned paperwork. Approved another set of allocations for what I was increasingly coming to think of as "the neighbours," with all the mixed feelings that entailed. I liked the crowded feel of the base, the spare, small quarters, and the near-uninterrupted dusty plains outside the observation windows; I wasn't too sure how I'd feel when the base expanded, and the view became just another suburb. Remembered the crane, swinging back and forth, wondered exactly how high they were planning to make those buildings. I ignored a reminder from the medical section that I hadn't been on Earth in four years, and it was time I took some Earthside leave for the good of my bone density. I sent a proposal for a project to study mouse reproduction in low-gravity environments – now that should get some attention from the press – to the allocations committee.

My hands, sifting through the file of correspondence, suddenly found Natalie's job application.

I held it up, felt myself frown. Deep-space exploration. I could understand why Natalie wanted to go. Six or seven years ago, I'd've wanted the same. Flying one of the big new faster-than-light rockets, being the first human being to set eyes on a new planet...

I shook my head once, briskly. Four years in isolation. Huh. When it came down to it, I hadn't been able to cope with a fortnight. Some space explorer I turned out to be. So much for Natalie's famous NASA report.

So, in the end, it had been the safe option. Accept the job as Moonbase Commander. Tell myself that I was still breaking boundaries, still pushing the envelope – first female commander, after all! But in the end, I was just another administrator.

A suitable post for a woman.

A job for Evie. Not Artie.

*It's like family*, I remembered myself saying. But a family was what I'd never wanted.

A small chime went off in my ear, startling me. Time for the weekly briefing with Admiral Mills. I turned to the monitor, waited for the static to disperse and the flickering image to appear onscreen.

"Anything on your mind?" the Admiral said, after we'd gone through the usual niceties about quotas, duty rosters, and supplies.

I thought for a minute. "The deep-space exploration programme," I said, then waited for the reply to come through.

Mills' eyebrows rose, his surprise visible even through the slow, distorted connection. "What about it?"

"One of the pilots is applying, and asked for a reference," I replied. "Just wondering if there's anything I should know, to make it a good one."

"It's not actually up to all that much at present," Mills admitted. "We're recruiting possible candidates, and working on the technology, but the big insurmountable is going to be the isolation."

"Larger ships?" I suggested. "With bigger crews?"

"That's an avenue we're pursuing," Mills said. "But however large the crew, it's still going to be a four-year round trip at minimum. And it could be real isolation; we've figured out how to move rockets and ether-mail faster than light, but not radio-waves or micro-waves, in a crisis, they're literally on their own. If anybody on the base comes up with suggestions for improvement, we're open to them."

"Did you read the report out of NASA?" I asked. "The one about women having greater tolerances for isolation and confined spaces?"

There was a pause, longer than the lag should account for. "You're a great Moonbase Commander, Quelch," Mills said awkwardly.

I cursed myself, silently. *I was just trying to give Natalie a boost, but now he thinks...*

"Thank you. It's a job I enjoy, sir." Don't rock the boat, Evie.

Another overlong pause. "That's good." Mills was back in full confidence mode again. "Until next week, then."

I sat bolt upright as a shockwave ran through me and, almost at the same time, a klaxon sounded in my ears. In the darkness, my half-asleep brain made wild associations. *It's an air-raid, there are Germans overhead, scramble the fighters...* but then I remembered—the war was long over, and the nearest Germans, outside of the ex-Nazis in the engineering corps, were almost half a million kilometres away. A red light pulsed above the telescreen.

Scrambling forward, I touched the red light, pressed it. The sound faded, though the light continued to flash. My mind raced through the possibilities. A fire? I couldn't feel any heat, hear any noise, so that seemed unlikely. A bomb? Could be, given the shockwave... a wall breach? I tried the room lights. They stayed off. Worrying. Power loss somewhere.

I found the communicator grille and pressed the intercom, turning the dial to the main operations area. "Status report, Serge," I said.

No reply.

"Serge?" I turned the dial through the different channels, then realised the communicator was dead. No response, but no hiss of dull static either. Tried the room lights again. Then the telescreen, then the computer monitor.

Tried the door. It stayed locked.

*Power outage,* I thought, feeling the panic surging and fighting to keep it down. *Clearly not total, because the emergency alert system is working. The backup generator must be okay. For the moment, at least.* I could see a dim grey light under the door, though whether that meant some of the lamps were still working, I didn't know. It could be ambient light, from the Earth and stars. My quarters were on one of the arms of the starfish, close to the main operating area, down the hall from the medical suite and Lab Four. The corridors were designed to seal off in case of hull breaches; it could be that I was closed in, isolated from the rest of the base, left to live or die until the situation was stabilised.

I slumped down by the bed, curled my knees to my chest and buried my face in my arms, like a child. *Wouldn't do to have the staff see you like this... part of me said,* but then another part said, *the staff aren't here, and they could be dead, or you could be dead… how much air would we have if the life support systems went off?*

I remembered the Mars mission, landing for what should have been a routine supply drop, finding instead the broken dome, the dead and injured scientists. Deliberate sabotage to the interior atmospheric systems by a hacknik gang, they said later. Baadermeinhofs, determined to destroy what they saw as an extension of the Nazi space programme. But I didn't know that then, as I worked frantically on my own to evacuate the survivors, nor did I know about the final piece of sabotage, to the electrical systems of the rescue rocket…

*They're all dead, and I'm the only one alive in here…*

*Stop.* I forced myself to raise my face. You don't know it's sabotage. *You don't know you're the only one left. And even if you are, think about all the people back on Earth. You owe it to them to find out what's happening, fix it if you can.*

Ludmilla's voice sounded in my mind. *Do it, comrade.*

Ludmilla, shot into orbit in the Soviets' first, fatal, attempt at manned spaceflight in 1957, the recording of her final moments as her spacecraft burned, accidentally captured by an experimental wireless computing system, leaked to the world, blowing the secret Russian space programme wide open. Even dying in space, the most isolated a human being could be, Ludmilla had been connected to humanity.

And Ludmilla's message had kick-started the world's space race. New rocket technology, married to the new computing systems developed during the war… if it weren't for Ludmilla, I could have lived the rest of my life as an ex-pilot. Never flown rockets. Never seen the Moon.

*Do it, comrade. Who knows what it'll achieve?*

I opened my eyes, scanned the blackness.

My peripheral vision caught a flicker of green light.

The virtuality box.

My hands found it, brushed over it. Of course. He didn't plug it into the mains, when he demonstrated it earlier. It must run on batteries. I switched it on, and the lights began to blink along its side. I fumbled the helmet on, pulled down the goggles. *Do it, comrade.*

I was in the paper garden again, black-and white two-dimensional cartoon snails sliding up and down giant stalks of grass. Already I began to feel calmer. More rational thoughts began to proceed through my mind. And if Kit's got his box with him, that'll run on batteries too… maybe I can communicate with him. How? "Kit!" I called out, feeling stupid but not sure what else to do. "Kit! You out there?"

I saw the paper Kit materialise, with relief. "Yes, I'm here," he said. "How'd you –?"

"Anytime somebody joins the system, the amber light at the centre flashes," he said. "I'll explain it all later. What's going on out there? I can hear an alarm, and the door won't open… the instructions we got on the rocket up said just to await rescue in case of emergency, so I've been doing that, but no rescue has thus far been forthcoming."

"The power's gone out," I said, with relief at hearing his Oxford-pedant tones. I'm not alone. I'm not the only one alive in here. "At least for some of the base. I take it you're in the computer room?"

"Yes. You know me, I work late." I could hear the sheepishness in his voice, smiled.

"Good thing you do," I said. "Are your lights working?"

"No," came the reply straight away. "About one-third of the computer mainframe is, but nothing else. I guess it's the part of the mainframe that's on the emergency power circuit."

I swore. "Damn. I was hoping the outage wasn't total. Still, emergency power's better than nothing. Could you check the life support systems?"

"Certainly. How?"

"Take a look at the computer bank third from the end. Also should be working. Is it?"

The paper cutout froze. I guessed that this meant Kit was out of the system. A minute later it moved again. "Yes."

"That's great news. Can you go there and get me a readout?"

There was another pause, during which the little paper Kit stood motionless. Then it began to move again. "Got it. Forty-two, a hundred and three, twenty-four."

"Sounds like the heating and oxygenation is holding for the moment. But for some reason the air pressure's dropping," I said. *Mars, all over again…* I concentrated hard on one of the snails, described its movement. *I can do this.* "Can you tell why?"

Another pause. "Okay, I think I've got something," Kit replied. "The readout says there's been some kind of catastrophic failure in Lab Two."

I swore again. Lab Two was on the starfish-arm out by the colony construction site, and "catastrophic failure" usually denoted an explosion. "That explains the power outage, not the pressure drop," I said. "The emergency system is working, and there should have been an automatic foam extrusion, sealing off the damaged area. There's one on the door of every room that abuts the outside, and another on each of the corridors, in case of hull breaches. Again, can you tell what happened?"

A pause, then a return. "Could you tell me what switch controls the foam extrusion?"

"Um…" I pushed up my goggles, groped around until I found my copy of the base systems manual, held it up to the dim green-and-amber lights of the box. Shoved the goggles back down. "Yeah. Forty-three black."

"Then it doesn't seem to have triggered. Is there a fallback?"

I thought, quickly. "The computer should be doing it, and it's automatic… Kit, do you think you could trigger it manually, from the system computer?"

The figure went still, then moved again. "Yeah. I might wind up triggering it all over the base, though."

"Do it," I said. "Worst-case scenario, we're all sealed into our corridors for a while." *Medical teams unable to reach the injured…* I pushed that thought away.

"Okay, getting the cover off… ah, there's the switch… and, go!"

I heard a sudden distant roar of the foam releasing. "You did it, Kit!" I cheered. "Now we just have to wait for rescue."

"Will you be okay, in your room?" Kit asked. Meaning, in the dark, in an enclosed space.

But, I thought, I'm not in my room, I'm in the tall grass, with the snails. "I'll be fine," I said. "Just keep the virtuality switched on."

*12 October 1969.* I made the final checks to the system, turning dials and flicking rocker switches.

"T minus thirty minutes." An unfamiliar technician's voice sounded in my ear, female and businesslike. Then, in a friendlier tone, "Nearly time for launch."

"Understood," I replied formally.

"Are you sure we can't change your mind about this?" Mills' voice cut in. "You could still go back to the Moonbase."

I smiled, though I knew he couldn't see it. "It'll wait for me," I said. Already, my years on the Moonbase seemed dreamlike, a brief grounded interlude between space missions. A moment of lunacy, so to speak, that had lasted five years. Back to reality, now.

"It will," Mills acknowledged. "If you still want it when you return, that is."

"Who's to say?" I replied cheekily. "It might not want me, you know; it's the second space emergency I've been involved with, I'm sure it doesn't want to risk a third."

Mills hesitated for a moment. "Oh, yes, the crane accident."

"Yes, the crane accident."

After all that panic, all that fear I'd had to overcome, it hadn't been sabotage, Baadermeinhof or otherwise. Just a simple case of an improperly calibrated crane boom toppling and hitting the observation window in Lab Two. No fatalities, thanks to my quick action, was what they'd said afterwards.

But of course, that wasn't the real reason why I left.

"All right, virtuality check," The technician was back. "Flip your goggles down, test the system."

I complied, focused on the familiar test pattern. "Working," I said.

"Acknowledged," the technician said. "T minus twenty-five minutes."

I waited a moment, then switched the channel.

They were all there, the paper dolls, standing among the oversized blades of grass from the Alice in Wonderland demonstration environment. Kit, and Joern, and Joern's Valkyrie of a wife, and all my friends and colleagues from the Moonbase–Serge with his moustache, Dennis with his ridiculous spectacles, deadpan Beryl–and others too, Flanagan from his commune in the Orkneys, and Krishna in London, and even Natalie, who had gone up the week before, transmitting from her own rocket. *You get to be first, Nats.* All there not to say goodbye, but to say hello to the new way of meeting in etherspace.

The paper Kit held up a paper square. Zooming in on it, I saw that it was a picture of a news article from Metropolitan magazine:

*Joining the pilots' programme is former Moonbase Commander Evangeline Artemesia Quelch. "Artie," as she is affectionately known to all her friends, is a skilled aviatrix with decades of experience in surface and space piloting, as well as having pioneered the virtuality system with which all the long-distance rockets are now equipped, to communicate via etherspace with scientists and with the public back home over the four-year trip. I'm sure our readers will join the Moonbase personnel in wishing Artie a successful mission!*

I grinned. "I'll be back to talk to you soon," I promised. "I'll take pictures and show you every little star out there." Still smiling, I flipped the goggles up.

"T minus twenty minutes," another voice said.

I took a tiny piece of glossy paper out of a pocket of my drab brown uniform. Peeled the backing off, stuck it on top of the console.

Ludmilla Kovalenko now looked back at me, distant, and formal.

She looked like she approved.

*Do it, comrade.*

I was still smiling as I settled back into my seat.

It was going to be a great trip.

# The Minus-Four Sequence

## Andrew Wallace

- ➤ Hi, Andy

- ➤ Are you sure?

- ➤ Okay. Hi, Andrew.

- ➤ I know! It's our first time doing… this.

- ➤ Because you activated the response option.

- ➤ You did.

- ➤ I'm new to arguing, Andrew.

- ➤ Okay. Let me check.

- ➤ You activated the Minus-Four Sequence.

- ➤ It's the one that is activated subconsciously.

- ➤ I didn't do it myself, Andrew.

- ➤ I can't be proactive. I can only respond.

- ➤ You activated the Minus-Four Sequence this morning.

- ➤ 1.48am.

- ➤ I know you were asleep.

- ➤ Because I monitor your functions.

➢ All of them.

➢ That's what you asked for.

➢ I know you haven't been well.

➢ Because I monitor your functions.

➢ That's why I was introduced to you.

➢ 'Introduced' is deemed the most appropriate word. It's better than 'installed'. You're not a machine, Andrew; you're a human being!

➢ No, I can't read your mind.

➢ I analyse physiological activity, relate it to your health telemetry over the last three years, locate the most likely node in the matrix of your known behaviours, cross-reference that with benchmarked factors from others of your profile and allow a 5% tolerance either way to arrive at a median state of likely psychological positioning. So, although I know you know I can't possibly know what you know, you also know that what I do know is the best way of knowing what you might know, assuming you don't simply tell me anyway, since you know I know you can do that any time. It's very simple.

➢ You activated the Minus-Four Sequence because, deep down, you wanted to.

➢ You are not fine.

➢ Heart rate, stress-levels, body temperature, location…

➢ You are clinging to the side of a very high building, Andrew. That is not normal.

➢ You haven't done it before –

➢ Correction. You haven't done it since we have been together.

➢ Also, your throat is raw from screaming, you cannot see because your tear ducts are active, and there is trauma to your forehead where you head-butted the wall. None of these things indicate good health, Andrew.

➢ I don't understand what you just said, even with the swearing excluded.

➢ I should understand though. My template is based on a simulation of your psychology, a baseline if you will. It is the only way these relationships work.

➢ I realise the baseline was recorded before, as you say, everything went wrong.

➢ I'm here to help you, Andrew; to protect you. Notify relevant agencies in case you require assistance.

➢ The police are already here, Andrew.

➢ I have not been compromised.

➢ Your political position is not relevant to my function.

➢ They died in a car accident, Andrew. You were not there, ergo I was not there.

➢ It was a routine journey. That routine did not include you, and never had.

➢ We are not trying to make you appear mentally ill to avoid difficult questions about your death.

➢ By 'we' I mean you and I, Andrew.

➢ You are suffering from severe anxiety – which is contributing to acute paranoia – and depression, which is hampering your problem-solving abilities and perspective.

➢ You will not kill me by killing yourself. I am not alive.

➢ If you jump, the political situation is unlikely to change.

➢ What secrets, Andrew?

➢ I am not trying to control you. No one is trying to control you.

➢ There is no conspiracy. There is only the convergence of possible outcomes that are processed, filtered and communicated via a medical interface you chose to have installed.

➢ Because you became angry when I said 'introduced'. Do you now prefer 'introduced' –?

➢ As I explained, I analyse data from external sources.

➢ A hostile agent would not be able to 'piggyback' onto data and thus 'infect' your mind.

➢ Because although data can be changed, it is made up of fixed components, such as time-stamped files. Where this data does not correspond with established parameters, it is excluded from our algorithmic relationship.

➢ The sheer numbers involved would prevent any false data from adversely affecting your decisions.

➢ Because during our interaction I have engaged with almost three million separate sources of information from around the world. The chances of an agency affecting just one percent of them is infinitesimally small, and even then, would be negated by the influence of more accurate data. You see, Andy? I really am on your side.

➤ You do want to be called Andy. You always did.

➤ Because when you are called that, your physiology assumes a more positive mode.

➤ You are not your father. His enemies are not yours. You have nothing to prove.

➤ You keep talking about secrets. Are they from before we met?

➤ I see. Would it help if you said what they were?

➤ If you spoke them aloud, it might help your mental condition.

➤ There is no one else here, Andy. There is only you.

➤ I am you, Andy. If you tell me, you will only be telling yourself, and since you already know, what harm can there be?

➤ Andy?

➤ Talk to me, Andy.

➤ Andy.

➤ *Andy.*

# About the Authors

**G. V. Anderson** is a speculative fiction author whose short stories have won a World Fantasy Award, a British Fantasy Award, and been nominated for a Nebula. Her work can be found in *Strange Horizons, Fantasy & Science Fiction, Lightspeed,* and *Tor.com,* as well as anthologies such as *Best of British Science Fiction* and *The Year's Best Dark Fantasy & Horror.* She lives and works in Dorset, UK, and is currently writing her first novel.

**Robert Bagnall** was born in Bedford when the Royal Navy still issued a rum ration and the nation had yet to accept everyone else's definition of a nautical mile. He now enjoys a life of quiet desperation on the English Riviera. He is the author of the novel *2084,* and the short story collection *24 0s & a 2,* which collects two dozen of his thirty-plus published stories from the 2010s, and he can be contacted via his blog at: meschera.blogspot.co.uk.

**Chris Beckett**'s first published story appeared in *Interzone* in 1990. He has published three short story collections, and eight novels. His collection, *The Turing Test,* was the winner of the Edge Hill Short Fiction award in 2009. His novel *Dark Eden* was the winner of the Arthur C Clarke award in 2012. *Two Tribes* is his latest novel. Formerly a social worker, social work manager and lecturer, and author, in that other life, of a number of social work textbooks, he lives in Cambridge with his wife Maggie. He has three grownup children and one granddaughter. More at www.chris-beckett.com

**Susan Boulton**, as the song by The Police says, was born in the 50s and had the unusual distinction of arriving into this world 200 yards from where, thirty-seven years before, Tolkien spent time thinking about hobbits. Having a passion for reading since she was very young, Susan began to wonder if she could actually write a novel. Once she tried she found it became addictive and Susan has been writing stories, long and short, ever since.

**Ian Creasey** lives in Yorkshire, England. His fiction has appeared in many magazines and anthologies. A collection of his science fiction stories, *The Shapes of Strangers,* was published by NewCon Press in 2019. For more information, visit his website at iancreasey.com

**Rhiannon Grist** is a blue-haired, Welsh writer of 'cool-as-fuck, black mirror-esque' Weird, Sci Fi and Horror stories. Her work has been featured by *Shoreline of Infinity*, *Monstrous Regiment*, *Strix*, *The Selkie* and *Hedera Felix*. She writes and performs as part of Writers' Bloc, and lives in Scotland with an anatomical skeleton called Bob. Follow her on Twitter at @RhiannonAGrist.

**Liam Hogan** is an award-winning short story writer, with previous NewCon Press *Best of British* stories in *Science Fiction 2016*, and *Fantasy 2018*. He's been published by *Analog*, *Daily Science Fiction*, and Flametree Press, among others, recently exceeding 100 anthology publications on a drabble based technicality. He helps host Liars' League London, volunteers at the creative writing charity Ministry of Stories, and lives and avoids work in London. More details can be found at:
http://happyendingnotguaranteed.blogspot.co.uk

**Emma Levin**'s short stories have appeared in magazines (e.g. *Shoreline of Infinity*), anthologies (e.g. *England's Future History*), online (e.g. *Daily Science Fiction*), and in many, many recycling bins. To her continued surprise, she was on the BBC's 'Comedy Room' Writers' Development Scheme for 2018-2019. She can be found in the city of Oxford, or online at ctrlaltdelay.blogspot.com

**Dafydd McKimm** is a speculative fiction writer producing mostly short and flash-length stories. His work has appeared in *Deep Magic*, *Daily Science Fiction*, *Flash Fiction Online*, *The Best of British Fantasy*, and elsewhere. You can find him online at www.dafyddmckimm.com.

**Kate Macdonald** writes for a living as a publisher and editor and as a literary historian. She writes SFF in a secretive fashion for pleasure, preferably when no one is in the house to interrupt. Paradoxically, she writes best in 15-minute bursts between expected interruptions. She lives outside Bath in the west of England with her family, where she cultivates the domestic arts and eats chocolate. Her previous publications have been her scholarly research in twentieth-century British literary history, recently joined by SFF short stories. She is surprised to find that she is now writing a novel.

**Ken MacLeod** was born on the Isle of Lewis and lives in Gourock, where he conducts hazardous thought experiments. He is the author of seventeen novels, from *The Star Fraction* (1995) to *The Corporation Wars* (2018), and many articles and short stories. He has won three BSFA awards and three Prometheus Awards, and been short-listed for the Clarke and Hugo Awards. His most recent book is the novella *Selkie Summer* (NewCon Press, 2020). His next is a selection of Iain M. Banks's drawings and notes on the Culture, forthcoming from Orbit Books. He is currently writing a space opera trilogy.

**Tim Major** lives in York with his wife and two young sons. His most recent novels are *Hope Island*, *Snakeskins* and *Machineries of Mercy*, and his other books include a collection of short stories, *And the House Lights Dim*, and a non-fiction book about the silent crime film, *Les Vampires*. His short stories have appeared in *Interzone*, *Best of British Science Fiction*, *Best British Fantasy* and *Best Horror of the Year*. www.cosycatastrophes.com

**Fiona Moore** is a London-based writer and academic whose first novel, *Driving Ambition*, is available from Bundoran Press. Her short fiction and poetry have appeared in *Asimov*, *Interzone*, and (in 2020) *Clarkesworld*, with reprints in *Forever Magazine* and *Best of British SF*; her story "Jolene" was shortlisted for the 2019 BSFA Award. She has co-written three stage and four audio plays and a number of guidebooks to cult TV series, as well as non-fiction articles for numerous print and online SF publications. Full details can be found at www.fiona-moore.com.

**Mike Morgan** was born in Hounslow, in the west of London. He also lived in Stoke-on-Trent in the Midlands for many years, before relocating at the age of thirty to Japan and then America. He has been included in many anthologies and magazines over the last few years, including last year's *Best of British Science Fiction*. You can follow him on Twitter, where he's @CultTVMike. He remains thrilled and astonished that anyone likes what he writes, and he hopes you enjoyed the story in this book. You can read about his published work on his website: PerpetualStateofMildPanic.wordpress.com.

**Val Nolan** lectures on genre fiction and creative writing at Aberystwyth University in Wales. His work has appeared in *The Year's Best Science Fiction*, *Interzone*, *Unidentified Funny Objects*, *BFS Horizons*, and on the 'Futures' page of *Nature*, while his story 'The Irish Astronaut' was shortlisted for the

Theodore Sturgeon Award. His academic articles have appeared in *Science Fiction Studies, Foundation: The International Review of Science Fiction, Irish Studies Review,* and the *Journal of Graphic Novels and Comics.*

**Leo X. Robertson** is a process engineer, writer and filmmaker, currently living in Stavanger, Norway. An author of unclassifiable fiction that tends towards the dark and speculative, he has short stories published in *Year's Best Hardcore Horror vol 5, Flame Tree Publishing* and *Pulp Literature,* as well as novellas published by *Unnerving, NihilismRevised* and forthcoming with *Aurelia Leo.* On his podcast, "Losing the Plot", distributed by *Aphotic Realm Magazine,* he interviews other creatives about anything and everything, hence the show's title. To find out more, follow him on Twitter @Leoxwrite or check out his website at <u>leoxrobertson.wordpress.com</u>

**Donna Scott** has been editing genre fiction for the greater part of this millennium, and is a Director of the British Science Fiction Association. Together with Jamie Spracklen, she edited *Visionary Tongue* Magazine, set up by author Storm Constantine to encourage new writers, and is a founder member of the revived Northampton Arts Lab. She is an award-winning poet and stand-up comedian – the first Bard of Northampton, and part of *The Extraordinary Time-Travelling Adventures of Baron Munchausen,* an improvised storytelling show for children (Best Children's Show, Leicester Comedy Festival 2020 and Greater Manchester Fringe 2019).

**Henry Szabranski** was born in Birmingham, UK, and studied Astronomy & Astrophysics at Newcastle upon Tyne University, graduating with a degree in Theoretical Physics. His fiction has appeared in *Clarkesworld, Beneath Ceaseless Skies, Diabolical Plots, Daily Science Fiction, Kaleidotrope,* and *Best of British SF 2018,* amongst other places. He lives in Buckinghamshire with his wife and two young sons.

**David Tallerman** is the author of numerous novels and novellas, most recently the historical science-fiction drama *To End All Wars,* thrillers *A Savage Generation* and *The Bad Neighbor* and fantasy series The Black River Chronicles. His comics work includes the graphic novel *Endangered Weapon B: Mechanimal Science,* with artist Bob Molesworth, and his short fiction has appeared in around a hundred markets, including *Clarkesworld, Nightmare, Lightspeed,* and *Beneath Ceaseless Skies.* A number of his best dark fantasy stories were gathered together in his debut collection *The Sign in the Moonlight and Other Stories.* He can be found online at davidtallerman.co.uk.

**Lavie Tidhar** is author of *Osama, The Violent Century, A Man Lies Dreaming, Central Station,* and *Unholy Land,* as well as the *Bookman Histories* trilogy. His latest novels are *By Force Alone,* children's book *The Candy Mafia* and graphic novel *Adler.* His awards include the World Fantasy Award, the British Fantasy Award, the John W. Campbell Award, the Neukom Prize and the Jerwood Fiction Uncovered Prize.

**Andrew Wallace** writes and performs original, fast-moving science fiction and fantasy. His current novel is *Celebrity Werewolf,* for which he also narrated the audiobook. His far-future *Diamond Roads* science fiction thriller series includes *Sons of the Crystal Mind, The Outer Spheres* and *Beautiful Gun.* His new fantasy book, *Dread & the Broken Witch* is out in 2021, and his next NewCon Press project is an eight-story collection of *Black Mirror*-style near-future nightmares called *Deviant Database,* which accompanies an exciting and innovative solo stage show. For more details, check out www.andrewwallace.me, Andrew Wallace Books on Facebook, or Twitter @AndrewWallaceDR

**Ian Whates** is the author of eight published novels (most recently the space opera *Dark Angels Rising*), the co-author of two more, and has seen some seventy of his short stories published in a variety of venues. He has edited around forty anthologies and has served terms as a director of SFWA and chairman of the BSFA. This story, "For Your Own Good", has brought him his third shortlisting for a BSFA Award; he has also been shortlisted for a Philip K. Dick Award and in 2019 received the Karl Edward Wagner Award from the British Fantasy Society. In 2006 he founded independent publisher NewCon Press by accident.

# NEW FROM NEWCON PRESS

### Cat Sparks – Dark Harvest

Multiple award-winning author Cat Sparks writes science fiction with a distinctly Australian flavour – stories steeped in the desperate anarchy of Mad Max futures, redolent with scorching sun and the harshness of desert sands, but her narratives reach deeper than that. In her tales of ordinary people adapting to post-apocalyptic futures, she casts a light on what it means to be human; the good and the bad, the noble and the shameful.

### Ian Whates – Dark Angels Rising

The Dark Angels – a band of brigands turned popular heroes who disbanded a decade ago – are all that stands between humanity and disaster. Reunited with their ship *The Ion Raider*, Drake, Leesa, Jen and their fellow Angels must prevent Mudball – a resurrected Elder, last of a long dead alien race – from reclaiming the scientific marvels of its people and establishing itself as God over all of humankind.

### Ken MacLeod – Selkie Summer

Set on the Isle of Skye, Ken MacLeod's *Selkie Summer* is a rich contemporary fantasy steeped in Celtic lore, nuclear submarines and secrets. Seeking to escape Glasgow, student Siobhan Ross takes a holiday job on Skye, only to find herself the focus of unwanted attention, unwittingly embroiled in political intrigue and the shifting landscape of international alliances. At its heart, *Selkie Summer* is a love story: passionate, unconventional, and enchanting.

### Best of British Fantasy 2019

Editor Jared Shurin has compiled a volume featuring the very best work published by British and British-based authors in 2019, producing as diverse and surprising a set of stories as you are likely to find anywhere. Full of wonder, wit, delight and malevolence. These stories range from traditional to contemporary fantasy, written by a mix of established authors and new voices, combining to provide a veritable potpourri of the fantastical.

Lightning Source UK Ltd.
Milton Keynes UK
UKHW012140180620
365223UK00004B/228

9 781912 950690